PHANTOM TEAM

PHANTOM
TEAM

JOSEPH P. CODY

A Mystery

Autotech Industries

St. Paul, Minnesota

This book is written, printed, and bound in the United States of America

First Edition: 2013

ISBN-13: 978-0-9791167-6-6

A Publication of:

Autotech Industries
688 – 11th Avenue NW
St. Paul, Minnesota 55112

Note: Autotech Industries is a publisher; it does not sell books.

This book may be purchased at Amazon.com or any bookstore.

To those who fought in the Vietnam War

— 1 —

Monday

"Double-Duce."

The words didn't send chills down my spine, they sent it to absolute zero.

A call from the past.

I had stopped to browse some late fiction releases in the window of a bookstore along the mall. It was a voice I'd never forget even with the inevitable shifting of the timbre over more than four decades. How had he found me? It was instilled with our code that we never spoke of our personal lives with others on the team so we would not be able to get together later. No matter, he had found me. Part of the training was to pass over what was done and move immediately to controlling the future.

It was not necessary for me to turn. In fact, that was contrary to training, too, even if I knew of the presence of the one achieving surprise. I wouldn't turn, that is, until intending to kill, which I didn't—yet, and I knew what he looked like. Five-eleven, shy of two hundred pounds. He would not have added any clay, no matter what the sacrifice—too much discipline. The strong face would be the same with a dimple on the right cheek having become a crease by now. The long white scar over the left eye would have darkened, but would still be plainly visible. It was too bad to have disfigured such a handsome face that way. Even a moderately proficient doctor could have sutured it so there would be no trace of the cut after all this time. There had been no doctor proficient or otherwise where we were.

In the heat of battle and the subsequent desperate retreat, he couldn't remember how he came to have the wound. The skin and muscles between the skin and skull had been cut or torn. The bone showed a shallow ragged grove. Later using what we had in our packs, I drew the skin together the best I could. Even at that I picked maggots out of the gash each morning with the tip of my knife until it skinned over and the scab fell off.

We had been running for our lives, the mission having been completed successfully. Of course successfully, or we would not have been running. The three of us had been living in the jungle on bugs and berries for days . . . . Stop it! Why reawaken that mental anguish now? Why had he searched me out? A deep breath, let it out slowly. Where there were no options, there were no decisions. I would hear him out.

Half way down the mall I located the sign for the restrooms. Turning down the hall I entered and went to use a urinal. The partition between my position and the washbasins was too high to see over. There was no sound indicating that he had followed me in, but there would not have been. He, as I, could move with no sound when circumstances so warranted.

"How many?" I asked to the "empty" space.

"Eight," was the reply.

That explained it. His legend was Nine Lives just as mine was Double Duce. He boasted that he'd succumb to old age at a hundred before he went through his nine lives. How he came up with the idea that he was singularly gifted with eight more lives than other mortals was never clear. Maybe he thought he was a cat, I don't know. It was enough that he believed it.

Now, he was living his last one and was scared, the voice betrayed that, too.

I walked from behind the divider that separated us and saw his reflection in the mirror with mine over his shoulder. He was as I had envisioned him, perhaps a little older. He was an inch shorter and he outmatched me in weight by five to ten pounds. I hadn't packed on any either—too much discipline. My face was longer than his with no scars. My eyes were blue, his gray-blue. His nose was a little wide, mine about average. Seeing our faces side by side in the mirror, it for the first time occurred to me that we could easily pass for brothers.

"Been a long time," I said.

"Seems like an eternity, doesn't it?" He studied my reflection. "Life hasn't been all bad for you. You look good."

Chatting with this man about inane subjects was not high on my list of things to do. "You found me. We agreed that was something we'd never do. I want to know why." Though, I tried to keep irritation out of my voice, it was there.

"When we promise to do things, we sometimes do so naively. Future events are still in the future. I don't mean to sound philosophical, but that's what has happened. Somebody poked a stick in that hornets nest that we were part of back then. I'm here to find out what you know about it."

He was serious, too serious, and that worried me. I had no choice but to take it the next step. "You know where I live."

"I do."

"Stop by in an hour. Park on the apron to the garage on the right so my wife can get into the garage on the left when she comes home. We'll talk on the patio."

The last glance I had at his face in the mirror—he had never turned to face me—revealed a man filled not only with hostility, but heavy with worry and pain.

Camilla, my wife, had already returned when I arrived home. We had a short discussion and she knew what was expected. I was seated on the patio when the sound of tires turning onto the tarmac reached me. The door opened and closed. No stealth now. The face I saw on the man coming around the corner of the garage was more relaxed which was a good sign. He even extended his right hand.

"You know my name and all the details so you have me at a disadvantage."

He nodded. "Let's keep it that way for now. It'll be to your benefit." Taking a slow breath he continued, "Vincent Wesson. That's a strong name. I suppose your friends call you Vin, and not Vinny. May I call you Vin?"

"You *are* in trouble or the years have mellowed you something fierce. The kid I knew wouldn't have asked. We were really kids then, weren't we?" I said as I motioned him to a padded chair.

"Yeah," he said as he glanced about. "We sure were. Thumbing our noses at the world, thumbing them at our own lives. They really got to us, didn't they. In such a short time turning us into tools where even we didn't care if we lived or died."

"You were serious about having gone through eight of your nine lives, weren't you?"

He smirked. "Not literally, of course. You know I jollied you guys around about that just as something to occupy the time we spent waiting between missions since we couldn't talk about our real lives. I've scared to death, though, if that's what you mean."

He was hurting, I could see that. He was reliving a nightmare in order to stay alive. "The thing is, we care about them now. Something must have really exploded to make you break cover. Want to tell me about it?"

"Why else do you suppose I'm here?—there isn't any choice. I need information from you and it's important that you take me seriously."

Most of his story was unnecessary to tell because we both knew it. It went back to Vietnam. We had been in a Phantom Team. That particular function consisted of a small number of off the books special teams who were trained for unique missions, most of which were illegal as in going into countries where the U.S. government had ordered us not to go and once there killing enemy commanders. Other times it meant nastier things, things we did behind our own lines, not that there was much in the way of lines in that war. My inner self told my outer self that I'd never take a mission involving the nasty things. There was always uncertainty that I would have been able to keep that promise to either self. And, it had always seemed odd to me that I could remember that there were such missions, but I was a blank as to what exactly they involved.

It all started when some bright bureaucrat got the idea that the men in the existing special forces units like the Army Green Barrettes or Navy SEALS had something special about them, something genetic. He found the files of these men and correlated the information with the results from the battery of tests each of them took upon entering the service. That testing was routine for each man entering the service to access the skills, talents, psychological stability, etc. so he might be employed most effectively. That was the theory, of course, but since there was always a shortage of infantry grunts, that's where most men landed, screw the tests.

Anyway, it seems that there are certain members of the male population who have an excess of what could be called warrior genes. From this he made a template and matched it against the test results of all the other men then on active duty. The computers of the time were not like they are today but good enough for that. Those with a high correlation to the template were approached with a proposition that sounded too good to be true and it was, though it was some time before they learned that hard fact. Those that passed muster for the rigorous training were kept, the others were dropped. Nine Lives and I met the standard of prodigy, so it seemed. We stayed. We were good, the best. In fact all the teams were good. No team ever failed in its mission even though frequently none of them returned alive.

All military training entails a fair amount of brainwashing. That is simply necessary if the average man off the street is to be turned into an effective killer of other human beings. We received that in spades. After our usefulness was expended we were expected to shake it off and reenter society. They played mind games with us on the way out too, just as much as going in. It left a few severely disturbed men being turned out to be predators on society. The cases where none returned from missions were obviously the easiest for the Army. Where they all returned it was harder because they stood a better chance of running across one another on the outside. We suspected in cases like that they'd be reassigned to dangerous operations in the normal Army in hopes at least some of them would be killed.

We were somewhat unique in that there were three of us left after our last mission, or I should say *my* last mission. There was no way for me to know if the others were assigned to other teams to conduct more operations. Things were winding down fast in the war at the time of that craziest of all missions so I had always suspected it was the last for all three of us. It was strange now that I thought of it. I could remember that last mission was unprecedented in its oddity, though I could remember nothing about it.

Since it was drilled into us never to tell other members of the team about our personal lives, and we were only known to one another by our legends, finding one another after leaving the team would be difficult. The out-processing from Phantom stressed this for obvious reasons. One was that a team that reformed in the civilian world could be a danger to society in ways ranging from running a drug cartel to assassinating presidents. We were honestly warned to stay away from any civilian job that could give us notoriety lest other team members or certain military officers recognize us. As a result of this none of us ever ran for public office, made a TV commercial, published a book or won a Nobel Prize. We never applied for work where a background check would be made. They told us we could lead normal lives, but never to break the rules. That's what worried me about Nine Lives.

"I've had a good life," he smiled and almost chuckled. "They said to stay away from police work and that sort of thing where our talents and training might be noticed or our history discovered. Do the opposite, they said. So, I went to college and took a history degree, then started as the assistant manager in a furniture store. Eventually, I owned my own place, expanded into kitchen cabinets, carpeting, and a lot more. I stayed away from meeting the public. Those around me thought is was because of my scar, that I'd scare away customers. It worked. During the real-estate bubble I did real well. Money is no problem if that would only solve it."

He stopped. Looked around. He said in a whisper, "Should we be talking out here? Anybody could be behind one of those bushes."

The fidgety look had returned which bothered me. When I handled the FBI agent the summer before, even though he was proficient in martial arts by their standards, he was nothing. Nine Lives would be something else.

"Yeah. You never can be sure. Let's go in. We can talk in my little shop in the basement. Would you like a beer?"

"Could really use one about now."

In the room I had set aside for fixing things, and making a model airplane now and then, he smiled. There were a half dozen planes hanging from the walls in one state of repair or other.

"This is tidy. Nice little hobby. Bet you're good at flying 'em. You were so quick."

"Surprisingly, it's taken me a long time to learn it. The thing I was good at was reacting quickly and correctly the first time in a dangerous situation. Under less than lethal conditions, I seem to be normal. Controlling the model to go up and down is easy because you always move the control stick the same way. But, left and right is hard. When the plane is going away you move the control stick the way you want it to go, but when it's coming toward you it's the opposite. Then, what do you do when it's moving across in front of you?"

"Strange world." He sat in an arm chair and popped the top of his beer. "I was down in South Carolina at a carpet factory working out the details of a new order."

It was clear small talk was over, time to talk business.

"When I was in my early teens I had spent a summer with some distant relatives on a small farm in the Smokey Mountains. I had some time so decided to rent a car and drive back in there and see if the place still existed. It's off the beaten path so the roads, while paved are curvy and have a lot of steep drop-offs. Coming over a ridge I started down and at that moment my brakes went out. As I remember, there were popping sounds as it happened. I immediately applied the emergency brake. That kept my speed in check but it wasn't enough to stop the car. Down I went leaving rubber on the sharper curves. Of course, there were several lights blinking at me from the instrument cluster. With a snap, the emergency brake was gone too and I was fighting for my life. I was already doing over sixty and accelerating so jumping out was not an option. On the last curve I almost bought it and then there was the bridge at the bottom of the gorge. I knew if I could stay with it until the car bled off speed going up the far side I'd make it.

"I was going over a hundred when the bridge leveled off in front of me, but it wasn't a smooth transition to the actual bridge, the bridge being higher than the approach to it. I was airborne for most of the distance across the river. Skidding and bouncing off rocky out-croppings I slowed. It was my plan to wait until I rolled to a stop and then slip it into Park. I was going to make it and was glad to be alive, but taking no chances, I unsnapped my seat belt and opened the door. There! Into Park. Nothing happened as the car started to roll back. I dove out and the lower corner of the door raked my ribs, but I made it. The car went over the side, bounced down the mountain for two or three hundred feet and exploded. Luckily, through it all I had encountered no other traffic. There was none now. I picked myself up and found a place in the bushes to hide not knowing how close they were. Somebody had deliberately tried to kill me."

When all I did was nod in response to his tale of horror he was taken aback, as I suppose would be normal. In response to his unspoken question I said, "About a year ago someone tried to kill me, too. I eventually found out who it was and mostly why he did it."

"He's dead, right."

"No. We settled it amicably."

"Maybe not as amicably as you think!"

"No. He didn't do that thing to you." Without giving him a chance to comment I proceeded to the question that was burning in my mind. "You found me, how about Blue Dog?" Blue Dog was the third man in our team from my last Phantom operation.

"Oh, yeah. I went to him first because he was easy. I knew his real name."

"How! That was the one thing that could get you sent to a killing zone in a blink." Everybody in Vietnam was aware that there were certain units that were regularly engaged with the enemy and took heavy causalities. Any screw-off that refused to behave was transferred to one of those units. He'd be dead in a fortnight.

"It just happened that we were both from the same company. We should have been assigned to different Phantom Teams. We were for our training and first missions. With our heavy attrition, though, new teams were always being formed, and they lost sight of our former associations. We weren't buddies, but we knew each other having pulled sentry duty and stuff like that together a few times. We played dumb not seeing how it could matter. After my 'accident' I looked for him on the Internet. He was working as the head grounds keeper of a medical complex in Massachusetts with a couple of guys under him."

"Well, what'd he say?" I asked. Nine Lives seemed to be trying to avoid something.

He finished the rest of his beer in a single draught. Slapped the can on the work table and looked straight ahead. "He didn't say anything!" The words were spat against the wall. "He died eleven days before I got there!"

The can crinkled as his strong hand crushed it.

"So, tell me about it. Obviously he didn't die of natural causes."

He looked at me as he shook his head. "They're smart. He was *murdered* of natural causes."

Though he looked like a coiled snake ready to strike, I wasn't sure he was ready to attack me. He was confused, and I was tense. It was unlikely he was packing a gun, or even a knife. Neither would be necessary for an attack on any normal man. I might be different, and even if I looked placid, I was ready to counter his first aggressive move.

"Want another beer?"

"Maybe in a minute. They were clever, but not perfect. Blue Dog died of a heart attack. I found the guy who did the autopsy. He said it was unexpected, but had plenty of precedent. After that I tracked down one of the guys he worked with. What they didn't know was that a few weeks before he died he had gone to see his doctor because he had discovered a lump. While there the doc laid on a thorough physical. Two days before he tipped over he gets the word that the lump is cancer, but a slow growing kind so not to worry except to keep an eye on it. As an after thought, the doc says the good news was his heart and arteries are like a teenager's—never die of that."

He had calmed noticeably as if by saying it some poison had drained from his brain.

"Normally, the heart attack would not be questioned, and it wasn't as far as I know. There was no point in exposing myself further by contacting his family. What happened to Blue Dog and then my experience must mean they're related—you agree?"

That was it. He thought the two cases had to be related, but on one level was questioning his sanity. I was the only other person alive who could corroborate his conclusion.

I nodded. "It would be unlikely they were random. The part I don't understand is why would anyone care after all this time?"

"How about that beer? But, don't offer me another one after that, okay?"

"Coming up and agreed."

It was necessary to leave him alone while I went upstairs and got the beers. There was no alternative so I hurried without giving the appearance I was.

— 2 —

When I returned with the beer, it appeared as if he had not moved.

As I handed him one of the cans he said, "That was quick."

There was no point in hiding it. "Can you blame me? This is heavy stuff. A man is dead, and you are a whisker from being the same. You're here looking for answers, I don't have any, and neither of us are men to be trifled with. Beyond that, I don't know about you, but my bones are getting too creaky for this sort of crap." Before he could respond, I continued, "I'm still curious, though, is there any reason this should be happening now?"

He sipped the beer. "Yes and no. I'll start with no. As long as the system stayed intact, there was no way they could find us. But, if there was even the slightest glitch, it would be a big yes. After I got out, I ran into another Vietnam vet. We traded war stories. His were better than mine, or better than mine would have been if I had stayed with my original company, which," he added with some regret, "is something I should have done. That unit was charmed in that it never seemed to get caught in one of those murderous operations of taking a heavily defended hill where most of 'em ended up wounded or dead. It was strange, some of those not in Phantom knew more than we did. I heard it like this.

"What we saw of the Army was nothing a person would want to do for his life's work. But, there were exceptions. If your father was a general, you could go to West Point. As long as you didn't screw up beyond the point that your dear ol' dad could fix it, you had a good life. The other option was to by hook or by crook get into the Point and then marry the general's daughter. Either way worked. The problem was that most of those who did it one of those ways were simply not cut out to be field commanders. The old rule is that during a war there are no promotions without having a command in-country. Each step up the ladder took another command the next rung higher up. The result was easy to see.

There were an awful lot of commanders who were inept, some so bad that almost anything would have been done to be rid of them. The problem was, they were connected. Guess what? They happened to take a stray bullet, drive over a mine in the road, get ambushed—lots of possibilities. That's what some of the Phantom Teams did or so went the scuttle-butt."

"I never heard that part of it," I interrupted.

Nodding at my comment he continued. "I don't know if that was true or not, but just having the rumor float around that there was a secret unit that got rid of incompetent commanders caused those gulf-club generals to try a lot harder. It's also why anyone who learned we were part of Phantom both hated and feared us. Well, the kids of the incompetent generals are no longer lieutenants, they're lieutenant generals, and may have a score to settle."

"Messy."

"More than messy—deadly. I've been over the last couple years of my life dozens of times. I don't think I slipped. There's no easy way to know if Blue Dog did without an investigation large enough to expose both of us and who knows how many others. I have to ask you, now that you think as I do, that my case and Blue Dog's are connected, did you do anything to start this?"

I wasn't willing to capitulate and reveal to him how I was likely the one who screwed up. There was more he wasn't telling so I ignored his question.

"It seems like they found Blue Dog first. There it should have ended."

"It's like I said, we were from the same company, and when I talked about my military service, I only talked about the places I was officially assigned. But, our company commander, Capt. Wilson, was a gossip. He was ordered not to tell that two of his men were listed as present but were not. If something Blue Dog said became connected to our company, they could have found Wilson who could still be alive or one of the clerks who did the morning report. That would have led to me. I agree, there it should have ended, and maybe it did. But, and there's a big question here, what got them looking in the first place. It's unlikely that one of those guys gets another star on his shoulder and immediately sees he has enough authority to go on a witch hunt. The more stars, the more of a political tight rope those guys walk. He wouldn't have done it unless he had expectations of a quick quiet success."

There was one possibility Nine Lives had not considered. "You're forgetting something. Having found one of us they could easily connect to the other two."

"How do you figure?"

"Remember on that operation when we finally stumbled upon friend-lies, about a day before we died of starvation, we had to give name, rank, and serial number. We had no dog tags or other identification. We were hardly recognizable as human beings, to say nothing of American sol-diers. Our cover that we had been POW's and escaped would answer the problem of no ID's. For you two it was halfway plausible. But, me, from the Quartermaster Corps? That was pretty thin. Just suppose that a guy did get another star on his shoulder and had the luxury of putting a man on digging through personnel records for the six months or so either way from when we reappeared from the jungle. He wouldn't know exactly what he was looking for, only something different, an event that didn't fit. That'd do it."

His earlier agitation, bordering on out right hostility, was gone. He was thinking out the possibilities. Undoubtedly, one of them was that I was hiding something. It's funny, not ha, ha funny, but odd funny, how it sometimes takes time for obvious things to become obvious. It occurred to me at that moment that he could easily think that with Blue Dog defi-nitely dead, and him maybe dead, that if I were definitely dead too it would all stop. Two confirmed and one probable might be enough to satisfy a delusional general's need for revenge.

He nodded slowly. "Yeah. They had us in that field hospital pumping fluids and food into us as fast as our weakened systems could take it. Es-caped POW's were so rare that G2 had the debrief team on the way. Then Blue Dog got that call through to our secret contact. The Phantom's Huey with us on it was just over the trees when the G2 chopper landed. The G2 guys would have been, well, enraged would be too mild, and made handsome reports about the whole episode. If somebody were looking for something odd, that would fill the bill."

He leaned back as if in thought again. He'd get there sooner or later. Then he said, "Once they stated looking, there's no doubt they could find all three of us. The fact that we weren't among those who did in the commanders, if that even really happened, wouldn't matter. They'd never be able to pin it down close enough to know what teams did what missions. Besides, we were all dirt. The question is, what happened to make them start looking?"

He was digging again. Maybe the attempts on Blue Dog and him weren't related. It was wishful thinking, I knew, but something I might as well explore.

"What happened after your car went over the side?"

He looked at me, probably for the first time, with real focus and intent, though his voice didn't intimate that he was scrutinizing me. "I was hurting and had a raw welt on my ribs, not bleeding much, though. I expected rifle shots any second. In hindsight, that was dumb. How'd they know the emergency brake would hold as long as it did? I went to cover fast taking in as much of the scene as I could, you know, from our training. After the initial fireball, it took only ten minutes before there was no more smoke than a camp fire along the river below. In the next hour only two cars came by, neither of them even slowed down. I worked my way up the rocks for a better view and waited. I stayed there the rest of the day. Nothing happened. With a half-hour of light left I started walking in the direction I had been driving. I recalled there was a small town five miles ahead. I arrived after dark, slipped the guy at the only gas station a fifty and he connected me with a truck headed out. Nothing's happened since. How'd they know exactly where to be waiting for me? I could have taken other routes to my destination."

He was either looking for information, or playing with me, so I played along.

"That was easier than you might think. Ever heard of the Global Positioning System?"

"Sure. We use GPS locators when we go deer hunting. You press the button for home when you're at the base camp. Then, it will always show you the distance and direction to camp. Slickest things you ever saw."

"Good. There are GPS receivers that are combined with a cell phone. These are placed on your car. Somebody a thousand miles away can call the cell phone and it will send back its location from the GPS receiver. The caller has a readout screen with maps of the whole country in memory, even contour maps. All that's needed in addition is an output circuit that will turn on when it receives a special code from the caller. It could be used to send an electrical signal to an explosive device. Did you rent your car the day before you went on your sentimental journey?"

"Yeah. Guess they rigged it that night, huh?"

"I'd say so. It's not surprising you didn't see anyone. They were miles away. It's likely they went back a few days later to check, though. They'll know they didn't get you."

"I've been hoping that wasn't true, I guess, but now that you say it, that's likely. Why all the stealth? I went home after finding Blue Dog. If they're so smart, why not enter my house at night and kill us all?"

"It probably means the one calling the shots is highly placed and has a lot to lose if he were to be exposed. They're being careful. That gives us some small advantage."

He raised his eyebrows, "What's this 'us' you're talking about? I came for information. Nothing else."

"No. You came because you're trying to stay alive. Now, that includes me as well. In case you've been blocking this from your mind, too, it means we have to reform the old team, with the two of us that are left."

The furrows in his forehead were more pronounced than I'd seen them. It wasn't making sense. His original hostility had turned completely to bewilderment.

"You've been asking yourself what happened to stir this up. Well, brace yourself, I did it."

That was another thing he hadn't wanted to face, that something really did happen to open this whole Pandora's box. It was now a fact that he hadn't been imagining things.

"So, let's hear it." He was curious, still refusing full acceptance.

"There was an old rich guy living in St. Paul, worth a half billion. He had two kids, a boy and a girl. For different reasons he didn't want to leave the money to either one. A PI firm he hired found me someplace in the relatives of his first wife. The son learned that he intended to leave the money to me—probably bugged the old guy's office. He tried to kill me with a bow and arrow like deer hunters use while I was out unwinding in some wild country north of town. He missed but I didn't get him. My nephew was with me so it would have looked odd if we hadn't told the police about it. One thing lead to another and the FBI became involved. The agent assigned was a loose cannon. Pretty soon he was accusing me of making up the story. He even showed up where I worked and tried to get me fired. I ran into him there, forced him into a conference room and beat him up pretty badly. I got his gun away from him, that wasn't so hard, but what to do with it?"

". . . You didn't!" he interrupted.

I nodded. "I did. I shoved a bullet up the muzzle of his gun the wrong way. I didn't mean it as the mark of Phantom the way we used it, but simply to make the gun unusable. You know that in those modern conference rooms where everything's electronic there isn't so much as a paper clip, certainly nothing to disable a gun."

He leaned back and emptied the second beer. "Our unique sign that said you had been visited by your worst nightmare."

From his expression I could see that it was almost a relief for him to know something solid, to stop guessing.

"Okay. From the training we know not to look back. What's done is done." With a double take his eyes were riveted on me. No matter how dire things might be, in this society, money was always the next thing to life. "Did you get the money, the half billion?"

He said he had done well, but a half billion would trump that. "No. When the old man died last fall his lawyer went to liquidate his assets. He found that most of the money was in an international investment that turned out to be a Ponzi scheme. In his will he left set amounts to various people and charities. I was to get the remainder which was the bulk of his estate, but in the end I got a little more than fifty thousand dollars."

He nodded with a smug grin feeling safe again on that score. "So, what do we do, and I most emphatically mean *we*."

I nodded, "The first thing I learned from that whole episode a year ago is that we really didn't get much training, especially anything that helps us now. If our mission required us to swim across a swiftly flowing river, we were trained how to do that. If there were no rivers in the scenario, they didn't bother. It was all narrowly mission specific. We had enough food with us to complete the mission and return if everything went perfectly. That's why we had such a hard time living off the land, even the jungle. They didn't bother to teach us that. In modern society it's even worse."

"But, you managed not to get killed by the arrow in the bush."

"Yeah, that's right. I was lucky. He missed with the first shot. Then, alerted, my ability to think quickly in a dangerous situations kicked in. What I did in the conference room to the FBI agent was totally wrong. Whoever's after us might be connected in some way with that bunch."

"Wait a minute. What you've just told me, that stuff from last summer, what's taking them so long to come back at you?"

"It's possible that the FBI agent was so bad that they were willing to let it go as if I had done them a service. Or, they're being careful. Like I said, this isn't like in a war where people are killed by accidents all the time, you know, truck roll overs, all of that. There are several people that know about last year. I've written it down in the most minute detail, too.

If I suddenly get run down by a Mac truck there'd be a lot of questions. And, my wife knows all the people's names from start to end. That took some work to get Blue Dog, and make the attempt on you. Now that I think about it, I'd say the whole thing started with the bullet rammed in the gun barrel the wrong way. But, there's more, and I don't know what it is."

"How do you figure? The idea that someone wants to even a score with you from last summer, or even the possibility that some general is out for revenge makes sense to me."

"Nah." I said. "They're like we are, especially the generals. What happened back then can't be undone so why risk your career with retaliation? However, if someone had a big dirty plan and they came to know about us, they might think we'd be good tools for them. Think about it, each one of us is living as Mr. Joe Average. Nobody suspects our profile showed us to have such unique talents to which was added specific training." After a pause I added, "And, it's possible it's not really us that interests them, but something that we did, or something they think we did or they think we know."

"That's why they did in Blue Dog. They'd be afraid to put the old team back together. And it wouldn't take three of us to remember something."

"It very well might take two of us, though," I added.

"They did try to kill me, too. How does that figure into it? It made sense if we were talking about revenge. This way it makes no sense at all."

"Exactly what did it sound like when the service brakes went out and then when the emergency brake cable broke?"

"Sort of a pop or snap, something like that. I definitely heard each one of them go."

"Remember that emergency brake cable was under a lot of tension. What if at the exact place they had predetermined, another explosive charge went off to break it?"

"Oh, I see what you're getting at. They first disabled the service brakes. Then, when I was far enough down the mountain to where I could make it with the emergency brake gone, too, they disabled it. I'd think it was lucky that it lasted as long as it did and thereby was alive when they intended to kill me. But, that's just the way they planned it."

The mood of Nine Lives had settled down to where he was looking at the situation like a vexing business problem, which was good. If only I could trust him. As this thought crossed my mind the door at the top of the stairs opened and I recognized the light steps of Camilla coming down. She smiled at Nine Lives and said, "Hi." He smiled and nodded. She handed me a manila folder and returned the way she had come.

Nine Lives tensed. I could tell he didn't like this, and it wasn't clear what he might do. But, it was also a test of how stable he was. Did he trust me, and could he control himself in a set back?

"What's that all about?" he blustered.

"Nothing to worry about."

Actually, it could be something for him to worry about a lot. After we had come to the basement, Camilla, as we had prearranged, went out and took the plate number off the car he arrived in. I opened the folder and saw that he had not arrived in a car, but rather a Cadillac Escalade. And he owned it, no lease arrangement or payments. He had the title free and clear.

There was no other way than to tell Nine Lives what we had done, so I did. "While we were talking on the patio you were unwilling to tell me your name. Since you knew presumably everything you cared to know about me, that put me at a disadvantage. After the events of last summer, we decided to use some of the money we had received from the ill fated estate of the old man to put a private investigating firm on retainer. My wife took the plate number off your Escalade and called the PIs with a rush request. They faxed the preliminary results of their search to us. You are driving your own vehicle, Mr. Harold Everett Auston. May I call you Harry, or do you prefer Harold?"

"Harry's fine." There was no question his voice told he was let down having lost any advantage he might have thought he had. "How much do you have?"

I flipped through the pages as I spoke. "Your home address with an aerial photo. That appears to be horse barn out back. Very nice. There's information about your company, its annual gross income and your take, number of employees, that sort of thing. Don't feel bad. It's a digital world. I've been wondering, how'd you find me?"

He smiled. "Sort of the same way only I had to do the looking myself since the only thing I had to go on was what you looked like back then. When I returned home from my experiences out East, I went on line. From your accent, I knew you were from this part of the country. You said you planned to go to college preferring engineering if you could cut it. I assumed you could and started my search with the biggest university in these parts, the University of Minnesota. We were both nineteen or twenty so I figured five years to get a degree. I called up one of those for fee 'find your classmates' websites and started looking at the Institute of Technology photos for a range of years. I found a probable. With the name I went to high school year books. Since I knew you less than two years after your high school graduation picture was taken it was a sure thing."

It crossed my thoughts that we now knew who each other was and that we had a problem. No, not necessarily. For sure *I* had a problem, and if what he had told me was the total truth, something I wasn't willing to concede yet, then *we* had a problem. There was one more thing to explore.

"If we are to get anywhere, we have to retrace our missions together in minute detail, with emphasis on recalling the names of those in charge of the operations, and in fact the name of every other person even remotely connected with us."

"Tough," he said. "Everybody used a legend, you remember that."

"True enough. But, I remember seeing a luggage tag on the duffel bag of one of the trainers. It was Sgt. M. C. Samulson."

"And, the captain who was in charge of our unit was Babbit. One of the NCOs called him that a few times. They seemed to go back a ways together."

I was rubbing my chin with my eyes closed as another odd thing came to mind. "You know," I said at last, "I haven't thought about those days much as they advised us not to. And, it has worked well. Now that I try to put things back together I'm having a hard time. What little I can remember of the missions seems all mixed up."

He looked at me as seriously as I'd seem him since we met. It wasn't fear, at least not fear of what lay ahead. It was something else.

"Over the last two weeks as I've tried to make sense out of all of this I've come to the conclusion that they did some serious messing with our minds before they let us go. I'm worried that they may have done something to us so it's impossible that we'll ever remember those missions. What do you think?"

"That's not out of the question. But, the fact remains if we plan to stay alive we must give it our best try."

The mood was getting too somber and we'd covered all the ground that made sense without getting into wild speculation. I needed him out of my house so I could think and do some planning.

"Tell you what. We aren't going to solve anything tonight. Are you staying in town for a few days?"

"Yeah, thought I might. What do you have in mind?"

"Write down every single detail you can remember about our trainers, the higher-ups and the missions. Give me a call in twenty-four hours and we'll get together and compare notes."

A thought struck me. We needed time to work this out, time together where we could throw ideas back and forth. He started to get up when I motioned him to stay seated. On a pad of paper I drew a crude map showing my house and a place to meet. Then, I said, "Might as well break this up for now," and motioned for him to follow.

Outside it was nearly dark. Near the garage I halted him and spoke in whispers. "If someone is really serious about all of this, they'll be keeping tabs on us in any number of ways. Here's what I suggest you do. Tomorrow morning, check out of your hotel. You do have a suitcase, I presume."

He nodded.

"Drive to the airport and park the Escalade in the long term parking. Buy a plane ticket to St. Louis. Then rent a car. What I say now is important. At the Minneapolis airport you don't take a bus to your rental car, you walk. So, tell the rental clerk you're in a great hurry and will take anything that is immediately available. If you have a choice, pick the most unremarkable vehicle they have. Get to it fast and start moving. Plan your moves to meet me at eleven in the morning where I've shown on this map. We'll talk and maybe take a little trip."

All he did was nod. He walked to his vehicle, got in, and drove off.

— 3 —

After Nine Lives—Harry Auston—it would be hard to think of him by that name, had driven away, I found Camilla in the back room pretending to sew. She looked up and I mouthed the word "walk." She nodded and put on a sweater. We started down the street toward the lake while not using a predictable route.

Through all the years of our married life, I had said relatively little about my military service other than a few stories from training in the States, and barracks life in Vietnam. These were all true so I could tell them with no fear of slipping and revealing things I shouldn't. For her part, she internalized the idea that I was a guy off the streets of America who had put on a suit of clothes that happened to look just like the clothes worn by a whole bunch of other guys and my job happened to be in a far away place where the cities had funny names. While there, I went to work every day in an office to process requests for people who wanted to buy stuff, some of which was dangerous. As far as my having any martial arts training, she had scoffed a time or two about how helpless I was in that respect. It would be hard to change that image though I now felt there was no choice but to try.

As we walked I said, "That man who visited this evening, was someone from Vietnam. He's called Nine Lives."

"The information from the PI said he was Harry Auston. Besides, what parent would name a kid Nine Lives?"

"His parents didn't name him that, he did. And, it's not his name, it's his legend."

"What you're saying isn't making any sense."

"I know. What I'm about to tell you will be a lot of stuff that doesn't make any *sense*, though it all happens to be true. My legend is Double Duce. Legend in this context is some times used to mean a completely new identity for someone starting with grammar school records and everything else. That's done for spies, people in the witness protection program, stuff like that. For us they were code phrases because we were engaged in covert operations, many of which were illegal. As such, our legends were not a complete life history of the type I mentioned, but were just as effective in keeping anyone from knowing who the real people were. He and I were part of a covert team during our Vietnam days. We were given special training to do special missions."

With hesitation in her voice, she asked, "Why haven't you ever told me about this?"

"First of all, it was top secret and it's a crime to reveal that kind of information. Beyond that, it was best that I didn't. What *you* don't know, *you* can't tell.

"Did you ever kill anybody?"

"Don't ever ask me that! It's not what you do to people who've been through the mill like we were."

"Okay, I'm sorry."

"And, after the missions we were thoroughly debriefed, and as both he and I are beginning to see that meant something more severe than what we think about as debriefing, we were sort of brainwashed to the point we aren't sure what we did. During that business last summer something happened to cause someone to take an interest in me and through me, Harry and the other member of our team who survived Vietnam. And, it seems possible it's not really us that interests them, it's something that we did, or something they think we did or they think we know."

"Is that the reason you decided to put that PI company on retainer? Did you think something like this would come up?"

"Not exactly like this, but, yes, I had a gut feeling that there was more to come."

"Are we in danger?"

"We wouldn't be talking in hushed tones on a dark street as I continually glance over my shoulder if we weren't. We must assume our house is bugged, and there are GPS tracking devices on our cars. The cars are probably bugged for sound, too. If you happen to find one, leave it alone but tell me about it. If we destroy it, they'll know we're on to them, and they'll just replace them, anyway.'

"Who are they?"

"No idea at this point. But, they have resources because the teams we were on were extremely secret."

"You mean like the FBI might be watching you?"

"It might be, but it goes beyond that. I plan to meet with Nine Lives . . . no. I have to stop that. I must think of him as Harry Auston. We'll get together tomorrow and see what we can figure out." As we walked in silence, I was thinking of the possibilities. "Of course, it's possible Harry's working for them."

Camilla grabbed my arm. "I'm frightened now. Can we go to anybody for help?"

"There's no one I can think of. It'll have to play out. Try to think of times I may have said something that seemed odd or didn't make sense. There must be a clue someplace. There were times I woke up after bad dreams. Sometimes I told you about them, and you'd hardly listen because they were so dumb. There might be a pattern, some common element. If we knew what they were after, we might be able to give it to them."

"No," she whispered. "You couldn't do that. If it's so important, they'd have to silence you, and probably me, after they got it."

I was a little surprised at how quickly she was picking up on the situation. "You're getting the idea. Let's head back."

Tuesday

The next morning I walked to the parking lot of a park a mile from the house and waited for him. A silver Ford Focus drove in at eleven with Harry driving. There was enough wild area with big trees near the parking lot to stay out of sight.

"Why all of this?" he asked as we started walking.

"We must assume they placed GPS tracking devices on our cars. If we were sure we found them all we could take them off and leave them home, but you never know if you're clean. By renting the car at random at the airport you got away before they could do the same to this car. If they check they'll know the car you're driving but won't be able to track it, though it still may have a cell phone in it that's active. But, we can hope that before they realize you didn't get on the plane and then figure out the car you rented, we won't care anymore. By the way, I approve of the make and color. It's about the most common type around here."

"That's good. We're working again, I mean like we did. Hope I can get into the groove to contribute my share."

"I'm wondering if just the two of us can make it work again. I really wish we had Blue Dog," I said.

"Yeah, that thought occurred to me, too. However, we'll have to define the mission, the constraints, resources at our disposal, all of that. The biggest thing we lack is information on the enemy. How do we do anything without knowing what they want?"

"Have you had any recurring dreams, flashbacks, even odd thoughts that came into your head the didn't fit anywhere? I'm convinced it has something to do with our missions with the teams."

"Let's start with what we know. I assume you remember the snake."

As we walked I guided us to the corner of an open field where there were some weeping willows. We stood behind a tree trunk where we could keep an eye on the car.

"Oh, yeah," I said. "That snake saved our lives. How long would you say it was?"

"Eight feet."

"That's about what I'd have said, maybe longer since it was twisted up in the grass. Remember, we'd spent a bad night, mostly because we were so hungry, but also because we though we heard Viet Cong voices in the area."

Harry continued the reminiscence. "At first light Blue Dog, who had the last watch of the night, pointed and whispered that there was something moving in the grass to our front, up close. We thought we were about to be attacked and were as good as dead. Finally the suspense got to him and he inched forward, his knife at the ready. I'll never forget the yelp he made as he almost flew back. He had come eyeball to eyeball with that big guy. From then on it was a running battle to kill the thing before it got away. Finally you whacked him on the head with a rock stunning him and we closed in for the kill."

"Boy, we spent all day filleting pieces of that snake and roasting it. That was a good idea Blue Dog had to cut the meat about an inch thick and leave the skin on and then just lay the skin on the coals until it was cooked. It was so good. The little they did tell us about living off the land—if it ever came to that—was never to eat raw meat, that we'd get parasites followed by the worst dysentery of all time. We did all right on that score."

"Agreed. That was something. We said then that this was the meal against which all others would be judged and found wanting. Gotta say, to this day never had a better one. Man, half scorched, barely cooked, no salt, no nothing. It was great! That was the right thing you said about eating it slowly and drinking water with it so we didn't barf it up. That night everyone of us took our turn at sentry, and everyone fell asleep. It felt so good to have some food in our stomachs."

"Yeah," I continued "And after each chunk we were moving about cutting branches to make better cooking and eating utensils." After a pause. "To come back from the dead, and we were almost that, really leaves an impression."

"Remember how we talked about ways we might save some of it to take with us? Nothing would work. Even later in the day there were signs of it starting to go rancid. The heat and humidity of the jungle were unforgiving."

"It was enough, though, it saved our lives . . . . Wait a minute. Did that really happen? Or, was that something they put into our minds as part of that debriefing process? We both seem to remember the exact same things. Try to think of some odd little things that only you'd remember."

"Well," Harry started, "I'd never dissected a snake before. I'd cleaned fish, but this was different. I remember thinking everything was so long. There was a small partially digested animal in what we assumed was it's stomach. And, Blue Dog and I did the butchering while you started the fire."

As he spoke, I watched the comings and goings of the people in the parking lot. There weren't many so it was no problem. A dark car parked and a couple with tennis rackets walked to the court. A man and two kids appeared along a paved path as it emerged from a wooded area. He followed the kids to the Jungle Jim.

The fire. It was there in my memory, but only a little. "Yeah. There was a dead tree on the bank just behind where we killed the snake. I remember that. At first it seemed like an impossible task to find dry wood, but there it was. After all, now that I think of it, it makes sense. It was the dry season. This is new, never thought of this before. I cut shavings of wood, but the wood was different colors as I cut deeper into the branch. This left some shavings with colored lengthwise stripes in them. Then I put small sticks over the pile of shavings in the form of a teepee followed by larger ones. I'd started camp fires when I was a kid. There were waterproof matches in my survival kit. Everybody had one of those. The fire started easily with almost no smoke. I remember nothing about the snake other than to go back and get another piece for the next round of cooking. How about the fire?"

"Nothing. We came over with the first meat, and you had the fire going like magic. We roasted the first pieces on green sticks over the open flames. You remember that?"

"Sure do. Charred, too hot. I think each of us burned his mouth on the first bite. It was really good."

We ambled over to some six-inch basswood trees, again not entirely exposing ourselves.

"So," Harry said, "it seems like we remember different things. It would have been a real job for them to have given us each a set of different false impressions like we remember. I'd say the snake incident really happened. How about you?"

"Yeah. Which logically means we were loose in the jungle and if we didn't starve to death, we'd come across some VC and either be killed or made POWs. But that wasn't part of the training. We were never sent on suicide missions as such. There were always provisions made to get us back, even pretty elaborate plans, though we were told there were times when entire teams went out and none of them returned. If we could remember the snake incident why can't we remember what the mission was about?"

Harry held up his index finger. "Because, my friend, they didn't *know* about the snake. We stumbled out of the bush, and were practically shot a couple of times by friendly forces. Finally, we managed to yell at them until they got the idea we weren't the VC attacking them in broad daylight. We were emaciated and that corpsman started feeding us. He was pretty good, now that I think about it. He gave us just as much as our weakened systems could handle. Nobody bothered to ask us how we had been able to live off the land, because it was all too obvious we hadn't been."

I nodded. "If we accept your premise, it means that everything *they* knew about the actual mission or anything else we told them has probably been erased from our memories, and our only hope is to remember little things here and there that probably won't help us with what we need."

"Is there anything else we both remember?"

"Carrying something heavy in sand is another snippet that came back to me from time to time, but the context is missing. Oh, and the smell of garbage."

"Funny, me too. It could have been an ocean beach, a gravel pit, a desert, just about anything except I don't remember anything about garbage. Unlike the snake, it ends there. This isn't getting any easier, is it?"

I shook my head. "No, it isn't. Let's do some driving. It seems like nobody showed up to tag your rental with a tracker."

I directed Harry south on the 35W freeway then on Highway 36 and exited at the Super Target on Snelling Avenue. I said, "We need some groceries, beer and a Styrofoam cooler. How do you want to handle it?"

"Obviously, you know what we're going to do and I don't. I'll get the cooler and beer. How much beer?"

"I'd say a twenty-four pack. They should have the cooler in Target so find the beer first, buy a cooler and then find me. This Target has a grocery section, and I'll pick up the ice with the food."

I watched Harry drive away. A light brown Honda followed. I recognized the driver. It was Camilla. She was good friends with a woman down the street and said her car was down and asked for a loan for a couple of hours. As we had made our way to the Target store, I knew where she would be parked and directed Harry to take that route. I had lowered my window as we passed her to let her know it was us. I marveled at how she had taken this in stride. She was scared, I knew, but the only way out was to see it through.

I walked slowly to the entrance of the supermarket trying to determine if there were anyone following her. Nothing was apparent. I knew our nemesis wouldn't have to follow us every minute, at least for now. It would be some time before we could possibly put together what was happening. As I entered and took a shopping cart, I thought it was possible we'd be given clues from time to time. I'd have to mention this at least to Camilla. I wasn't sure of Harry yet, probably never would be. I hated shopping but started anyway.

Ten minutes later, my cell phone vibrated, and I answered it. It was Camilla.

"He drove to the Har Mar Mall parking lot and parked. He slipped into the passenger seat of the car he parked beside and is having a conversation with a man. I got the plate number of the other car, and am headed for the Barnes And Noble bookstore. I'll watch through the window until they leave."

"Wow! That's really good. What do I call you double-oh something or other?"

"Don't joke. I don't think you can trust him. What will you do?"

"Don't see that I can do anything other than what I had planned. He knows we're going somewhere, and not just the two of us to cook out in the park. It means somebody's either following us or tracking us, probably following to be so close at hand. He had no idea where I would direct him to go. When you're home, have the agency run the plate and see what we get. If it's bad call the house where we're going."

"Okay. Be careful."

Five minutes later there was another call.

"I watched from the entry of the bookstore. They finished and the other car went south on Snelling. Harry drove a half-block and stopped by a liquor store. It's odd the other guy left and won't be following you."

"Yeah. Either there is a whole team, or they know all they need to know for now. Wonder that the story is with Harry?"

"Now that you mention it," she continued, "when Harry drove away from his meeting another car backed out one row back. It seemed to be following him, or it's my imagination. When Harry stopped at the liquor store, the other car parked a ways off and an Asian looking man got out. Now that I think of it, that doesn't fit. The Asian guy only drove fifty yards. Then, he went into the same store Harry did."

I saw Harry waiting as I was in the check out lane. He stood back and followed me out giving no indication we were together. I slowed and Harry moved off to the right. The cooler, with beer, was already in the trunk. I dumped in two of the three bags of ice, then the half dozen steaks still in plastic trays with clear plastic wrap, then the rest of the ice. With the calls from Camilla, I scratched the idea of stopping at a fast-food place in the area for our lunch before we started our drive. Instead, I bought a few things at the deli in the grocery store. I took this bag and a six-pack of bottled water into the car with us.

— 4 —

Once buckled in our seats I said, "Now we do a little driving." From there on I gave only left and right directions and never mentioned a highway number. We went east on Highway 36 until we exited to North 35E. We were headed to Wisconsin by way of Taylors Falls.

After we were moving, I asked, "Do you have a cell phone?"

"Sure."

"Can I see it?"

"What now?"

"Come on. I'll show you something."

Harry reached into his shirt pocket and produced it. I used the blade of my pocket knife to pry the back lid off, and removed the battery after which I placed the three pieces in the cup holder. Then I did the same with mine.

"You may or may not know, but it is possible to track the location of a cell phone even while it's turned off. It makes sense, you know. Once you have turned it on in a certain area the cell system knows where to find you. The cell system doesn't look for you all over the world, just in the system where your phone signaled its presence. That means your phone will "hear" a call when it comes. It's only a small step from there to have the phone respond with a signal saying that it heard the call even though it's turned off. At this point, we don't know who we're dealing with or how sophisticated they are. I don't want to take unnecessary chances."

After a pause I added, "Make sure you don't push the 'road service' button or the car will call some central location saying you need a tow, and give the location of the car."

"I know about the car, but the cell phone, that's interesting."

We rode in silence for some time. After that we talked about our families and our work. As we crossed into Wisconsin, Harry said, "I don't want to seem nosey, but since I'm in the car too, in fact, driving, would it be too much to let me in on where we're going?"

I smiled. "We're going on what might be a wasted trip because I don't know if the guy will be home. I didn't want to call ahead in case my phone is bugged."

"You're really paranoid, you know that."

"A few times in the past when I was being paranoid, the thought occurred to me that I was being ridiculous. The only mistake I made was in not being nearly paranoid enough. You see, they could have the entire FBI and who knows what other agencies keeping tabs on us, or it could be the work of two or three guys. If it's a very small group, we should be able to stay ahead of them if we're careful.

"Since we still have some driving time ahead of us, let me tell you about something I read recently. Out in the Salt Lake City area the Federal Government built the all-time biggest computer complex which is at least partly up and running. Anyway, it will consume as much power as all of Salt Lake City and it will have more memory capacity than all the computers in the world combined. They are building another one in Texas somewhere. The NSA already has the largest computer system in the world. They intercept all the cell phone calls, bank transfers, airline reservations, credit card purchases, etc., and check them for flag words like bomb, explosive, or a person's name. The messages with the flag words are saved and sent to the person who put up that particular word or group of characters. The rest of the information is discarded. That means that under that scheme they could only automatically track you from the time you become of interest to them. Of course, they could still look into your past, but it'd be expensive and time consuming.

"I think the new system is intended it save all the data that is now dumped so it can be searched in the future. So, if you happen to come up on their radar screen, so to speak, they can not only follow you from then on, but they can also go back and look at everything you did in the past, who you called, where you went, what you bought. If they are really the big time, they could be using the NSA intercept system to watch us now, and maybe go into our pasts as well."

"This is becoming so complicated I'm starting to feel physically sick. Why don't we just give it up and let them do what they want?"

"Because, it's not that easy. If we give up, they'd break your wife's legs or something like that. It will keep getting worse until we do what they want."

"Come on! We don't even know for sure *they* are out there. Maybe we're making this up."

"If you've been honest about Blue Dog and what happened to you in the Smoky Mountains, they're out there. The Question is who and how many. If it's a group of thugs we have a chance. And, I think that's what it is even though they might be highly placed thugs. If it were a case of infiltrating a drug cartel, or exposing a mole in the CIA, *we* are not the people to do it, right?"

"Right. And it logically follows," Harry continued somewhat lethargically, "that it has to have something to do with our long ago activities that we both admit, probably for the first time, were secret enough or bad enough for somebody to go to the considerable work of erasing those events from our memories."

"You got it. Now they want our memories back and don't much care if we're interested in helping or not. They will make us help."
"Darn it!" he slapped his hand against the steering wheel. "We always get back to that, don't we. So, you never said who it is we're going to see."

"It's someone I met awhile back who just might be able to help us in an indirect sort of way. We'll leave it at that for now."

As we drove there was no point in not working the problem. Harry apparently felt that way too as he initiated the discussion.

"I've been thinking. Whoever they are, they must be after something valuable. It could be gold, stock certificates, cash, cut diamonds, or art works. I'd put my money on cut diamonds."

"Why not gold?"

"I did some figuring last night. Even at two-thousand dollars an ounce, a ton of gold is only worth fifty-eight million. If you want to be rich without working for it, you have to score at least a half billion, better a billion because you have to cut it so many ways. No two man team does a big job like that. Look at all the expense they've had so far in doing in Blue Dog, and trying to do in me. It adds up fast. With a hundred million clear, that's nothing. You buy your own jet, there's at least five already, and a million a year for pilots, fuel, landing fees, that stuff. Then you need someplace to go in it. More millions. Before ya know it's gone. When you travel in those circles, *if ya ain't got a billion ya ain't nothin'.*"

"Well, then I don't see diamonds as being any better. Granted, dollar for dollar they won't weigh as much as gold. But, still a billion dollars worth is a lot. And, cut diamonds that are big enough to be worth that kind of money are traceable. And, think about this. There are a lot of people who have made at least a billion on Wall Street selling these credit default swaps, derivatives and stuff like that. Why not just steal it from one of them? If you made them the proposition of 'your money or your life,' sooner or later you'd find one who'd opt for his life."

"We aren't getting anywhere."

"Yeah, we aren't. It has to be something else. Maybe they want us to do a job for them, like we did back then."

"Mr. Wesson. Are you smoking something? Even if we were the world's best operatives when we were nineteen or twenty, we, at least speaking for myself, I'm most certainly not anymore. That is the worst idea either of us has had yet. Please, try again, sir."

I smiled. "Pretty bad, huh?"

Harry let it go. "Even if we stole some secret codes or something like that, it would all be useless by now. That's not it."

"Okay. So, it's something some hotshot special ops guys did or stole forty years ago. And they think these hotshots still know about in it the back recesses of their minds, and only they can call it to mind and redo, undo, find, or something like that, even if they are now old and decrepit."

"Not that bad! You know what I mean."

"What if they really did erase it from our minds, and there is no way we will ever recall it?"

"Then we're screwed."

We drove in silence with me giving Harry directions from time to time. It seemed to me that Harry was really who he said he was, and was genuinely trying to solve the problem. However, maybe it was only me who knew the secret and Harry was working for *them* and he was pretending to be working the problem as if we could both contribute. Harry's meeting with the other man in the parking lot would add credence to that theory.

It was mid-afternoon when I directed Harry to slow down and turn into a farm driveway. We stopped near the house and got out to stretch our legs. There seemed to be no one around, not even a dog. The lawn had been mowed recently so the place didn't appear to be deserted. I knocked on the door. No reply.

I walked around a little. "It looks like there, under that tree, next to the back-hoe on the trailer is where a vehicle is normally parked. We'll wait a couple of hours and see if he shows up."

"He in the construction business?"

"I don't know. If he shows, we'll ask him."

After walking around and taking in the layout of the place, we went to the bench on the porch and waited.

"What's in the field?" Harry asked.

"Soy beans. He had been growing corn for several years in a row. Because of the increased use of ethanol the price of corn is up. But, corn's hard on the soil and beans are legumes and help to replenish the nitrogen."

"Farmer Brown, I do thank you for the treatise on husbanding the land."

I shrugged. "Gotta talk about something."

We discussed inane things for an hour and a half drifting back to our situation now and then. Finally a powerful pickup that had seen better days pulled into the yard with a small row boat stuck in the bed, point facing the rear. There was consternation on the face of the well built man a little past forty. He was hard and muscled out with a strong, wide chin. His hair was black and recently trimmed, though a little unevenly. He did it himself.

I got up and said, "Dutch, hi. It's Vin Wessen from last summer. Remember? The place in Arden Hills were we met. I was mowing the lawn?"

The man's dour expression lightened a little as he approached. I held out my hand and he somewhat uncertainly grasped it.

"Yeah. I remember you. That was some miserable business. Almost got myself killed out of it. Why are you here, and who's that guy?"

"This is Harry, an old army buddy. Dutch Tuley, meet Harry Auston. We thought you might show up sooner or later and decided to wait until you arrived and then stay for supper."

Dutch's dour expression returned. "Well, it would have been nice if you could have given me some warning. I caught a three-four pound northern, but that won't go far."

"Sorry. Forgot to mention it. We ran into a cow on the way and rather than leave it for road kill threw it in the trunk. You wouldn't have a charcoal grill around where we could char-up a few steaks, do you?"

"Now you're talkin'! Yeah, back in that shed," he said pointing. "Hope you thought to bring some charcoal."

"We did. And, by the way," I said walking to the car, "you look thirsty. We ran down a beer-beast on the way, too. A shame to leave it beside the road, so we picked that up and threw it in the trunk, too."

As I hefted the cooler out of the trunk I saw a smiling man. I handed him a can and he popped the tab.

"Now, that's right neighborly," he said after a long pull on the beer. "I'll have to fillet the fish or it'll go bad. See what you guys can do about the grill."

The grill was in the shed, sort of. It was more like buried in the shed, but we found it. I asked Harry if he'd clean it up as I talked to Dutch about fishing. Harry looked a little skeptical but shrugged and grunted his approval.

Near the barn, a plank was set up at a convenient height for cleaning fish. It seemed to be well used. I walked up and set another beer at the end. "Mind if we talk a little fishing?" I asked.

The knife was sharp and I watched as he expertly filleted the long fish.

"Sure if that's what's on your mind?"

"Not really. But, some day I'd like to fish with you. Haven't done it in quite a few years because I don't have enough time to learn a lake. But, you're right. We have an strange story to tell you in hopes we can get a little information. Problem is, I'm not sure I can trust Harry. What I need is this. Last year you said the FBI mentioned three names and they were wanting to know if you knew them and you didn't. I was the only one in the phone book and that's why you came to me. I need the other two names."

"Sure. They were Joab Feinstein and Flavian Cutter. Feinstein's dead as far as I know."

"Then, tell me about Cutter."

"He's a well built guy about six feet tall, two hundred pounds, with blond hair with the vertical scar on the right side of his mouth."

I nodded. That sounded like the guy by the Mustang on Ford Parkway from last summer. I hadn't gotten a look at his face, but he was connected with that affair so that must be the man.

"Okay. We've been talking fishing and when we get into all of this, tell us about the two guys, but not Cutter's name or description. If Harry checks out, I'll pass that along to him. Help me here. What we're into doesn't look good."

After dumping out the spider webs and what looked like a mouse nest, Harry scraped out the crud from grilling in the historic past. Then he added the charcoal and had the lighter fluid burning. I saw him approach.

"That'd be nice," I said. "I could sure use fresh local fish. It's been a long time."

"Yeah," Dutch said. "In the fall there's a hole in a little lake a couple miles from here where the big crappies congregate. Doubt anybody else around here knows about it. We'll pull out some of those big slabs."

Dutch filled a shallow pan with water from a hose and washed the fish fillets. We followed him into the house and watched as he wrapped them and slid the package into the refrigerator. The three of us went out and parked our back sides on the bench, each with a beer.

Dutch's curiosity was really itching him, as I had hoped. Finally he said. "Okay, out with it. All this sudden attention is really nice, but I ain't won the Miss America pageant or nothing like that. It has something to do with last summer, doesn't it? That's the only thing that makes sense."

I nodded. "Yeah, in an indirect way. The first and main thing I would like from you is the other two names. You remember when you stopped by the house and I was mowing the lawn, you said the FBI guy had asked you if you recognized any of three names. And you said no to all three. I was the only one in the phone book so that's why you were there."

Dutch nodded. "I sure remember the two guys who were here, but I'm not too sure about their names. You think they'll come around to visit me?"

It made sense, he'd put himself first. Who wouldn't. "No," I answered. "I honestly don't think they care about you. But, they might care about the two of us. Something happened recently that makes us think it's connected to last summer. Can you give me the names?"

"The small guy was Joab Feinstein. You won't have to worry about him, though. He's dead."

"How do you know that?"

He smiled. "Looks like the charcoal is ready to go and I'm hungry."

That about ended the discussion for the time being. We slapped three steaks on the grill and set about putting together some of the trimmings. The store had some early sweet corn so we put some of that on in the husks. I'd never done that before, but had decided to give it try. Dutch set the table in the kitchen. He said as the evening came on the mosquitoes would become vicious as there was no metro mosquito control district out here.

The meal passed pleasantly and half way through my steak I asked, "Are you in the construction business? We couldn't help seeing the backhoe parked outside.

"Yeah, sort of. The 'hoe belongs to a friend who is a for real construction contractor. I do a lot of the digging for him so to save trips I park it here sometimes—saves on gas."

Everybody told a few jokes that got funnier as the beer supply dwindled. Finally, I had to push back before I exploded. Dutch said he'd clean it up in the morning. His living room was nothing special, the furniture was old, and probably needed a good sucking off with a vacuum cleaner. It didn't matter, though.

With that it was back to business. "How do you know the guy Feinstein is dead?"

"You remember the two of them rented the truck in my name. The guy at the rental place said he didn't care who rented it, my name was on the contract and if I didn't return it he'd take my farm in payment. I finally found the warehouse where they had it, which is where, it turns out, they made the bomb. We, that's Feinstein and me, fought it out for awhile and I beat him up pretty bad. I took some lumps, too. He was a tough little guy. I left him tied up, but still very much alive, and took my truck back to the rental place. The next morning there was a news item on the radio. I only heard it once and later when I found a newspaper there was nothing about it. The story said that Joab Feinstein, a member of the President's inner circle of advisors, was found dead of a congenital heart defect in the place where the terrorists built the bomb. Supposedly, the guy was sent by the president to oversee the investigation into the explosion. I guess if you have some way to dig into things you could find out if that's true."

"How about the other guy?"

"When Feinstein arrived with the truck to get the fertilizer, the second guy was sneaking up through the woods behind the house with a rifle. I had expected Feinstein might plan something like that so I had my friend waiting back there. My friend got the drop on him and broke his right arm. Man, it makes my skin crawl when I think of it. That piece of crap intended to kill me as soon as the fertilizer was loaded."

I nodded. "Ever get his name?"

"Nah. When my friend marched him up to us, neither one even acknowledged they knew one another. I asked Feinstein if he'd give the poor lost man a ride to town. He took him along. Mind telling me what's going on? Why the interest now?"

I looked at Harry and he shrugged so I decided to tell just enough. "When we were in the army, we were on some highly classified missions. After them they debriefed us until we can't remember most of it. Somebody thinks we remember, or can be made to remember if they scare us enough. Since there is one thread that links this to last summer, we thought it might be the same guys. I guess, it can't be Feinstein. But, if he was a close advisor to the president, and he was out here, it means this goes right to the top. Just knowing that helps."

"Yeah," Harry interjected, "but, not with what's going on. We still don't know what they're after. We can run some checks and see what we can find on this Joab Feinstein. Wish we had the other guy's name."

Something occurred to me. "Dutch, did you ever get the idea there was anybody else working with the two who were out here?"

"Nope."

We answered a few more of Dutch's questions, and that about did it. It was getting close to nine so we thanked Dutch and he thanked us for the meal. At the front door, I stepped out on the porch first and saw movement by the car. It was still twilight and I thought it might be a man with a gray jacket or possibly a deer.

"You see that!" I said. "There was something or someone by the car." The sound of twigs snapping in the woods were unmistakable.

"The deer wander up here from time to time," Dutch said. "They're smart, though. Come fall, they won't be near the buildings."

Harry and I walked to the car. Before opening his door he looked at the sky. Stars had begun to appear and he said, "Look at how bright and sharp they are. With the lights and pollution of the city you never have a chance to see something like that."

He stood there apparently enthralled for five minutes while I was go-ing nuts. If it had been up to me we would have been in the car spitting gravel down the driveway to see if there had been a car parked on the highway opposite the house. I couldn't help but think he was deliberately stalling to give whoever I had seen by the car a chance to get away. There was the sound of a car, though it might only been one driving past on the road.

— 5 —

As we drove away from Dutch's place, Harry asked, "Are we safe? I mean, what was that you saw by the car when you stepped out on the porch?"

"You'd know as much about that as I would." I said it casually though my intent was to see his reaction. Glancing at his face, dimly lit by the dashboard glow, there was a sudden twitch of the muscles around his mouth that immediately returned to normal.

His responded with a hint of indignation in his voice as would be expected after a implied accusation like that, "What's that supposed to mean?"

"Oh, I don't know. Only that your imagination is as good as mine, at this point probably better. You were the one who could easily have been killed on the mountain road. This is all so ethereal for me. Swatting at ghosts would be bad enough; these seem to be imaginary ghosts. Are we sure this is even happening?" After a pause, I continued, "Look at it from my point of view. I have your word for what happened in the Smoky Mountains, and for the fact that Blue Dog is dead. I can't verify either case. It seems there would be no accident report of a car crashing off the road if nobody knew the car is down in the ravine. And, I don't know Blue Dog's real name."

He didn't volunteer to allay my concerns by giving me the name so I could check. He was driving too fast for the conditions so I said, "The road is good enough for this speed, but your headlights aren't. There are a lot of deer in this part of the country, and if you hit one it'll at least disable the car if you can manage to keep from rolling it. He slacked off a little.

"I thought we were in this together, but you don't seem to be working with me. What were you and Dutch talking about when I was working on the grill?"

"Like I said, fishing. I gathered that he fishes quite a bit, and he's a local, so I managed to wrangle an invitation to go fishing with him."

"What does being a local have to do with anything?"

That made me smile. "Let's start with this. You mentioned that you hunt deer, but I doubt you fish, is that right?"

"Yeah. So?"

"First of all, deer leave tracks and make noise. Fish don't. And, when you find a deer, you shoot it. You can't shoot the fish. You have to convince the fish to eat your lure or bait. What that means is first of all it takes a lot more patience to fish, and you have to go fishing when they are hungry, that is, when they're biting. The only thing that evens out the two sports is that you can only take one deer a year and the law allows several fish a day."

"Okay. I still don't see your point, though."

"Look at it this way. It is a well know fact that ninety percent of the fish are taken by ten percent of the fisherman."

"I never heard that before, but it makes sense. That's because some guys are crazy about fishing and the rest only fish for a week or two a year when they are on vacation."

"True. But it goes beyond that. The people who fish a lot know the lakes, what species to fish for at what time of year, in which part of the lake, with what bait, etc. A local, like Dutch, knows these things. He even knows the game warden and where he's likely to be on any particular day, so he can decide when it's safe to use a few illegal techniques. Now, do you see?"

Harry laughed for the fist time since I met him the day before. "Yeah. Now I understand."

Driving in silence a deer appeared beside the road. Harry was startled enough to drop his speed to the posted. More time. Finally he said, "You're right about cut diamonds. That's not it. We have to think of something else that's really valuable, but for the life of me, I'm coming up empty."

I agreed with him, and added. "Maybe we're thinking too narrowly about this. Gold and diamonds would be valuable to anyone. Maybe it's different, like something that only a few people would find valuable. This isn't what I mean exactly, but a keepsake could be extremely valuable to one person, but have no intrinsic worth, you know what I mean?"

Harry slowly nodded without taking his eyes off the road. "It could be a geological report showing where a rich deposit of oil could be found. It would be meaningless to all but a very few experts who deal in things like that."

"That's good except that's not likely it. If one oil exploration outfit made a good hit, it seems likely that after all these years others would have stumbled on to it, too. In addition, either our team or another one would have had to kill all the people who knew about the finding. I'm still trying to believe that we would not have done something like that."

"We're getting closer, though. What you just said figures in a twisted way. We were trained and ordered to perform a mission. And, the mission was successful or none of this makes any sense. That means there is, or more importantly, *was* someone else, probably a whole chain of command, who knew about what we succeeded in doing. Why aren't those guys the object of this harassment? We were 'debriefed' but they wouldn't have been. It was *their* idea. It follows that due to natural causes or assassination the others who knew about what we did are dead."

I had a feeling we were getting close, too. "The whole matter lay dormant until I brought attention to our team last summer. With some research, they were led to classified information and things started falling into place. There was only one problem, we were the only ones left alive who were associated with the mission, and, darn the luck, we had been lobotomized where that mission was concerned."

Harry was intently starring out the windshield as his foot pressed harder and harder on the accelerator peddle. Finally I had to say something. "Too fast, Harry. How about using the speed control."

He didn't protest as our speed slacked.

"Just had a blinding flash," he said. "What if we stole a weapon of mass destruction, stashed it someplace, and then something happened to those calling the shots. That means the people after us are terrorists."

"That's good except it still could be someone in the government who's worried that terrorists will get to it before they do. If there are spies in the government, and there are, when they learned about it, the information could have slipped out to some unsavory types about the same time."

Harry laughed nervously. "That's even worse. Maybe there are two factions looking for it, and we're the focus of both."

By this time we had crossed into Minnesota. I suggested we stop working on it of the evening and we'd both sleep on it lest our imaginations get the best of us. We also agreed he might as well go home and we'd keep each other informed if anything happened.

There were a lot of things ripping at me. During these discussions Harry seemed so totally involved in solving the problem. Yet, it could be a front. His idea about a WMD was such a case. It could have popped into his mind at that moment, or it might have seemed to him to be the right place in the discussion to interject it. If he were faking it, his timing was perfect.

Friday

The day we went to see Dutch Tuley I had taken vacation. It was a Tuesday. The rest of the week had been normal. The week was ending with everybody letting down a little in preparation for the weekend. Other than that, nothing. My suspicions of Harry were all over the place with the dominant one being that he was simply ringing my chimes—a practical joker. I was still convinced he was Nine Lives which left nothing but over forty years of empty road as far as we were concerned. He could have escaped from a mental institution for all I knew, though, it would have been an up-scale one since the Escalade was in his name, and the DMV photo matched the man who visited me.

That all changed that Friday afternoon when, after work, I found a note under the windshield wiper of my car. In block letters it said:

> **THAT WAS A WARNING. FROM HERE ON IT STARTS TO HURT. YOU KNOW WHERE IT IS, WE WANT IT. GET TO WORK!**

If bafflement were worth a penny a pound, I would've been a rich man. What "WARNING" and what was "IT?" Had I missed something? Before I opened the car door I looked in front of and behind all four tires to see if someone had placed nails there for me to drive over and get four flat tires. There was nothing I could see. I opened the door expecting to be vaporized in a blast, though that would have been counter-productive to their desire to get "IT."

Driving home it hit me hard. This did not have the marks of a practical joke perpetrated by a nut case who had escaped from a booby hatch, though it seemed somebody has his timing off. *Nothing* had happened.

When I entered the garage the thing that struck me was that Camellia's car was gone. I wasn't sure, but I thought this was a day off from her volunteer job. Oh well, she might have gone shopping, or I was wrong about the day off.

When I entered the back door she was there to meet me and I could see in an instant that something was wrong.

"What happened? You don't look so good."

"Please don't be mad at me, but I totaled my car this afternoon. Or rather, another guy totaled it for me. I called the police and the insurance agency so everything was taken care of. I didn't see any reason to call you at work."

"Slow down. Are you all right?"

"I was shaken up a little, but I'm okay. I had gone to the supermarket to pick up a few groceries. You know, the parking is two rows of cars parked ninety degrees from the traffic aisles between the rows of cars. I had pulled out and was proceeding along when this old car shot out backwards and mashed into my passenger's side front wheel and fender. The wheel was laying flat on the road so the stuff under the hood was all crunched up."

"What did the other driver have to say?"

"That's the problem, he shoved it into drive and was off in a second. Where he was parked, his car was along the row closest to my line of travel. But, the space in front of him was empty. It was as if he had planned to drive forward real fast like he was mad about something, and put it into reverse without thinking. I suppose if he were upset that would be a common enough mistake to make. We all start out in reverse most of the time by backing out of the garage or a parking space.

"The insurance agency told me what towing company to call and the tow truck came and picked up the car. The driver dropped me off at home."

"Did you get the plates of the other car."

"Of course not. It all happened too fast. It was a dark blue car from the eighties, I'd say, an Oldsmobile or something like that."

My mouth suddenly fell open. She saw it and said, "Are *you* all right?"

"Just a minute," I said. "I left something in the car."

Before she could say anything, I was gone. Back in seconds, I was staring at the paper. "What do you make of this?"

Looking at the paper, she slowly settled on a dinette chair. "We've talked about it a few times, but what is it they think we should be doing?" She was shaking her head. "Are we expected to wander around looking in random places for something that we wouldn't know we had found even if we tripped over it? This is madness."

"Not completely," I said. Then I related how I had remembered cutting the shavings to start the fire to roast the snake, how I had not thought of that in all the years since it had happened, yet, while Harry and I discussed the incident, it had come back to me.

"Maybe, that's from another time like when you were out camping with the boys when they were young."

"We have no choice but to assume it is as I remembered. They seem to think there are a whole lot of memories like that stuck away in my head. If I don't start pulling some of them out, they will start breaking somebody's legs. And, from what happened today, it's your legs they'll break first. They want my legs to be in good working order to lead them to the treasure, whatever it is. So, we don't want any negative vibes about this. Do you see?"

"I hate this!"

"So do I. But, think hard about anything I may have said over the years that was out of place, out of character. There has been a time or two when you've snickered about how inept I was in the area of self defense. Remember the FBI guy I beat up in the conference room at work last year. He was twenty years younger than me, out weighed me, and didn't have an ounce of fat on him. He was also trained in martial arts. I took him down without him landing a blow because I knew I could. But, that's only an example. We need different odd things."

A look of something between horror and excitement crossed her face. She was on her feet tugging at my sleeve. I followed her out the back door and around to the end of the house facing the side street. We lived on a corner lot. In whispers she said, "What if the house has eavesdropping things in it?"

I shrugged, "I suppose it could have."

"Well," she said, "there may be times when we must have conversations at odd places other than in the house, garage or even on the patio. Anyway, this is what occurred to me. First, remember I called you while at the Har Mar Mall shopping center and said it seemed like an Asian looking man was following Harry? I just remembered there was a guy who could have been the same man taking an interest in my accident in the grocery store parking lot. What does that mean?"

"I'll have to think about it. But, we'll have to keep an eye out for him."

I went to my workshop in the basement and started writing down all the things I could remember about my secret life in the Army. There wasn't much, at least a first. As I worked, more came. In a way, it didn't surprise me. For all these years I had accepted what they had told us, that our safety lay in not remembering the missions. With an effort to reverse that, it came a little at a time. I could put together fragments from what I thought were four missions. With that I tried the best I could to put the collection of facts with the missions.

The sound of Camilla coming down the steps made me pause. She laid a page in front of me. She had written down things she remembered from when I'd awakened in the night. The list wasn't long, only a half dozen items. Three were about the snake, one was drugs, another about an aluminum case or cask or something. The last was "night." After that she had written that it was as if I were trying to put night together with something else but was frustrated in not being able to come up with the connection.

I nodded and whispered, "Thanks."

Looking at my watch I said, "I have to call Harry."

She nodded.

It was late enough that Harry might he home so I called there first. A woman answered.

"Harry, thank goodness you called. I'm scared! Come home as fast as you can."

"Sorry," I said. "This isn't Harry, but Vin Wessen in Minneapolis. What happened?"

"Wessen?" After a pause, "What's wrong with you guys? Are you trying to get us all killed?"

"Slow down. Is this Carol, Harry's wife?"

"Yes."

"Tell me what happened quickly. Then call Harry."

"A bomb came through the front window! It made a hole in my favorite chair and smashed the coffee table. That's what happened!"

"What?"

"It's lying on the living room carpet ready to kill me."

It took only a moment for me to put it together. "Does it look like a rocket, and what color is it?"

"Yes! A rocket with a big fat head. And who cares what color it is."

"You do. What color is it?"

"Light blue, smart guy. So, that's important?"

"Yes. Very important. Light blue is the color of training munitions. They don't explode. That was shot at you as a warning. Something like that happened to me, too. That's why I'm calling. Where's Harry?"

"Still at work, or on his way home." The voice was losing its tone of terror.

"As soon as you get your situation under control have him call me. He has my number. Will you do that? It's important."

"Yes. I guess so. He told me not to worry, that everything would be all right. Was he lying to me?"

"We both thought there was a good possibility there was some mistake. Now we know there wasn't. Be sure to have him call."

A half hour later, Harry called. "Vin, this is really starting to irritate me."

"Yeah. I know how you feel. Was there a note on it? It sounded like a three point five inch anti-tank training round."

"Yes to both. He used an electric pencil like you use to mark tools and stuff to write the note on the side of it, said to make progress or people would start to hurt."

"The same with me. Looks like we have to get together and work this thing out. How do you see it?"

"Eventually, yes. But, give me a couple of days. There are a few things I've thought of that I can best check out while I'm here with my own resources. I'll probably make a quick trip to Kansas City. I might get a lead there."

"Okay. Don't take too long, though. We have made exactly no progress, don't even know what it is they want."

"Give me a little time. I'll be in touch."

— 6 —

Saturday

I was up this morning at the usual time because I had not slept well. There was a light knock at the back door. I swept back the curtain and saw Harry. He motioned me out. I saw a brown car parked on the tarmac leading to the garage as I walked to the patio. We sat on a bench against the side of the garage.

"Surprised to see me?"

I nodded.

"Didn't know what else to do. As you said, our houses and phones are bugged so I let them think I was still in town or somewhere else."

I raised my eyebrows.

"Yeah. They did a good job of it. Not real good but not bad." He pulled an electronic device from his jacket pocket. Still in a whisper he replied, "This is a bug sweeper. I found four in my house and I'll bet we'll find some in yours. When did you get hit?"

I still hadn't told him what had happened to me. "About three yesterday afternoon."

"Makes sense. They have at least one man on you and one on me. They're watching to see what we do. I don't think they saw me leave town or arrive here. The old instincts of survival are coming back. I'm really watching everything around me."

"Why *are* you here other than to sweep for bugs which we assumed we had anyway. We still have nothing to go on. What do you propose to do?"

He leaned over near me and whispered in my ear, "We have to catch one of them and find out what they want."

I snickered. "Great idea. How do we do that?"

"We find a bug, pretend we don't know about it, and lay out a plan that will draw the guy out. Then we grab him. But, you see, we have to move fast before the guy in St. Louis can get here to help."

He was assuming that there was only one man watching each of us, a big assumption.

I was whispering now, too. "Got a better idea. We'll spend the morning like nothing was happening. Then, I'll tell Camilla about something I thought of, a good lead or something. They must continue to think you are in St. Louis to keep the guy watching you down there. Then I'll go to find something or other and the local guy will think I'm alone so he'll see no problem. But, there'll be two of us."

"Yeah. That's good. You were always good at stuff like that."

"Sweep the garage and then come in and do the same with the house. You'll have to lay low for the day."

"That's fine with me. I'll get a cheap motel room because I'm tired. I was driving most of the night."

He found a bug in the garage, and three in the house, and the phones.

All morning I tried to think of something I could search for, probably in a local park, but was coming up dry. If I was so good at this, why wasn't I doing better? There were two problems. The first was I had to be looking for something that would seem important enough to draw our adversary out, without saying what it was for the simple reason that I didn't *know* what it was. That meant it had to be a map or some general clue like that. The second difficulty was I had to pick a place that would not have been developed since the early seventies. Even the parks would be hard. Where there had been nothing but dense woods when we arrived in the city, there were now ball fields, picnic pavilions, and paved trails. But, that wasn't the biggest problem. Why would there be anything around here to find? There was no indication that what they wanted would be in this metropolitan area.

In the mid-afternoon I went to the garage to get something. Harry was there waiting for me. This surprised me because there was no car. We went to the side of the house away from the street. On one side of us was my fence, and on the other were bushes. We sat on the grass while we leaned against the side of the house.

"How long were you there, and where's your car?"

"Just arrived five minutes ago, and I parked by the lake a couple of blocks away and walked."

I nodded and said in a whisper, "Harry, I don't think this is going to work. Think about it. We were in Vietnam. This is Minnesota. What could we possibly find here, a treasure map?"

Harry whispered back, "No. Not a thing, a person. We have to invent someone they don't know about, someone they missed. Maybe one of our handlers or even an instructor. Or, even the fourth member of our team."

I stared at the fence in front of me not wanting to move lest I lose my train if thought. "Harry, where'd you come up with the idea that our team had four men?"

"Hey," he said, "that just popped into my head. But, I think it's right. How about you?"

"Yeah. I think there were four, but then, why were there only three of us alive until a few weeks ago?"

"I don't know. In any case we need a legend for the new guy and a story of how one of us ran across him. What do you remember about the legends of other men we knew. Some were even worse than ours."

"Well, during training I remember Snake Eyes, Jack Rabbit, Tom Cat, Big Hand—he said Big Foot had already been taken—Tree Frog, and that's all I remember. Maybe more will come to me later."

"There was Hoot Owl and Night Hawk. Why does Night Hawk tug at me?"

I could feel something squirming around in my brain. It started with Night Hawk. It was like a dam ready to burst but simply would not crack loose.

"You look funny. Did you remember something?"

I shook my head. "It was close but nothing I could grasp. It had to do with Night Hawk." After a long pause during which Harry didn't interrupt me for fear that I'd be distracted at the moment something important came to mind, I said, "It's gone for now. I'll have to work on it. I like your idea about another guy. We need a legend."

"How about Horse Fly, Ground Hog, or Big Buck?"

"Big Buck. We'd have called him Buck. He was always dirty, liked to drink and was always quoting cartoon characters. How's that?"

"Works for me. How'd we find him?"

"We didn't. I was buying some nine millimeter pistol ammo at a sporting goods store and had a case of déjà vu, like I knew this guy who was waiting on me. I really did buy some ammo for my son last Christmas. He's taken up target shooting. Anyway, to continue with our fantasy, there seemed to be sort of a connection between us so we chatted for a few minutes. I remember him but didn't get his name. With all of this happening, I now realized he was a man from one of the teams I was on. Later this evening, I'm going to the store and try to find him. How's that?"

"Wow. That's good. We're doing it, we're back in the team."

"Not all that good. What do we do, accost everyone in the store who happens to look my way as I'm inquiring about a clerk? And, what happens when I give a description of him to the department manager, who by now I'm talking with, and he says there's never been anybody like that working in the whole store."

"Simple. You talk in conversational but hushed tones so nobody next to you can hear. It doesn't matter what you say or what the other guy says. If someone moves up as if to eavesdrop, I'll know that. Maybe I can follow him out and get his car license number. Even if he's driving a rental, a good PI firm will be able to find out who's driving it."

"Good luck on that. He'll be using false credentials. Remember, Dutch said one of the guys from last summer was a close advisor of the President. We must assume these guys know how to do a covert operation in the real world."

The sun had moved enough to shift the shade off me so I stood up and brushed the grass from my pants. Harry stood, too, as he said, "I agree, we might not catch the guy, but we have to do something and this sounds like a good start. Along the way we could use our fictitious partner whenever the need arose. We'd only refer to him as Buck so no real person could be in danger."

". . . except possibly somebody at the store."

Harry shrugged.

I went into the house and brought Camilla out and explained what we intended to do. Not having any better suggestion the three of us went into the garage.

"I've got to tell you something sweetheart, and since the house might be bugged we'll talk out here. A few things have been coming to mind about the time I spent on the Phantom Teams. When I was shopping last Christmas I ran into a clerk in a store who seemed familiar in an odd way and we spoke for a few minutes. After that I thought nothing more about it. Since this whole thing started, he's been on my mind and it finally registered why. He was on one of the teams with me."

She responded using my name so there would be no doubt to an eavesdropper who was talking. "Vin, I thought there were only three, you, Harry and the guy out East who's dead."

"Oh, no. The people who are doing this to us obviously don't know that the Phantom Teams always had four men. If one team was not enough for a job, another whole team would be assigned. And, this is significant, no team of four stayed together for more than two missions so we wouldn't become too familiar with one another. That means I was on missions with a dozen guys at different times. The same with Harry. If I can find this man at the store, we might be able to put together three of us. That'd help a lot."

Up until now Harry was nodding, though not saying anything since he was supposed to be Missouri.

Camilla nodded. "What if he won't help? After all, he hasn't had a rocket shot through his front window or his car demolished."

"Maybe he won't, but I'm pretty sure I can convince him it will be in his interest to go along with us. And, that's not the best part. Harry said he had a lead to run down in Kansas City. I'll bet he ran across a Phantom man, too. If we could reconstitute a full team, we'd be unstoppable."

At this point Harry was emphatically shaking his head and mouthing the work "stop."

I continued. "With a full team, we'd be able to find one of the operatives and force him to talk. We're very skilled at that. Speaking for myself, there was nobody that didn't talk when I interrogated him. From there, we'd simply work our way up the chain of command. We'd find them all and put an end to this."

By this time, Harry had grabbed my arm to stop me from saying any more. I shook him off glaring at him. He saw the look and immediately stepped back.

As a final shot, I said, "You see, it's really not so hard. This is precisely the type of situation we were trained to handle."

On cue, Camilla replied. "Well, if that's the way it has to be, so be it. After all, they started it, they'll have to suffer the consequences."

"I'll go to the store after supper and see if I can find the guy I met last Christmas. Let's eat a little early."

Leaving the garage, I slammed the door hard enough to ensure the listener would know we had left. Outside, Harry motioned me to a bench as Camilla went to the house to start the meal.

"You really put your foot in a size sixteen cow pie, buddy. This will scare them to death. If they really did kill Blue Dog because they were afraid to let even three of us work together, you now effectively told them we could have a full team that will hunt them down and will kill the lot of them. They'll come after us loaded for bear."

I shook my head. "I don't think so. You're forgetting, they still want *it*. And if we're dead, they'll never get *it!* Sure wish I know what we were looking for, though."

"Wait a minute," Harry said. "None of this makes sense. Presumably, we did a mission in Vietnam that involved something valuable. That something was hidden someplace by us, or so they think. But, Vietnam has been ruled by the communists since 1975. Even if we remembered everything and told them every detail, as in exactly where it is, how will they be able to recover it?"

"That's exactly what I was thinking about all day, and I don't have an answer."

Camilla brought a plate of food out for Harry.

After supper we drove separately to a sporting goods store a few miles away. I stopped at the gun counter and asked a few questions the clerk would expect from a naive suburbanite. He showed me some guns, I felt them in my hand and kept him occupied for fifteen minutes. After that I drove home, Camilla and I took a walk to the lake like we frequently did. We caught up with Harry in a shaded area.

"Anything?"

He shook his head. "Nothing. Maybe nobody was listening when we were in the garage. The guy who sold me the bug sweeper said most bugs transmit to a recorder located within a half mile. The snooper stops by and down loads the recording every day or so."

"If that's true, it puts us one step ahead. It means they don't have enough people to have someone listening to the bugs round the clock."

Harry nodded. "That would also mean this is not a legal operation. If the FBI, Secret Service, or any such organization learned about a missing WMD that anybody might find, especially terrorists, they'd have unlimited access to manpower."

"Good. That makes sense. So, we have this to go on. Somebody in the Federal Government who has access to highly classified information is after something valuable for an illegal purpose. That means the team is small. The old problem of keeping secrets would dictate that the fewer people who knew about it the better. Besides, they started out thinking there would only be two of us. You might be right. There's probably only one or two guys watching each of us."

"It also means that when the guy does listen to the recording from the garage he might go nuts. You really set them up with that stuff about putting together a whole team. Maybe they'll kill the other guy on sight."

"Not if I set it up as though we can't possibly figure out what they want without him."

"I still wouldn't like to be *him*."

"Wait a minute, Camilla said. "Think hard. Did you notice anyone special while you were in the store watching Vin? Anyone you remember who wasn't moving along as fast as one would expect. Even someone who seemed to be unable to make up his or her mind about which of two products to buy?"

Harry stared up at the sky as he recalled the scene in the store. "I can say for sure there was no one close enough to overhear what Vin said to the clerk."

"That's not what I meant. What about someone who was simply watching the situation, someone who knew you and Vin and was only keeping tabs on what you did."

"There was a guy an isle over looking at bows and arrows. He seemed to pick up each one a half dozen times."

"Describe him."

"Can't much. His back was to me most of the time and I wasn't interested in him. He was shorter than me, but most people from Japan, China, you know over there, the Pacific rim, are shorter than us."

"Definitely Asian."

"Yes to that. Why?"

"He's shown up twice before, that's why. He followed you into the store to buy beer the other day, and he was in the parking lot when my car was crunched."

"The plot thickens. What! How do you know he followed me into the store to buy the beer?"

"Because I was following you," Camilla said in a smug voice as she smiled and raised her chin.

A cloud came over Harry's face. "What's going on here?"

I raised my hand, "Settle down. Remember, before Camilla's car got crashed and you were visited by a flying object, we had only your word to go on so we took a few precautions."

Harry frowned but nodded. "I suppose so." Then he did a double take. "Anything else?"

"Well," Camilla continued, "you got into a car and talked to another man. Who was he?"

Harry's mouth twitched. "Might as well say it. At the start, neither of us knew what was going on. I had a PI follow me that first time I was in town. Then it seemed there was no need."

"Was he out by the car that night at Dutch's." I asked.

He shook his head. "No. In the parking lot where Camilla saw us, I told him to call it off. The guy at Dutch's, if it is was a man and not a deer, is still a mystery. What's our next move?"

"I'll talk to Camilla in the garage again when we get home. I'll say I found the guy at the store but he's not sure he wants to break cover. It may be necessary for me to go back to the store again and buy something. This may take a few days before we can get things set up.

"As I see it, I have to meet him in a hidden place like back further in this park. I'll have to work on the place. It'll have to be a location that can be described exactly, but is secluded so he'll have to be close by to have any hope of seeing the guy I meet. But, I need someone to meet. If I go to a rendezvous and nobody else shows up, the guy will never reveal himself."

"Then we're stuck. It can't be me because they know all about me. Who else is there?"

I took a deep breath. Harry looked at me. "You know somebody, don't you? Want to tell me about him?"

"It's a long shot, but it might work. His name is Fred Clements."

Immediately Camilla interrupted me. "Oh, no you don't! Not that man!"

"Yes, that man. He's a loose cannon, hates everybody, and would think this would be a way to get even with me. He'd fit the part of a Phantom man who had been cheated out of life because of the job he did for his country. The biggest problem would be to keep them from identifying him. If they learned he was ex-FBI they'd question his having been in Phantom. He's also too young so we'd have to meet at dusk or he'd have to disguise himself."

"Do they ever throw anybody out of the FBI?" Harry asked incredulously.

"After he made the mistake of coming after me they do."

"Ouch! It sounds like there's bad blood there. Will you be able to control him?"

"I have no way of knowing. But, if you have a better idea, I'm listening."

"Well, then, ex-FBI it is. Can you find him?"

"Our PI firm should be able to track him down. It's a long shot getting him to help, though. I'll have to work on him so it'll take time. You can stay around or go home. That's up to you."

He thought a minute. "I guess I'll go home. It'll be time for me to be getting back from Kansas City, anyway. Before I go, let's set up a few simple codes so when you call me, you can tell me to come up and give you a hand when you have it set up with the FBI guy."

This we did and Harry sauntered away toward where he had parked his car.

At home in the garage, for the benefit of the listening device, I related to Camilla my trip to the store where I supposedly contacted the man from one of my Phantom missions. Then I continued, "I wasn't mistaken, this man was in Phantom with me. And, I'm pretty sure he remembers something that would help us though he didn't admit anything. My approaching him about our past was a complete shock to him. I know the feeling from when Harry contacted me. It sends a person back to a place best forgotten. I could tell by the look in his eyes that he knew, as I did, that now that it's been opened it won't end until something had been resolved. I'll give him a day to think about it and then contact him again so we can set up a meeting. Unless I'm mistaken, this is a big break for us. So far we're getting exactly nowhere. Neither Harry nor I can come up with any idea about even *what* we're looking for, to say nothing of where it is."

We went to the house. After five minutes I returned to the garage and sawed on a board with a hand saw for a few minutes. Then I carefully removed the bug wrapped it in a towel and put it in the basement. I needed to contact our PI firm and had to drive to a shopping center to make the call, and I didn't want the sounds of my car leaving the garage to be on the recording the bug made. Harry had also found a tracking device on my car so I removed it before I left.

The private investigators were good because they had what I needed while I waited on the line. Fred Clements was a night watchman at the Northtown Shopping Center. That was a break since it was only six or eight miles from where I was at the time. They gave me the type of car he drove, its plates as well as his home address and phone number.

I assumed the shopping center closed at nine and it was close to that now. If I hurried, I might get there in time to catch him coming to work. As I drove my thoughts tripped and tumbled over what I would say to Clements if I were fortunate enough to run across him. It had to pique him enough to let me meet with him the next day.

At ten minutes before nine I tuned off Highway 10 being lucky to get the left turn arrow without stopping. I didn't frequent this shopping center as a matter of course but knew the basic layout well enough. Driving around I knew it would be a long shot. If only I could make contact tonight so he could think about it. With any luck we could meet tomorrow before he went to work.

All shoppers were walking away from the stores so my attention was on anyone headed the other way. There, a man came up a sparse line of cars against the flow wearing a uniform. He looked to be the right size. I stopped, backed up and turned toward him. Ten yards away I was certain. Lowering my window, I stopped as he came along side my car.

"Mr. Fred Clements?"

He was startled, having been in something of a reverie, his thoughts miles away. From habit he shifted his hand so as to be ready to draw his gun except that it was fully enclosed in a holster high up on his belt. It was worn as display rather than an armament to be readily accessible.

"Vin Wesson," I said. "We met last summer. Do you remember me?" It was unlikely he'd have forgotten.

He grimaced and retorted, "What do you want?"

"In a word, your help. That thing from last summer isn't over. They're after something big, and I need your help to find out who they are and what they want. There'll be a substantial reward, and you can have it all if you'll help."

"Who are they and what is it they want?"

"I'm not exactly sure who they are, but I think it's a nuclear bomb that's gone missing. They want it and God knows what they'll do with it."

Bing! What did I just say? Did I remember something or did I say it to get his attention? Have to work that out later.

"So, call the FBI, stupid. In case you haven't figured it out, that's not me." He turned and took a few steps toward the shopping center. I put it in reverse and backed to stay even with him.

"Because they might not want it found. No, that's not right. There might be someone in the Bureau that doesn't want it found or its one of them who's doing the looking. It's confusing beyond what you can imagine. That thing from last summer involved some people highly placed in the Federal Government. One of them was killed. The others are back."

He stopped and faced me. "Who? You mean Feinstein? He died of natural causes."

"I know for a fact that he was killed. You want to know how I know? You want to get your old job back, you want a raise, you want a big reward? Meet with me. Yes, I might be a nut, but don't decide until you've heard the story. And, don't mention this to anyone. I'll stop by your house at six-thirty tomorrow evening."

There was no point in giving him a chance to reply so I shoved it into drive and sped away.

As I drove home, my words came back to me. Was it an atomic bomb? That made as much sense an anything else. Most of our missions had been to kill or capture enemy generals. For some reason that stuck in my mind. At least one time we were sent out to place a sophisticated electronic listening device in the area of the Ho Chi Minh Trail. If one of our missions had been to place an atomic land mine, and if it hadn't been found after all of these years, why do anything about it now? We had been told about small man portable atomic explosives during our training. Their existence wasn't even classified. In fact, at the time, they had atomic artillery shells weighing about eighty pounds.

It still didn't add up. Why us, why now, why here? That was Vietnam. Hey, guys, that's way across the Pacific Ocean. Try looking at a map. We had to catch one of them and find out what this was all about. And, as far as I could tell, I needed Clements to do that.

It still bothered me that I didn't remember anything about this. There were at least little things about other missions I could remember. But, now that I thought about it, I remembered the briefing from before the missions, not the missions themselves. Like placing the listening device along the Ho Chi Minh Trail. I could remember what it was in general terms, how we were told to deploy it, and the few tests we were to make to be sure it was working. I even remembered what it looked like. That was it. I remember doing the self-check test on the device, but in my mind it was setting on a table in a tent. That was where we were shown how to do it. But, there was nothing about the actual mission. There was no memory about actually doing the self-test in the field. The only mission specific event either Harry or I remember was the incident about the snake. And, as Harry had figured out, that was because they didn't know about the snake.

There was, of course, the long ride on the C-130 as part of one of the missions. I guess they didn't think that was important enough to erase. It was only the commute to the job, as it were. No reason to care whether or not we remembered that. Yet, it was odd.

There had to be someone I could talk to about how a person's memories could be erased, and if it were possible to make it permanent. Was it still all in there and just couldn't get out, or was it gone for good. I sincerely hoped it wasn't gone for good because *they* seemed to think I could recall it.

About to turn off Highway 10 onto Interstate 35W South, I was trying to think of someone who could tell me about lost memories and what the chances were of recovering them. Henni Froom came to mind. He knew a lot about things like this. Even though he was a microbiologist by profession, he had spent a great deal of time studying philosophy as a hobby. Well, no. Not so much a hobby more as an obsession. Something had happened some yeas back that changed the way he looked at life, especially his own. He seemed reluctant to discuss it with others, though he mentioned this event had made a deep impression on him.

It was shortly after nine and if he were home he shouldn't mind if I stopped by for a half hour or so. This wouldn't take long. He lived in Maplewood so I stayed on Highway 10 until it intersected I-694 East and some miles later took I-35E South.

— 7 —

The door opened to reveal a Japanese man. I was pleased he was home, having no idea what he might be doing on a Saturday evening. Henni was of slight build, very Asian looking, and spoke with no hint of an accent being second generation American. Having never known another Japanese man, I couldn't tell how typically Japanese his features were. It always seemed the various nationalities played in movies overly accentuated the variations that set the races apart. And, for my part, I rarely saw the facial features clearly of a person I met being drawn more to their attitude and the other psychological features of the person.

"Hi Henni. Sorry to arrive unannounced so late in the evening, but I need your advice on something. It shouldn't take long."

"Not a problem, Vin. I'm always glad to see you. From the look on your face, something's bothering you. You always seemed so completely in control of your life. Please, do come in."

The house was of typical Minnesota construction with the main floor all on one level and a full basement. The exterior was covered with lap siding. It sat on an almost flat lot with a couple of tall trees, shrubs, and a few flowers around the front. The living room had polished wide board floors with area rugs covering most of it. On one end were beautiful built-in china cabinets. The furniture was contemporary, or would have been for the eighties and was comfortable. Henni motioned me to an easy chair at the end of a marble coffee table. He sat on the sofa. If others in the family were around I heard no sound of them.

"I'm a little embarrassed to be here," I began. "But, some things have happened and I thought you might to be able to help me. Are other members of your family home? This should be kept confidential which you'll understand in a minute."

"My wife is away visiting her mother and the only son still at home is studying—his last year in college. We can change the subject if he interrupts us." After a pause, "That was some opening, and your have my full attention to say nothing of my curiosity."

I tried a thin smile. It wasn't a smile and Henni saw this. "When I was in the Army in Vietnam, I was part of a small cadre that we can call special, special forces. We normally operated in units of four men. Our missions were off the books and not always legal or even moral, I think. After the missions we were debriefed so thoroughly we couldn't remember most of what we did. Now, someone thinks that on one of the missions I was part of, we stole something valuable and hid it. They want it, and are threatening another man and myself with bodily harm to members of our families if we don't produce it. The two of us have come up with the rationale that they feel the stress of imminent danger to our families, and eventually to us if we fail, will make the memories come back."

Henni looked perplexed, though he appeared to be accepting at face value what I was saying. Still not knowing where I was headed he said, "Continue."

"Well, I thought since you have made a serious study of philosophy and related topics, you might have some knowledge of what I think is called philosophical psychology that would speak to how the brain and mind work together, and especially what affects memories, why we remember certain things and forget others. In short, is there any hope of my recalling what I did all those years ago?"

Henni nodded. "Is there any way you could go to a professional? Psychotherapy and related remedial treatments are likely to help more that I can?"

"That's not really what I need. If the memories are there, I'm pretty sure I'll recall them at the rate things are progressing. But, if there's no hope, the two of us will have to take steps to stop this."

Henni shifted his position to face me more directly. "I don't like the sound of that. What do you mean, exactly?"

The whole affair fell on me in a second, in a way it hadn't any time up until now, and I was angry. My eyes flashed and Henni's reaction told me he hadn't missed it. "I mean, exactly, that the two of us are exceptionally capable men. We were chosen out of thousands because we were so good at, for lack of a better term, being hunters. We will track them down and kill them to the last man!" I unconsiously rubbed my hand across my mouth as if I could erase the words.

Henni didn't flinch, but he responded, "I'm in no way a psychologist, but you just remembered something, didn't you?"

It was like a crack in a rock wall. Yes, I had remembered something. "Yes," I said slowly. "At least on some missions, we were sent out to find and kill enemy generals. We'd injun up behind them and cut their throats."

"Why'd you use the word injun?"

Another flash. "Because . . . there was an American Indian on our team. Yes, that's it. His legend was Night Hawk. He was so good he hardly needed any training. The rest of us were from average American upbringing. Night Hawk had already been trained as a hunter. But, for all of us, the trainers frequently remarked at how quickly we learned. It was the best assignment they had ever had. They had only to tell us how to do something and we'd do it right the first time. That was because of our natural talents. But, that guy. He was ahead of the trainers most of the time."

There I paused but Henni didn't prod me. "Okay," I said trying to organize my thoughts based on the new bits of information I had remembered. "We were told that our lives after the special teams would depend on our forgetting everything, and like I said, they did a lot to help. What do you think, will it come back?"

"My guess is most of it will come back." Henni was choosing his words carefully. "You must accept that there is an involved connection between your physical brain and your mind which is part of your spiritual soul. My dog remembers the sound of my voice. That memory is in his brain because he doesn't have a spiritual soul. Abstractions you form like 'treeness' after seeing many trees is in you mind, that is, your soul. A dog or a monkey can't make those abstractions. When you think the equation two plus three equals five you are operating on the level of abstractions. You have an abstract notion of what the numbers two, three and five stand for. You also know the meaning of the two operators "plus" and "equal." However, you still need your physical brain to process that equation. A person with a certain level of brain damage might remember how to speak but could not do simple arithmetic because of the part of his physical brain that had been damaged. From this and other considerations, we know the brain is always involved."

"Wait," I said. "I thought after death souls were aware of themselves and even people who were still alive. With their brains rotting in the grave, how can they think?"

"The only answer I've ever heard to that is if God could make us in the first place, he can figure out how to do that. And, it's only a temporary state because after the General Judgement we'll be reunited with our bodies again. Back to your problem. Do you remember what they did to make you forget your missions? Did they hypnotize you, use drugs, or something else?"

I leaned back in the easy chair. This was going to take longer than I had thought. It was complicated. Why wouldn't it be? "The best I can figure it was something like hypnosis without being put to sleep. We were warned of the dire consequences of ever telling anything about the missions. They also forced us to say and sometimes even yell statements as true that were the opposite of the truth. There were probably drugs, too, because my recollections of the debriefings have an ethereal feel to them. They didn't hit us in the head nor inject stuff into our brains to kill some of the cells that I can remember."

Henni sat without moving thoughtfully listening to every word as I spoke letting me say what I wanted without interruption. He waited until he was sure I was finished. "I would say that whatever you abstracted into your mind is still there because your mind has almost unlimited capacity. It's the links from your brain to your mind that are in question. With time and effort, most of those should come back."

One of his statements struck me as odd. "Why did you say that about my mind's capacity? I forget things all the time as does almost everybody else."

Now, he leaned back and looked straight ahead. "It's getting a little late, but I think I must tell you something that happened to me several years ago. It's what got me started on the study of theology and philosophy in general. Normally, I don't tell people about this because it hardly makes any sense. But, in you present circumstance I think it might help you."

When I arrived he said I had his interest and his curiosity. Now, he had mine.

He continued, "I was praying in church, actually a prayer to St. Joseph, when I had a spiritual locution. A spiritual locution is where God speaks directly to your mind. You don't see or hear anything, but the experience is totally unmistakable, something you never forget. It's not a dream, hypnotic suggestion, or anything like that. There's simply no mistake—it's from God. If you have never experienced it, you wouldn't understand. In this case it had nothing to do with memory, but I hope you'll see the relevance in a minute. It was about peace. I was given a few moments of deep peace that is most difficult to describe. We all think we know what the word peace means but mostly we understand it only as the absence of its opposite as in war or conflict. This was the presence of positive peace. Think of sitting by a lake shore at sunset with perfect temperature, no wind, no bugs, no intruding noises, just a relaxed state where all is right with the world. That is about as close as we can normally come to peace. The experience I'm describing was a thousand or a million times greater than that. After a few seconds it was as if I were told, 'You think that's something, how about this.' And, the peace went a million times deeper than that. Then, yet a third time it happened, still immeasurably more. Associated with it was the clear understanding that any one of us could do that at any time, but we just don't.'"

He paused to see my reaction. "You're right, I don't understand it. I do believe you, though, because of some of the odd things that have happened to me. Most of them deal with the fact that I'm alive when I should be dead. I appreciate you telling me this, but how does this help with my lost memories?"

Henni nodded. "In this way. That experience showed me that we are much more than we normally think we are. We were created, not infinitely more than we see ourselves, but so much greater that in our notion of "infinite" it might as well be infinite because we don't really grasp what that word means. In Genesis it says we are made in the image and likeness of God. Few people give any thought as to what that means. But, if God told us that, it is our duty to take it seriously. Since we cannot be God, who is infinite, anything less allows for an extreme range of possibilities. That is, we could range on the infinity index from a little more than a crumb of dirt to a tad less than God. What I'm saying is that we tend toward the higher end of the scale. And, now to your problem. All of this means that there is a lot more to you than you imagine there is which by extension means if it happened to you, you can remember it *if* you can reconnect your physical brain to your mind in the necessary ways. It's all in there, all you have to do is get it out."

I took that as good news, though, there seemed to be a lot of memories to resurrect. It was hard to believe they'd all come back. The statement that we can all do what he had described, but we just don't nagged at my mind so I mentioned it to him.

"It has to do with what is called detachment" he replied. "If you can detach yourself from all your worldly attachments you can experience some part of heavenly bliss while still alive. The great Catholic mystics did this and wrote books about their experiences. It's too extensive a topic to cover tonight. Did any of what I said help?"

A crazy situation had taken another crazy turn. So, I said, "I suppose it helps from the point of view of positive thinking. You just told me it's all there to be remembered, all I have to do is one little thing, as in doing the remembering. It's certainly not bad. Looking at my situation optimistically, I can say I've crawled out of the dumper."

Standing up, I made as if to leave, but Henni motioned me to stay. "I suppose you not only don't know where you hid it, but don't even know what you're looking for."

"Right on both counts."

"Any ideas about either question?"

Shaking my head, I said, "Nothing at all on where, and as to what, only logical deductions. And, that has led me to nuclear fissile material or even a complete ready to go bomb."

He asked, "You said this is about what happened in Vietnam, right?"

I nodded. From the look in his eyes, it was obvious he was conflicted about what he wanted to say.

"Well, go ahead and say it," I said.

He smiled. "Yeah, might as well. It doesn't matter where you got it, you hid it around here somewhere. That's partly logical deduction and also sort of an odd feeling I have. From the logical point of view, they wouldn't expect you to fly to San Francisco and start digging in the Golden Gate Park or any other place in the world. They must have clues from documentation about the case. But, there's something else. Maybe seeing you so short of information, I responded to the remotest of stirrings in my subconscious. These things do happen but we normally discount them because we're accustomed to dealing only with concrete situations and ideas—things that are certain and solid."

"The other guy and I have discussed how hard it would be to recover it if it were in Vietnam. I was assuming that if my memories came back, I'd be able to draw them a map for anyplace on earth and let them go after it."

"No. I wouldn't count on that if I were you. Think about it. Even if there had been no attempt to make you forget, that was a long time ago. You wouldn't normally be expected to draw a detailed map. And from what I gather that's what they want. And, don't forget this. After all this time things have changed a lot."

He laughed. "Sorry," he said apologetically. "I remembered a rather funny movie, though, I don't recall the title. A man had robbed a jewelry store and was pursued by the police. He ran into a building that was under construction. Not knowing what to do, he hid his loot in a heating duct in a partially constructed room. He was caught and went to prison. Five years later he's out and immediately sets about to retrieve his booty. To his dismay he discovers that the building where he hid his ill gotten goods was the new police station that was under construction at the time. What I'm saying is, what if you do remember where you hid it, and there is now a skyscraper on the spot?"

Shrugging I said, "*They* are obviously assuming that while digging to put in the foundation for the skyscraper it would have been discovered. Since it hasn't turned up they expect us to find it where we put it."

He looked away for a few seconds and then back at me. "I know this is hard on you, but it is kind of exciting, isn't it?"

It wasn't exciting at all, but I didn't want to offend my friend for his lack of understanding of what it meant to me. I closed my eyes for a moment and it was there in all its horror. I heard the sounds a few feet to my right and glanced over. Night Hawk was laying in the wet leaves twitching with part of the top of his head blown away. I could not see his full body because of dark green undergrowth blocking the view. Some of the slick wet vegitation beyond him was stained with blood, hair, and bits of brain. He didn't cry out, but there were gagging sounds for a few seconds. Then he lay still. It could just a well have been me. I clearly recalled thinking at that instant that this was a throe that I'd endure another time. It appeared this was that time. I sank deeper into the easy chair holding my face in my hands. We were so close, having saved one another's lives multiple times. It was the only way any of us came back from those missions. They were so dangerous, so deadly. Why all the death? What was wrong with this species we call *Homo Sapiens*?

In a soft empathizing voice, Henni said, "You're remembering, aren't you?"

I nodded without looking up. "More than remembering, I'm there. A member of my team, one of my best friends, just had his brains blown out. I saw him thrashing around on the wet leaves. We were both prone returning Viet Cong fire. A ricochet hit him in the head. He was gone instantly. I hope he was ready to go."

I looked up, right into Henni's eyes. "The two of us were putting up a delaying action while the other two made off with it."

"And, do you recall what *it* was?" Henni almost whispered.

"It's not clear what it looked like, but it was heavy, maybe three to four hundred pounds. They were rolling it down the slope toward the truck."

"Any more?"

I took a deep breath and leaned back, and said slowly, "No. This is going to be tough. If I have to remember more things like this, I'll go crazy. I just now saw him die, his life gouged out of him. He was so expert, such a loyal partner. One second he was an superb warrior, the next . . . nothing. And now these goons are driving us like some cavemen driving wooly mammoths off a cliff. Well, I'm about done being driven!"

My face was red, I could feel it. Henni didn't say anything as I let it pass. The one thing we learned, and had stuck with me all me life, was never to go into battle if you are angry. I was now in battle again, and I had to hone my old skills, this one in particular. As I had aged, I had become less and less able to clinically deal with society. As politically correct fetishes, each one dumber that the one before, were foisted upon us, I became increasingly riled. That had to stop. Only by cold calculated cunning was I going to defeat these monsters, and that I was intent on doing.

Standing up I said, "I've taken up enough of your evening. Thanks for your concern. It has helped to tell someone about the situation. And, in telling it I have recalled several things. I can only hope that regardless of the pain, I continue to bring back memories. If I'm ever totally stumped, I'll give you a call. But, I must warn you to say nothing to anyone about my visit."

Driving away from the manicured lawn in front of Henni's house, it was nearly dark. The visit had taken far longer than I had planned, though I should have realized that it would before I stopped. Maybe I did but felt the situation went beyond my friend being inconvenienced. It had been disturbing on a deep subliminal level. We all live with our inner life that no one else sees. It seemed like these miscreants not only would care nothing about physical torture and murder, but wouldn't hesitate to rip a man's soul apart. How far would this go before it was over? The good thing to come from my visit was I now felt certain most of my memories were at least available to be recovered, whether or not I'd, in fact, manage to do that.

That night I was tired, but found sleep illusive. The flashback to seeing Night Hawk die as he jerked about in the undergrowth was hard to deal with. How many more times had that happened? Would I have to relive all of them, too?

— 8 —

Sunday

That evening, at six-thirty, I left my car in a school parking lot a block from Fred Clements' house. It was a neighborhood that had been built as a tract in the fifties. The houses were all in the thousand to twelve hundred square foot range. This was an area that had been potato farms and the trees were planted at the time the development had gone up resulting in most of the trees being fifty to sixty years old. The streets were shady and the places well kept.

The front door stood open so I opened the screen door and stepped in. Closing it behind me I knocked on the oak molding around the door frame. "Anybody home?" I inquired.

The living room looked like a bachelor's pad, though I had a sense he had made a pass through it and picked up thrown about clothing, towels and half eaten bags of snacks. The vacuum cleaner hadn't had its chance to help beautify the environment, probably twenty-two hours was too short of notice. Through an archway in front of me was the eating area where a bare table and chairs pressed up against the wall.

"That you, Wessen?" a voice asked from down a short hallway on my left leading to bedrooms.

"Yes."

"Well, have a seat. I'll be there in a second."

He hadn't offered me a beer, but then we weren't exactly friends. The last time I'd seen him I had provided him with a trip to the hospital. That, and his rather forward attitude of assuming everyone was a criminal with only the lack of evidence keeping the entire population from serving life sentences, had lost him his job with the FB of I. My being here at all only gave credence to the saying that life sucked—for both of us.

He made his appearance still buttoning the shirt of his rent-a-cop uniform. "The great Vin Wessen," he said with sarcasm. "Never expected to see you again, especially with the offer of gifts. This outta be good."

His attitude was as I had expected. At least we were starting off on the wrong foot, which was the only way anyone could start with this man. Anything else and I'd have been suspicious. "Yeah," I said. "I suppose the feeling is mutual. But, life does have its little ups and downs. There's somebody out there that's going to start killing certain members of my family if I don't deliver a particular item to them. The tiny problem is that I don't know what it is they're after or where it is."

"So, tell certain members of your family to bend over and kiss their backsides good bye. Why aren't they going to kill you?"

His deep concern for other members of society was touching. "Obviously, if they did, that'd end the game. There'd be no fun in that, would there? And, there's no question they'll get to me if I fail. But, I don't intend to fail and that's why I thought of you."

He responded with a sneer, "You're even more obnoxious than I remembered."

"Thank you. I try to meet the expectations of my fans. But, this isn't getting us anywhere. I'll give you a truncated account of what has happened. While in the Army in Vietnam, I was part of a special forces group that was sort of off the books. For the most part, we did illegal things. I hadn't signed up for that, but once you were in that particular club and well trained, it wasn't an easy matter to walk away, and stay alive, that is. After our missions we were debriefed so thoroughly that we hardly knew our names. And, when we finally got out they told us that if we started talking about what we did remember, they'd hunt us down and take us out of circulation."

"As in," he interrupted, "a tour of duty in Fort Leavenworth."

"Actually, they had a more permanent idea of 'out of circulation' than that. As a result, we were told that we could lead normal lives if we made an effort to forget everything. For all these years I've been doing my best to do that. Now, decades later, somebody wants to dig it all up again for their own purposes. On one of our missions we were told to recover, steal, or whatever a valuable item. Over the past few days I've been remembering a few fragments here and there. I think it was the size, for lack of a better description, of a casket and was quite heavy, as in several hundred pounds. At some point we were attacked by Viet Cong. Two of us stayed behind to fend off the enemy while the other two worked the thing down the hill to where we had left the truck. Of the two of us left behind, I was the only one to survive. That's all I remember. I don't recollect any other mission that even comes close to our coming back with something. Sometimes, we were told to capture an enemy officer, and if possible return him alive. But never a thing, except that once. Therefore, I'm assuming that's what they want."

He interrupted me again which I did not find objectionable. It meant he was getting into the spirit of things. "Do you think it was full of gold?"

I shook my head. "No. I immediately though of that, too. At two-thousand dollars an ounce, a ton of gold is only worth fifty-eight million. The whole thing couldn't have weighed five hundred pounds or we could not have been expected to carry it. And, with a hundred pounds for the case that gives four hundred pounds of gold or about fifteen million. These days that doesn't go very far. I've come to the conclusion it has to be something that's valuable to only a few people. If it were a chemical or nuclear bomb, it's likely the people who are after it are terrorists, and of course they'd die, literally, to get their hands on something like that."

By this time we were both sitting in well worn stuffed chairs. He leaned back. The wheels were turning in his head. If what I said was true, and he managed to control the situation to his advantage, he could really, in fact, be a hero. This reaction was totally predictable and was fine with me, but only to a point.

Finally he said, "That's some wild story. Why should I believe it?"

"There's no reason at all unless you want to go the next step with me."

"Which is?"

"We have to flush out one of them. So far it's all been indirect. They totaled my wife's car in a parking lot while she was driving it. She wasn't injured, but the guy got away. As I left work the same afternoon, I found a note under my windshield wiper saying the accident was only a warning, and that it would get worse if I didn't make progress. Stuff like that."

"Let's cut to the chase. What do I get out of this?"

"I like that. You've got your eye on the ball."

He shifted nervously. It's not that he minded a compliment, but he was on his guard lest he start liking me. I had the same feeling toward him.

I wanted to keep things moving so I said, "If it's something nefarious, and I can only assume it is, the story would be that you were not really let go from the FBI, but it was made to look that way so you could more easily work under cover. Due to my past, I must avoid public recognition at all costs, so if there is any credit to be handed out, I want you to get it. That includes any rewards. I'm serious about that."

From his expression, I could tell he was working on it so I let him take his time.

"What if it blows up in our faces, figuratively I mean, you expecting me to take the blame?"

I hadn't worked it through that far, but his concern made sense.

"If it goes badly wrong, there's no chance I'll be able to remain anonymous, so I'm toast any number of ways. There'd be no reason to involve you as long as you weren't the one causing the problem. I want to stress that everything must be kept totally below the surface, no shooting, or injuring people, that sort of thing. We also won't be involving the authorities at any level, at least as long as possible."

More cogitating. Then he said, "What I'm doing is pushing me more toward a vegetative state every day. This sounds like a break in the routine if anything. If I agreed to help, when would it be? It's difficult to take time off my job. There're five applicants for every watchman opening."

I just about had him. "It would be as soon as possible. What's you schedule for the next few days?"

"By my normal routine, I'll be working tonight and be off the next two days. But, one of the guys asked if he could trade his Wednesday for my Monday. I have to let him know tonight."

"Then, tell him you have to have your Monday off and we'll make our little get together tomorrow evening—the sooner the better. We don't want them to have time to plan. When I get home, I'll let them know it'll be Monday evening at the regional park north of Lake Johanna, in Arden Hills."

"What's this!" he demanded. "You'll let them know? What's going on?"

I held up my hand palm towards him as I smiled. "It's part of the game. We assumed our houses were bugged and the other guy got hold of a bug sweeper. We found three in my house, plus my phones, and one in the garage. When I want to tell them something, I take my wife to the garage and talk to her there. I've said we had to assume the house was bugged. From what we can tell the bugs are the type that only transmit when someone is talking, and they send to a recorder located within a half mile of the house. They're downloaded periodically, I assume daily."

He was now smiling. "Oh, this is really good. Do your imaginary friends ever answer you? You know what they say, its not so bad if you talk to yourself, but when you start to answer yourself, then it's loony time."

I nodded. "As I said, they smashed our car and left a note. They shot a rocket propelled grenade through the other guy's front window. It didn't explode but there was a note engraved on it saying the next one would."

"Wait a minute. You've alluded to others before. How many other guys are there?"

"Only one. We have to make it look like you are another man from one of the teams we were on. The idea is they would want to see who you are, so they could go back to the records and find out who they are dealing with. We are pretty sure there is only one man watching me, and one keeping tabs on the other guy who lives in St. Louis. You and I will meet and the other man will be in the background hoping to catch the one who comes to observe our meeting. Are you in?"

He screwed up his face as he considered it. Then, "Yeah, for tomorrow evening, then we'll see. How do we do this?"

"First we'll use our legends. I'm Double Duce, and called Duce. The other guy is Nine Lives, called Nine. We've decided you'll be Big Buck, and called Buck. Here's a sketch of the park and where we'll meet."

He took the page with the sketch as he replied, "Were you that certain I'd go along with this?"

"Not at all. But, I decided to come prepared in case you agreed. Luring them out is the only thing we could think of. We're getting a little desperate because neither one of us had much of a clue as to what they want."

After that I went into the details of what he had to do. I could see that he had something of an amused expression on his face at times. I had read the novel *The Prince and the Pauper* by Mark Twain a few years past. His attitude reminded me of the way people treated the young prince when they thought he was a common pauper as he kept insisting he was the King of England. Clements just couldn't bring himself to believe I could be so important as to know where a nuke was hidden.

My parting remark was, "By the way, there'll be a lot of mosquitoes."

* * *

When I returned home, I placed the tracking device back on the car and returned the bug to the garage so I could make a "phone" call. Actually, there was no phone, but I had to let them, whoever they were, know where the meeting with Clements would be.

"Hi, Buck? Glad I got you. What do you say, will you meet me?"

After a pause, "Good. I'm glad you decided to hear me out. What? Oh, don't worry. I bought a non-contract cell phone a few days ago. They don't know the number so they couldn't possibly listen in. Okay?"

I left a longer pause this time. "I want our meeting in a secluded place so there's no chance of being overheard. Here's where you go. In Arden Hills is Perry Park just off Fairview Avenue. Park your car in the parking lot. There're four ball diamonds, two north of the parking lot, and two south of it. It'll be Monday evening so I don't think there'll be any ball games. Walk east out of the lot to a tree line. There's a rough path down a steep slope in the woods, it's kind of a wash for the rain water. At the bottom of the slope is the foundation of where a small building once stood. I'll meet you there."

I waited a half minute. "Well, you may have to walk along the tree line ten yards left or right if you don't see the path right away, but it's easy to find. The meeting place is only a couple of hundred yards from the parking lot." Short pause, "Good, see you at seven-thirty tomorrow evening. And, thanks."

After that I took a short walk down the street, and with my real cell phone, I made a call to Harry. Using a code word we had set up he knew to be here tomorrow afternoon.

With that done there was nothing to do but wait. If the man watching me down loaded and listened to the fake call about tomorrow's meeting as soon as this evening, there could be a whole platoon of guys waiting for us in the woods tomorrow. But, we'd assume there would be at least two. If I had waited until tomorrow to make the pretend call, there was a good chance that the bad guys would not know about the meeting in time. But, two would not be bad. If Harry were to capture one it made his chances better. There were a lot of woods, and the brush was thick. With only Harry and one bad guy, it was possible Harry wouldn't find him.

Monday

As he had planned, Harry left his office at nine to attend a business meeting, but instead went to the airport and took a plane to Minneapolis. He was at the back door by one o'clock where Camilla met him. She give him the maps and detailed instructions that I had written out the evening before. I warned him about the mosquitoes, too. Harry parked at the Lake Johanna end of the park and walked the three-quarters of a mile through the woods to the meeting site. As with any city park there were a plethora of trails leading nearly anywhere. Perry Park and Lake Johanna Park were part of a larger regional park. The land had been set aside because it was at least half marshland.

In my instructions, I indicated the general area where Harry should position himself because I needed to know where he would be in case I saw movement anywhere else. This he understood from our training all those years ago. I'd be packing my nine millimeter pistol, and Clements would be armed, I had no doubt of that. Harry would do as he thought best, which I was sure would mean a camouflage suit, trip wires, his jungle knife and enough fire power to handle the platoon that might be there. The trip wires were just that, wires that were strung between two trees across a trail to trip someone.

The main thing about the location was the dense foliage all around it. For anyone to get a look at the mystery man, to say nothing of hearing our conversation, he would have to be less than ten yards away.

At seven-fifteen I left the house. Camilla had at one point wanted to be part of it, but I convinced that she did not have the skills needed for something like this. Stuck in the back of my mind was always the possibility that they would want to kill Clements just as they had Blue Dog, though I sincerely doubted it.

The trick I left for them was that I'd be the one arriving at Parry Park. My instructions for Clements had been for him to park by the Valentine Hills Elementary School a half mile to the northeast of the meeting place. This would leave it to him to walk south along a road reserved for the twig-pigs, known to others a park rangers and other assorted park workers and tree-huggers. He could have then made a right turn onto a causeway across the swamp and approach the meeting place from the east. The causeway itself was shielded on both sides by fifteen foot willows and other brush. Here too was a little surprise.

If all they wanted to do was identify our new member they would have stationed a man beyond the ball fields to the south of the parking lot because just past the outfield fence the land rose sharply for twenty feet. A good telephoto lens could easily capture the arriving man. And, in June, there would be plenty of light at that hour.

Locking my car I put on a baseball cap, and started walking at a brisk pace, but giving no indication of hurrying. Immediately, I started down the path knowing exactly where it was having used it many times. At the bottom was the old building foundation. I hesitated momentarily and looked around. Then I started across the causeway. Where I walked the roadway was less than a foot above the mucky stagnant water. The meeting was actually to take place on the east side of the swamp rather than on the west by the remains of the old building like I had said. Oops, what an evil world—can't trust anybody. How would they react?

It was only a hundred yards across the causeway. As I crossed there was no sign of Harry or anyone else. However on the other side there were two boys about twelve with bikes. It seemed they had made a sort of competition out of peddling up and down one of the steeper trails that terminated in the small clearing east of the swamp. To my left a branch of a small tree moved and I saw Clements also wearing a baseball cap. He was not in camouflage clothing, but his choice of colors could not have been better, all dark greens and browns. I turned my head toward the boys, then back to Clements. He stepped into full view.

The boys, who had paid me no notice, now saw that there were two of us both looking at them. They stopped talking as Clements approached them. "There's some police business going on here, and the two of you had better go home."

I had to admit, he had a way of saying a few simple words that sounded like the crack of doom. They were off peddling as fast as they could, and not looking back. It even made me want to get away from him. I raised my eyebrows. "Lots of practice," was all he said.

We were standing where we could not see down the causeway and all was still. The gnats and mosquitoes were buzzing about our heads, but with the prior liberal application of bug spray, we were reasonably comfortable. It was too quiet. Then I heard it—a train was approaching from the east. Not a hundred yards to our south, a railroad track cut through the park, and it was a busy line. With all the vegitation, a person didn't realize it was there. And I had forgotten about it. If someone had taken the time to check schedules, they could have known when it was due. With a hundred car train rumbling past, all sounds, even gunshots, would be largely drowned out.

I turned to Clements. "If anything's to happen, it'll be while the train is coming by. The tracks are just beyond those trees." As I spoke the noise increased.

As the locomotives were opposite us, I fell to a crouching position. "Out of sight!" I said as I pointed to my left. Then sensing there wouldn't be time for that I lunged over and swept Clements' feet from under him. A shot cracked, then another. They had come from the direction of the train. I had my gun out and shot twice keeping them low so as to hit only legs if I were lucky and miss the train if not lucky. Clements didn't need any coaching as he scrambled to the cover of the foliage pulling a pistol from behind his belt in the small of his back. I took a rolling dive in the direction of the swamp.

I heard the snapping of branches in the direction of the train. I smiled. If he were to make his getaway in that direction it would be hilarious because the bank leading up to the tracks was covered with blackberry bushes that had some of the sharpest thorns in the world.

The train passed. There was rustling to our south and what I thought was a muffled curse. After that it was quiet. I looked in the direction of where Clements should be. All I saw was his cap where it had fallen as he went down. Knowing they would not be shooting at me, I was up and in a crouch ran to the general area where Clements had taken cover. He wasn't there. I waited and listened. In the deepening shadows under the dense foliage I couldn't see more than ten feet in any direction. I started moving in the direction of the railroad tracks. I intersected a trail that led to the clearing where Clements had been shot at. To my right across the clearing I could see the causeway and Harry coming my way along it.

Footsteps in the leaves across the trail caused me to draw back. Clements cautiously appeared ten yards up the hill from me. I whispered, "Buck," I'd never get used to calling him that, "see anything?"

Stepping onto the trail, he came my way. "As soon as the train passed he scooted across the tracks. Looked like he was leaving, but who knows."

I motioned for him to follow me. We met Harry in the small clearing at the end of the causeway. His first words were, "Is anybody hit?"

We both shook our heads. I inquired, "How about you, did you do any good?"

"Yeah. I think so. We have to move, though. There were shots and even with the noise of the train, somebody heard them. I'm parked by the lake to the south and that's a lot of bush and woods to get through."

I nodded. "Buck saw the shooter head that way. My car's the closest. Let's go."

Clements was returning from retrieving his cap. He was holding it up to the light looking through a hole in it.

Jogging across the causeway to the west, we all had a hand on a gun. They had meant to kill Clements. I wondered how he'd react when that occurred to him.

Once out of the trees at the top of the hill behind the outfield fence near the foul line of one of the softball fields, we walked very fast, almost ran to my car. Once out of the lot and on the street, I went north to County Road E2, and the east. We'd pick up Clements' car at the school. Nobody was talking.

— 9 —

I stopped at a dark blue Trailblazer. We all got out looking for a tail, and any movement as far as we could see in any direction. Clements said, "Mind telling me what's really going on? The guy in the bushes tried to kill me. If you hadn't clipped my legs out from under me at that instant, I'd probably be dead." He was looking at the hole in his cap again. Apparently as he fell his head jerked and his cap flew up and took the bullet.

"You got something against a stimulating experience every now and then? Just helping you keep your head out of the Vegematic."

Harry looked puzzled. "What?"

"Later. What did you get, Nine?"

"When I saw the setup, I knew you had picked a good spot. Even though you said the meeting would be at the west end of the causeway, I assumed you were likely to improvise, as did they. It forced them to split their force by leaving one man on either end. So I found a spot midway across and strung a slack trip wire across the road, and then hunkered down in the swamp beside the road in a bunch of willows. My legs are soaked and covered with mud, but it was a good setup. I watched as you came past me knowing what you were doing. Two minutes later, sure enough, the guy stationed on the west end came along. I pulled the line taught, he fell, and I was on him. If I do say so myself, after all this time, I did pretty good. He was gagged and his hands bound before he had a chance to cry out."

At this he pulled some plastic zip bags from his pockets. "Exhibit one," he said solemnly. It was a pistol magazine. "There should be prints on this. I whispered in his ear that I was throwing it in the swamp as I tossed a small rack. The splash convinced him. I found his spare clip and, being out of rocks, really did toss that one in. Then I asked him what they were after. He didn't want to cooperate, so I took some DNA evidence."

Harry produced a second bag. Clements stared at it not believing what he saw. Laying the clear plastic bag carefully in the palm of his hand Clements said incredulously, "That's a finger!"

"Right you are, sir. But, not a whole finger, only the last joint of the little finger of his right.had. You see, he was right handed."

Clements handed it back without saying more.

Harry was looking a little smug seeing how an FBI, well, former FBI agent reacted to what to us was only the real world. "You're probably thinking that was a little severe. But, first, I needed information and exposed the way we were on the road, I didn't have much time. Second, he'll experience difficulty handling a gun for the next month, hence the right hand. Also, as I already mentioned, it's totally prefect for DNA identification if it comes to that, and it contains a complete pinky print. Lastly, and most importantly, these guys had the audacity to screw around with Phantom, and that would not go unanswered!"

Clements' mouth dropped open. "Phantom Teams! They really existed! After the happenings last summer, everybody was talking about that. It was finally put to rest as nothing more that someone's fertile imagination, like Sylvester Stallone as *Rambo*."

We were both nodding. I said, "Fertile imagination or not, we existed." Turning to Harry I said, *"Forsooth, my dear Nine Lives, it doth seem thou spake rightly about poor departed Blue Dog."*

"Where'd that come from?"

"I don't know."

"What're you guys talking about?" Clements demanded.

Before I could answer, Harry gave the narration. "Before all of this started, I was nearly killed while driving along a mountain road. Thinking there was a possibility it had something to do with the teams, I looked up another member of our team. A week before I found him, he had been murdered in a way that made it look like it was from natural causes. Blue Dog's death looked suspicious so with more effort I found Duce. Neither of us were really sure that what happened to Blue Dog and me was connected. That's why Duce came to you. We needed a reason for them to show themselves so we let them think we had located the fourth member of the team and you played the part of him."

"And," Clements interjected, "this evening was to see if they'd kill me the same as they did Blue Dog! Is that it?"

We were both feeling rather sheepish, not looking him in the eye. Finally, Harry said, "We never expected they'd go that far, but it shows how desperate they are. The idea was to lay our hands on one of them. It seemed like the only way we could get information to make the progress they demanded. And," he added, "I did. After I cut off the finger, the guy was motivated to talk. He said we were looking for a "madam." I hope that means something to someone, because it means zip to me. He said only we knew where it was hidden."

We all stood with blank expressions on our faces.

"Great!" Clements almost exploded. "You almost get me killed, and got nothing. Just great! This whole thing is nuts. Did I happen to step through a *Looking Glass* and not notice it."

Harry replied, "Another literary reference. What is this a book club?"

I looked at Harry. "Do you have a hotel room?"

He shook his head. "No. But, I know where to go that I'm sure they'll have rooms available at this hour."

"Does it have Internet access in the rooms?"

He nodded. "And, I do have a laptop with me."

We set up a plan in a couple of seconds and left. Clements would follow me and I'd drop Harry off at his car. Then, the three of us, driving separately, would go to Harry's hotel. Once he had a room we'd get together and see what we could find on the Web. On the way, I called Camilla to say we were all okay.

Past nine, we were together in Harry's room. He had taken off his wet clothes and wore a pull over shirt, and khaki shorts with bare feet. He put MADAM in the search engine. Most of the hits were what one would expect from that word. We were looking for something that was a little off. Harry worked the keyboard while the two of us looked over his shoulder offering suggestions from time to time. Nothing. Page after page of MADAM produced nothing but MADAM.

"Maybe," Clements suggested, "it's an acronym and some of the letters aren't there."

Harry tried MDAM and didn't do any better. Then MADM, and there it was, Medium-Atomic-Demolition-Munition. It wasn't long before we had all the government was inclined to say about the MADM. It was an atomic bomb using Plutonium 239 that was adjustable to produce a yield of from one to fifteen kilotons. It had been used on atomic antiaircraft rockets, as well as several other weapons. According to the information on the Internet, all 350 of them that had been built were decommissioned by the late nineteen-eighties. It was the demolition munition that interested Harry and me.

"That's an atomic land mine," Harry said.

The exploding device itself weighed 150 pounds. It was a cylinder eighteen inches in diameter and sixty-five inches long. The land mine version, with protective carrying case was four hundred pounds.

"If memory serves, fifteen kilotons is about the yield of the bomb dropped on Hiroshima," I said. "And, from this, it appears they've all been decommissioned, which means they're all gone—except one."

Clements added dourly, "That's the one nobody wants to talk about, because nobody want's to admit they lost it. And, you guys took it, or they *think* you did."

"Pull the plug," I said to Harry. "We don't want to be on the Internet too long looking at stuff like that. Besides, we have to talk."

There were three chairs and a round table which suited our purposes as we sat around it. I began, "First off, I hope it's clear that if any one of us is a snitch, we'll all die including the snitch. Buck, I came to you out of the blue, but you could have talked to someone after that. I'm not singling you out, because it goes for Nine and me, too.

"Secondly, we did take it. I visited my friend the other night to see what he knew about memory loss and how to get it back. Don't worry, he knows it's serious, and I didn't tell him much. He helped me a lot, though. He said it's fairly certain the memories are in our minds, and all we have to do is make the brain connections to our minds. While talking about it, I had a short flashback and last night a lot more came back. I now know Night Hawk was the forth member of our team. These flashbacks are painful, but it seems there's no other way it'll come back.

"In my flashback we were all together digging it up. We were on a mountain not far from Cam Ranh Bay in Vietnam. We had it out and were on our way with it when the Viet Cong attacked. Hawk and I stayed behind to hold them off while Blue and Nine manhandled the thing down the hill to the truck. Hawk took a ricochet to the head and was gone. That's as far as I can remember. I still don't remember what it looked like, but the description on the Internet seems about right." After a pause I looked at Harry. "We could use some help. Don't you remember anything?"

He shook his head, then looked at Clements. "I don't think you have too much to worry about if they managed to identify you. Maybe they got the plate number off your car or something. When they find out how old you are, they'll know you couldn't be with Phantom, and were used as a ploy."

Clements wasn't happy. "But, *I* can't assume something like that. Of all the dumb things I've done in my life, this is really it. Now, I'm stuck with you guys."

"Look at the bright side," I said. "We know we're looking for a lost nuclear weapon. If we find it and you are the one seen as responsible, you'll be a genuine modern hero. People will make up folk ballads about you to sing as they sit around camp fires at night. Well, maybe not. Let's say they'll share them on their I-Pods, or it'll go viral on FaceBook."

Clements wasn't amused. "As I said before, this is just great. We know what they want, but still have not the faintest idea about where it is. I'd like to start knocking your heads together. Maybe that'd help you remember.

"How about the prints on the clip?" Clements asked. "It might help if we knew who we were dealing with. Did you get a good look at the man you took down, Nine?"

Harry responded, "Yeah, I did. And, from what I saw, we aren't dealing with ragheads, at least not directly. That guy looked like he was ex-U.S. military, maybe Marines, something like that."

"Describe him," Clements said.

"He was what you could call a good looking man of six feet, maybe a little more, and in good shape. He has reddish hair and fading freckles, blue eyes, probably of Irish descent. I didn't notice any distinguishing marks—oh yeah, he had a round brown spot or mole on his right cheekbone about the size of a pencil eraser. His nose was a tad wide, it seemed. I only had a couple of glances at him, and we were in shadows."

I stood up and started pacing the room. "We know that thing last summer was strictly Federal Government, though obviously a rogue element of it." I looked at Clements, "Did anyone mention a man by the name of Flavian Cutter concerning that business?"

He looked down and shook his head. "No. It was all over by the time I was out of the hospital. They really had their noses bent out of shape and were looking for a scapegoat as much as anything. And, I was handy."

"You were more than handy," I said. "You were the one who managed to get the Speaker of the House of Representatives connected with it. That'll bend some noses out of shape if anything will."

He didn't respond. In fact, I was beginning to worry about him. He could have been killed earlier this evening. It was the latest incident in a life that was spiraling down. He was feeling sorry for himself, looked depressed, may even be on antidepressants, and could become a loose cannon at any moment. It was important to keep him involved.

I sat down and said to him, "Do you still have any contacts at the Bureau?"

Without looking at me he responded, "A few that would at least acknowledge they knew me, but I wouldn't expect them to do anything for me like run the prints on the clip. That's what you're asking, isn't it?"

"That would be useful, but we should be able to put a name to the prints. It's finding out where that person works, or how he's connected that we'd need help with. I very much doubt that someone who's part of a professional assassin team has his utilities and credit card under his real name. He'll be hard to pin down."

He shrugged. "Give me a name and I'll give it a try. Since I'm loosely in law enforcement, they may not laugh too loud."

We decide Harry would take the clip to his PI firm for lifting and tracing prints. Since there were two men in the Twin Cities now, they may see that's where the action is and wouldn't follow him back to St. Louis.

I had an idea. "Nine, how about slipping a few of the cartridges out of the clip. We'll leave them with Big Buck for safe keeping. If it came to it, we might be able to lift prints off them, though it would be hard. Since he's not part of Phantom, he's the safest."

Harry nodded, I think, knowing what I was doing. He produced another plastic bag and carefully ejected four cartridges out of the clip and let them fall into the bag as Clements held it.

"The other bag too," I said to Harry. "They seem to slip into our houses and plant bugs whenever they want. How about putting it in your freezer, Buck?"

He whispered, "I'll label it ground beef."

Clements and I drove away at the same time, but in different directions. A quarter mile later I turned around and returned to the hotel. Something had been hanging at the edge of my thoughts and finally come to the fore. I knocked lightly at Harry's door. He could see it was me through the peephole yet he opened the door with the security chain attached.

"You alone?" he asked.

I nodded and he opened the door. There was a towel around his waist as if he had come from the shower a minute before. I could tell he was a little embarrassed by his caution when admitting me. "This is starting to work on me," he said as he entered the bathroom taking a pair of jeans with him. He reemerged wearing the jeans, a sweatshirt and combing his hair back. "I'm too old for this. I have a wife, a couple of kids, a big house and own a business. What happened to a sane life where all I had to worry about was being shipped shoddy merchandise by a supplier?"

"Our past is what happened," I replied. "I don't like it anymore than you do." He sat on the edge of the bed and I dropped into one of the chairs. "The reason I came back is I remember from the operation where we dug the thing up that there was an Air Force major running things. When we were assigned the job in the operation tent at the helicopter base he had green tape over his name tag. It was odd because he wasn't with Phantom, and being Air Force didn't make any sense at all. Do you remember anything about him?"

"Major Bruce Holt," he said without hesitation.

When he didn't continue, I prompted, "And . . . ?"

Nonchalantly, he continued. "I'm not sure he was connected with that operation. I remember being in the back of a truck covered with canvas, maybe a duce and a half, or three-quarter ton—we rode in a lot of trucks—and he and I were the only ones. His hands were free, but his wrists were raw like he had been bound and spent a lot of effort trying to free himself."

"Who was driving?"

"I don't remember. It could have been any one of the three of you guys, I suppose. We dropped him off in a seedy part of Saigon. It seemed strange as I recall, but strangeness was what we did."

"How'd you get his name?"

"There was a patch coming loose from over his left shirt pocket. . . ."

"Could it have been tape falling off?"

"Yeah, I suppose it could have. Anyway, he pulled it off and said it didn't matter anymore because what he had done would get him killed. Then he said he was Major Bruce Holt, a C-130 pilot, and he was telling me this so that if he disappeared maybe I could contact his family and tell them he was dead so they wouldn't hold out hope that he was MIA."

"Anything else? How were you to contact his family?"

"I don't know except he mentioned the 133 Airlift Group. How do you suppose I remember that?"

"Maybe it was like the snake. It was something they didn't know you knew so they couldn't make a special effort to make you forget it."

He raise his index finger. "Now, that's sort of making sense. Being a C-130 pilot had to mean the major I was with in the back of the truck was Air Force. And, you remember the man who ran that operation was also an Air Force major. Somebody with a lot of pull managed to get some Phantom teams, or at least one, us, assigned to the Air Force to do something. If it was to dig up an atomic land mine, which it seems it was, and the person in charge was a C-130 pilot, it could only mean the intent was to fly the thing out of country."

We were both silent. Almost simultaneously, we both started to speak. I motioned to Harry who asked, "Where would they take it?"

"Plug in your computer again and look up 133 Airlift Group."

It seemed like the Net was unusually slow this evening as we waited. Wow! That was a surprise. The 133rd flew out of the Air Force Reserve Station at the Minneapolis International Airport. Harry went into the history part of the 133 Airlift Group's website and found that reserve units like this were put into service for varying lengths of time to fly personnel and vital supplies to Vietnam and take various cargoes the other way. The reserves were used to augment air transport capability without having to increase the number of active duty units since congress put limits on the size of the active duty forces.

"Think about it," I said. "What could be more natural than a plane from the 133 Airlift Group making a flight from Vietnam to Minneapolis. That means that sucker is here someplace."

Harry nodded. But before he could say anything, I continued, "And . . . if it had been deployed on that mountain where we dug it up, it was a complete weapon. If we're not careful we could have fifteen kilotons explode under my house, or this hotel."

Harry grinned. "But the good news is, he must know where it is. I think we've done it. All we have to do is locate him and convince him to let us in on the little secret."

We both laughed. It was more than a *little* secret. If he were inclined to tell where it was, why hadn't he done so in the last forty years?

We agreed I'd use my PIs to locate Major Holt, and Harry would look for the owner of the ammunition clip.

— 10 —

Tuesday

Shortly after I arrived at work this Tuesday morning I called my PI firm. The man I normally worked with had been gone for several days. Luckily he had returned so I could talk to him personally. We had met a year before and he had left me with a impression that he would be trust worthy. For some things I didn't mind asking anyone who answered the phone, but in this case I wanted him to handle it because Holt represented such a break for us. When I asked him to locate Major Bruce Holt, formerly of the 133 Airlift Group he took it in stride, though I could tell that by this time he was becoming almighty curious about what was going on.

While I was eating lunch at my desk I received a call. This was the time my PI had been instructed to contact me. He had an address for Holt in Hopkins, a suburb southwest of Minneapolis. That wasn't far from where I worked so I decided to work a little late and stop by his home after work. It was five-thirty before a found his house. There was nothing I could do but use the direct approach so I parked in front of the house, a well kept up two story with small dormers facing the street. The lawn was lush with the appearance that a service fertilized, watered, and cut it.

The chime sounded in the house as I pressed the doorbell button. It was impossible to know what sort of reaction I'd receive which made me apprehensive. After a minute with no response, I pressed it again, after another shorter wait yet again. Finally there were sounds of foot falls and the door opened a crack.

"Hello," I said, "I'm looking for Bruce Holt. Is he here?" I made an effort to keep my voice low but understandable. Any nosy neighbor could have moved up behind a shrub to eavesdrop.

"Not again! No. He's not here."

"Ma'am, I'm sorry, but what did you mean by 'not again?'"

"The Secret Service men who were here earlier today. Are you some more of that bunch?"

I paused for only a few seconds. The PI firm had been compromised. So much for my feeling of whom I could trust. But, in the man's defense, all those guys had to do was walk in and flash real or fake credentials and the whole place had no choice but to play ball with them which in this case meant contacting them whenever I called asking for something.

"No ma'am. Are you Mr. Holt's wife?"

She nodded.

"I'm not with them, and I doubt very much that, in spite of the badges they showed you, they are with the Secret Service. It is imperative that I speak with you. I knew your husband in Vietnam and this is very serious. Please, will you talk to me?"

She opened the heavy door and we looked at each other through the screen. She was in her fifties, dark blond with blue eyes. The face was narrow, but pretty. She was wearing beige slacks and a flowered top. Her hair was at shoulder length with a nice wave. Her face was made up as if one never knew who might show up during the day.

I stepped back on the landing, down one step, and motioned for her to come outside. She didn't understand so I said softly, "Come out on the lawn."

Uncertainly, she did as I bid her. When we were half way to the street, I said, "Your house has had listening devices installed in it by the men who visited you."

A wildness appeared in her eyes. "What's happening? Am I in danger?"

"No. But your husband is."

Then, spunk appeared in her face. "What's going on. Listening devices? Ha. What do you take me for? You had better leave or I'll call the police."

My next utterance would either hook her, or all was lost. "In Vietnam we were both part of a highly secret operation to collect and dispose of a valuable item. This item would not be valuable to you or me, but certain people would kill any number of people to gain possession of it. I was part of a team that acquired it, your husband was involved in hiding it though he may not know precisely where it is. The important thing is that the men who visited you *think* he knows where it is. That's all that matters."

Small creases between her eyes became evident as she was working on what I had said. At least she was considering it. "Why would they bug the house?"

"Because they would know that within twenty-four hours I'd show up and they'd want to know what you told me."

She was shaking her head. "I don't know. That's pretty flimsy. Show me a bug," she said assertively. There, she had me.

I nodded because after Harry had located the ones in my house I knew where to look. "Did they talk to your husband in the house?"

"Yes, of course. Bruce and the two of them sat around the dinette table."

"Good. I'll follow you into the house and, without a word, you point to the places the two men occupied. Is that okay?"

"Wait. How do I know who *you* are?"

That was a fair question. I handed my driver's license to her and told her to hang onto it. She compared the photo to me and nodded.

"You watch me all the time so you are certain I am not the one placing the bug. Do you understand?"

That had not occurred to her, but she grasped the idea immediately. In the house, we traversed a short hallway toward the back of the house. There were irregular slate tiles on the floor covered with area rugs. The walls were adorned with framed children's photos. The kitchen and informal eating area were separated by a counter with hanging cabinets above it. She pointed to two wooden chairs with a padded seats neatly tied to them. On hands and knees I looked up under the table as she stood back watching me. I motioned her to open the drape across the patio door. The patio was on the west of the house and the afternoon sun streamed in thoroughly illuminating the room. Nothing was obvious under the table. The underside of one of the chairs was different. I backed away and stood up motioning for her to tip the chair over and look. She saw something about the size of stick of gum. I stooped down and pointed to what looked like a strand of hair which was the antenna. I motioned for her to stand and pointed to the patio door.

Outside with the door closed, I said, "That's a listening device. The reason I know is there are some in my house, too. I had called a PI service to locate Bruce. The men posing as Secret Service obviously have gotten to them with their impressive badges so they arrived here before me. Where is your husband, I must speak to him."

"He's gone. The reason he was home today was he and our youngest son, Bud, who's twenty, were leaving on a canoe trip to the BWCA. Do you know about that?"

The BWCA is the Boundary Waters Canoe Area Wilderness in northern Minnesota along the border with Canada. It had so many lakes that with short portages between lakes and around dangerous rapids, a person could travel for tens of miles by canoe. With ever increasing use in the nineteen fifties and sixties regulations were placed on it. Camping was now only allowed at designated campsites, and an entrance permit was required. This permit listed the number in the party, which was limited, the entry point and the day of entry. This controlled the number entering so the number of parties never exceeded the number of designated campsites.

"Yes," I said. "My sons and I went up there a few times some years back. Did he tell them about his plans?"

"I could tell he didn't want to, but he told them their entry point. He had to explain all of that to them. They had never heard about the canoe country. He told them they would be leaving shortly. Bruce and Bud left about eleven."

"Was there any warning that he should not leave town, anything like that?"

She looked at the ground as she shook her head. Finally, looking at me she replied, "Nothing at all that I heard. Now that I think about it, it seems odd. If this is as important as you say, they'd demand that he stay around in case they had more questions."

I didn't want to alarm her more than she was, but it was obvious that a wilderness setting would be the perfect place to ask more questions.

"Returning to the trip, did they intend to enter today or stay in a motel tonight and enter tomorrow morning?"

"Why is any of that important."

Ignoring the question I asked, "Did the Secret Service men say why there were here?"

"I was in the kitchen making coffee part of the time and they were talking in low voices so I'm not sure, but I assumed they did."

"So, they talked briefly to Bruce and then left?"

"Yes. They were gone before the coffee was done. What are you driving at?"

I looked away thinking about Blue Dog, and how they tried to kill Clements. "It was unlikely they could conclude their business with you present. What I mean is, if they think he has the information they want, they mean to get it."

A cloud came over her complexion in contrast to the clear sunny afternoon. "You mean to say they would torture him is he wouldn't tell what he knows?"

"I rather think they might," I replied. Now, it was important to get what I could. "Please, describe the men as well as you can. That's important."

The wild look was back, but she was in control. "One man looked very strong. His biceps were positively huge. He had hair that was longer than normal, but not to his shoulders. It had a natural wave to it."

"A white man?"

"Oh yes. They were both white.

"Any particular marks that you can remember?"

She thought. "Why, yes. He had a scar running up and down on the right side of his mouth and chin."

I nodded.

"You know him?"

"Not personally, but yes, I do. So you understand this is serious, I know for a fact that he was one of the men that built the bomb that exploded on Ford Parkway last summer."

Her eyes were wide. "Oh, my. I had no idea. We felt the shock wave way over here."

"How about the other man?"

She proceeded to describe the man Harry had taken down in the park including the mole near his ear. I nodded again.

"It's important that I know where your son and husband were going. Can I look at what there is in the house that has to do with the planning of the trip? There must be some information about their entry point and which day they're going in." I held up my index finger. "Not a word in the house."

She led me to what was sort of an office where there were still several papers lying about concerning the trip. The entry point was #30 for Lake One. I found a scrap of paper and wrote, "Did the SS guys come into this room?"

She shook her head so I whispered, "Is that the entry point he told them?"

"I'm not sure," she whispered back, "but, I think so."

"Did you hear him mention the town of Ely?"

"Yes."

Ely was the small town that was the gateway to the BWCA on the west side. Rather than follow them on the five hour drive to Ely, and take the chance of being spotted, they'd immediately hit the road to get there first. Then, they'd park near the entry to the town and wait for them. From there, they could follow and be sure they had been given the correct information.

There was a large scale map of the canoe country in a file and I located the entry point. Is was not one my sons and I had used. I asked if there were any particular lakes they talked about while they were planning the trip. She thought. "Yes, something like Insulate Lake, but that doesn't make any sense."

I scanned the map. "Lake Insula?"

"Yes, I think so."

"Why that lake?"

"It was because they had very good fishing in that area two years ago and they planned this trip to be there during the same week as last time."

"Did he mention that lake to them?"

"I'm pretty sure he did."

I sorted through the maps from the file and located a well worn detailed map that looked like it had been used on the previous trip. The officially designated campsites were shown by red dots. One was circled. The dates of the trip were written on the margin. It was two years ago to the day.

Taking the large scale map and the detailed one, I asked, "Can I borrow these maps? It's important I reach your husband before they do."

She nodded and I got up to leave. She followed me out the front door. In the front step she asked, "How do I know who the good guys are?"

There was no really good answer so I did the best I could. "I'm your husband's age and we both served in Vietnam. Those men are too young for that. I'm not flashing a fancy badge, and I'm not the one who bugged your house. If you think of every place one of them touched, you'll likely find one or two more bugs. That's all I can say other than if anyone asks you must deny that I was here. Your son is in danger, too. I have a lot to do, so I'll leave you. Thank you, you've helped a lot." Pausing I asked, "Could I have my driver's license back?"

Driving away, I palmed my cell phone. I hated people who talked on the phone while they were driving, but this was a special case. I supposed everyone else would say that, too. It didn't matter. First, I called Harry at his cell phone and he answered.

"Harry, Vin. Did you deliver the clip to your PIs?"

"Yeah, and a short time ago they called me and said it had been wiped clean, the bullets, too."

"Figures. Our PIs have been compromised. They wiped off the prints under orders from the Secret Service. The man who shot at Buck was the man we learned about in Wisconsin. You get that?"

"Yeah. Bad news. What now?"

"I'll call you back later, have a lot to do. Bye."

Next I called Clements. It was early enough so he wouldn't be at work yet, and if I remembered right he said he was off work today. To my surprise, he answered.

"Buck, this is Duce. I'm on my way over to your place. Don't leave. Don't let anyone else in the house. Have your artillery handy. See ya."

Since my destination was on the opposite side of downtown Minneapolis, I took the freeway leading into downtown Minneapolis which was moving well this being evening. The one headed out was full, but staying above forty, so rather than try alternate streets, I stayed with it. Shortly before seven I parked in front of Claimant's house. The living room drape was open a crack as I assumed he was keeping the front walk under observation by standing back in the room. He opened the door before I could press the doorbell button.

Inside, I began. "I located a Major Bruce Holt." In a few sentences I told what we knew about him. "Two guys were out to see him this morning shortly after I called my PI and told him to try to locate him. When I got to his house after work this afternoon, he was gone. But his wife talked to me and described the men. One was the man Nine Lives took down in the park and the other was the man we learned about in Wisconsin. That means, of course, that this thing goes to the top levels, even to the president. And, it goes without saying that the PIs are no longer useful."

He let out a low whistle. "You called the same PI to locate me, right?"

"Yeah. That means they know about you, too."

"So, if Holt's gone, did the wife know what he told them?"

"They had Secret Service credentials and talked to him while they were seated at the kitchen table and she was making coffee. They mentioned they wanted to ask some questions about his military service. At first they were a little pushy until Holt told them he and his son would be leaving on a camping trip yet that morning. When they learned where they were going, they backed off and were affable, talking about hunting trips and stuff. As they left, they said they'd be in touch when he returned."

"I get the picture. With the wife there, they couldn't get rough, but out in the woods it'll be different."

"My thoughts exactly."

"Too bad we don't know where they're going."

"But, we do. And that's where we're going, too. The only problem is you just about can't get there from here. Ever hear about the BWCA?"

"Why, yeah. I made a trip up there when I was a Boy Scout."

"Get ready for a Merit Badge. She let me look through the stuff he used in planning the trip, and I learned their entry point and even the exact camp site that's their goal. If we really move, we might be able to get there while Holt and his son are still alive. Are you supposed to work tonight?"

"As I mentioned Saturday, I'm off tonight, but work the rest of the week."

"You'll have to make arrangements for tomorrow, now. We should be back by Thursday. Make your call while I work on our time line."

Holt would have arrived at the entry point about six. It being Tuesday, there should have been campsites available on the first lake where they entered, which was called Lake One. At the worst, they'd have to portage into Lake Two. By afternoon tomorrow they would be at their targeted campsite. If we put into the lake at first light, we could be in Lake Insula later tomorrow, though we'd have to work hard. But, we needed our gear yet tonight.

When, Clements was off the phone I said, "We have to move. We'll take your vehicle because it'll be easier to haul a canoe on it. I'll put my car in your garage. But, we have to find a canoe and our gear yet tonight before the stores close. There's a big Gander Mountain store out by Forest Lake. We could be there before eight. If they close at nine, we'd make it."

As he drove I made a list. We both had credit cards and would each buy part of the list, while leaving the impression we were not together. If there had been time for me to go home, I had all the equipment we'd need except for the canoe, but there wasn't time.

They were announcing that the store would close in five minutes as we were checking out. The big thing we had was the canoe. It was a two man size, very light, and very expensive. In the back of my mind was the hope I'd be able to get Harry to help defray the costs, since he would have been my partner of choice if he had been in town.

Luckily, Fred—I had reluctantly taken to calling him by his first name, as he had me—was the proud owner of two hand guns. One was a forty-five and the other a nine millimeter. The thing nagging at my mind was I had no idea how Clements—Fred—would behave in a desperate situation. With Harry I'd know. There was no point in discussing it with him because it was unlikely Fred had ever been in one. You can talk and train forever about that, but still you know nothing until it happens.

It was shortly after nine as we entered Interstate 35 headed north. I had decided to stop in Hinckley, which was about an hour ahead, to gas up and buy food. There was a casino a few miles east of that town so it was likely gas stations would still be open when we arrived. There were a few fast food places that might still be open, too. In our mad dash through Gander Mountain we had grabbed a few packages of beef jerky and several other items of dried food. I hoped the gas station would have a store with it so we could get granola or power bars as well as soft drinks.

Clements had provided me with a medium weight winter coat that was a few sizes too large, but would do. We bought backpacks, ponchos, a couple of compasses, a knife for me, mosquito repellent, and a variety of miscellaneous items. A tent was not necessary since it was unlikely we'd want to use one even if we had it. And, we'd likely not be stopping at designated camp sites, anyway.

Traveling light, we'd be able to single portage. There were a total of ten portages between the point we'd enter and Lake Insula. Nearly all the campers were forced to double portage. This meant they traveled across a portage with what they could conveniently carry. Then, it was necessary to retrace the portage to get the remaining equipment. In single portaging it was necessary to traverse the portage only once rather than three times. My boys and I always double portaged. It was simply a matter of common sense. I, along with most people, went into the wilderness to get away from things, to have a change of scenery, not to do saintly penance. Therefore, one brought along a good tent, sleeping bags, air mattresses, and cooking utensils, to say nothing of fishing gear, cameras, and a fair gob of other things, most of which were not needed. We had only light sleeping bags that we could slip into as we leaned up against a tree. With no cooking and no, that is emphatically no amenities, we would be roughing it in the most abstemious of hermit traditions. But, we'd make much better time than Holt and his son.

Since our adversaries had never heard of the canoe country, it was hard to tell how they would be accouted. By the map, I saw that there was an outfitter on Lake One less than a half mile from the official public Lake One entry point. This was all considered the same entry point according to one of the documents I had found in Holt's office. We made the assumption that they would have a normal outfit from the outfitter, which would mean double portaging for them, too. They had no entry permit, but the Secret Service IDs would handle that if questioned.

One other expensive item I had purchased beyond the canoe was a high end Global Positioning System, that is, GPS navigator of the type that had a moving display showing the user's position and the terrain around him. I made sure it had the BWCA maps loaded in it. Now, as Cements drove I worked with the direction booklet to learn how the thing worked. I had figured in my planning that with normal rest stops, we would arrive at the entry point at about three a.m. Since we had no entry permit, I intended to hit the water as soon as possible and by first light be lost in the maze of lakes. It was unlikely that there'd be a DNR enforcer waiting where we'd have to leave the car, but it was all too possible that someone from the outfitter would be around to check permits. The old business of tipping off officials about the wrong doing of others in exchange for a nod at your own, could easily be in play.

In Virginia we stopped for gas and in a lighted area away from the pumps, we put together our packs. It was imperative that we be quick and quiet in getting underway once we arrived at the entry point. Clements did not argue since not only did we not have an entry permit, he was well aware of the fact that there were people out there that would kill either or both of us with no compunction, especially him. He was the one who was in the way because he had none of the information they sought.

— 11 —

Wednesday

It was two-forty when we arrived at the entry point neither of us having had more than three hours of sleep. It didn't matter, the job had to be done. It would be obvious to anyone coming at dawn which car arrived that morning by the lack of dew on it. But, it was a calm clear morning and there may yet be time for dew to from. As prearranged, I unlashed the canoe and carried it to the water while Clements hustled the packs and paddles to the same place. I loaded the canoe while Fred parked the car. To the east of the road into the landing was a loop a couple of hundred yards long for parking. When he returned we used water proof flashlights we had purchased to check the area for dropped items. Minutes after arriving, we shoved off.

I paddled stern, since my experience in a canoe was more recent than Fred's. Away from shore I switched on the GPS navigator which made some beeps and tones. I had been unable to find how to mute them in the time available to work with it. I placed it on a small pack in front of me beneath the gunwales so light from its display would not be seen beyond the canoe.

Our first leg was a half mile jaunt headed northeast. Where we put in was not technically Lake One, but the extreme easterly end of a chain of lakes called the Kawishiwi River. There were several cabins to our left since that shore was not in the BWCA but bordered on it. At the end of this half mile we'd be leaving a narrow channel a hundred yards from the outfitters. From there our course took us south into a long arm of Lake One. Our canoe was dark green since it was of Kevlar construction which was fine with me. That material was what made it the lightest available as well as the most expensive. We both wore the darkest clothes we had. We saw security lights from the outfitter shortly before exiting the channel. Clements was to watch as carefully as possible for obstructions as I had no idea how accurate the electronic gadget would be. It was advertised to be good to within three feet of one's exact position, but then, there are known to be rare cases where sellers of merchandise exaggerate the attributes of their products slightly.

The docks and overturned canoes, mostly aluminum, lined up on shore were easily visible as we rounded the point of land at our nearest approach. My fears of seeing Flavian Cutter or the other man standing on the end of the dock with a powerful flashlight were unfounded. It had even crossed my mind that they would have turned out some law enforcement officers to be on guard under the subterfuge that we were escaped convicts or something equally despicable. With no sense of disappointment, I saw a serene shore—not even a dog barked. Fred had to hiss at me as a shore line loomed ahead. With my concern with being apprehended, I had lost my concentration on navigation and nearly ran us up on the rocks. There was no telling how well a carbon fiber hull would handle a solid smashing against jagged rocks as there were few sandy beaches in this part of the world.

With relief, we lost ourselves in the night heading in a more or less southwesterly direction away from the last permanent habitation. We had a total of about three miles to cover as the canoe flew, that is paddled, until we made two short portages from Lake One to Lake Two. Our route would take us from Lake One, to Lake Two, Lake Three, and then Lake Four. The person naming the lakes appeared to have been imagination challenged. Lakes Two, Three, and Four were all connected with no portages. After Lake Four, there were several more portages before we'd arrive at Lake Insula. Our total paddling distance to where we thought Holt would camp was about ten miles.

The early morning was peaceful. We made a point of not speaking since voices could be heard for miles across the calm water. We slid across the surface of an ethereal medium with only the rhythmic swishing of our paddles breaking the silence. Fred had the best of it because his eyes could become completely dark adapted while mine were inhibited from that by constantly watching the GPS navigator even though I had the light emission set low. The stars were bright and the air fresh. I would have liked to try some fishing at first light, but there was no time for that, and we had no equipment in any case. That in itself would make us look suspicious when we met other parties on portages, to say nothing of our sparse gear. If anyone commented on it I had it in mind to reply that we took our pain seriously, or some equally dumb retort.

I felt it was important to cross the two short portages into Lake Two as soon as possible. Less than a quarter mile into Lake Two was a small island with no campsites on it. I planned to stop there to rest and perhaps sleep a couple of hours. We'd pull our canoe up into the trees so no one would know we were there. It was located such that anyone headed toward or from the portages to Lake One would pass close by.

In the dark the portaging was difficult. These were not like city park trails. I carried the canoe and a light pack while Fred carried one hanging in front of him and one on his back. He went in front with a flashlight turning to point the light at places where I might stumble, which I did once to muffled curses.

The sky to the northeast was hinting of dawn as we pulled the canoe up to the rocks on the east side of the small island in Lake Two. A low mist hung over the lake which was good since there was a campsite in sight of this location, whether or not occupied we did not know. With the canoe out of the water and into the shrubbery we fell exhausted on the soft pine needles under the trees.

During our travels to this point, I had tried to figure out how things would be once we got this far but had come to no conclusions. Deciding how to handle each stage of the trip as it came upon us had taken all of my attention. I scratched lists constantly trying not to forget things or make obvious mistakes. Clements had provided helpful suggestions, but he was not a mission planner. I supposed it made sense because his function in the Bureau had been to chase down leads in cases, not to plan operations. We had done well, it seemed, by arriving deep into the BWCA without having met a single person or forgotten any critical item, or none that we were aware of.

After giving ourselves fifteen minutes to revive, we moved to an observation point where the second portage from Lake One was visible and sat on the soft compost leaning our backs against trees. Fred had the pack with most of the food in it. He took out and ripped open a pack of beef jerky, took a piece for himself and offered the package to me. As I munched, waves of fatigue came over me. There was go escaping the fact that we'd have to sleep, which meant, I'd learn the true mettle of one Mr. Fred Clements. If he still harbored resentment towards me from the summer before, or our recent incident in the park, he could take all the gear and abandon me on the island. True, it had been his decision to go to the meeting in the park, but then, he had not been told he would come within a inch of having a bullet in his head, either.

It was important I focus on the job at hand so thinking out loud, I said in whispers, "You know, if Holt and his son did leave at eleven o'clock, and they didn't push it, they would have arrived at the entry point between five and six o'clock. I didn't ask his wife if he owned all his gear, but I'd guess not. I found it the most cost effective to buy packs, sleeping bags and stuff like that, but to rent the canoe. Canoes are bulky to store and transport. It would be my guess he'd rent it at one of the outfitters. That would have taken another half hour at least. That means they would certainly not have progressed further than we are now. They might even still be on Lake One. When arriving that late, a person is wise to take the first open campsite he runs across."

Fred had taken one of the two heavy plastic quart sized water bags, sort of a collapsible canteen, and slipped off to get water from the lake. When he returned we filled plastic cups and drank.

"Where does that leave Cutter and the other man? They couldn't have rented their gear at the same outfitters as Holt did unless they waited until they were on their way. If Holt had seen either of them, he would have suspected something."

I replied, "Holt's wife was pretty sure he had mentioned Lake Insula to them. If so, they would be in no hurry. My guess is they waited for Holt to be on his way and spent the night at the outfitters. Most of those places have cabins or a bunkhouse. They would have selected the gear last evening, and planned to shove off at first light expecting to locate Holt along the way or back on Insula." I gave Clements a wary look and said, "I'm going to have to ask you to take first watch because I'm beat. Stay awake if you can and shake me after two hours." I was asleep in two minutes.

I jerked awake to the sound of voices nearby. It took five seconds to remember where I was. The thud of a paddle on an aluminum canoe made the connection. There was a party coming past the tip of our island not a fifty yards away. I stood slowly and spotted them through the branches. The occupant of the bow was a woman with a halter top her skin noticeably red already. I shook my head. Greenhorns. Clements was rolled nearly onto his stomach snoring softly. At least we were still together. I suspected that if he had wanted to abandon me, he was forced to wait for another time since he had been as tired as I was. It was after nine and I was sure he had not stood his post for long. That meant we did not know if either of the parties of our interest had passed by.

I studied the map again. There were two short portages getting from Lake Four to Hudson Lake. Then, there was a long, 105 rod, portage from Hudson into Insula. A rod is five and a half yards. That portage by-passed a river with rapids. That was it. It was a long portage and there were rapids to make covering noise. That's where they'd set up an ambush, snatch them off the trail, and force Holt to talk. If they left them alive it would be no blessing, because it would mean they would be bound and gagged to die slow deaths. We had to get there first.

Clements was a deep sleeper. I had to shake him several times before he was a wake. "Time to hit the deck," I said. "We have seven or eight miles to paddle today, and it's already after nine."

We ate and drank again and when we could see no other canoes on the east side of the island, set off. Now that it was light we could talk. My arms were tired from paddling stern the day before, so I had Clements take a turn. It was slow going at first as I instructed him.

Paddling a canoe was not a simple matter of the one in the bow and the one in the stern sticking his paddle in the water and pulling. That was true for the bow, but not the stern. First of all both paddlers must never paddle on the same side. If they both dig their paddles in at the same time for a hard stroke it could easily overturn, i.e. swamp, the canoe. That means they must always paddle on opposite sides. The man in the stern determines this.

If the man in the back is paddling on the right, say, the man in the front will paddle on the left. This will cause the canoe to turn to the left. It's simply the physics of the thing. To counteract that rotation, the stern paddler divides his stroke into two distinct parts. The first is with the blade of the paddle perpendicular to the long axis of the canoe, and this is called his power stroke. Part way through the stroke he twists the paddle so it is parallel to the long axis of the canoe and pushes out. That last motion counteracts the rotation of the canoe to the left. Depending on how much of a correction is needed he may not twist his paddle at all, or he may use the whole stroke to contract the rotation. Since the two actions cause the paddle's motion to be in roughly the shape of the letter "J" it's called the j-stroke. In any case, the muscles used to push the paddle out are seldom used by most people so they become tired before long. As a result the stern paddler will say "switch" so the bow paddler will change to paddling on the other side. That's why the stern paddler decides which side both will paddle on.

Fred had a faint recollection of having been taught the j-stroke in the Boy Scouts, so his learning curve was steep. In twenty minutes we were making good progress. It was easy to pick out novices because the stern paddler was constantly switching sides in order to keep the canoe headed the way he wanted. We were looking for someone like that because I didn't think Cutter and his side kick would know how to paddle a canoe.

Things were going well so far. I was pleased to see Fred fully into the operation. We had even discussed mission planning and he admitted he was no expert there, though I encouraged him to make suggestions which he did.

Two people paddling a canoe can make about three miles and hour, and it doesn't matter too much if they are headed into a light wind or not. A heavy wind obviously makes a difference. As a result we were at the long portage between Huron Lake and Insula at twelve-thirty. We had discussed the situation as we paddled, and decided I'd take my pack and the canoe across the portage and set it off in the bushes where it could not be seen. Fred would wait at the start of the portage out of sight with his gear and watch for either party approaching the portage. If they were clearly not Cutter and the other man, and they looked about right, he'd ask if they were the Holts. Meanwhile I would start back across the portage as if going back for a second load and look for signs that someone and their gear had been stashed off the trail. We were assuming the Holts would be double portaging, so if the Cutter clan had ambushed them, they would have to dispose of gear at both ends of the portage and probably along the way, too.

— 12 —

The portage between Hudson Lake and Lake Insula was one of those grueling tests of endurance meant for super humans, or so it seemed to me. I exercised regularly and considered myself to be in reasonably good condition, but the lack of sleep, the stress, and pushing myself so hard was taking its toll. As I struggled along under my burden I began to think about it. It wasn't even twenty-four hours since we had started. It settled hard on me just how much the passing years had weakened the old body. In Nam, I wouldn't have been breathing hard yet.

At last I saw it, the halfway rest point. Now and then a scout troop or other do-gooder group came along and made small improvements to the situation. Here was a horizontal pole lashed to two trees eight feet above the ground. It was the place where one could rest the bow of the canoe and lower the stern to the ground to relieve the load and rest. The muscles where the yoke rested on my shoulders were sore and tired. Dropping my light pack, I walked around the small area, no more that a widening of the trail, twisting my shoulders to ease the cramps caused by the canoe. This deep in the wilderness, we were leaving at least seventy-five percent of the canoers behind, but still there was plenty of traffic. This rest area was well worn and one had to expect that every other person who made the stop here took to the bushes to relieve himself. Therefore, if the small plants on the floor of the forest were bent and stomped here and there it would be expected.

Of course! What better place to do it. Accosting a person at either end of the portage would invite the observation of others approaching it. In a depraved situation like we were considering, that would be a bad thing. And, tripping someone as he carried a canoe, especially an aluminum one, would make a noise like a church bell. Yet, here, hidden from all sides, with the background noise of the rapids nearby, and the canoe on the rest, it was prefect. The noise of the stream was not as loud as I had expected, though that was likely because my more recent memories were of rivulets cascading down the slopes of the Rocky Mountains.

As far as I could see in either direction on the trail, there was no one coming. Yet, I took the precaution of working my canoe out of sight in the bushes. That done, I took the small pack and dropped it by the canoe after extracting the forty-five Fred had bequeathed to me. He knew it had more knock down power than the nine-millimeter, but he was more comfortable with the smaller bore weapon. I went fifty yards back on the trail and started into the rugged terrain perpendicular to the trail. I planned to make a one-eighty arc around the rest stop.

This part of the world was as broken a country as it was possible to find anywhere. There were no thousand foot drop-offs or anything like that, but from the standpoint of traveling overland it was excruciating. The low branches of the pine trees, the dead falls, and the under growth were one thing. The up and down terrain was another with rocky up thrusts and swamps and sloughs of all sizes everywhere. Seldom did the land rise more than fifty feet above the ubiquitous lakes. Even at that, a person could become disoriented and lost in two minutes.

I knew what I was looking for, a recently broken branch or bent weed. Nobody was so paranoid about their toilet habits as to go this deep into the bush to do his business. It took fifteen minutes for me to make half of the circuit I had planned and there it was, a flattened plant, what in the spring we used to call a jack-in-the-pulpit. Looking to left and right I saw no more signs. Proceeding ahead ten yards, there likewise was nothing. I backtracked and located the crushed plant. Some yards before first encountering the plant, I had traversed a relatively open place beneath one of the larger pine trees. The mat of pine needles was disturbed. Following the indistinct path past the tree, there were broken twigs in the thicket.

Stock still, I listened. Not a sound other than a red squirrel objecting to my presence in its territory. Proceeding on, there were more signs. Here was a ten foot high rock formation with wiry pine trees sprouting from fissures in the nearly vertical wall. Over or around? To the right, a scuff mark. I followed around the rock. On the far side under another large pine tree were two lumps of clothing inhabited by men. They were on the opposite sides of the spread of the tree's boughs. Crouching, I scanned the area, my gun in both hands with the safety off. One of the lumps moved and the whites of eyes seemed to bore into me. Inching over to the closest one, I whispered, "Holt?"

There was a nod. Slipping my hunting knife out of its scabbard, I slit the gag. The blade was sharp like it should have been on a new knife. Replacing the knife, still looking all around, I felt for the strip of cloth and pulled it free.

"Speak only in whispers, okay?"

The head nodded. "Are they gone?"

"Yes, I think so."

"Why do you think that?"

"Because they made a call and ordered a float plane to come and get them just before they left. They discussed it. One of them had to climb that rock behind you to get a signal."

I looked at the man for the first time. He had to be the son. "Bud Holt?"

"Yes."

"Hang on a minute."

I went to the other man who could not be seen from Bud's position due to the trunk of the tree. I cut the man free who, not surprisingly, turned out to be Bruce Holt.

"Thanks, and who are you?" were his first utterances. "We thought we might die here, and we're free in less than an hour."

"How much less than an hour?"

He thought a minute, "It might have been forty-five minutes, more or less. Is that important?"

"Yes. The men who did this to you, were they the Secret Service men who came to your house yesterday morning?"

"Yeah, they were. What's going on? And, again, who are you? not that I'm complaining."

"In time. Are you injured? Can you paddle you canoe back out of here. As you might guess, there have been some changes to your vacation plans."

"They beat on me quite a bit. I'm bruised and hurt a lot, but, yeah, I can manage."

By that time we were beside Bud and I was cutting him free. "This is important, did they give any indication which way they were going, on to Insula, or back to Hudson?"

"Back to Hudson," Bud said.

"It makes sense. Insula is too big. Hudson is long enough to land a plane and small enough so they'd be easy to find." Insula was a huge lake, though there were no large expanses of open water. It was filled with dozens of islands, large and small. It had many long narrow bays, hooks of land, isthmuses, and peninsulas, to say nothing of over forty campsites so there would likely be several canoes visible from the air.

"Here's what I want you to do. Gather up as many of your belongings as you can find in a reasonable amount of time and collect them at the end of the portage on Hudson Lake. Stay out of sight until you hear the plane come and then leave. After that start making you way back across Hudson. We want to find the men before the plane arrives, though if its coming from Ely or anyplace around the BWCA it'll be here any time."

"Once again, what's going on?"

"You obviously told them something or you'd be dead. That means they have to be stopped at all costs. We'll meet on Hudson whether or not I manage to stop them. Then, we'll talk. Find a campsite along the north side of the lake, there must be at least one."

I was up and about to leave when I turned. "Do you have fishing poles?"

"Sure. That's why we came out here."

"Bruce, you make it back to the trail as best as you can, Bud, come with me now and we'll try to fine a pole, okay?"

"Sure."

As I had started my circuit of the rest place along the portage, I had almost stepped on some of their gear, but the brush was so thick in places that you couldn't see two feet in any direction and that included down. Bud kept asking what was going on, but I had to say there wasn't time. From their relative locations when I found them, it was reasonable to assume Bud had not heard what Bruce was asked or what he had told Cutter so he was totally in the dark.

As I lowered the canoe at the edge of the water at the end of the portage, Fred appeared. "What, we're going back?"

"Yeah. I found Holt back in the woods. Get the stuff in the canoe fast, we'll talk as we paddle."

He was good in that way. He could tell by the tone of my voice that I was decided on a course of action and there was to be no discussion. As we loaded up he looked askance at the fishing pole and small tackle box.

"Are you a fisherman?" I asked.

"Haven't fished in years."

"Okay, you paddle stern."

It wasn't a minute before we were on our way.

He wasn't, of course, about to be left out entirely. "I don't want to sound negative, but do you think this is the best time to go fishing?"

I had the small pack on the bottom of the canoe in front of me, with the zipper open. Just inside, was the forty-five in easy reach. On top of it was the map.

"Have your gun so it's east to get, but not in sight," I said. "And, it's not fish you'll be shooting."

I turned so he could hear better. "Cutter and pal accosted the Holts on the portage, beat some information out of Bruce, left them bound and gagged back in the bushes, and called in a float plane to pick them up on this lake. That was about an hour ago. If the plane were coming from Ely or someplace in the area, it would've been here by now. So, I assume it's coming from the seaplane base in Lino Lakes or some other place around the metro. That means we have about a half hour to take them down and get all of us out of sight. Got it?"

"Okay, but why the fishing?"

"There's a small island less than a half mile ahead. It has a campsite on the far side which is where I'm guessing they're waiting. As we approached the island I will start fishing as you paddle around it. We need to be fishing so we look normal prowling around the island. You have to get me close enough so I can cover them with my gun before they can take defensive action. If they're not both in sight, it'll be messy. Pull your hat down as much as possible so they don't recognize us any sooner than necessary. Maneuver the canoe so I can get out as easily as possible."

— 13 —

Fred was game. I suspected it was as much because of the chance to even the score for Cutter having tried to put a bullet through his head as anything else.

The fishing rod was expensive, with a modern spool type reel that was not supposed to get backlashes. There was a large spoon lure in the tackle box which I clipped to the line and got the feel of the reel. It was a good one, no doubt about that. I had set the map aside and had the forty-five laying on top of the pack. It was in my mind that when the time was right, I'd throw the fishing rod over the side so it was out of the way.

Rounding the island, I immediately saw two things. The first was expected, a canoe pulled up at the water's edge. The second could spell trouble. The top of a tent was visible above the bushes which meant there was a party camping there. Nobody was near the water which made sense, now that I thought about it, because they'd wait back in the trees for the plane to land and then paddle out to it leaving the canoe to drift. After all, they rented it with a false credit card so why would they care. But, what about the campers?

I turned my head and said, "Campers on the island, and there's no movement."

In a whisper between strokes, he replied, "I'll pretend to be about to pass by and at the right moment turn and head right for the shore."

I nodded.

Fred did as he had said as I reeled in the line. Holding the rod in my left hand and the gun in the right, low and out of sight, I watched as the shore approached. As luck would have it, there were a few feet of sandy beach between rocks with an aluminum canoe hogging most of it. Fred drove the canoe precisely onto the sand leaving two inches from the other canoe. Throwing the rod I leapt out raising the gun. As I did a voice from the left said, "Drop it!"

I threw myself on the ground, rocks, of course.

With a thump, Fred was out of the canoe, followed by a shot, a ping of bullet on metal and a grunt.

"On your face!" It was Fred with that commanding voice of his. The man went down. I rolled twice and came up behind two foot high rocks, looked about and dashed for trees behind the tent. A figure came up as I dove for a tree between it and me. Two shots. I rolled and fired. My bullet hit something but I was moving and out of sight in a second. The pine needles were soft. Holding my gun in one hand, I thrust the right half of my face around the tree where I had come to rest. The other man was not down, but rubbing his eyes. Raising with all my strength I rushed toward him. My bullet had barked the tree sending splinters into his eyes.

"My eyes, my eyes," he kept repeating. I didn't wait to let him try a trick, as I kicked one foot out from under him. He was down with me on his back. From my left pocket, I pulled a four foot piece of nylon rope and bound his hands. Then another around his ankles. The training from all those years ago was as fresh now as then. He was bound and would not be getting free. Phantom guys were good at that.

Shoving his gun behind my belt, I was up. Fred, keeping his distance, held the other man, Cutter, in submission. His right hand was bleeding as half of the third finger on his gun hand was missing.

"That was a pretty gutsy shot, shooting the gun out of his hand," I said.

He shrugged. "I do a lot of shooting. The only hobby I have left. Guess, it helps to stay in practice."

"Remind me to remain friends with you," I replied.

"Wonder where the campers are."

One canoe was well up from the water to protect it from being thrown about by wind in the night, and Cutter's canoe was beside ours.

"Either dead, or bound. In either case we don't have time now, care about them later." After a quick search of Carter's body for concealed weapons, I bound his ankles so they were loose enough to shuffle, went to the tent and found an article of clothing, a woman's blouse, and threw it to him.

"Wrap your finger in this, but be sure your hand is free because you're going to paddle or die, got it?"

He nodded with a sour expression.

Hustling back to the other man, I searched him and rebound his legs shackle-wise, too. "Get, up. It doesn't matter if you can't see, and rubbing those splinters further into your eyes will only make it worse."

Fred got into the aluminum canoe in the stern, I loaded Cutter in the bow, handed him a paddle, and shoved them off. The other man wasn't putting up a fight as his only concern was his eyes. I loaded him in the bow with a paddle. Getting wet feet, I turned my canoe around after which I shoved off and joined Fred and his bosom buddy. As I pulled up along side, I said in a subdued voice, "Not a word from here on, not a sound," and pointed to a narrow bay to the south of the island. The only other thing I said was, "Now paddle you worthless pieces of dirt."

Five hundred yards from the island we were behind a small point of land that put the campsite out of our line of sight. It was good enough. I motioned to pull in. There was waist high brush nearly to the water and small rocks on the shore. "Remember, no sound." I hissed.

Our two captives were behaving better than I had expected, almost too well. Yet, losing a finger hurt a lot. If there had been any initial shock to deaden the pain, that had passed by now. And the other guy continued to blink copious tears from his eyes.

With everybody on shore, and my small bag beside me, I pulled more nylon chord from the spool and bound both to trees.

"Now to get the canoes out of sight, quietly," I said.

Fred nodded. He lifted the bow and pulled the aluminum canoe in as far as he could without scraping the rocks. I waded into the water since my feet were wet anyway, and lifted the stern out. We thrashed into the thicket until it was out of sight. We repeated the action with the second one and sat down to rest.

"Why all the concern with sound?" Fred asked.

"We'll have to go back and find the campers. If they heard us making plans to hide in this bay, or even guessed from the sound of things where we went, they might come and investigate. If you haven't figured it out, we will be leaving those guys here, bound and gagged. Oh, that reminds me."

I got up and went to the two men and gagged each in turn. Fred wasn't the operations type of guy and I couldn't fault him for that. If Harry had been with me he would've had them gagged and thoroughly going through the two men's gear looking for nasty tricks they might have packed for us, or looking for a more permanent place to leave the two men.

"Fred, take those guy's packs out of their canoe and go through everything looking for anything that might be a tracking device. Then thoroughly search them, every crevice, and remove their boots and everything in all pockets. I've some scouting to do.

Twenty yards further into the woods I found what I wanted. It was a cut in the rocky ground, four feet deep and six feet wide. The rocks in the area were covered by moss and pine needles except for the bottom of the channel which was spongy earth. Returning, I motioned for Fred to help me with the aluminum canoe. We slugged our way back to the shallow gully. We over turned the canoe in the depression and propped one end up on a tree that had fallen across the ditch so it formed a lean-to. I threw fifty pounds of pine needles on it so there would be no reflection for someone in a airplane to see.

Returning to the men, I helped search our two scumbag pals. We collected all of the suspect gear and took it back and put in under the canoe which would form a type of Faraday shield to trap any electronic signals. I had Fred help me move the two men inland to the canoe.

"Here's the plan, boys and girls," I began. "You will first give me the name of the man or person you are taking orders from. You first Charlie." I had learned the second man's name was Charles Divner from the wallet I had taken from him.

"Not a chance," he retorted.

"Yes, more than a chance," I snapped back. "We intend to leave you here bound and gagged under the canoe. When we get out of here, if we are in a very good mood, we'll call your boss and tell him or it where you are. If he decides it's worth the trouble to come and get you, you can live. Otherwise, you'll die of thirst. You tried to kill Fred, and you tried to kill me so we are not happy with you. *Comprende*?"

"When was that?"

"You, Flavian," I said looking at Cutter, "tried to put a bullet in the head of a man in the park. That man was Fred. Last summer I was forced to drive a truck bomb to Ford Parkway where the plan was to make a red mist out of me when it exploded. The explosion was delayed so I got away. You put us both on borrowed time, as it were, so don't expect mercy from us."

"And," Fred interjected, "this is the orneriest man you've ever met. Give him what he wants."

They were silent. "Nothing to say? Want to die of thirst?"

Still nothing. All they did was stare a me.

"Now what?" Fred asked. "Do we start cutting parts off them?"

I shook my head. "No, we missed something. They don't look at all worried. They still have some sort of tracking beacon on them. Ah . . . the belts."

Their belts were as wide as possible and still fit through standard belt loops on slacks and blue jeans. After removing them I examined one carefully. It was apparent both belts were constructed of split leather in two layers. With the tip of my knife I cut the stitching and slowly parted the two halves. The miniaturized electronics were neatly laid out on a flex circuit between the laminations. Near the buckle was a place to press that would close a contact and activate the device.

"Nice work," I said. "Without these things for them to locate you, your only hope of getting out here is us. Even if you phoned them before you left the outfitters and told them which lake to come to, there's a lot of wilderness, unless you haven't noticed. We could even move you to a different lake. They'd never find you. Now, if you want to live give me the names and numbers to call."

Divner looked at Cutter. "We have to give them what they want. What other chance do we have?"

"No," Cutter responded. "We simply can't."

"Screw it. The man you want to call is Sal Khruz."

"Who's he?"

"A helper around Washington. Does a lot of things."

"Who does he work for?"

"Oh, no. That's not what you asked."

"Well, I'm asking now."

"No. I can't say."

"How are your eyes doing?"

"Better, thanks." The thanks was sort of a instinctive response tinged with a note of surprise that I would suddenly be solicitous of his well being.

"How about I stab them both out?" I pulled my knife from its sheath.

"He'll do it!" Fred snapped with as much feeling as if I had stabbed his eyes out ten minutes before.

Horror transfixed the man's face. "He reports, indirectly to the president."

"You fool!" Cutter spat out.

"Another name," I said. "I'll only call once and if the first one doesn't answer there had better be a backup."

"You can't!" Cutter was frantic.

"Seth Goldman. The President's National Security Advisor."

"That's better. We're getting someplace. Now, the . . . ."

Suddenly I lifted my head. The faint sound of an airplane. It came from the south and passed nearly overhead. The pilot circled the lake low. He had to be crazy or had a gun to his head, the latter was the most likely. All of these lakes had places where there were rocks whose tops were at water level. If the submerged rocks were in heavily trafficked areas, they'd have silver markings on them where aluminum canoes had slid over them. Since this lake was never used for pontoon landing, there would be no notations on air charts of where the hazards lay.

"Right on time," I said. "Now the phone numbers. And, I won't tolerate gate keepers, recorded messages or any of that crap. The man himself had better answer or you guys are so dead."

He gave me two numbers for both men. I wrote the names and numbers in the little notebook I had been using for my lists as we were on our way up to the north country. I agreed I'd try all of them before giving up.

"You told them to pick you up at that little island with the campsite, right?"

Divner nodded.

After checking their bonds, I motioned to Fred to follow me. Out of earshot of the others, I said, "There's a game trail headed toward the tip of this peninsula. Lets see what's going on."

It was only two to three hundred yards to the end of the point of land where we found an observation point behind some rocks. Not surprisingly—rocks were in plentiful supply. The plane had landed from east to west and was now taxing toward the island, not two hundred yards from us. If memory served, it was a Beaver or Otter, both planes manufactured by a company in Canada. The Beaver was the smaller of the two, and I decided that's what it was. It had a five or six passenger capacity, and there was at least one of them frequently present at the Rice Lake Seaplane base in Lino Lakes, a suburb north of St. Paul.

I was imagining their perplexity in not seeing anyone ready to meet them. There was no canoe lashed to the pontoons. Cutter and Divner were to paddle out to the plane. But, there was no sign of them.

The plane made a circuit of the island and stopped on our side. The pilot killed the engine. A man emerged, and stood on a pontoon. He reached in and pulled out a device. As he extended claws on one end, I could see is was a collapsible anchor. The wind was light and blowing our way. He swung the anchor underhand and after it sank to the bottom he jerked the rope until the claws grabbed the bottom rocks, after which he lashed it to a pontoon strut.

The pilot had slid the cockpit window open and said, "We can't stay here. I told you that campers will call in and report the illegal landing of a plane. The DNR will have someone over-flying us in no time. Then we're stuck."

"We can't leave without our men, so shut up. There's a canoe on that campsite. I'm taking the dingy in for a look. No argument!"

"They ought to lighten up," I whispered to Fred.

He looked at me still not knowing what to make of this.

"That was good how you kept reinforcing what I said to Divner to make him talk."

"I meant it. You *are* the orneriest man I've ever met."

The man on the pontoon had pulled the lanyard and the rubber boat inflated. He clumsily paddled to the shore. In his defense, it's hard to propel a small rudderless craft with only one paddle. He had a pistol out as he proceeded to the tent. The plane was off to the right of our line of sight to the island and a second man had emerged from the plane to stand on the pontoon with an automatic assault rifle. If I was not mistaken he was a light black man, maybe half white.

"Notice the increased fire power," I said.

On the island the man found the tent empty and in a few minutes, emerged from the trees with two women in front of him. He endured the full wrath of their ire. We heard their screeched obscenities clear as a bell. In turn, the participation of his mother in the oldest profession was asserted, he was likened to certain animals, and then to an unsavory part of the human anatomy. And, it didn't stop as cries of battle zone and death camp were thrown in. The man holstered his gun, stalked to the dingy, shoved off, and paddled for the plane.

The second man slung his rifle over his shoulder and helped the man up on the pontoon. We could hear every word.

"After our guys tied up the women they were in turn captured. It was that damned Wessen, I know it!" He looked up and said in defiance to the trees on shore. "I know you're there Wessen and we'll get you!"

I pulled the hammer back on the forty five and shot low so they would see the splash of the bullet real close. I fired again. The second bullet ricocheted off the water and hit the man who had yelled at us in the calf of his leg.

"You're dead, Wessen!"

"Start the engine," the second man snapped as he heaved his buddy into the plane. He produced a long knife, stabbed the dingy and cut the anchor rope. The engine cracked and came to life with a small cloud of blue smoke. It was still warm so he gunned it immediately as the second man scampered into the cabin. The plane swung around the island and the pilot shoved the throttle full open. In a minute it was gone.

"You have a strange way of making friends," Fred said.

"Yeah. Do you suppose he'd like me better if I had only shot his finger off?"

Fred shook his head as he laughed.

— 14 —

There was feverish activity on the island. The two women had the tent down, and were stuffing things into bags. One of them pulled the canoe to the water and threw things in at random. It seemed that some to the edge was off the rough, tough outdoors woman thing. The second one shoved off, got her foot wet, cursed like a stevedore, and they dug in their paddles heading west. They knew how to paddle so the one in the stern was not continuously switching sides.

"At least, that's one problem out of the way," I said to Fred. He nodded as we started back to our prisoners.

When we arrived Divner said, "You certainly made a good impression on those boys—heard it way back here." Cutter wasn't talking, obviously in pain.

"Yeah, I'm good at that. Do you know who they are?"

"Might."

"It's not a good time to play the coy game. If they make good on the threat to kill me, you'll die here. You seem a little slow to grasp what's at play."

"We know 'em," Divner said. "We both recognized the voice of the one who yelled at you."

"So?"

"His name is Jimmy Hook, as in his middle name is Meat. Get it?"

"Childish and ever so clever. And, the other one?"

"Iceman Jones. They're an assassination team."

I thought a minute before responding. Then, "I find it hard to believe your Mister Hook is an assassin—too emotional. What I learned in my military training is to never go into combat angry or with revenge in mind. To be successful it takes a detached mindset. Emotion probably is an asset when charging a hill with a bunch of other guys, but in a one on one hunt it's deadly for the one who succumbs to it."

"Then, you're in luck because the other guy has no concept of emotion. He's a total psychopath. His emotions have been flat-lined since he got knocked in the head playing college football. They're a team with Hook the wheel man, and Jones the trigger man. And, they *will* get you."

"It's still not making sense," I said. "And, if it doesn't pretty soon, I'll start breaking bones because they will not kill me until they find what they're looking for. Even if the man you beat and left to die in the woods back on the portage told you exactly where it was, neither they nor you could eliminate me until you knew that the information was good."

I was tired and not thinking as clearly as I should have been. Another odd thing came to mind. "Why would they send an assassination team to pick you guys up out here? It seems like that isn't their line of work."

Cutter snickered even as he winced from pain. "I wouldn't be too sure about any of that. It sounded like you really pissed off Hook, and Jones will be just as intent on getting you because you caused him to fail in his mission. A time or two I've heard it mentioned that even though he's very good at what he does, he might have to be eliminated because he was too hard to control. He'll take any assignment, even if it's to go buy Chinese take-out. As long as the Chinese place is open, and the clerks don't try to dick around with him, it all works. But, if he feels slighted, watch out. It's not so much that he gets angry, it's like there's an animal in him that wants to feed on something. Being sent up here was like Chinese take-out. I think he'll kill you because you made that inner beast hungry."

Cutter continued, "There're some pain pills in my pack. Mind pulling them out and giving me a couple?"

"My, my," I said. "I could almost hear a 'please' and 'thank you' in the tone of your voice. What's this world coming to?"

I found what he wanted and looked at the bottle of prescription pills. "It says they may cause drowsiness so you get one since I'm not sure what we'll do with you." He had no choice but to take what he was given.

We had to locate Holt and find out what he knew so we tied the captives to trees again and set off. Across the lake, north of the island were a couple of camp sites. In fifteen minutes we found the two men.

After pulling our canoe up I made introductions, then got to business. "They wanted to know the location of a lost item, didn't they."

Bruce nodded. "The problem is, I didn't know what they were talking about. They said it had to do with a mission I was part of while in Vietnam. I did recall having made an unscheduled flight from Nam to the metro area and thought that might have had something to do with it. I was in the reserves during most of the war, but they were using us more and more. After two call-ups in six months, it was hurting my job, so I went Air Force full time."

"You made the flight in a C-130. You were a C-130 pilot, right?"

"Yeah. It was then, after I was full time and stationed at Cam Ranh Bay, that I was ordered to make the trip. I made a straight in landing at the Anoka County Airport from the north. Back then, it wasn't as busy as it is now with no control tower coverage during the night. We arrived a couple of hours after midnight. The conditions were good, and the C-130 can be stopped pretty fast with full brakes eliminating the engine noise of reverse thrust. I managed easily. I was familiar with the airport because back then one of my friends based his plane there and we flew together quite a bit."

"It was sort of like someone had been checking and found the perfect man and the perfect place."

"It's beginning to look that way. Anyway, these two seemed to want any information even if it was doubtful, as if they were under pressure. So I told them the cargo was hidden a couple of miles southeast of the airport. At the time it was a large open area used by an RC model airplane club. South of it was wild land belonging to the county or the state. Now, I think it's the Rice Creek Regional Park, or some such name. That's what I described to then. I mean, I said it was near the north boundary of what is now the regional park. The thing is, I never left the plane."

"Why did you pick that place?"

"Because it's close to the airport. There was a three-quarter ton truck in the cargo bay, the only cargo, and some men. As soon as I landed, I taxied to the east gate. It was not locked or even closed back then. As soon as I was stopped and lowered the ramp, they drove off. They were gone such a short time, like a half hour or less, that they did whatever they had come to do in the local area. Since they were assuming I knew where the cargo from the truck was, it made sense that they buried it. If they had transferred it to another vehicle, how would I know where to find it?"

"But, saying you or someone else transferred it to a truck would mean for sure you didn't know where it was and would be of no further use to them. Why didn't you say that?"

"Every time I seemed at a loss, one of them gave me another bruise. They weren't interested in learning I couldn't help them so I made something up. By the way, we heard shots and saw the plane. I suppose they're on their way to Minneapolis. What happens when they don't find what they're looking for?" He paused, then added, "How could they expect to find anything with the information I gave them?"

"They were not on the plane." I said. "The shots you heard were our shots. The plane had no choice but to leave or we would have disabled it, and them, until the authorities came. We have the two men who accosted you tied up in the woods across the lake."

Bruce settled himself gingerly on a rotten log someone had pulled up to the fire ring for that purpose. He looked at me with hard eyes. "I would like for you to tell me just who you are. I admit, I am most grateful to you for coming to our rescue. But, since then, I've been thinking. You were there so soon that it seems unlikely. Care to explain that to me?"

"You think we're working with the others, is that it?"

"It would explain things. What happens when the others find that I've given them bad information? It would mean they'd have to come back here and 'interview' me again. But, if I were freed by some friendly passer-by, I'd make my way back to civilization maybe even have to call in a plane to fly me out and all at my own expense. Then, if they wanted to question me further, I'd be handy. You have to agree that it makes sense. Leaving people to die in the wilderness is a despicable thing to do and someone just might have a conscience attack. So, get the information and then have a surprise rescue."

Here was a typical modern man. You put yourself out to help someone and they immediately assume you are the same as they are, namely a cold self-serving wolf. "All I can say is this, my suspicious 'maybe' friend. When you get home—if any of us manage to get home alive— your wife can tell you that I was at your home yesterday afternoon. If she would not have told me where you were going, you'd still be tied up in the woods. Fred and I were following them knowing they were after you. We are missing work, and paying for all of this out of our pocket to save your sorry lives. I had to buy a new Kevlar canoe and hundreds of dollars of other equipment because I didn't even have time to go home. Most of what I needed for this trip I already owned."

Bruce shifted around. I was beginning to think he was more seriously injured than even he knew. I added, "It's understandable that this is all unexpected and you're not a little angry. Your vacation's ruined, and you're hurting, to say nothing about wondering what this is all about, and what worse calamities the future holds. Take it from me. It's not over and the future is uncertain. I can say this because it's been happening to me a lot longer than you."

"Do you know what this is all about?" Bruce asked.

"Yes," I said. "And, I think you do, too. We'll go into it more later."

I turned to Bud. "When the guy was making the call to order the plane to pick them up, did you hear him say anything about where something was hidden, anything like that?'

Bud shook his head. "I was too far away to hear clearly what he said on the phone—only a few words here and there. That's how I heard about a plane and Hudson Lake. The reception must not have been good because he repeated himself a few times. The call took several minutes so he might have told where to find something. As his voice faded in and out he must have been turning to get the best reception."

That was not the best news, but not terrible. If Holt were telling me the truth, and if he was not able to tell them where it was, they'd need Holt alive. It would make them at least a little cautious. The main problem was getting everybody back to civilization so I said, "For now, let's see if we can get out of here alive."

The three of us were standing in a circle around Bruce and Bud said, "I can understand why they seemed so pleasant after they learned where we were going. They didn't want to do this in front of my mother." After a pause he asked, "Why would men from the Secret Service use such bullying tactics? You'd think that they'd be grateful if an ordinary citizen could provide information that would help in an important investigation. I could see why they might compel us not to tell others what we knew, but, as it is, we don't even know what this was all about."

Fred spoke, "Because we do know they are not Secret Service. Vin, here, has a knack of making people feel it's in their best interests to talk."

Bruce Holt was walking around working his muscles and gingerly touching sore spots. "What do you intend to do with the two guys in the woods?"

"We need them out of circulation, so we must move them at least to another lake, or take them with us. We can't leave them there because the guys in the plane know where they are. Here's what I'd like you to do. Start making your way out. By the way, do you have a cell phone on you?"

Bruce looked a little sheepish. "Yeah, I do. My wife is a worrier and made me take it. I don't know if it works out here, though. I've heard that some of them do, depends on the service, and I assume the two men that beat me used one to call the plane, or else it was a sat-phone."

I took the phone since I wasn't sure I trusted him. Of course, Bud might have one, too, but I didn't want to get into searching them. Holt was peeved, but I said I'd explain later.

"Okay," I said, "We'll paddle to Lake Two near the portages to Lake One and camp on one or the other of these islands." I pointed them out on the map. "There are only three short portages between here and there and the two of you should be able to make it. Start now and we'll catch up with you. We'll be in two canoes with our new friends, at least to start."

As we headed back to where we left the maggots, I suggested that we stop at the campsite where the women had been. I'd have Fred try to locate the gun he shot from Cutter's hand while I made an attempt to find Holt's fishing rod. It would be a shame to leave such a fine rod and reel behind.

The gun was too damaged to use, so we'd drop it overboard in the middle of the lake. The rod was another story. The water was clear and it was easy to see. But, it was six or eight feet down. It took a half hour, but I finally snagged it with a long stick. It was dumb to waste so much time, but sometimes when things are desperate it helps to completely switch one's attention to another activity.

Though Cutter and Divner had wiggled around and tried rubbing their bonds on the rocks to cut them, the had made no progress. As I checked the cords, I noticed Divner's little finger, the one that Harry had shortened. "That pinky is healing well, I said. If you think I'm mean and ornery, you don't want me to let the other Phantom man lose on you." His expression was strange, like he found my statement hard to believe while having no doubt that Harry had cut off the finger almost as sport.

We spent another twenty minutes eating beef jerky and granola bars. It was time to go. "Okay, you two will now earn your keep. Remember, neither one of us has the slightest compunction about shooting you so no fast movements, no moving close to either of us."

I hated to do it, but it was up to Fred and me to carry the aluminum canoe out of the woods. I didn't trust the other two in such tangled conditions. When we returned to then, I loosened the bonds on their ankles so they could shuffle. If they deliberately overturned a canoe, they wouldn't be able to swim far and would drown. It would sure make things a lot easier if they did. I loosened their hands saving the cord for later use.

I'd put Divner with Fred because Fred had too much reason to even things with Cutter. I covered then with my gun as they launched, and Fred stayed in easy range while we did the same. He was getting the idea of operations.

"Now, paddle," I said. "And, especially you Cutter, don't break your paddle, we don't have a spare. Without a paddle you'd be useless to us, and anyone who can't pull his load gets left behind in the woods."

As we sped along I saw how strong Cutter was. I'd never take him in a fair fight. That was neither hear nor there as I didn't expect it to come to that. Which reminded me, I still hadn't decided what to do with him.

The Holts were ahead of us somewhere and I hoped we wouldn't pass them unawares. It was unlikely, but anything was possible. We'd probably run into them on the portages between Hudson Lake and Lake Four, which we did. Bud was doing his best, he was young and hadn't gone through the training I had by his age to toughen him up. Bruce was not doing well. He could walk and carry paddles and miscellaneous light items but that was it. He couldn't paddle. That was about what I had expected so when we were launched past the third portage into Lake Four, I cast a line to Bruce and we towed him with Bud doing as much as he could to help. My dilemma about Cutter was answered. He'd be our main source of propulsion.

It was now nearly four and we had five miles to go. We'd make it by six and hope we could find a campsite. I'd prefer to leave the Holts on their own camp, fewer people to trip over one another. We'd see.

With nothing to do but dig in the paddle I had time to think. The assassins were an odd couple. One given to emotion, and the other with none at all except when thwarted, then he became an animal. Iceman was in the business because he had no aversion do doing the most heinous things. That did not mean he was particularly clever. In fact, he may require micro management to do his job. If he were really a psychopath, he wasn't much good at figuring things out. I had read a long article about a politician some years back who was reputed to suffer from psychopathy. The writer went to some length to show that it took psychologists a long time to make the connection that psychopaths, who were frequently criminals, and others who had sustained brain injuries, really suffered from the same illness. That was because the criminals were housed in prisons, and the mentally incompetent in asylums.

Normal people make decisions by attaching an emotional tag, positive or negative, to each piece of information needed for the decision. For example, assume you are in the market for a used car. You go onto the lot and the salesman greets you with a warm smile. His demeanor has a very slight positive tag attached because you expect him to present himself that way. It's better than if he had a scowl. He shows you three possibilities and you are particularly taken by one. It is the exact model you want so that has a high positive emotional tag. It has lower miles than you expected, also positive, and it has certain luxury features you did not expect to get for the price—more positive tags. But, it is bright red inside and out and bright red gives you a headache, a huge negative tag. Using the emotional tags, you make a decision. But a psychopath could go over the various pieces of data, even write them down and assign positive or negative numbers to them. At the end, he would still not know what to do.

As one would expect, there are many levels of severity with psychopathy as with any illness. If the Iceman were totally unable to make decisions he couldn't function in society let alone in his profession. But, it was a weakness that might be exploited. His normal victims likely were people who did not know they were targets. And, he normally operated in a city or other structured environment. It was unlikely, though always possible, he had training in stalking his prey in wild country.

The emotional one had promised they'd get me. The question was, would they try out here? If they did they'd be waiting where we left the cars. If I assumed that, would we be better off arriving during the day or at night? The options tossed around in my mind and I wasn't getting anywhere. I was tired so I let go and concentrated on paddling and my muscles which were hurting more with each passing minute.

— 15 —

At six-thirty we pulled up to the area of the islands. There were at least a half-dozen sites in the near area so we pulled all three canoes up to the same one to the south of the portages to Lake One. I immediately bound the hands of Cutter and Divner while Fred held a gun. They grumbled, but we all knew what they'd do if given half a chance. Bruce was worse than he let on when I found him on the portage so it was well that we had him with us. Bud immediately set up their tent so he could have his dad lay down where the misquotes weren't so bad. As it was, we were all liberally applying bug repellent minutes after setting foot on land.

Cutter had a tent, but we did not. It didn't matter because the four of us would sleep under the stars, if we were lucky enough to have any. That much I had figured out. If we slept in the tent, and one of them should get free, all they'd have to do is collapse the tent and roll us up in it. If they slept in the tent, it would mean they were together and could help one another get free. When one of us came to look in on them in the morning, they could surprise us. With everybody outside, I'd tie them to trees well separated from each other, and Fred and I would sleep a short distance from our respective paddling partner.

Bud was good around camp. Immediately after seeing to his dad's comfort, he opened several packages of beef jerky and cut it into bite sized chunks and put it in a pan of water to soften. He then started a fire in the fire pit that was part of each designated campsite. Fred took the folding saw and went into the brush for wood. Since Bud seemed to know what he was about I functioned as his assistant, getting water and finding stuff in the packs. He carefully measured out water in the biggest pot and set it on the fire. He said they liked to make meat in gravy and put it on mashed potatoes. They had pre-measured out enough potato flakes in zip shut plastic bags for two, so he planned to make three bags worth.

It was a study watching him work with such concentration. He had poured several packets of dried gravy mix in with the meat that was simmering in the smaller pan. When the water in the large pot was boiling, he dumped the potato flakes in, pulled it off the fire and stirred like crazy with a wooden paddle he had asked me to carve. It only took thirty seconds for the potatoes to be ready. I had six aluminum plates arranged on the ground and he plopped a huge lump of potatoes in each. I followed with the pan of meat and gravy. I stuck a large spoon in two of the piles and took one to each of our "guests." I had previously freed the left hand of each of the captives.

We all dug in. You never saw a pile of food disappear so fast. The hot food tasted good after all of the power and granola bars we had eaten. There were assorted cups of one kind or another and we all just drank water as it came from the lake. That was the customary thing to do up here, especially this early in the year.

When the eating utensils were scraping empty plates, Bud went around dividing up the remaining potatoes and gravy. As he walked away from Cutter, Cutter said, "If I ever hear that anyone has laid a hand on the young man, I'll personally kill him. You never harm a good cook."

I caught the expression on Bud's face as he walked to the fire. It was beaming. He could only imagine the rough pasts these hardened men had lived, the rotten food they had eaten only to stay alive. Cutter's comment was praise supreme.

In one of Cutter and Divner's packs, I had found some fruit pies that were not badly crushed which we had for dessert. It was a heavy meal, but we were all big guys and had been working hard. Bud and I washed dishes and Fred continued bringing in wood. I was surprised to see that he had remembered some of his scout training. He piled the wood, twigs, and chips by a rock and put one of the Holts' ponchos over it. That was so if it rained during the night, we'd have dry wood for breakfast.

With the camp chores done, I walked back in the woods and using Holt's cell phone discovered we were close enough to civilization to get a signal. I called home and Camilla answered clearly worried. I told her I was okay. It was a relief to learn that she had not had visitors, but I said she must get out of the house as soon as she could. Without using any names, I told her to go the Henni Froom's house for a couple of days. She could tell them as much as made sense, but not so much as to endanger them. She didn't argue. I said I'd try to be there within twenty-four hours.

Back in camp I saw Bruce sitting with his back against a tree swatting a mosquito now and then. The bug spray was good, but not perfect. I checked the ropes on Cutter and Divner and motioned Bruce and Bud to follow me. Bruce got up heavily and we walked away from camp. There was a faint trail along the shore where campers had walked many times to cast a line in the water. As soon as we were out of earshot of camp I said to Bruce, "You must call your wife and tell her to get out of the house. Do you have somewhere you could tell her to go that would not let an eavesdropper know where it was? You know, like where we went for the birthday party last week, or something like that?"

He thought a minute. "Yes. I know just the place."

"Good. When you head back to the Cities, go there, too. And, tell me where it is and a phone number if you can so I'll know where you are. We aren't done with this by a long ways in case you haven't figured that out. Don't leave a message on the answering machine. Our prisoners told us there were two assassins on the plane plus the hired pilot. They may try to get to us through our families."

Holt didn't seem to be believing all this was necessary. "Are you sure you have this right? It seems over the edge."

"He's understating the case if anything," Fred said. "One of the guys we have tied up tried to put a bullet between my eyes. As it was, they only ruined my baseball cap due to his man's quick action," he said nodding to me. "Wesson's pal, who you will likely meet, made Divner talk by cutting off his pinky. I saw it, not the act but the finger afterwards. I now have it in my freezer at home for safe keeping. Don't forget, they would have left you back on that portage to die of thirst. Are you computing this?"

Neither Bruce or Bud were looking so good.

"Something came to mind that I had overlooked." I said. "Things may be worse than we've presented them. Look at it. The plane left here and if they were of the mind to harass our families they can find out were we live. I called my wife a few minutes ago and they had not found her yet. Maybe, they are more interested in you for the time being."

Holt nodded and took the phone. His wife was still unmolested, too, and she was receptive to the idea of leaving the house.

After the call, I said, "They could still make it back in time to be waiting at the entry point as we come out tomorrow. "So, how do we get out of here without running into them?"

We returned to camp and took out our maps. There were some options. In all of them we had to go over the portages and get back into Lake One. Once there, by means of some short portages, we could pass over to Kawishiwi River, the series of long narrow lakes. With that route we could stay well clear of the entry point where we came in. Then by means of a long portage to Triangle Lake we could exit at one of the lodges on that lake. However, if we did not exit where we came in, we would not have a vehicle. Holt's car was parked at the Lake One outfitter, and ours was at the public landing. All of the other places we could exit were located at or near a lodge or outfitter located on the edge of the wilderness.

As I pointed this out, Bud said, "So we exit someplace where we can walk through the woods to a road. One of us hitches a ride into Ely, rents a large vehicle and comes back for the others."

I nodded. "That's not a bad plan, but the down side is it leaves our assassins on the lose. We'll have to deal with them some time. One of our prisoners assured us that they would succeed in killing as many of us as was necessary. We'll keep your plan in mind and see how we feel in the morning."

I gave two of Cutter's pain pills to Bruce and two to him. They both needed sleep, but for different reasons.

I unzipped sleeping bags so they were open blankets for both Cutter and Divner and threw one over each man. I found a place near Cutter with a good mat of pine needles and slipped into my sleeping bag. My poncho was in easy reach in case it started to rain. I twisted and turned to get comfortable feeling I'd never sleep, but I eventually did.

Thursday morning

I awakened at dawn which came early this time of year. Cutter was still leaning against his tree, dozing. I suspect he had spent a miserable night, but the wages of sin and all that. Turning over I tried to sleep but knew it was pointless. I slipped out of my sleeping bag and put on my shoes. I had spent the night wearing my hat, more or less. Cutter was silently following me with his eyes as I inspected the camp. Everybody was still where they were supposed to be.

Holt's rod and reel were still drawing me so I decided to try some serious fishing. Since the trip was completely unplanned, I had no fishing
license, but then our circumstances were a bit different from that of the
average camper. I began with the red and white spoon I had used the day
before with no results. The reel was a fine piece of engineering, though.
Trying another lure with a spinner up front, and yellow and black hair
covering the treble hook I tried again. On the second cast I hooked into
something, a northern pike, I assumed. He was decent sized and it took
five minutes to tire him out before I landed the five to six pounder.
Throwing it well up on shore I went for another one. Around the side of
the island where Holt had made the call to his wife, I got another one
about the same size.

It was common that a given part of any lake will have the same size
fish. I had always supposed it had to do with the type of food that was
available. It also might have been because some species were cannibalis-
tic and if they were all the same size they couldn't eat one another.
Mother nature is wonderful that way.

In camp, I began filleting one of the fish using a canoe paddle as a
cutting board. When my boys and I went out, we always carried a spare
paddle in case one broke or was lost. I owned the spare and it was made
of wood so it worked well for cleaning fish. I made do with a plastic
paddle making sure it was one of Cutter's.

Fred was soon up and he rousted out the two in the tent. Bruce had
spent a bad night, and looked like he was running a fever. Bud immediately started a fire. I consulted with him and we agreed he'd fry the fish
and let it go at that. Normally, we'd have had pancakes as a second
course, but time was becoming important for Bruce. I let Cutter and Divner know in no uncertain terms that if Holt died, I'd get both of them for
murder, no matter what their bosses in Washington thought.

We ate in silence, sipping coffee between bites. It was all good. Bud
had brought along a prepared light breading for the fish that was sea-
soned perfectly. I had it in mind to give him a call when this was over
and get some of his recipes and tips. I could hold my own when it came
to camp cooking, but it's given to some people to be really good at it.

We swished off the plates in the water, packed up and were paddling
by six o'clock. On the portages, one of us had to help Bruce walk. Once
in Lake One we set off as fast as we could reasonably paddle. The air had
been heavy since first light, and now a steady rain began. We all donned
ponchos, and that was only a marginal improvement. With the exertion,

the perspiration could not escape the impervious surface, so our shirts were soon wet with sweat. Cutter threw his off and let the rain patter on his considerable physique. I cast off the line to Bud's canoe a quarter mile from the outfitter's dock. With the rain and mist, we were still not in sight of the landing. He agreed he could make it the rest of the way in short order. I had given the cell phone Holt had been carrying to Bud. He agreed to call me when they learned about Bruce's condition.

Up to that point, we had all stayed together, and now Fred and I turned our canoes around. We could have taken Bruce and Bud directly to their destination and then continued through the narrow channel and approach the public boat landing from the northeast. That would be the way we would be expected to arrive. Therefore, we backtracked a mile and by means of three short portages were able to approach the public landing from the southwest. With the rain and general gloom, this could give us the small advantage we needed, and maybe not. I had considered that there might not be a reception committee because one of the team had been shot in the leg by me. They knew who we were and would have ample time to practice their assassination arts at their leisure. However, I considered the extra effort to be worth the marginal advantage.

I had also considered going ashore a couple of hundred yards from the public landing and stealthily making my way through the woods and brush to the landing. But with the rain, it was too miserable to move, wait, listen, and move for several hours. The landing with its loop of road a quarter of a mile or more around with parking spaces on either side would make things difficult enough so I decided on the direct approach. Five hundred yards from the landing we pulled to the shore. I bound Cutter's hands in front of him so he could still hold a paddle, but not paddle, then pulled his poncho over him. I did the same with Divner and we set off. I rammed the bow of the canoe into the sand beside the dock. Cutter laid his paddle on the ground as I had instructed so as not to make noise by hitting the canoe with it. He then got out. I was behind him with the forty-five under my poncho. The rain has slacked off but was enough to make the use of ponchos seem reasonable.

If Cutter weren't sweating, he was crazy. I had made it clear to him that if I took a slug, and had the slightest twitch left in me, he would be dead, and I meant it. The hammer was back, all safeties were off, and my finger was on the trigger. The gun remained pointed at Cutter's heart from the back. While we made our hike, Fred had taken Divner immediately to the trees to the left of the landing.

I was sweating, too. It was impossible to know what to expect. If the Iceman were waiting in ambush he could let us pass and plug me in the back. The walk up the main road was uneventful. Then, we took the branch to the right into the loop. It was on that section of the road away from the main drag in, that I expected trouble. When trouble came, it was not as I had expected. There were a couple of young guys unloading their canoe from a Lincoln Navigator where it was parked, a hundred yards from the water. Everybody, drives to the landing, unloads, and then parks the car. These guys would have to carry everything all that distance for no reason. This was the type of thing I had learned to be immediately wary of all those years ago. It was something out of place, it didn't fit.

Looking at us as we approached, not from the landing, but the opposite way, one of them asked in a smart voice, "Forget where you parked your car?"

If it were a ruse, it was perfect. I was losing my concentration so I had to play it the way I saw it. We were headed toward the lake. The vehicles were angle parked as if they had come from the water. Immediately beyond the Navigator, was a pickup and past that Fred's car. I assumed the assassin would be in the trees at the front of Fred's vehicle.

I almost stumbled over the packs lying about behind the Navigator, and the other of the young guy said, "Watch where you're going, old duffer."

"Shut up," I retorted. "The man in front of me is my prisoner, and I have a cocked forty-five under my poncho aimed at his back. There's an assassin in the bushes around here someplace."

The one who had spoken first snapped back. "You're an Alzheimer case who spends too much time in his rocking chair watching old movies."

"Between the Navigator and the pickup," I said nudging Cutter with the barrel of the gun. Between the vehicles, I threw back the poncho so my gun hand was free.

One of the guys said, "No kidding the jerk really has a gun. Hey, what's . . . ."

I was concentrating on the area in front of the vehicles when my instincts made me grab Cutter's upper left arm with my left hand and we both swung around. Across the parking area a leaf moved. It might have been a bird or squirrel, but I knew it wasn't.

The shot came from a silenced pistol. The slug hit Cutter in the right shoulder as I pushed him to the cover offered by the navigator. The next two found a home in the shiny new vehicle. The sound of the shots and the pings as they landed in the Navigator sent the smart mouths to the ground. I raised the forty-five above Cutter's right shoulder and fired at the point where the leaf had moved, then to the right and to the left of it. A final shot I sent low in the center of the pattern. That one hit. It always surprised me how even with the sound of my own gun so close to me, I could hear the sound when a bullet hit flesh and penetrated muscle, cartilage and bone. It was a thump like none other. And, the magnitude of the sound told me I had gotten a solid hit. The bushes shuddered ever so slightly followed by a faint thrashing sound in the wet leaves

I pushed the muzzle of my gun into Cutter's back and he started to walk toward the trees. I jabbed him twice more. He got the idea and started to run. With a fist full of his shirt in my left hand, I pulled him up short under the first branches. I pulled him to his knees. He was shaking with fear. And, no wonder. He knew the assassin would think nothing of killing him to get to me, if in fact it was me he had shot at in the first place. We were both breathing hard, not from exertion, but from adrenaline surge.

I prodded Cutter forward on his knees until we were a foot from small trees. On one knee to Cutter's right I pushed on the back of his upper arm. He got the idea, raised his bound hands and moved the slender stems to the side. In the gloom of the forest floor, I saw a patch of something lighter than the surrounding damp decaying leaves. It might have been a large fungus growth on a decomposing log, or a man's face. It was the latter. Pushing Cutter aside, gun at the ready I took two steeps into the deepened shadow.

There he was lying face up, a forty-five bullet hole in his forehead, a little to the right of center, his right. After he had shot at us, he had crouched down, and that's when my fourth shot had struck home. What kind of mess was I into? This was not Vietnam a half world away. This was paranoid, politically correct America. A white man would have been one thing, a minority was the end of the world.

I pulled his fingers off his weapon one at a time, pulled out my handkerchief and relieved him of his weapon. Being careful not to add my finger prints, I safed it, and slid it behind my belt under my poncho. Behind me an engine roared and I spun around. It was the Lincoln Navigator peeling out as the tires slipped trying to gain traction. Leaving Cutter I ran with all I had to where the loop met the main road into the landing. Just in time I saw the big SUV speeding away on Highway 169, rather than making the right turn that would have taken them to the outfitter's premises. Their main concern was to put distance between us and them rather than sounding an alarm.

That gave us some time, though it was hard to tell how much. In the still, damp air the sound of my shots would have easily carried to the business east of me. It was a fact, though, that a lot of guys packed guns into the wilderness as sort of a macho thing and after carrying it all that way discovered it had been nothing more than useless baggage. While packing up to leave, if there was no one else around, they'd take a few shots at a tree to assure themselves that if the need had arisen it would have worked. With that in mind, I felt it unlikely anybody would investigate based on the shots alone.

Rushing back to Cutter who seemed dazed, I pulled him to a standing position, and told him to cooperate.

He shook his head. "You shot that gun right beside my ear—can't hear a thing."

Bringing my mouth near his left ear I said, "Cooperate or I'll leave you in the bushes in the same condition as the assassin."

He was a believer, and in spite of the pain in his shoulder jogged ahead of me to the lake. Fred had pulled both canoes out of the water and carried them to the tree line and turned them upside down with Cutters gear under his as if someone planned to be back for it. Mine was over turned near it with our gear beside it. It was good he was trying to think on the fly. But, we needed my canoe.

"What happened?" Fred asked as we neared.

"The assassin tried for me and hit Cutter. He's dead in the bushes. Run and get you car. I'll watch them both. We have to load up, including my canoe, and be out of here, now!"

Fred ran. I had them sit on the ground back to back ten feet apart. Pulling back his shirt, I took a look at Cutter's wound. He was covered with blood front and back, but not as bad as I'd seen a lot of other times. I ran to Cutter's canoe and pulled a handful of clothes out of his pack. I ran the sleeve of a long sleeved shirt under his right arm pit and tied it to the other sleeve where his left shoulder and neck joined. Then using some underwear, clean or not I didn't care, I stuffed one between the shirt and the wound front and back. It was the best he'd get until we were well away from here.

Fred had the Blazer backed beside my canoe. Leaving the motor running, he was out, opened the rear hatch and pulled out the car-top carriers and threw them on top. I hurried over and helped him hoist the canoe onto the carriers. While he worked at securing it with nylon ropes, I threw packs in the back. I put additional loops of rope around Divner's whole body pinning his arms to him so he had little movement. Then I pushed Cutter into the rear on the near side, the driver's side, and slammed the door. Divner went in the other side. Fred slammed the rear hatch as I dashed for the passenger side. We were driving out as a van drove in with a canoe on top.

"Wave at him," I said to Fred. He did and got a wave and friendly smile in return.

"In case you haven't figure it out, that's why we bothered with the canoe. We could *not* have been seen driving away without one."

Fred nodded. "You're quick with stuff like that, aren't you?"

I shrugged. "That's what got me sucked into Phantom."

— 16 —

Driving away from the public boat landing at Lake One, I asked, "How are you doing, Cutter?"

"Been better."

"The wages of sin and all that. You might consider reforming. You aren't doing so well. Broken arm last year, shot off finger and bullet in the shoulder this year. It seems to be getting worse."

"Stuff it!"

"Sure. But, I'll give you a choice. We'll drop you off someplace in Ely where you'll be able to beg a ride to the hospital, clinic or whatever they have. Or, we'll take you back to the metro and drop you off at a shopping center or something. What'll it be?"

"I'll let you know when we get to Ely."

We rode in silence. Half way from the landing to Ely we met the Lincoln Navigator going the other way.

"Did you see that SUV we just met?" I Asked Fred.

He shook his head.

"The assassin put two bullets in their new Lincoln Navigator right after he hit Cutter. They had equipment all over the parking area like they owned it, like they were a bit more equal that the rest of us. Their first impulse was to get away from there. But, after thinking it through they realized all of their stuff was still there. Besides, if they were from money the way their smart mouths indicated they would expect to elbow in and make sure those responsible were caught and made to pay for the damages."

I considered it was likely they had no idea which vehicle was ours. They might have thought it was the pickup, but other than that, I doubted they took note of the other vehicles parked in the area and by noting which one was missing discover which one was ours. But, they'd go back and probably do some snooping around. They'd in all probably find the assassin with no gun. At the time I took it, my concern was to not leave it lying around for someone to pick up. It was wrapped in one of Cutter's shirts in my small back pack along with the personal effects of our two guests.

The reappearance of the Lincoln Navigator meant we had to get at least as far as Virginia as soon as possible. And, we would not be dropping off a man with two gunshot wounds in Ely.

Once past Virginia, it would be good to dump the canoe. That would be devilishly hard. A canoe was a valuable and bulky thing. On one hand, nobody discarded something that they could sell for money, good old money, no one passed up any of that. On the other hand, it could be considered littering. Anyone seeing us doing that would consider it so odd that they'd take an interest in our activities, note our plate number, even call the police. Nobody, simply nobody, left behind for the first taker a piece of valuable property. That aside, if someone saw it being deposited or came upon it soon there after, and he personally wanted it and felt he can get away clean with it, then the precious environment would be free of that piece of litter in a microsecond. Worst of all, it had a serial number that was traceable to me.

It was fifteen miles to Ely, and another fifty to Virginia. Fred was meticulous about observing the speed limits in and around Ely. It was maddening how the city speed zones extended well beyond the last houses—speed trap heaven. Finally past the last speed zone, he set the speed control at fifty-five. Though, excruciatingly slow, and causing no little consternation to the couple of cars hugging our bumper, there was no other option. We could not take the chance or having a cop stop us with all manner of weapons, and wounded men.

Five miles out of Ely we saw flashing lights ahead. As Fred slowed we came upon an accident. It didn't appear bad, though it had part of our lane blocked. A state trooper was on the scene sorting things out. The way people were walking around it appeared there were no serious injuries. As on coming traffic cleared, cars in our lane could ease around trying to avoid glass on the pavement. When our turn came there were cars approaching so Fred had to stop. The Smokey was acting professionally though his expression showed he was bored. He turned to watch traffic, both as a caution, and as something to do. He looked at me and made eye contact—big mistake on my part. With that he took an interest in us personally. Taking in the four unshaven men in a vehicle with a canoe on top, we looked normal enough. Then he saw the ropes tied around Divner and the blood on Cutters clothing.

He motioned for me to lower my window. "What's going on here. You have that man in the back seat bound. Lower the rear window," he said as he backed away a step while moving his right hand in the direction of his sidearm.

"That other man's hands are tied, too, and he appears wounded. When on coming traffic clears, pull around the accident and stop on the shoulder."

"Yes sir," I said.

In a few seconds we were able to move. "Trouble," I said in a subdued voice. "Where possible, let me do the talking. We don't want to make contradictory statements. Drive ahead another ten yards so nobody from the accident hears what is said."

Fred complied. When the car stopped I immediately got out and slammed the door, being careful my hands were empty and visible.

The trooper approached and stopped five paces away. He looked to be in his forties, over six feet by an inch or two, and looked like he worked out. Under the brim of his Smoky the Bear hat, I could make out gray eyes and balanced features except that as I caught the light along the side of his head his left ear protruded more than the right. His uniform was impressively pressed with creases visible in his shirt, military style. "Did I see that right?"

"Yes, sir, you did."

"Mind telling me what's going on?"

"It's a long story, sir."

"Try me."

"The two men in the back seat are Secret Service agents. There was a shoot out and the wounded man took a bullet in the shoulder, and the assassin took one in the head. We're on our way to get medical help for the wounded man. It's quite complicated, sir."

"Assassin, you say. How did he know the other man was an assassin? I need to see some identification, you first."

I pulled out my wallet and handed over my driver's license. He held it between his fingers and snapped the edge of it with his thumb nail, like he wanted to shake off cooties. "I want everybody out of the car."

"I would advise against that, sir. The wounded man is not in good shape."

"Why didn't you take him to the hospital in Ely? We do have medical facilities, even out here in the bushes. You," he said to me, "stand back from me and no fast moves." From the rear he looked in.

"How about you, the bleeding one. Don't you want to get to the nearest hospital?"

Cutter only shook his head.

"This is a very long story, sir," I interjected.

"Driver, get out. Let's see the ID."

Fred slowly got out, closed the door and came around the front of the car. He produced his driver's license.

"He's FBI," I said.

The trooper stopped short. Looking at Fred, he said, "Let's see the badge."

Fred took a short breath and I hoped he would follow my lead which he did.

"I'm sorry sir, but I don't have it with me. I didn't expect to need it on a canoe trip into the wilderness. That's why I go on vacation, to leave stuff like that behind for a few days."

Bravo. Some great lines.

"Yeah, I know how that goes. How about the credentials of the two in the back seat?"

"They're in the back in a pack," I said. "I'll be happy to get them. I'll be careful to make no fast moves." He nodded. Fred pressed the button on his key fob and unlocked the back. I had to dig a little before I found it. The assassin's gun was in the bag too, and my mind was racing about what to do about that. I carried the bag to the side of the car.

"I'll look," the trooper said.

I backed away. "Be careful because the assassin's gun complete with silencer is in there, too, wrapped in a shirt. Don't smear the fingerprints."

He found the shirt, lifted it out and laid it on the ground. Finally he dumped out the whole bag. With his left hand he sorted through the pile of stuff. From his expression I could tell how conflicted he was. If Fred was an FBI agent, the other two were Secret Service, and there was a murder weapon wrapped in the shirt, he was in way over his head and wanted to be free of all this as soon as he could professionally do it.

He found two folded identifications, flipped one open with his thumb and saw I had not been kidding. Then he did the other one. Standing up, he went to the vehicle and compared the photos to the men.

My cell phone sounded and I said, "Mind if I get this? I'm expecting an important call."

He made no response either way so I took the call. It was Bud as I had expected. He updated me and I said he should call his mom, that he should be careful and ended the call.

Looking at Fred, I said, "That was Bud. They decided they couldn't handle it in Ely and they're medevacing his dad to Hennepin County General. He's in critical condition." Looking at the trooper, I said, "That was a call from the son of the man the two in the back seat nearly beat to death. That's why they're both wearing ropes. It's a long story."

"Just a minute. Nobody leaves," he said as he turned his attention to the accident.

I said to Fred, "This is a good time to dump the canoe. How about untying it and I'll help you with it." He did as I had suggested. After all, it was my canoe.

After a few short interchanges, and the arrival of a tow truck, the trooper returned, the conflicted expression had not left his lined face. He picked up the shirt and carefully unwrapped the gun. There it was, silencer and all.

"Just what part of the Secret Service do these guys work for?"

"They report directly to the President of the United States," I replied.

That was it, his mouth dropped open. Drawing himself up, he asked, "Where'd you get this, where's the dead assassin, as you call him?"

"Do you know where Lake One is?"

"Sure. Everybody around here knows that."

"He's on the parking loop associated with the public landing, on the east side of the loop, east of the parking area, about a third of the way from the north end of the loop, back in the bushes twenty feet. He has a bullet hole in his forehead, a little right of center, his right. You'll probably be getting a call about it pretty soon."

This was one state trooper who had met his match. "If I could make a suggestion," I said. "Take prints off the gun and match them to the cadaver. Do it locally, here, for your own piece of mind. If you send the gun to St. Paul and the case gets into the system, there will be no prints on the gun, and the prints off the dead man will be from someone who died fifteen years ago. And, if you're really unlucky, the gun will end up being registered to you. It's a long story."

"What are you talking about . . . ."

"Unit fifty-one."

It was the remote radio from his belt that transmitted to his car and from there to the dispatcher. We had been hearing cryptic messages from time to time as we talked.

He pressed the talk button and said, "Unit fifty-one."

"We have a possible 10-89. How long before you're through with your 10-51?"

"Is that the 10-89 at the public landing at Lake One?"

There was a long pause. "Unit fifty-one, how did you know that?"

"Ah . . . . It's a long story. I'll be finished here in a few minutes, and will respond."

"Roger, fifty-one. Dispatch, out." The female voice had a pronounced tone of bewilderment.

When the officer was off the radio I told him we were leaving the canoe in the bushes along the road, and that if he came and retrieved it, he could have it.

"Why'd you do that?"

"We can't drive into the metro with that thing on the top. Up here it's normal, there we'd stand out and be remembered."

Along the way, Fred began replacing the contents of the back pack while I wrote on a page of my little notebook.

"Here are my address and phone numbers, and those of the driver on the other side. Could we please have our driver's licenses back?"

Reluctantly, he returned them.

"Don't call us at these numbers for a few days."

"Why not?"

"We won't be home—too dangerous. Do you have a business card and a number where I could call you this evening? It's possible you may need a few more details."

Shaking his head he said, "That's possible."

He produced a card and wrote a number on the back.

I was itching to be away from here so I made a desperate plea. "Can we please leave now? You have work to do and so do we."

He nodded.

Once up to speed we relaxed. "How are you in the back doing," I asked.

Divner spoke, "That was the craziest thing I ever saw. You admitted to a murder, at least by one of us, you gave him what could have been the murder weapon, a highly illegal one, you gave no motive, and we drive away."

"The Secret Service credentials were bad enough, and when I told him who you worked for, well, I guess you didn't see his expression. He didn't know what to think. It was all so unbelievable that it had to be true."

"Are you dead yet, Cutter?"

"I need a couple more of those pills."

"Whatever you want."

There were some cans of soda left from our trip to the peaceful northland so he washed them down with a Gatorade.

— 17 —

Two-thirds of the way from Ely to Virginia, at Cutter's request, we pulled off at a crossing road and drove a mile into more forest. On a deserted stretch of road—a lot of that up here when away from lakes—Fred stopped and we all relieved ourselves. Back on the road, we were headed back to town, non-stop. Three hours later we joined Interstate I-35. Cutter was asleep and I was driving. The wheels in Divner's head had been turning.

Finally, after nearly an hour when no one had spoken, Divner said, "When we get to the metropolitan area, it would be a help to us of you'd take us to the downtown area of St. Paul. We know a doctor there that looks after us. I don't think Cutter will do well if we are left off at a shopping center and have to wait for a taxi. He's hurt pretty bad. In addition, we would surely draw attention and I think you want to avoid that as much as we do."

"Where in St. Paul?"

"Take I-35E to downtown and I'll direct you. It isn't far off the freeway."

I nodded. "We'll see." The situation had been working on me, too, so I said, "This is rapidly getting out of control, you can see that. Just how far are you guys going to push it?"

Glancing over my shoulder, I saw the look. There may have been a time after the Iceman had been iced and Cutter shot, or when I could have given him over to the trooper when he might have been having second thoughts. He was reverting to type now that he was free of the law and was in all likelihood going to be released.

"We have our orders." Flatly, that was it. No thinking, only a robotic response.

"We all know what it is we're looking for, don't we?" It was a rhetorical question so I continued immediately. "It's a complete, ready to go, nuke the size of the one dropped on Hiroshima. The folks you work for are terrorists, we all know that, too, don't we? If this were on the up and up, people wouldn't be dead, shot, or beaten to an inch of their lives. Therefore, they intend to use it for terrorist purposes. They'll of necessity have to kill you as soon as they have it in hand. I'm sure you've figured that out." I said it with the intent that I was pretty sure he hadn't thought that far ahead."

"How do you figure that? We're reliable foot shoulders who have provided services for them that not many men would have done. We can't be replaced in a minute, or even a month."

I was right, he hadn't figured it through. He also said something that he had not intended to say. I'd mention it to Fred later.

It was time to play with his mind so I said, "It would be one thing if the U.S. had granted citizenship to some raghead because he had helped the CIA in one of the interminable wars they always have going, and then in return he had gone rogue and blasted a U.S. city with an atomic bomb. But, these guys are so highly placed that they have to clean up all loose ends. Not only will they eliminate you, me, and my family, but they'll have to get rid of the trooper who stopped us and probably the outfitter who rented you the canoe. You see, every possible connection to recovering that thing will have to be eradicated, period."

I glance back again. He wasn't saying anything so I continued. "As soon as I turn you lose, it's my thinking that you'll be on the hunt to get me. But, there's something you should know. Bruce Holt told me that he had no idea what you were after nor where it was. He flew the plane into the Anoka County Airport, but he never left the plane. You think you know where it is, but he lied to you."

Without giving him a chance to reply again, I continued. "One thing I didn't mention when the trooper had us stopped was that you beat Holt so badly that he'll likely die, so you have made a dead end, literally, out of the only real lead you had. Neither Nine Lives nor I were on that mission. He was all you had. Nice going."

Divner started to bristle, and Fred shifted a little so I suspected Fred was awake taking it all in. Divner said, "What makes you think he lied to us? He lied to you. He needed you to get him out of the lakes. You were his only hope which meant he would say what you wanted to hear. Did he tell you where he told us to look for it?"

I hated to lie, but there were times when it seemed like the right thing to do. "No, he didn't. He was in bad shape and I saw nothing to be gained by interrogating him. I figured there'd be time enough for that if he lived."

There was smugness in his voice, "Just as I thought."

"Does that mean that you will kill me after all?"

"You really have a high opinion of yourself, and a low one of everybody else. We don't have to take that risk. A word from the right highly placed person and you'll be in a dungeon so deep you'll never see the light of day again. We can make it happen. You are so gone."

As much as I resisted the feeling, for the first time terror set in. They could make good on a threat like that. The assassin, the gun, the trooper, it could all be brought together in a minute and I was "so gone." No matter what training I had there was no possibility I could fight the juggernaut of the combined criminal fighting forces of the entire nation.

I swallowed hard and he saw it. He snickered. One thing I knew for sure, he would not be the one to take me down. It would be an expensive snicker for him.

When we exited 35E in downtown St. Paul it was nearly three. Divner directed me as Fred pretended to wake up and stretched. He was right, in a mile we pulled into the driveway of an old part of town that had been the upper class district a hundred years ago. It was still reasonably well maintained. The two hundred foot driveway curved and near the garage had a place to back out and turn to the left so the driver could turn around and not have to back into the street.

"This is it," Divner said. I pulled up to the garage and backed into the turn around that was hidden from the street by tall shrubs. "Sound the horn."

What? He was thinking that since he had made the threat to me, I was his chauffeur? Wrong. "No need," I said. "I'll help you guys."

Fred and I both got out and as Fred went to Divner's door I said, "Better let me help you with him."

Coming round I helped Divner out and cut his ropes. Before he could take a step, I grabbed his right wrist and rammed my fist into his gut. Before he could make a sound, I smashed his head into the door jamb and he went limp. I let him slump to the ground. Turning his left hand palm down on the pavement, I took the forty-five from behind my belt and beat on the back of his hand making sure to break at least one bone in each finger. I did the same with the right hand. I swept out my knife, pried open his mouth and made a couple of good cuts into his tongue. Leaving him on the ground, I slammed the door.

"Get in," I said to Fred. He did. On the other side I opened Cutter's door, grabbed his sore shoulder and threw him out on the ground. Walking over, I had it in mind to whack him in the side of his head with my fist, but he was unconscious already. I slammed his door, got in and driving to the street sounded the horn.

A block away from the house, Fred said in a subdued tone as if he couldn't believe what he'd just seen, "You *are* the orneriest person I've ever met."

Grimacing, I said, "I don't enjoy doing things like that, never have, not even back in Nam. But," I continued, "nobody's perfect."

Fred glanced my way, his mouth open.

Before he could speak I said, "You were awake to hear Divner and me talking, weren't you?"

"Yeah, I heard most of it."

"There were two things he said that he should not have said. The first was that they'd sic the law enforcement on me and nail me for good. They could easily do that. All they have to do is take the information from the state trooper and twist it together with the dead man, the gun and the circumstances. Failing that they could always plant illegal drugs in my car. You know how it works."

"Are you saying I did things like that while I worked with the Bureau?"

"Don't go defensive on me. No, I did not mean to imply that. But, it is not without precedent that some law enforcement officers push the limits now and then to get a particularly obnoxious person off the streets. Other than that, if this really does go to the top, there are ways to make people disappear nice and legally."

"Okay. And point number two?"

"You remember that he said it would not be easy to replace him in a minute or a month? I believe that means he, Cutter, the assassin, and a few others had been doing the dirty work for that gang that now runs the Federal Government while they were still in Chicago. That explains why the Iceman and Jimmy Hook were sent to the BWCA to pick up Cutter and Divner. That pair is not really qualified for that sort of thing, but the big shots have a limited pool of trusted underlings. It would be no problem finding men to do the most atrocious things. The difficulty is in determining their loyalty. When you are so far into illegal activities as these guys are, the other side, or several other sides for that matter, could be working counter deals with your operatives making double agents out of them. Only when you go way back together, and have all shared the risks and rewards of many conspiratorial affairs, when each one knows where all the bodies are buried, does an atmosphere of trust exist, and then there are limits, as I believe there are in this case."

Fred was nodding his head. "And what you did was further reduced their limited pool of trusted thugs."

"And, kept them from talking for a few days so we have time to work this out. Cutter was running a high fever so my hope is he will be either comatose or delirious for quite awhile. Last summer they had their top terrorist running things. That was Joab Feinstein. He was born in the U.S. went to Israel where he was trained by the Mossad, and eventually joined the bunch in Chicago. Well, he died last summer. Now someone else is running things and he isn't doing so well. Jimmy Hook has a bad leg, the Iceman is dead, and Cutter and Divner are both laid up. They'll have to start sending in the second string if they have one."

"What about Holt?"

"He's a big unknown as is Harry."

"Harry?"

"After we left Harry in his hotel room that night, I returned and asked him about the major we had with us at the end of one of our crazy missions. He immediately remembered his full name and that he was with the 133 Airlift Group operating out of Minneapolis. The major's name was Bruce Holt. He said he had not considered Holt since he had been assuming he was part of another mission. When I arrived at Holt's house Cutter and Divner had already been there. I immediately assumed they had flashed their badges at my PI firm and learned about Holt. But, it might have been Harry who tipped them off."

"He seemed like a solid guy who is in this as deeply as you are. Why would he do something like that?"

"He owns a company that sells carpets, cabinets, etc. He said he did very well during the housing bubble and if money could solve this thing he had it. But, that might not be true. A lot of those guys are going bust these days. He might have needed a pile of cash to tide him over and guess what, Cutter and Divner show up with a suitcase full of money. You see, they would have researched each of us to see how we were doing and picked the weakest one as the patsy."

We had been ahead of the main rush hour traffic and made good time on our drive to Fred's house. He had a two car garage, but one bay was full of junk and my car was in the bay he normally used. I pulled up to the junk. We went in not knowing what to expect so we covered one another as we swept the rooms. All appeared to be in order. Our clothes were not the cleanest, but neither was his living room furniture so we both sank heavily into an easy chair.

We both jerked awake at the sound of the phone. It was a little after six. We let it ring until the answering machine kicked in. Typical of a bachelor, Fred had not changed the greeting that was pre-programmed into the machine when he bought it. It simply said no one was available to take the call and to leave a message.

It was Harry. "Hey, where are you guys? Vin called me Tuesday afternoon and said he had things to do and would call me back later, but he never did. It took me awhile before I decided to find you."

I was beside Fred listening and said, "Answer it. Tell him we were out of town and are back. Ask him where he is now."

Fred picked up the phone, "Harry, sorry, I was in the basement. We've been out of town. Where are you now?"

"Still in St. Louis. Didn't seem reasonable to come up there not knowing what was going on."

Fred had caller ID and I pointed to the 612 area code which we both knew was for Minneapolis.

Fred continued, "I'm not sure where Vin is now, but I'm off to work in a few minutes. I'll call you tomorrow. Do you have a number where I can reach you?"

After jotting down a number, Fred said. "The case has taken an odd turn, though we still don't know any more than we did before. I've really got to go now. I'll call. Bye."

"That was good," I said. "It means that he's local and either he or others will be here soon to 'interview' you about the 'odd turn.' You have to get out of here so pack fast, go to work and don't come back in the morning. I have your cell number. It looks like Harry might be working both sides."

There was no reason for me to keep his forty-five since I still had Divner's nine millimeter pistol, so I returned his forty-five. I waited until he was packed so we could both leave together. That would give anyone watching the house two cars to follow.

Traffic had lightened up so the drive to Henni Froom's house went well. I knew Camilla would be going nuts wondering what had happened to me. I parked in front and the door opened before I was half way up the walk. She waited for me to get into the house and hugged me.

Henni and his wife were there as was his son. We sat down and I gave them the highlights of the trip to the BWCA leaving out the shooting parts. I was pretty scruffy so while I showered the women put together some food. While I ate, it was clear everyone was dying to know the gritty details so I relayed a few of them, about the plane landing and how we had captured Cutter and Divner.

As tired as I was, there was one thing left to do. The state trooper would be waiting for my call, and it was imperative that he be let into the affair as far as possible so the whole legal system didn't fall on me.

They gave me directions to the Maplewood Mall that was nearby. At a drug store I purchased a phone card, and with it used a public phone. It rang three times and was answered with a tense, "Yes."

"This is the man from the accident earlier in the day. Is this the officer who was present?"

"Yes. You took your time in calling!"

"I suppose so," I said. "A lot has been happening."

"Tell me about it. You landed me in as rotten a situation as it's possible to imagine and I need information."

"Before you go too nuts, remember that you didn't have to pull me over. I'm not blaming you, because it was your job. But, don't dump on me for dragging you into this. Enough, though. I dropped off the two men in the back seat at what looked like a private residence in St. Paul, near the downtown area. Apparently, that's where a doctor lives who does off the record medical work in his home. The man who was shot was unconscious and running a fever, and the other man has broken hands so neither will be much danger to any of us. But, you can count on the fact that they have contacts. How about you?"

"By driving like a maniac, I managed to arrive at the scene first. The body was as you said, and I planted the gun under some leaves near it. The sheriff's department arrived a few minutes later. One of their guys found the gun. There are two problems. The young guys from the Navigator were still there and gave a clear description of you and the wounded man. There was a canoe off to the side near the landing that was from the outfitter nearby. When he was questioned he remembered the wounded man, too, and the descriptions matched. The scar on the chin was a no brainer."

He paused so I interjected, "And, what else?"

"I was getting to that. You remember I got the call about the 10-89 while I was talking to you and suggested where it might be. The dispatcher, being the gossip that she is, told everybody about how I was clairvoyant, was hearing voices and seeing visions, maybe even could be in more that one place at the same time. All those calls are recorded, of course, so it was easy to verify her story. Now I'm in trouble for letting you go. Why did this have to happen to me?"

"Stay with me. There's a lot more going on than you can imagine. Right now we need each other. Do you ever have reason to come to the metro area?"

"That's why I was waiting for your call so impatiently. I have a meeting with the head of the State Highway Patrol at ten tomorrow morning in St. Paul. They wanted me to come yet today, but I put them off. The FBI and who knows what else will be at that meeting. I have a lot of explaining to do. At the very least, I need those Secret Service IDs."

"That's easy. You'll have them along with the men if you want them. Obviously, we have to meet before your meeting. You'll probably be followed. Can you leave town in a car that nobody would suspect? You can pack along your uniform and change into it before the ten o'clock meeting. But, you must wear one part of your uniform at all times."

In a quizzical tone, he asked, "And, what part is that?"

"The part with the bullets in it. Here's where we'll meet, say at seven o'clock."

It was ten o'clock when I returned and I was beat. I'd have to be up early to meet the state trooper. Henni showed us to a guest room in the basement which was nicely done, except that the furniture didn't match. There was a bathroom in the basement that made it convenient.

Henni indicated he wanted to say something to me so while Camilla showered and brushed her teeth, we had a short discussion.

He began. "The last time you were here you remembered the name Night Hawk. I could see by your expression that it connected. Has that helped you recall anything else?"

My mind was frazzled and I knew he was only trying to be helpful, but at this particular time it was hopeless. "No. I said. Nothing of any value. There have been a few times when some things came to mind, but they were incoherent. I remember we dug something up. It's frustrating that there's no detail, nothing that really helps.

He nodded. "You're tired and should fall asleep quickly. Think about Night Hawk as you do. It might help you remember in the morning."

Ten minutes later we were in bed with the lights off. I tried to think about Night Hawk, but mostly I was wondering what would happen next. I didn't wonder for long because I hardly had time to pull a blanket over me before I was asleep.

— 18 —

Friday Evening, Vietnam

"Echo Team!"

"Yo."

"You're with the major in the corner in the back." The speaker was a master sergeant we knew as Sergeant Crag, one of our TIs, Technical Instructors.

As one, the four of us spun our heads around. A short man with a hard, intense, almost angry expression gave the slightest nod. His gray eyes were steel balls as he seemed to size us up in a second. I could almost hear his mind clicking. The two on the end will do. The next one is weak, and the last, me, I hate from all time, but he'll pull it off. And, that's all that matters.

They say you only have one chance to make a first impression. I wish that saying had never been invented because first impressions never worked for me. There is something about me that engendered instant dislike in anyone who was my superior, like hate at first sight. It's always been that way. My teachers were no exception. In grade school, every year would start the same. The teacher saw a new batch of heads full of untrained gray stuff, hers to mold in the ways of righteousness and learning. My head seemed to be filled with something else because nothing took. I always looked forward to a new school year about the same as a trip to the dentist. And, back then, the dentist didn't use novocaine. You bucked up and took it. I hated that drill!

As each year went on, I never turned out as expected. And, why should I? I never paid attention in class because I was bored out of my gourd. "Look, look. See Dick. See Dick run. See Jane. Jane runs, too. See, see. See Spot run," . . . out of my gourd! When I wasn't drawing pictures of airplanes, I was talking to the boy across the aisle, or looking at my shoes as I sat in the cloak room supposedly considering the debt I owed to society for my crimes against humanity. Actually I was thinking about shooting sparrows in the barn with my BB gun when I got home. I'd stand in the hay mow and wait for a sparrow to fly in. One had better come pretty soon or my toes will freeze so hard they'll fall off. Finally, the unmistakable flutter of wings. It perched. Slowly now, raise the gun. Pop. The bird would drop to the hay. It was satisfying, but not a cause for elation. It broke up the boredom. I'd pick it up with numb fingers and find a barn cat and throw it in its general direction. It'd find it. Those cats loved sparrows. Man, talk about fun. Ugh. Back to school. The teachers scolded me, laughed at me, ridiculed me, even talked nice to me once in awhile. Didn't work. School was boring and I have always had the lowest threshold for boredom of any person I've ever known.

I wondered what that major thought about boredom. From appearances, I had to conclude that he was never bothered by it. The only thing that intrigued me was how something chipped out of granite could move.

Who am I? I'm Double Duce. That's not my real name, of course, but my legend, or code name. We used legends so when official reports of our doings were sent in nobody would know who we were. That was good because a lot of what we did was bad, but not boring, which for me was good—the not boring, I mean, not what we did. We never knew the real names of the others we worked with. It was a security precaution so we could not get together after we were discharged and take over the government. We were all exceptionally capable men, young men, well just more than kids.

Let me introduce the other members of the team. Night Hawk is an American Indian. Strong, steady, and reliable. He can lie in one position without moving as he watches the enemy for a whole day. Boredom has no meaning for him. We are total opposites which is probably why we landed on the same team. Blue Dog is quick and resourceful, that is, more so than the rest of us. That trait would only stand out to those of us on the team because resourcefulness was something we all have in spades. He's six-two, and strong as an ox, clearly of Germanic stock, blonde, blue eyes, strong facial features. Nine Lives. Our best all around man, good at stealth, and taking out enemy guards, not as good as Night Hawk, but good. Not as muscled as the other two, but hard, and has real staying power. I'm the runt of the litter being five pounds lighter than Nine Lives, but can carry my share. What I lack in muscle mass I make up for in cussedness. My specialty is technical things, like setting explosive

charges, picking locks, and breaking things—intentionally and uninten-
tionally.

We're in a army issue field tent that has wooden pallets for a floor and
olive drab steel folding chairs to sit on. That takes a little getting used to
because if you unconsciously shift your chair a leg will slip into a crack
in the pallets causing you to tip over causing much laughter and ribbing.
It's normally the only source of amusement in these meeting tents because meetings are boring. I can rattle off the Federal Stock Number,
FSN to us in the service of our country, for every item in sight because
before I volunteered for a Phantom Team I had been in the Quartermaster
Corps filling out requests for that stuff—Boredom with a capitol "B."

The other four Phantom Teams have their leaders assigned in turn.
We're the only team that will work under a major. The others were all
assigned to senior sergeants. I take that to mean that the major is in overall charge of whatever we are to do. It's apparent that all five teams will
do the same basic thing because the assignments are all being made at
the same time. All Phantom Teams consisted of four members and today
there are no double teams as there sometimes are. That was it, the briefing ended. We all stand and are dismissed.

Granite man was gone by the time I looked around. We glanced at one
another and piled out of the tent. In the fading light we spotted the major
nearing a three-quarter ton truck. As we approached him he said, "At
ease."

His name tag sewn over his left shirt pocket was covered by a piece of
green tape. We watched over his shoulder as each of the sergeants directed their teams to waiting Huey helicopters. One thing was obvious.
They would fly to where they were going, we would drive. The major
took in the four of us with his steely eyes. Since when on operations we
wore no rank insignia there was no way of knowing who among us was
the senior man. He looked at me.

"You."

I knew from training that he meant that I was to be the leader of the
team. I walked over to him.

In a subdued voice he started, "In 1968 after the Tet Offensive, some
of the top brass became edgy about something like that happening again
so they took precautions to protect key installations. As such, certain devices were emplaced near said installations for that purpose. With the
troop draw down and America's role in this war ending, the same top
brass now wants their items recovered." He carried an eight by ten inch

brown water resistant envelope with TOP SECRET stamped on it. It had been slit open along one end. Reaching in he retrieved a topological map, opened it and placed it on the hood of the truck. Using a flashlight he continued, "We're here," he said pointing to a circle on the map. "An item was buried at this location." He pointed to another circle over rough terrain as indicated by the close contour lines. "Your mission is to recover it and return it to the Cam Ranh Bay Air Base," he parted the end of the brown envelope and produced another sheet of paper, "to the building shown on this sketch."

I looked at him with an air of expectation at which he responded.

"You're looking for an olive drab aluminum case with dimensions as shown on the diagram." On the bottom of the sketch of the air base he pointed to a hand drawn rendition of the shape and size of the case. He continued, "The team that placed it was given orders to bury it at least fifty meters from the road you'll be driving on." He indicated the road on the map. "It was to be deep enough to be covered with a foot of dirt, and camouflaged to look like the surrounding area. The displaced dirt was disposed of by scattering it around the area. He produced yet another sheet of paper with a diagram and instructions on it. "This shows how it was rigged. The sensor will be about flush with the surface of the ground. Once the sensor and the cable to the top of the case are uncovered, but before you move the case, unscrew the sensor cable from the case and replace it with this." Here he reached into the brown envelope and produced a round olive drab cap an inch and a half in diameter and three-quarters of an inch long. "Be absolutely sure you have installed this connector cover before you move the case. Is that clear?"

I took the device and pocketed it as I looked at him to see if he were serious. It seemed he was so I ventured a comment. "Yes. I understand those instruction. But, that's rugged terrain and that grease pencil circle represents an area a half klick in diameter. The probability is we won't find it if that's all we have to go on. Is there any marker they left, or directions from landmarks?"

He nodded. "There's a little help from some notes they made." He reached into the brown envelope and removed that appeared to be the only remaining item and handed it to me. "That's all the additional information I can offer."

With that he folded the brown envelope and put it into his jacket pocket. This I understood. It was stamped as classified. The items he gave me were not stamped. It was standard procedure on operations like this. There was no point in advertising the fact that you were on a secret mission, especially if you were captured. The sheet of notes was messy, obviously done in haste, with dried mud smeared on it.

After a pause he continued, "The other teams left this evening because they have further to go and their own planning to do. Since your destination is near here, you will stand down until tomorrow. This base has orders to billet and feed you." He tapped his knuckles on the hood of the truck, "This is your vehicle for the operation. Do your own backward planning from what I tell you now."

Backward planning is where you start with the time the objective must be completed, that is, the end time, and work back in time taking into account all the things that must be accomplished to reach the goal. That results in the time the operation must start.

"The other teams will return their items here tomorrow afternoon and a truck will haul them to the Cam Ranh Air Base for transport out of country. You will be, as I have said, returning yours directly to the base. You must time your operation to arrive at the building on the sketch at precisely 2200 hours on Friday. No deviation is permitted. Is that clear?"

"Yes, sir," I replied. A simple nod of the head does not suffice in situations like that.

"Good. I will see you at that hour." He turned, strode away and departed the air field in a quarter ton truck, that's a Jeep to people on the outside.

After the major drove away, the four of us got together in the tent we had been assigned. During the briefing the clouds had been thickening and now the rain came in torrents. Nothing new about that. This area of South Vietnam was under the influence of what were called the southwest monsoons which lasted from May to October. This being June meant it would be raining a good portion of the time. Our training allowed for that so we'd take it in stride. It could even be helpful to our mission if there were heavy precipitation, our sounds would be muted. It was also only human nature that the enemy would be hunkered down trying to stay dry. At other times it could be a negative.

In the light of a Coleman lantern we discussed the mission. The map showed the location of the helicopter base where we were as being west across Cam Ranh Bay from the large Air Force base. Our destination was less than ten kilometers away, though the terrain became broken after five. We had arrived in the afternoon and had picked up enough information to know that the VC, Viet Cong, were active in this part of Vietnam as they were everywhere in the country. Though, after the pounding the North Vietnamese had taken in what our side called the Easter Offensive, just now mopping up, they were less of a threat than they would have been six months before. We were going into a patch of rough terrain in an area of South Vietnam that was about half arable and half mountainous. Our destination was on the side of a ridge that snaked its way up a 5,000 foot mountain.

We decided it would be necessary to depart the helicopter base at first light and park the truck one to two kilometers from the location of the case. Two of us would stay in the area of the truck and reconnoiter that area while the other two proceeded into the location of the target with the purpose of locating hostiles and our objective in that order.

At 0500 hours we were standing in line outside the mess tent in the rain inching our way toward the cover of the canvas. Our ponchos shed most of the rain, but our boots and lower pants legs were soaked—a common condition. The atmosphere had relented somewhat as it was not slopping water on the landscape as hard as it had been through the night. Army days always started early and went late. That was one of the things I disliked most about the military—never enough sleep. Helicopter ground crews had already eaten and were out sloshing around in the mud readying the green and brown craft for another day of flight. The slippery wet surfaces of the birds reflected distant lights as they sat forlornly in the rain with drooping rotors.

The line moved fast as everyone had a schedule to keep. The steaming pans of reconstituted scrambled eggs, thinly sliced ham, soggy toast, and pineapple chunks right out of the gallon can were a welcome sight to us. Though, the pilots groused about the fare, we didn't because we spent an inordinate amount of time eating food like substances out of foil packages.

By 0600 hours we were on the road. I know, we planned to leave at first light, but that term was something of a misnomer under these conditions. Some days were even rather pleasant during the monsoon season, but not most of them. Today was in the "not most" category.

Nine Lives drove as I directed him from the map. After a half kilometer, we turned onto Highway 1, the main paved north-south road running along the coast. In fifteen minutes we were to our turn-off and it was still dark. We drove a click through what the map said was lightly inhabited country on the north side of a village. We stopped where the land became hilly with no dwellings shown on the map, though the map was woefully out of date. There was no point in going further without light.

Immediately we were all out and taking up defensive positions, two on either side of the road. The rain had stopped. By 0700 it was becoming light and the clouds were showing a few breaks in them. We had seen no local activity so climbed in and were off again. The road was nothing more than a seldom used overgrown track. The vegetation helped with the traction, but also meant the roadway was not maintained leaving washouts at places that were barely traversable. Twice we were stopped by brush that had fallen on the road. That being a perfect set-up for an ambush forced us out of the truck to clear the surrounding area of possible hostiles to say nothing of booby traps. All the effort was in vain which was fine with us.

A klick and a half, more or less, from our destination we stopped. This was as far as we were going without having a careful look-see at what was up ahead. I doubted we'd be driving much further in any case because the terrain was becoming severely broken and steep with frequent switchbacks in the road. As a whole South Vietnam was only ten percent arable meaning that most of it was unsuitable for sustained human habitation, certainly not dense population. The coastal regions were better, but even those were punctuated with rugged terrain as we now experienced. We were on the approaches to the mountain that held our objective, and it was only a few miles from Cam Ranh Bay. The abandoned road we were on was probably built for access to a now unused antenna farm on top, or possibly for logging at some time in the past when prices for timber made it worthwhile.

Night Hawk and I would proceed in a more or less straight line to the area where the case was supposed to have been buried. Nine Lives and Blue Dog would scout ahead on the road, such as it was, looking for trip wires and other signs of mines. It was important to know as early as possible how far up the road we could drive the truck.

I was on Hawk's left with him slightly ahead of me. On my left the outline of the road was visible now and then when we slipped over one or another of the innumerable minor ridges. We each carried a silenced nine-millimeter pistol and a silenced M-16 set on three round burst mode. I carried a short handled shovel strapped to my backpack while Night Hawk's pack contained sundry equipment we might need.

At the end of two hours we were nearing our approximate destination. We were all trained in the art of moving silently through the jungle and what that meant more than anything was moving with the utmost caution resulting in painfully slow progress. As our line of travel brought us within fifty meters of the road, I signaled Night Hawk to stop as I wanted to check the road where it crossed a steep cut in the hills. After twenty minutes of working myself down the steep bank I was on the road where it crossed the cut. I was glad to have made the detour. This was the end of the road for vehicular traffic and likely had been for a long time.

Arriving in sight of Night Hawk I motioned him to me. Talking in a whisper, I said, "No truck has gone past that cut in the hills in five or more years."

He nodded understanding the implications of the information. In our briefing from the major we were told the case had been taken in to be placed by truck, not delivered by helicopter. I suppose it made sense since helicopters were noisy and attracted attention. We were also told it weighed 350 pounds. We were up hill from the road. Down hill the land broke off sharply approaching vertical in places. The case was not down from the road. It also meant that regardless of where the destination circle had been placed on the map, the case was not too far from where we were crouching at the moment.

The sheet of notes I received from the team placing the case said the digging had been difficult and they had found a hollow that had collected wash-off soil. It was still difficult, but after three tries they had succeeded. That had obviously been a Phantom Team, too—succeed at any price.

We were about to start scouring the area when Night Hawk clutched my arm. Slowly he stood up sniffing the air. Frequently, our first awareness of Viet Con near us was from their smell. The lack of any sanitary conveniences as well as the spices they used with their food, left an unmistakable odor that could be sensed at considerable distances, the wind being in your favor.

Though, I hadn't smelled anything, nor heard an unusual sound, it didn't mean anything. Night Hawk had sharper senses than I. In a minute, making his way up hill and forward he was lost from sight among the vines and broad leaves that by now were more home to us than the places where we grew up. He was on the hunt. I'd seen this before. It was an animal thing with him the way he could stalk his prey.

With Night Hawk out of sight, I started off to my front and then angling up hill hoping to stay on his left flank close enough to lend assistance if needed. As always, after every half dozen steps I stopped to listen. I head it, a faint gagging sound and the rustle of foliage. Then nothing. It had come from the direction I had last seen Night Hawk moving, perhaps thirty meters away. I froze and slowly went to a stooping position. Nothing more happened so I came to a crouch and advanced five slow steps alternating scanning the area to my front and looking where I'd place my foot on the next step. Repeating this sequence a half dozen times I stopped. Slowly pulling aside a small branch, my pistol at the ready I saw the unmistakable hooked nose profile of Night Hawk's head. Sensing me, he looked my way and motioned to me.

Arriving at his side, he had a small man—the VC were all small which did not detract from their deadliness—lying on the ground face down with hands bound behind him and a gag in his mouth. His pants were down. Night Hawk pointed. I passed behind him and went to his right a few steps. The guy had been doing his daily business over a cat hole when an American Indian had appeared out of the ether and shackled him before he could take a breath.

With one eye on his prisoner, Night Hawk was at my side. He stood and gazed into the hole for fifteen seconds without moving. Finally he looked at me and raise two fingers. I nodded in agreement. The Viet Cong had a lookout or listening post near where we stood that was manned by two. Coming across an enemy latrine was a good way to estimate the size of the force you faced. It was also clear the other member of the team was within a radius of fifty meters, give or take. Nobody liked to walk a half mile to relieve himself, especially in driving rain.

By this time the man on the ground was looking at us wondering why he wasn't dead. It wasn't that we were squeamish about that, because we weren't. The fact was, we might need him. Night Hawk produced more cord from a pouch, bound the man's feet which wasn't all that necessary because his pants were still down around his ankles. He then bound an arm to a four inch diameter tree.

We looked at each other. This was no longer just a scavenger hunt, it was war. We both felt the fear welling up. At the start, it had been possible to internalize the idea that this being so close to a strong concentration of U. S. military forces, the area would be pacified. That illusion was gone. Anyone who goes into harm's way and is not afraid is either mentally deranged or doesn't understand the situation. Our training had stressed this. Discipline is needed to manage the fear and keep the senses sharp, not to let fear rule you.

From our inspection of the less than edifying portal in the ground, certainly not a subject for small talk around a banquet table, it was also clear this position had been occupied for some time. That being the case the location of the other man would not have been difficult for a blind man to find—the path was well worn. By understood agreement, each of us moved out perpendicular to the path. It would be dangerous to walk on the path or alongside of it. Something as innocuous as a branch lying across the trail could be a trip wire for a buried mine. Or, to deter someone lying in ambush of the trail, there could be mines along either side. Night Hawk had not encountered such a deterrent as he approached the man during his meditation. He would have been watching for trip wires, of course. Maybe there were no such defenses, or maybe he had been lucky.

— 19 —

The camp was in a hollow, roughly fifty meters in diameter. And, logically it would be here because there were few such depressions on this part of the mountain. The rocky land sloped into it from three sides. It appeared well drained, probably with the aid of the past and present inhabitants, though in the long past it might have been a pond filled with water at least part of the year. It was free of large trees, and some of the vegetation had been trampled or otherwise removed. A small hooch was set off to one side. There was a large flat splinter from a tree trunk laying across a couple of rocks. Two wooden rice bowls sat on it, bowl side up. They let the rain wash the dishes and at the same time collect drinking water.

The second man was not is sight, though I assumed he was in the hut. About to move to my left to come up on the side of the shanty, movement on the far side of it caught my eye. It was Night Hawk. With a stick he reached out and upset one of the rice bowls that made a rattling sound as it toppled off the makeshift sideboard. There was a grunt of displeasure followed by movement in the doorway. No sooner had the man stepped into the open when Night Hawk had him. We were all trained in taking a man down and securing him, but this man was so quick and moved with so little lost movement that it was hard to see how he did it.

Three seconds after Night Hawk made his move I was beside the door and went in low with my silenced pistol out-stretched in front of me. There was enough light to insure we had been correct in our estimation of the number of men at the post. Besides the meager housekeeping items one thing stood out, a field telephone. No doubts here. It was used to make periodic reports, and also it was likely that if the reports did not come others would be sent to investigate. We hadn't been born yesterday, and that was the reason the two men were still alive.

Not being one to let down his guard Night Hawk had disappeared into nearby foliage. When I reappeared from the hooch, still in a crouch, I heard a faint sound to my right. Night Hawk motioned me to him. In whispers, he asked, "Read those notes to me about the location of the case."

Out of my buttoned down breast pocket I produced it and as I scanned it realized my companion's interest. "Located in a small hollow. Two rocks, flat on the bottom mark the spot."

Night Hawk pointed toward two rocks. It made sense. Dirt from the surrounding mountain had washed into the hollow over eons, and left the only place on the mountain where it was possible to dig a hole several feet deep.

He had already unstrapped the shovel from my back pack and with a grin handed it to me as if presenting a trophy. Well, somebody had to do the digging and if we were to find our elusive, and much valued treasure, there would be ample time for everyone to take a hand in it.

The rocks were separated by two feet so I scraped away the soil and plant debris from that area remembering that there was supposed to be a sensor of some kind flush with the surface of the ground. It didn't take a minute and I had it. From there I dug out several shovels full and in a few minutes more heard the unmistakable sound of metal on metal. Bending over, I scooped a few hands full of dirt out of the way and saw the olive drab case.

A glance at Night Hawk was all it took. I went to him. He pointed in the direction of the latrine and then back to where we stood. Yes, that was necessary. He'd do that. Alone, I went into the hut and examined the phone. It was connected to what looked like a twisted pair of WD-1 field communications wire used by all U.S. forces. The phone was familiar too. It was a standard issue sound powered telephone with a range of five miles that needed no batteries. With the VC so intermixed with the general population, and with the South Vietnamese selling anything they could lay their hands on, it was common to find the enemy using as much U.S. equipment as their own.

There was a coil of excess wire behind the bench on which it rested. Convenient. Inspecting the phone for trip wires, I saw none so moved it to the door of the hooch. Night Hawk returned with his prisoner, pants pulled up.

We had a short strategy session, short was all that was possible with my compadre. Of the two of us, he was better at noiselessly traversing the jungle so he could return to the truck faster than I could. He'd have

Blue Dog and Nine Lives back the truck in to the place of the washout. I'd stay with the prisoners. Without a sound he was gone.

We decided to put the lowest ranking man to sleep and keep the other one awake to answer the phone if a call came in. Frequently, higher authorities wanted to "interview," that is, interrogate the VC we captured. And, there were times when we didn't want any trouble from them so we had a sleep drug that was easy to apply by automatic syringe.

All U.S. soldiers knew about the automatic injection technique. In basic training recruits were given rudimentary CBR training. That stands for Chemical, Biological, and Radiological warfare. For the chemical part there was the ever present danger of nerve gas. Thankfully, there was a good antidote for it, called atropine. But, it had to be administered within seconds after coming into contact with nerve gas or the soldier lost control of his limbs as he went into spasms. In the canvas satchel that contains the man's gas mask was a small pocket with three automatic applicators in it that are about the size of a fat crayon with a rounded end. All that was required was for the soldier to press the rounded end against his thigh. The pressure released a spring that drove the needle through clothing and into the muscle. Another internal spring forced the atropine into the tissue. The whole process took only a second. The needle was an inch long and as thick as a No. 2 pencil lead so there was no worry about breaking it off. The special forces people had adapted the devices for the administration of the sleeping drug. There was a second type of applicator with the drug's antidote. We carried these devices as standard equipment on every mission.

With one man asleep, I blindfolded the other in addition to his gag. I went to the place of our find and carefully scooped out the dirt around the sensor cable where it connected to the case. I carefully unscrewed the cable connector and taking the device the major had given me, I screwed it on over the cable connector. It was a little difficult because I had to compress what felt like a spring to start the threads. But, all in all, it went okay. Now we were ready to dig the case out and vacate the place as soon as they returned. Looking at my watch, it was five minutes to ten.

At one minute after ten the phone clacked. A field phone clacked because a clacking sound was easier to hear over battle noise than a ringing bell. I had expected this. The man from the latrine was left awake so I removed his blindfold and gag holding the phone receiver to his ear with my left hand. With the other hand I pressed the cold steel of my silencer against his temple.

He knew the story. If others were sent to rescue him, win or loose, he'd be the first to die. Though I didn't understand the language, I would be able to detect uncertainty or excitement of snapped orders. The receiver was tilted away from his ear enough so I could hear the other side of the conversation, too. Boy, these guys really smelled bad. There were a few exchanges and the line went dead. I replaced the receiver and then his gag and blindfold.

Waiting was the hardest, especially in a dangerous situation. It was hard for me to remain alert, the old boredom thing, though the fear of enemy reinforcements arriving and finding me alone took the edge off it. To stay alert, I moved back from the two men. From time to time I'd change locations to take in the surroundings from other angles. Things had been going too well. The worrisome thing was the listening post right on top of our prize. Time would be critical. There was no telling what the guy had said on the phone. Maybe a situation like this had been anticipated so that even if I had fluently understood Vietnamese, I would have missed the code word that meant he was a captive. Maybe the men at this post were the ones who were supposed to initiate the report. One case of a late call and the higher echelon having to call instead might be put off as lack of attention. But, not another time.

I glanced over at the captives and from what I saw now or could remember, neither man was wearing a watch. Maybe there was a time piece in the hooch. I dared not be out of sight of the men long enough to check. And, again, maybe the timing wasn't so important other than a call in, say, midmorning. Boy, I wished those guys would get back.

Using the waiting time to best advantage, I began planning the retrieval of the case. The size wasn't too much of a problem, the weight was—over 350 pounds. It would be hard lifting it out of the hole especially with dirt and rocks jammed in along the sides. It was unlikely they had dug the hole even two inches larger than needed. All aluminum cases the Army used had handles on the sides. This one would, too. I had noted a heavy handle on the top that was more like a lifting eye. Okay, it was taking shape. We'd cut eight or ten foot poles. We'd dig around it as far as we could. Then, putting ropes in the lifting handle, we'd use the two rocks as fulcrums and lever the case up. But, that would only lift it six to twelve inches so we'd need a means to hold it up as we shortened the ropes on the levers. More rope, and a third pole perpendicular to the other two across the hole. Two such cycles and we would have it up enough for two of us to hoist it out. Any one of us could lift two hundred pounds in a dead lift, especially Blue Dog and Night Hawk.

I moved to a new position. There had been no sound except the sound of the trees as the wind gusted through the upper branches. That was not good as it would mask the sounds of the enemy moving up. It had been an hour and a half since I had been left alone. Leaving a man alone was something almost never done, but with such a small team there had been no choice. The rain started, only a sprinkle but that would change as the sky darkened.

There, movement to my right! In practiced fashion, I rolled back and came up with my pistol in the right hand. Then I saw the teeth. It was Night Hawk grinning. The rat, took ten years off my life. He edged over to me.

"We're all here, how do you see it?"

I told him my plan. I also told about the call. He nodded and held up a hand extending three fingers. I didn't see anything nor did I expect to. He knew where the other two would be. Three fingers meant to expect hostiles to be approaching. He checked the bonds on the prisoners. Satisfied, we attacked the problem. The two of us working together managed to move back each rock a foot or two, then we started digging. In ten minutes we had it uncovered far enough to determine there were two handles on each side as if it were meant to be carried by four men. Looping a rope through the top handle we both lifted. It was stuck. The lever method would be needed. Our standard tools included only one small folding saw, but it would have to be enough. While Night Hawk went for pry bars, I continued digging around the case.

The team that buried it had worked hard. They must have had to pry loose and heft out a lot of rocks as they dug. As a result various shards of rock lined the sides of the hole making it impossible to dig much away along the sides of the case to free it from its lodging. It had started raining harder and I used removed dirt to build a dam around the hole so it wouldn't fill with water. Nigh Hawk returned with one pole, taking deep breaths. There was strain showing in his face. It was taking too long. He returned to the thicket. Minutes later he returned with another one. By this time I had ropes reeved through the top handle and was ready for a pole.

He slipped one pole through a loop of rope and let it rest on a rock with the far end six feet in the air. Again on the other side. We both grabbed a pole twisting and shoving it to the highest part of our respective rocks. We made eye contact and he whispered, "Together." The case scraped but it came up twelve inches. I had rolled a third rock to the approximate place where the end of my pole would come to the ground. I knelt on the end of the pole and worked the rock in place to hold my pole down. This permitted me to go to the hole and jamb dirt and small stones between the case and the wall to prevent it from sliding back and losing our gain.

I nodded to Night Hawk who let up on his pole. The case settled a few inches but our gain was good. I was retying the rope for another lift when he whispered, "The phone."

Being occupied with the work, and with the rain I had not heard it.

I was up and dashed to the two men, yanked off the gag and put the receiver next to the ear of the same man. He started talking in the same conversational tone as he had the first time. Suddenly he blurted out what sounded like some expletives. The butt of my pistol landed on his head ending the conversation. Night Hawk was beside me.

"The alarm is out," I said. "We have to move!" He gave a low trill like a bird call and it was answered. In a half minute we were all at the location of the case. With the poles slipped through the ropes, and one man on the end of each pole, we all lifted. It wasn't coming. We worked it side to side. It was coming up when one of the poles snapped.

I said, "Nine, the saw, another pole. We'll worry away at this and try to wiggle it out if we can." He snatched up the folding saw and disappeared. Using the longer part of the broken pole, we levered up one side a few more inches. We were back to prying it up by shortening the ropes every few inches. After ten minutes we had it up high enough so we could roll it out or the hole. Blue Dog ran in the direction Nine Lives had gone and was back in seconds with him. We each grabbed a handle and starting trotting to the edge of the hollow in the direction of the truck. On the hillside out of the hollow Night Hawk suddenly released his hold and disappeared back the way we had come his M-16 at the ready.

The snap of silenced shots was unmistakable. Enemy reinforcements had arrived. It was my call so I said, "You two will have to get the case to the truck while we hold them off. Once its loaded get out of here. It's close enough so we can make our way back in a few hours."

There were no argument since the success of the mission was all important. The last I saw of them they were rolling the case down the slope. Lucky it's not up hill, I thought.

Night Hawk was ten meters up hill from me. I went to him and told him the situation. He nodded. If it had been put to a vote the same action would have been agreed upon. I hated to admit it, but this was exactly by the book. With only the four of us, there was little room for improvisation. He motioned me down the hill a short distance as he indicated he'd move up hill.

The rain slacked off to a sprinkle after a particularly hard downpour. The intensity of the rain didn't matter since hard or light, both had advantages and disadvantages. I caught movement and fired a three-burst. There was a grunt followed by substantial fire. It came as no surprise that we faced a superior force. I fell behind a low course of rock and slid along on my belly, then in a crouch ran ten meters stopping behind a tree. Up hill there was sustained fire, some returned by Night Hawk, I thought, but it was hard to tell with his silenced weapon. Using more rocks as cover I worked my way up hill until I saw Night Hawk lying behind a rock. He was sliding on his stomach to a point of cover behind a tree. As soon as he was away from the rock I heard the shot buzz of a ricochet. This was common because most ricochets impacted something before traveling far. Night Hawk slumped flat on the ground. It could have been because he realized he was exposed and was attempting the lowest profile. His body quivered. I had a dark feeling as I inched up behind the rock he had moments before left and whispered, "Hawk!"

No movement. The leaves of small undergrowth plants made him only partially visible and some were covering most of his head, or so I thought. Then I realized what I was seeing, most of his head wasn't there. He had taken a close ricochet and was dead in less than a heart beat.

There was no time to waste, but I stayed a moment without moving as I whispered, "May God give you angel's wings to fly to the light, oh Hawk of the night. Good bye, brother warrior."

I sat on the edge of the bed wiping the perspiration off my face. Camilla moved beside me and said, "Are you all right? You cried out, 'Night Hawk.' You had a flashback, didn't you?"

She flipped on a small reading light. I nodded as I held out my hand palm toward her so she wouldn't say anything more. The whole chain of events was clear to the minutest detail as if it were yesterday except that the shape and size of the case were not there. The more I tried to recall it, the more frustrating it became. Yet, it seemed the way we were handling it, the size and weight were right for the MADM we had learned about.

Finally I said, "Yes. A large part of a mission came back in detail, and I think it was the one about the thing they want. The only information missing is what it looked like. Everything was so clear. I'm sure it was the thing we have been assuming."

She was lying on her side supporting her head with her hand. "Well, does that matter? Do you remember what you did with it? That's what we need."

I shook my head. "No. The dream, flashback, or whatever you want to call it, only went as far as my teammate, Night Hawk, being killed. We had located it, dug it out, and were under attack as we were attempting to get away. Night Hawk and I were holding them off while two others of the team were tumbling it down the hill to where they had left the truck. It's possible I may never have seen it again after that." I paused and looked around the room. This was a fantastic journey, slipping from the present to the past and back again. "I suppose it stopped where Night Hawk was killed because that particular few seconds came back to me as I was talking to Henni a few days ago. That was painful, but it might mean that I have to recall further traumatic events before the rest of the story fills in."

She tugged at my arm and I fell back in bed even more tired than the evening before. It seemed like I should have been more upset, but I was soon asleep again.

— 20 —

7:15, Friday

I was waiting in the parking lot of the old Arden Hills Library. I chose that place because it was a public space, with a secluded area a couple of dozen steps to the north, and it was easy to find. All my state trooper friend had to do was exit I-35W at County Road E2, turn left and two blocks later there it was on his left. He was late, but it was a five hour drive from Ely, and he had to do all the driving himself. He would have had to leave home at two in the morning. The small late model Toyota pulled in and stopped beside my car with an empty space between. From my first glance I could see John Witherton, the name from the card he had given me, was a tired man. He probably had little sleep the night before.

When he was talking to us at the accident outside of Ely I didn't see his features clearly as one normally doesn't when talking to a cop. One got the feeling that the uniform with the rank and unit patches on it along with the weapons belt provided them with a personal aura of invincibility just as it was supposed to render a feeling of submissiveness in those they faced. Here, stripped of his physical and mental crutches, he looked like a man who was alone and vulnerable. The crows foot creases on the outside of his eyes were pronounced as if he had spent his entire life squinting, which was the case now. His lips were a little thin and absent of color. With no hat, his light brown hair with specks of gray was obvious. His grooming was impeccable as one would expect. He was not smiling, though it didn't seem that he was particularly angry. It was more a look of bewilderment.

He did not offer to shake hands as he approached, a sign that he didn't particularly trust me. That was fine as I felt the same about him. We knew where we stood. I said, "Let's walk a little so we are out of sight of the street."

He nodded. As he turned his left arm swung back drawing his jacket tight against his chest revealing the lump that was a shoulder holster. That was fine, too. He was armed. I was not and as he was the law and I didn't have a permit to carry—you never knew. As soon as we were down the slope toward the pond that lay a hundred yards from the cars we were out of sight among bushes and trees. I withdrew the two Secret Service IDs from my pocket and handed them to him.

He flipped them open and recognized the faces on the pictures as the men in the back seat of the Blazer. "It would have helped a lot if I had these yesterday," he said.

"I'm not so sure. Those two guys are not regular Secret Service agents. The IDs may be authentic because they work for people at the very top and could get anything they wanted." After a pause I asked, "Were you able to do anything with the prints from the gun?"

"Yeah. I managed to convince the sheriff to print the man and the gun. I learned later in the day that they matched, no problem there."

"How about the identity of the assassin?"

"What can I say, you were right. They are from a man who died in Iraq in 2004. As for the registration of the gun, nothing came up, it was clean—never existed."

There were no trails in this part of the wild land that was mostly swamp so we walked slowly talking in low voices as we ducked around branches. I gave him a short version of the Phantom Teams and the story as current as my flashback from the night before. Then, I described what had happened to Harry and me in the last few days leaving out certain items as I saw fit.

"Have you ever heard of an M-A-D-M?, "I asked.

He shook his head.

"That's what this is all about and what makes it so scary. MADM stands for Medium Atomic Demolition Munition. It's an atomic bomb made in the sixties and was placed on antiaircraft rockets, as well as being intended as an atomic land mine. It's the latter version that we're talking about. We looked it up on the Internet and it really did exist, the last of them being decommissioned in the early nineties. It has an adjustable output from one to fifteen kilotons. There are highly placed sources in the Federal Government who think that if I'm stressed enough, I can remember where a missing one is hidden. Maybe they're right. I have been under a lot of stress lately and did have a detailed recall last night as

I mentioned. From that it seems likely I was part of the team that dug it up. Maybe I had something to do with hiding it, too."

He stopped walking and looked at me. His face had gone a few shades whiter. "If I draw a few conclusions here, what you're saying is that if they simply wanted to find it so they could dispose of it before terrorists got their hands on it, they would not be sending assassins who have been dead for years nor other men with fake Secret Service credentials. And this just to stress you so you remember where it is?" The incredulity of the situation was evident.

I nodded. "You've drawn the same conclusions we have. A further inference we can make is that some of those at the top of our government are—there's no other word for it—terrorists. The remaining questions are where is it, and what they intend to do with it? Therefore, you have to understand that we must find it first and make a big public display about the finding—by total accident if we can manage that—so the whole world knows about it. And, in the process it would be best if the whole world also knew that those very people in the government had taken possession of it so they could never, ever, use it. You can see the problem we face. If any of us, including you, flubs up in any way so that the death of the assassin up north can be swept under the rug, they'll keep looking until they find it even if they have to fry my brain in the process. Then, they will clean up loose ends with extreme prejudice, and you will be one of those loose ends."

He was looking like a defeated man. "I have a wife and three kids. Law enforcement doesn't have to be dangerous if a man keeps his focus. But, this is so far beyond anything I ever mentally prepared for, I can't get a hold of it. I'm floundering."

His pain was obvious, as was his despair so I had to pump him up. "No. You are not floundering! It's just an outrageously unlikely situation. You are still facing men who put their pants on one leg at a time, just like a murderer or drunken driver. Life has risks and law enforcement has more than most professions. However, being a roofer is far more dangerous than being a cop."

He looked at me askance. "Are you kidding me about roofers?"

"No I'm not. At one time I looked up the most dangerous professions in the U.S. and law enforcement didn't even make the top ten. However, this situation *is* dangerous, make no mistake about that. In a way it was fortunate that you were drawn into this because at some point we were going to have to get legitimate authorities involved. Better state than something like the FBI. They are by definition Federal, and hence owned by the bad guys."

We had started making our way back to the cars. "Why did I ever tell you to pull over by that accident?"

I had the urge to smile, but didn't. He was tired and a little too close to the edge. "Just before we made eye contact I saw an expression of total boredom on your face. There you were, the authority figure who had to remain in charge, and of what? A little more than a fender bender. The people were stunned and walking around dazed. You needed any excuse to keep yourself from screaming at the klutzes, something more demanding of your talents and training—you found it."

He offered no comment because I suspected I had hit pretty close to home. I handed him a slip of paper with the address of where we dropped off Cutter and Divner. It also listed the phone numbers I was to call if it had become necessary to abandon the two of them in the wilderness.

"Try to meet with the head of the troopers before the meeting at ten and do your best to convince him to keep the Feds out of it, or at least keep them from knowing what's really going on. If this makes it back to Washington by official channels, there's no way of knowing what'll happen. We have to find that thing and open up their whole sordid plan to the news media before they can make any more moves. If any of your people have some suggestions, I'm listening. If you think you're scared, think about me. This has been going on for longer than I care to remember."

It seemed he was in better shape now that he had been briefed. We were about to go to the cars when I thought of something. "There's one more complication. You remember the FBI agent who was driving when you pulled us over? "

"That's another thing. You lied to me. He wasn't and FBI agent, he was an *ex*-FBI agent. We checked him out."

"Well, maybe I stretched the truth a little. We were in a tight spot. If you had hauled us in Cutter or Divner would have made one phone call. They would have been released and Clements and I would have been in jail. If this thing exists, one way or another they'll find it. You have to believe that so we must get there first. Anyway, Clements has been quite helpful in getting as far as we are. Without him I couldn't have done it. He wants his job back with the FBI. When this is all done it would be nice if it could be made to look like he was not ex-FBI but it was made to look that way so he could work under cover. It's important the people in your organization take that seriously because this in not over by a long way. He is one of a handful of us who know what's happening. If he feels snubbed, he could go public prematurely and really screw things up. So it isn't so much a request as a fact that must be dealt with, and dealt with carefully."

He nodded. By a bit after eight, we were standing by his car. "I need a place to change into my uniform."

"Follow me home. The garage is empty so I'll open the garage door and you drive in on the right and I'll come in on the left. You can change in the garage."

Our place looked undisturbed as we drove up. He changed as I made a quick check of the house. All was in order. As he was about to leave in his spiffy uniform, I could see he looked better. For a lot of guys like him, the uniform was more a benefit to them than the public. "Try to keep me informed about what happens, if you can. We all have jobs and I'm taking vacation again today, but I'm about to run out of time I can take off. We have to move ahead. I just don't know what to do. It's maddening."

When he drove away, I decided that there was little reason to stay with the Frooms. First, if someone wanted to find me, especially after meeting with the trooper, they would. And second, it might put them in danger. It was also obvious that I'd have to meet with Harry. It would be nice to know what was going on with him. I was about to call Camilla and tell her to come home when I had another idea. There was something that had to be taken care of. I'd be home about noon and I'd call her then.

The PIs office was in downtown Minneapolis. I hated to go there because the buses owned the streets in true politically correct style. After all everybody should be riding the bus and saving the environment except that the members of the City Council, and State Legislature who made the rules wouldn't be caught dead darkening the door of a bus. They were better then the rest of us slobs. After the bus problem it was the general feeling of coldness about that particular part of the city. From the number of police visible it also appeared that it was a war about to happen.

After finding a parking space in a suitably inconvenient and exorbitantly expensive parking ramp, I exited the elevator at the seventeenth floor of what I hoped was the right steel and glass palace. A bronze plaque announced the suite number of the gum shoe business that was the objective of my sortie into piled high land.

The entry to the sleuth lair was lavishly appointed, or so it seemed to me. Perhaps a more discerning eye would have perceived that the Persian carpets were commercial polyester floor coverings sold by the acre, and the ornate lamps by the sofas were production line plastic straight from the sweat shops in Mexico. One of the sofas was occupied by a man whose face was hidden by a newspaper.

The receptionist was middle aged and suitably frumpy. She had the requisite head set with a small microphone to the side of her mouth. After taking a nip on her diet soda that was suitably accouted in a fuzzy cozy, she said in a guarded tone as if she wasn't sure I was worth talking to, "May in help you?"

"Yes, I hope so. I'm here to see Avery Fallon."

"What's your name?"

"Vin Wessen."

"Do you have an appointment?"

"No. But, I've been having him do quite a bit of work for me lately and this is very important. Is he in?"

She responded with her best condescending glare. After a pause long enough to let the expression of disdain register with me she replied, "You need an appointment. We are not some back street operation. Our agents are very much in demand and very busy."

"Well then, maybe you will not be so *very* much in demand when I put word out on the street that you can't be trusted to keep your client's business confidential. Is he in!"

The sound of the newspaper crinkling behind me was obvious.

"There's no call to raise your voice, Mr. Wessen."

Only her fingers moved as she pressed a series of keys on the phone board. In a voice that was nearly inaudible to me, and certainly to no one else in the room, she said, "Mr. Fallon, you have a client, a Vin Wessen, who demands to see you immediately. I suggest he might be worth a moment of your time."

His reply, of course, was not audible to me, but his response was. I had met Fallon only once and almost didn't recognize him as he approached me seconds later. The sandy haired six foot man of thirty-five was trim and from appearances was in good physical shape. His blue eyes had no sign of warmth, but then I always found blue eyes, like mine, were hard to discern. Maybe it was a blue eye on blue eye thing.

His hand shake was cordial as was his greeting. He led the way to his office. He took a seat in an upholstered swivel chair behind a desk leaving that customary piece of furniture as a psychological barrier between him and the people he met. The room was moderately Spartan with a few pictures of landscapes on the walls, probably off the wall of the furniture store that supplied the desk.

He spoke as soon as he was seated. "Gladys expressed that there was a certain urgency in your visit. While we, as a firm, certainly do appreciate your business, I do have a crowded schedule today. How may I help you?"

So far his response was exactly as one would expect from a competent professional who had all the business he could handle. It was a situation where I had to get him to reveal the truth by his expression and body language.

"Monday morning of this week, you had two unexpected visitors, didn't you?"

His expression was neutral. "I wasn't in the office Monday morning."

Great. It was hard to learn anything from a reply like that. Certainly, he didn't seem uncomfortable.

"Please ask Gladys to step in here. It'll only take a minute."

He hesitated. "That will leave the front desk unattended, I can't do that."

Was that true, or a ploy? "The two men I refer to were from the presidential detail of the Secret Service. If they were here it is most important that we both know. Call her in here."

Fallon jerked his hand as if to reach for his phone, then pulled back, then reached for it. He pressed a button. "Gladys. Please come to my office for a few seconds. It's important."

There was no response, but in the time it took to walk from the front desk there was a light knock on the door which opened immediately.

"Come in and close the door." Noticeably agitated, Fallon asked, "Were there some unexpected visitors here Monday morning asking for me. And since I was out, did they perhaps ask for the person in charge or anything like that?"

The smugness was gone. Slowly, shaking here head, she said, "No. I would remember that. Nobody. I will, of course, check the log, but I'm certain there was no one."

"Okay. Thank you. Check the log and if something shows up let me know. That's all."

Fallon seemed to sink into the stuffed chair in relief. If he were lying, it was a perfectly rehearsed act.

After a few seconds he leaned forward. "Does that answer your concern?"

"Possibly. You almost certainly don't know the implications of what I asked. If those two men would have been here, they would have sworn you and everyone else in this outfit to secrecy, national security, imminent threat, and all that. You understand?"

He nodded. I continued. "What I have said and am about to say is extremely confidential. Not from the national security stand point or anything like that, but from the 'your staying alive' stand point." I raised my eyebrows as if in a question to see if he understood. Again, he nodded, though his expression had changed to revealing apprehension.

I continued, "There was a vital piece of information that got out and I'm not sure how that happened. This firm was one possibility. For now, I'll go on the assumption that you were not the leak." He was noncommittal in his expression and said nothing.

"However, on another matter, I need some immediate help. You remember that over a week ago, my wife called this place in the late afternoon asking information on a Mr. Harry Auston. In fact all she had was a car license number."

Fallon turned to his computer and made some entries. It took less than a minute. "I was out, but one of the technicians did the data search your wife requested. Was the information satisfactory?"

"Yes. It was more than adequate at the time. Now, I need something more that should be easy for someone with your resources. Harry Auston owns a business. Is it in financial trouble, or is he generally financially stressed? Is he behind on his home mortgage payment, anything like that? Can you get that for me while I wait?"

Fallon was business a usual now. "I simply don't have the time. You must understand. How about if I fax it to your home in a couple of hours? I could put a technician on it and he will be thorough."

I thought a minute and said, "Yes, that will be fine. Also, if he has been in difficulties, try to determine if he has had a recent infusion of cash."

"Will do."

I got up to leave and he stepped around the desk to say good bye. As a parting remark, I said, "First, tell Gladys not to mention anything about my inquiry about the unexpected visitors. And, if by chance they, or similar types do show up, will you please inform me regardless of what they say. All is not as it appears in this case."

He did a second take, and then I think he got the idea that I was implying that there were rogue elements at play. He nodded.

— 21 —

After lunch I was sitting on the patio when I heard tires on the tarmac. My position was such that I could see it was the Toyota. This was no surprise, in fact I had rather expected it. John Witherton strode over to me and said, "You wanted to be kept up to date so here I am. I've been assigned to stay around town for a time to be determined."

I suggested we go in the house and he readily agreed. I asked if he wanted a bite to eat and he said he had had a sandwich downtown. With that he let go as if a cork had popped out of his head.

He started with this, "Do you suppose your house is bugged? I'd hate to have any of this get out past you."

"It's bugged, but I've swept the place and found them all and I keep moving them around. Whoever placed them—I assume it was Cutter and company—still hears things but only what I want them to hear. Where we are now is completely safe."

He didn't bat an eye as if he were in the head offices of the CIA.

"That's good. You're on the ball. That was the most intense morning I've ever spent. The head of the state police—that's what the troopers are—took what I said without too much comment. Apparently, he goes back a ways with the Sheriff of St. Louis County. And, the Sheriff is spooked. The Secret Service IDs were whisked off seconds after I entered his office."

I sat on the sofa and while he started relating the morning's events seated in an easy chair, he had stood up and was pacing the floor.

"Wow, you were right. We have some pretty good people who looked at the 'paper.' Then, they called in some experts they knew from the St. Paul Police Department, too. They all agreed, the IDs were not forgeries. But, get this. When we had a routine check made of the numbers on them it turns out that they were from a series that had never been used. Perfectly legitimate credentials, and totally fake!"

They were *told* the numbers came from a series that had never been used. But, where they? How honest were the Feds when dealing with state agencies?

As he was speaking, the gestures of his arms augmented his words. He was worked up, in fact, too worked up. The stress and lack of sleep were taking their toll. I began to feel that some of what he was about to tell me was stuff I was not intended to hear, and which I probably didn't want to hear. I'd have to take it all to get the information I needed, though.

I nodded and he continued.

"The part I can't figure is when I mentioned that you said it involved an atomic bomb, they didn't argue much. They asked how you would know and when I told them the story about your meeting in the park and that Harry pried that information out of the Divner guy they bought it. By the way, both Cutter and Divner are real people who are alive, or at least are alive as far as anyone can tell."

Here I stopped him lest I forget to ask about something he said. "Why was the Sheriff of St. Lewis County spooked?"

"Well, okay. The evening of the day before yesterday a couple of tired women paddled out of the wilderness at Lake One and first thing they called the Sheriff's Office. They reported how they had been bound and gagged earlier in the day on Hudson Lake followed by a shoot-out and then an airplane that landed on the lake, another shoot-out and the plane taking off. And, just before the plane took off a guy from the plane yelled the name Wessen. Anyway, that had all the marks of illegal entry."

"Wait," I said. "The U.S. borders are like sieves. That must happen all the time."

"Yes and no. Yes, the borders are poorly guarded but most of the illegals come across from Mexico. But, ten percent of them are caught. For high value terrorists, ten percent isn't good enough odds so they try novel methods, like paddling across the Canadian border in a canoe at night and then being picked up by a float plane. So, no, that method is not common and as a result it raises all kinds of flags.

"Anyway, the Sheriff was about to call the INS when the report of the dead man in the bushes came in. He rushed off to the scene and what does he find? A dead man shot in the head by someone who knew what he was doing, like by an assassin. Yet, he had a silenced pistol himself that had been shot three times. An assassin who had been assassinated. That changed the picture. Then I get into the game with my wild story about Secret Service agents, one of whom was wounded, and both are the prisoners of an FBI agent who turns out to be an ex-FBI agent. And the man who seemed to be in charge had the name of Wessen. Now, it's all connected and not as simple as illegal entry. So, they agreed to sit on it until you called me in the evening. I almost busted a gut waiting for your call."

No wonder he was wound up. He was the key to what could be one of the biggest stories of the decade. And, guess what, it was a big story, bigger than anything any of them could have imagined.

"What came next really blew me away. Well, in retrospect maybe not."

He stopped pacing and put his hands on his hips focusing his eyes on infinity. With a snap he was back into his narrative.

"They wanted the whole pie for themselves, the state police, I mean. 'If the bomb is in our state, well, the darned thing is ours.' There were two others at this initial meeting and as they discussed it I never heard so much bad-mouthing of the FBI. When I said you suggested that we keep the Feds out of it they said, 'No brainer there.' Apparently the FBI is quite politicized."

He paused and I asked, "How many people know about the bomb?"

"The three at the first meeting and me. The chief and the other two are buddies from almost childhood, I gathered. So, I got the feeling they won't spread it around, at least, not for awhile. But, they are political animals, make no mistake about that. Me, I hate that garbage and am happy to be as far away from that St. Paul snake pit as possible."

I shifted my position on the sofa and he took it to mean that I thought the report was over. He raised his index finger as if to warn me not to move.

"By ten o'clock, the time for the real meeting, the three of them had hatched a plan, a pretty good one it seems to me. The FBI guys were late as our guys said they'd be. You know, make the state boobs know that they were second class citizens. There were two men from the FBI and a woman from the ATF, you know the silencer on the gun. That alone will keep a couple of hundred easily amused bureaucrats busy for days." He held his hand out palm toward me. "Those aren't my words. Boy, when they're in the mood to let go at federal agencies, they can really do it."

He was letting down as the story came out, but wasn't done yet.

"A short time after I arrived they sent someone out to check on the doctor's house where you said you left the wounded man. He was back before the ten o'clock meeting saying there was no answer at the door. From records they found that a semi-retired doctor lives there so that figures. There was nothing else they could do but keep someone in the area to watch the place. A search warrant would require revealing too much so that was out for the time being."

I suggested that since I had dropped the men off there, they would know the place was compromised and would have moved them by now. He said they had come to the same conclusion.

"The meeting wrangled around with the FBI suspecting they weren't being told everything. They were left with a strange set of circumstances that looked like an INS case. The INS would undoubtedly try to locate the plane and pilot and other witness. All the people going into the BWCA legally have permits so they will be contacted when they came out."

I was glad when he finally sat down.

He looked at me with a special intensity. "Now for the best part."

I could hardly wait.

"You gave me those phone numbers from the Divner guy, you know, the ones you were to call after you left them in the wilderness to die of thirst. With all the fuss preparing for the meeting, I forgot about them until after the meeting. The guys I was talking to knew what they were doing when it came to things like that. One of the underlings said, 'Lets go for the gold and call Seth Goldman.' It seemed that they had all heard of him. Well, what can I say, right again. He told Goldman that Flavian Cutter had been shot in the shoulder. After a short pause he said, 'Yes I assumed you knew, but I doubt you know how bad off he is. He'll die if he stays with that retired doctor in St. Paul.' After another pause when I got the impression that Goldman was asking who was calling and how he got the number he replied, 'Where else, Cutter gave it to me. He said you'd want to know. That's all. Good bye.'

"After the call they decided not to call the other number for now. The guy said that from the voice it had to be Goldman. Now it began to sink in that the two fake Secret Service men really did work for the Oval Office. They slumped back in their chairs and for the first time nobody had anything to say. It was like a morgue. I kept looking from one to the other. To me it made sense. Everything else you had said checked out from the location of the dead man who had been killed years ago to the match of the cadaver's finger prints to the silenced gun to the fake IDs that were not fake. This really hit home, though. It was like they had been humoring me about the bomb and didn't want to be laughed at by the Feds if they mentioned it. Now, it was real and guess what, it was in their lap. And also guess what, they couldn't go to the Feds because the Feds had become the enemy. Who was it that said, 'We have met the enemy and he is us?'"

"The cartoon character, Pogo."

"Never knew that."

There was one more item. "How about Fred Clements?"

"Oh, yes. That really made them squirm. I mentioned it early on, and it was also the last thing we discussed. They accepted the requirement that he be kept in the loop so he doesn't go rouge. As for him getting his job back at the FBI, once the Feds are left out of the glory it will be hard to call in any favors. At the worst or maybe the best, he might get a job with the state police, who knows? Right now his future employment is not high on their list of priorities."

"What are those guys going to do while we wait for something to happen?"

He leaned his head back in the easy chair and I was afraid he'd fall asleep. "Hey, John."

Jerking alert he looked at me not really focusing. "What does anybody do? More specifically, what are you going to do? There are high expectations. Those people are already spending their pay raises, basking in their accolades, and looking at the next rung to climb." After a pause, "I'm played out—got to take a little nap."

"No," I said. You need a good sleep. Come on, we'll dump your tuck-uss into the rack where you can zonk out properly." I had seen the condition many times in the army. A man goes too long on no sleep, too much caffeine, and a lot of stress. Finally the brain shorts out and the mind shuts down. That was happening. I had to get him to a place where we wouldn't trip over him while he was out.

I was up and pulled on his hand until he was standing after which I led him down the hall and into the spare bed room. The front of our treadmill sort of blocked part of the side of the bed, but I threw back the spread, blanket and sheet. "Take your gun off. You can lay it on the treadmill so it'll be handy."

He did as I bid him, sat on the side of the bed and fell over, his head luckily hitting the pillow. I lifted up his legs and slipped off his shoes, pushed him further on the bed so he wouldn't fall out, and flipped the sheet and blanket over him. He was down for the count.

Back in the kitchen, I took the business card he had written his home phone on and called it. His wife answered. I explained as much as I dared and said he'd call when he woke up which might not be for awhile. She was worried but accepted it and thanked me for caring enough to call her.

After that I called Camilla and told her to come home. When I told her we had a guest, she said she'd stop and pick up some groceries and would be home in an hour. From experience, I knew that meant more like two hours. I never knew anyone who could take so long shopping for groceries. She had to pick up every tomato on the pile before taking the first one she touched. What works, works, I guess. In any case I locked the front and back doors sat in my favorite easy chair, and put my feet on the ottoman. It didn't take long before I was asleep, too.

— 22 —

The rattle of the back door being opened jerked me awake. From the rustle of paper bags I took it to be Camilla rather than a SWAT team. After all, they smashed doors down.

"Why didn't you have him park on the other side? He's blocking my side of the garage."

"I didn't expect him to be staying and he's asleep fully clothed in his crisply pressed uniform. I managed to get his gun off, but that was it." I explained what had happened, that he hadn't slept last night, and the turbulent morning he had.

She nodded and said for the hundredth time she was sick of the whole business. I took her to the sofa and we sat down together. I put my arms around her and we just sat there. Finally she said, "The ice cream is melting in the car." It seemed that's the way it always was. We couldn't even relax for a minute. I went out to get the rest of the groceries looking for anything out of place in the neighborhood. It seemed too normal.

When I went back out to close the trunk lid and lock the car, I saw a car swing around the corner. I knew it had to be Harry, and it was. He stopped behind the cars and lowered his window.

"Am I crashing a party?"

I shook my head. "Park in front." My voice exuded discouragement. I could even hear it myself. Why wouldn't it be Harry? All the players had to check in so the viewing audience didn't forget about them. I half expected to see Bruce Holt being pushed around the corner on a gurney with IV bags swinging from hooks above his head. Might as well get the whole cast together and we could sit around and wring our hands together for all the good it would do.

I leaned back on a padded lounge chair on the patio with my feet up. Harry sauntered around the corner of the house like he owned the place. The egotistical look that he had the first evening we had talked was back.

"You've been avoiding me," he said with a hardness in his voice.

While I was helping put away the groceries, the report from the PI had come in on the fax and I wasn't in the mood to play games. "Have a seat," I replied with an equal amount of hardness.

He was shaken for just a second and was about to say something further when I spoke first.

"Time to cut the crap, Harry. On the first night you said that if money could solve this it would be easy, like you were rolling in it. In fact your business is on the edge of bankruptcy, and you are close to losing your house. You are strapped for cash, or were until a week before you came to me. Then, guess what? A gob of money. I have to ask, where did that come from? And, it isn't a rhetorical question, where *did* it come from?

"The PIs, huh?"

I nodded.

He moved his chair closer to me. He was literally wringing his hands. What a pathetic sight for a guy go from a confident mover and shaker to groveling in less than a minute.

"What can I say? They got to me. If they had just threatened to kill me or my family if I didn't play along with the hunt for the nuke I probably would have let them do it. I was so stressed out from worry and fatigue about my finances that I wasn't thinking sanely. Through their digging into my past they knew how hard I had worked to get where I was. And they knew that if a wad of cash was dangled in front of me I couldn't refuse it. Once I had the money there was no way I could give it back because in a couple of days half of it was gone. Worst of all, now I was back in business literally and figuratively. I had my old confidence back and was on the move. Too late, it had become obvious to me what changes in my business plan were necessary to prosper in these times. With the money I could make the changes I should have made a year ago. And, it really will work, it's already working. The only price I've had to pay is that they now own me."

His face fell like it would go smack flat onto the patio bricks. "I'd do anything to go back to being bankrupt."

He was a tough proud man, and to see him brought to this was painful. At least the air had been cleared and we could go from here.

"Okay. From our training, we accept what has happened and don't dwell on it beyond what lesson can be learned. I doubt they'll try that trick on me. There's still a bomb out there and we're in a race to see who gets it first. Are you with us?"

"Who's the 'us?'"

I smiled. "Things have been happening. First of all there's Fred Clements from the meeting in the park. You remember him?"

Harry nodded.

"Then there's the State Highway Trooper who's presently asleep in my guest room. After that there's the head of the state troopers, and the head of the state Bureau of Criminal Apprehension. All of these guys are part of the Minnesota Department of Public Safety. The overall head of that department isn't in on it yet as far as I know. The FBI suspects there's something going on and the State Dicks aren't letting them in on it. Of course, there's Bruce Holt and his family. Bruce was nearly beaten to death by Cutter to make him talk and may not make it. Better get comfortable it'll take awhile."

Without giving all the details, I sketched in the story. I saved for last what Holt had said about the flight in the C-130 to the Anoka County Airport in hopes it would jog some memories. "There's a friend of mine who also knows the outline of what's happening. He's done a lot of reading about the mind-brain connection and offered some helpful insights about our remembering enough to find the thing. Aside from that, he gave an opinion that it was hidden around the metro. It was only a hunch, and though there were no facts to support it, he seemed fairly certain. At that time I had not met Bruce Holt. Then, Holt says he was here, and you remember him from one of the missions."

"Yeah . . . yeah. That could be. We took a long plane ride on a C-130 once but that's all."

"How about the part where I remembered we were all together digging it up? Does that connect with anything?"

Harry said he remembered nothing, and maybe he was telling the truth.

"Are we going to talk to Holt some more? It seems like that's the best lead we have."

"No for two reasons. The first is that I called his son and Bruce is in no condition to talk, but they are now guardedly optimistic that he'll live. The second is that I'm not sure he knows anything. When he related to me what had happened with Cutter, he was too busted up to invent another story so told me the same thing. In time, if he manages to recover, I'm certainly going to pay him a visit."

Harry was pacing now and kicking his toe against things, not hard enough to hurt his toe, but like he was angry with the world and wanted to inflict pain on it. The pleasure-pain centers of his brain were in conflict. He knew that if he kicked the table leg with enough force to even move it, he'd feel pain and it wouldn't care. On the other hand, maybe he wanted to feel physical pain to keep his mind off the psychological agony he was experiencing. "So, what do we do? We're at a dead end, again, still, and the world is caving in on us. Cutter and company want us to give them information so they can pick up a nuke that's lying around somewhere. Now, the state cops want to find it first which is fine except that we are their link to it. And, I don't expect the Feds to sit idly by when they think something big is going down so we're their point of their spear, too."

Something came to mind. "Let's do the opposite of what they think we'll do as in nothing. You go about your job and I'll do the same. Maybe all of these players will sort of trip over each other's feet and that'll be enough distraction to keep them busy. Meanwhile, try to remember something, anything, what might help. Somebody has to eventually find this thing or the harassment will never stop."

Harry sat down again. My idea appeared to please him. "Whether or not they'll let us do nothing, that's the best for me by a long way. Running a business is like balancing a pyramid on it's point. You look away for an instant and things start to fall apart. And, especially now that I'm restructuring, it takes even more attention. There are a lot of people relying on me for a pay check. It's a serious burden, not that I'm complaining because I do like the rat race. Anyway, I could really use some time when I could forget this shadow world we're working in."

With that he stood, "I wish we could have accomplished more, and this seems like a wasted trip for me, but you know how it is."

I followed him around the house to his car and we shook hands as friends though I doubt he was aware of doing it. As he drove away he had his cell phone slapped up against his ear probably making airline reservations for a flight back. I had to smile. In a way I supposed his life was one of the likely outcomes for a member of Phantom. He'd be good at handling unexpected difficulties in his business. When things changed, he'd be going in a new direction before his flat-footed competition had a chance to think. His one blunder was not reacting correctly to the real estate bust. Even at that he held it together for a long time and probably came close to making it anyway. That's why he was so susceptible to Cutter's overture with an infusion of cash. Given a second chance, he was not about to drop the ball.

* * *

My newly acquired friend, state trooper John Witherton, found a motel and stayed in town for a few days. On Saturday we went to the Rice
Creek Regional Park to see what was there. The State Bureau of Criminal Apprehension had a meter for detecting x-rays given off by weapons
grade nuclear material which they had loaned to him.

When we finally decided it was a nuke we were looking for, I went on
the Internet and looked up how one detected nuclear material, since I
figured the time would come when I'd be doing that. The main fissile
materials were uranium 235, and plutonium 239. U-235 gave off 80 keV,
and 185.7 keV x-rays so was relatively easy to detect. Pu-239 was much
harder to detect since it gave off weak gamma rays and neutrons. However, all weapons grade plutonium contained several isotopes. In addition
to the dominant Pu-239, there was always a small amount of Pu-241. Pu-
241 beta decayed, with a half-life of 14.4 years, to americium 241. Am-
241 subsequently decayed in a half life of 470 years with the emission of
a 60 keV x-ray which, like the 80-keV x-ray of uranium, was relatively
easy to detect under field conditions. Thus, the most sensitive technique
for detecting weapons grade plutonium was to detect the contaminant
Am-241 and infer the accompanying plutonium. The detector Witherton
had was designed to use that stratagem. And, since the fissile material in
a MADM was Pu-239, it was Am-241 we'd be detecting. Witherton
didn't know what the instrument measured and didn't seem to care other
than being intent on finding a place where the little needle behind the
round glass window moved away from zero.

Witherton and I spent several hours trying to walk a pattern in the tall
grass, weeds and brush of Rice Creek Park but never did the little needle
waver from its comfortable resting place above the zero. The difficulty of
our task settled in as we climbed into his borrowed car. We spent the rest
of the day together driving around the Anoka county airport, out to the
Carlos Avery Wildlife Preserve, and just wandering around. The patch of
land known locally as the arsenal caught his attention. It was officially
called the Twin Cities Army Ammunition Plant, TCAAP, located in Arden Hills within a couple of miles of the Anoka County Airport. It was
two miles on a side and had been purchased from the Army by Arden
Hills for a song. The intent was to develop it since it was prime real estate. But, the real-estate bust of 2008 pretty much ended that plan leaving
the city of Arden Hills with what amounted to a white elephant. Not to

worry, Ramsey County subsequently took it off their hands so the whole county was now on the hook for the contaminated property.

However, during the Vietnam War and many years after that, it was used to make military ammunition. There was a time after my family had moved into the area when they were making artillery shells. Every day at five in the afternoon they would shoot several of the shells as a quality check, something that could be heard for miles.

On Monday evening Witherton stopped by and for the twentieth time I told him there was nothing new. Bruce Holt's family was adamant that no one was about to interrogate Bruce in his weakened condition. I was trying as hard as I could to implement the plan I had discussed with Harry. Tuesday morning my trooper friend headed back to northern Minnesota, much to my relief.

After that things settled down. Witherton called every couple of days to check in. He implied that people were getting nervous, but I said that was too bad. In so many words I said they were free to find the darn bomb without me any time they wanted. Then Fred called, just checking in so as not to be left out of getting his job back with the FBI if things started to move. Though the respite was good for us all, something inside me said this wouldn't last, And . . . it didn't.

— 23 —

Friday afternoon, two weeks later

Harry was at the back door and not looking so good. He motioned me out, and in a hushed voice said, "The skunks are back, and mean as snakes. Whatever you did to those guys wasn't as bad as you thought or else they've made miraculous recoveries. He showed up with the Divner guy and knocked me around in my own living room in front of my family. It seems like they don't care who knows about them or what they want. *They want it!* He said no more of this crap about bugging houses, cars, phones, no more warnings. They don't care. I am to give them a report every two days and there had better be results or people will get hurt, people will die!"

We were standing on the patio and as he took a breath I motioned with my hands palms down and fingers spread to slow him down. He was scared. "How did Divner look?"

"He still has casts on both hands and as I recall he didn't smile once."

We sat down and I asked, "What do you make of it? I mean the overtness."

"Yeah. I've been figuring on that. From one point of view it isn't so unexpected. If the state trooper saw them and checked out the fake Secret Service IDs, their cover's blown so they might as well take the direct approach. However, that being the case, why are they back at all? Why not someone else? If something went seriously wrong and the story got out, it could bring down the president. It's like they don't care if the whole world finds out about what they're up to."

I closed my eyes and leaned my head back. Harry didn't say anything more. Then, I said, "It looks like they plan to take over. All they need is a defining event like a huge earthquake out West. But, you just can't trust an earthquake to happen at the right time so they plan to make the event like a nuke going off in a major city. They would declare martial law, suspend the Constitution, and that bag of dirt in the White House would become dictator. It appears they are confident they can get away with it and are working to a schedule. That's why they've started pushing so hard."

From Harry's expression I could tell what I said didn't come as a particular surprise to him. He replied, "That or something equally bad. But, for us it doesn't really matter. You can see that. If we don't get them the bomb, we, along with out families, will be dead. We absolutely need to have results to show them. That means no more thinking about the big picture, only the little one with just us in it, okay?"

The fear was back and I felt it too. "Have you remembered anything at all about the mission since trauma is supposedly what jars it loose?"

"Hot chow."

"What?"

"Hot chow. That's connected with it. Something about hot chow."

"I already mentioned that. We spent the night before the mission at that helicopter base and that pleased us because we could get some hot chow for a change."

"No. After we came out with the case the three of us that were left went to get hot chow. And wooden crates—wooden crates getting mixed up."

"Forklifts and wooden crates."

"Yeah. Forklifts and . . . that's all. How about you? What else?"

"Dammit! Nothing else. Think! Who else was there? If there were wooden crates and forklifts there must have been others. We didn't steal forklifts from the North Vietnamese. And, where were we with the forklifts? That had to be someplace other than the bush or even the helicopter base because that base was all mud."

"We were in a huge building with one side missing. We could stand there and watch the rain lash down. You must remember that."

"Nothing. But, a large building with a side missing had to be an aircraft hangar. Why can't we remember? It's so maddening!" I was holding my head in my hands thinking it was like when you can't remember the name of a movie star. You can see the face, even remember the movies they starred in. You knew that it would pop into your mind sooner or later. Only this was different. There was a lot more than a name, a whole series of events that made up tumultuous times in our lives. Plus the fact that a determined effort had been made to make is so we'd never be able to remember.

Neither of us said a thing for five minutes but nothing more was coming. "Okay," I said, "let's give it a rest. Oh, by the way, there's a thing I forgot to mention last time because I assumed I knew the answer after you admitted taking money from Cutter. But, I'm going to ask it anyway, because I'm pretty ticked off about it. You were the one that tipped off Cutter about Holt so they got to him before I did, right?"

"Wrong! I've been a rat, I admit that. But, I'm not into stabbing buddies in the back either. The night after you filled me in about what had happened it occurred to me that you were thinking I ratted on you. At least now we've got that cleared up. And, us rodents aren't stupid."

The hardness was back in his voice. It was something I was starting to notice when he was honestly angry with me. Then it clicked as we looked at each other. "Then who?"

"How'd I know? Yeah, I took their money and had to play ball with them, but Holt was a piece of information that could genuinely help us stay ahead of them. As we both know, as soon as they have their hands on the bomb, they'll probably kill us to clear their back trail. In case you missed it, that was probably why the assassin tried to kill you. Cutter probably told them where to look when he called in the float plane. They thought they had it."

"Okay, I accept that, but I ask again, who told them about Holt? It seems unlikely that Cutter knew about Holt all along and just by chance went to see him a few hours before I did. Who knew about Holt at that point?"

"Well, I did and so did you, and you had your PI locate him."

"Yes. But, I told you I went downtown and looked him in the eye when I asked if he leaked the information to anyone, especially a couple of guys flashing Secret Service badges. He wasn't in the office that morning and the woman who was at the front desk said she is required to keep a record of all visitors, and that no one was there asking to see my PI, and no Secret Service badges. They could both be lying, but it didn't seem like they were. Who else knew about Holt?"

"Holt."

"Nah. He no sooner got into the game when he was nearly beaten to death. How he's connected, or even if he is, remains unknown, but it hardly seems he would have let on to anyone that he was involved in something like this, especially after all this time."

"Did you mention it to your wife?"

"She wouldn't blab something like that."

"That's not what I meant. What about listening devices?"

"Well, in the first place, I didn't tell her. And in the second, since you swept the house I know where they are and keep moving them around. Which reminds, me, do you still have that bug sweeper with you? I never thought that they may have added some more."

"Sure. I never leave home without it."

"Then, let's sweep the house and since Cutter said they don't care about the bugs anymore, we'll remove all of those things."

Harry nodded and went to his car. He opened the trunk and pulled the small cardboard box containing the device from a side pocket of his suit-case. We did a thorough sweep of the house, garage and the cars. When we were done we had more bugs than were there the first time we did it. We left them on the kitchen table and went out back again.

"What do you make of that?" I asked. "If they said they don't care about the listening devices anymore, why did they plant additional ones?"

He was puzzled. "They were sure emphatic about only relying on my reports from now on. Neither one was fully recovered, that was clear. It was like they didn't want to bother themselves with the effort to monitor the bugs. Now we see this."

"The one on the phone wire seemed different. Lets go in and examine them again. No talking."

First we separated out the ones that were definitely there the first time Harry swept the house. These were like the one I found in Holt's kitchen when I went to see his wife. The others were clearly of a different design, but they were placed in locations that might require another type. We went outside for another consultation.

Harry was first. "What do you think?"

"I think Cutter has competition. If he wants to see progress, you might tell him that. Who knows, maybe it will make them back off."

"Or," Harry interjected, "it'll cause them to push even harder to find it before someone else does. Somebody else planted bugs and yet another person knew about Holt who told Cutter because there's no reason Cutter's competition would tell him that piece of information. Try to figure all of that out."

The next morning, Saturday, Harry and I drove out to Hopkins to visit Holt. We hadn't called ahead because we didn't want to give him a chance to get away. We were assuming he had recovered enough to do that.

Holt's wife answered the door. I could see after a second she made the connection. Before she could say anything I said, "It's important we talk to him or you will all be hurt. They're not going to go away and hiding won't help."

The pain was obvious in her eyes, but she opened the door. "He's doing better. He'll only have one fully functioning kidney and his liver will never be at full capacity. But, with drugs, they say he'll be mostly all right in time."

Her hair was a little frizzy, and her face had a haggard look in spite of her makeup. This had been a hard time. Recovering in a hospital or a half way house is hard because of the hired help. To them it's a job. They see people in pain and discomfort all the time so are immune to it. It's always best to get the patient home as soon as possible. To the family members, this can be a hardship. Anyone who had ever been a primary care giver knows how true that is.

"Thank you for letting us in. Time is the one thing we don't have much of. We'll try to be as brief as possible."

She led us to the master bedroom. The room was well lit from outside through sheer curtains. Dark blinds behind had been drawn aside. Holt was sitting in an easy chair with his feet up on a makeshift footstool. He wore a bathrobe and was a couple of days overdue for a shave. He looked weak.

I entered first and Holt acknowledged me. "Sort of expected you'd be around since this whole thing is way out. You really expect to find a nuke? Doesn't seem possible."

His attitude was to be expected whether or not he knew anything. In one case he'd think it was science fiction, and in the other he'd want me to believe he thought that. Sitting on the end of the bed I said, "Yes, we really do expect to find a nuke. And, I'm pretty sure you can help. By the way, I brought along a friend who's in as much trouble as I am, and you are."

His grinned slightly as if he didn't buy my assertion that he was in trouble. I turned and said, "Come in, Harry."

When Harry stepped through the door the light was full on him. I watched for Holt's reaction. His shock was unmistakable. If he had ever seen Harry before the scar on his forehead was unforgettable. "You recognize him, don't you."

Holt was shaken as I saw it all connect in his mind. There was now no possibility that he could maintain he knew nothing about the mission.

"Why, yes. I've seen this man before, though I'm not sure where."

I shook my head. "Not true. You know because there was only one place you could have seen him." I slid to the corner of the bed and looked intently at Holt. "We're not here to hurt you, but if we don't get results there are people who will. And, from experience we know they will start with your wife and son. They want to keep you as able as possible so you can do their bidding. That business in the woods was out of character. They must have gotten over confident. We need to know what you know, and now."

He violently shook his head. "No. I can't do that. I never wanted to be a part of that."

"You must! They mean to find it, and when they do they are intent on using it. Minneapolis could become a mushroom cloud. Don't you get it? We have to stay a step ahead of them and find it first so we can let the whole world know about it."

He slouched back and closed his eyes. The weakness was obvious, but I had no choice.

"How about telling us the story of your involvement."

His wife was taking this all in. "He's weak. Can you come back another time. And, what about listening devices?"

Harry held up the bug sweeper and began going over the room. He found nothing so went into the hallway toward the kitchen. Five minutes later he returned. "Just two of the original type that are now stewing in a pan of water."

Holt's hands had started to shake and I was afraid we'd lose him. "I don't even know who the good guys are."

"In case you're forgotten," I said, "I'm the one who saved you from dying in the wilderness."

He drew in the sides of his mouth as if disgusted. "As I said then, that could have been part of the plan."

Harry had been standing by the French style triple dresser. Mrs. Holt came up behind him with a chair which he graciously accepted. It was obvious she was resigned to the fact that it wouldn't end until he told what he knew.

"Bruce, tell them. It can't hurt. This won't end until that thing is found, you can see that."

Looking at Holt, Harry said, "Tell us the story and maybe things will start to come back so you'll see that we never were the bad guys. We can fill you in on the few things we remember. You probably don't know this, but we were both members of a Phantom Team. As such, after the mission we were given a memory loss treatment. There are a few things that are coming back, but we need more of the pieces so we remember what happened. We may have been the ones who hid the bomb."

It was in the back of my mind that part of his weakness sprang from his holding back some awful truth, that if he got it out, he'd recover a lot faster.

Holt slowly nodded his head. "Why not? I'm too weak to fight. It seemed to start shortly after that jerk was promoted to brigadier general."

— 24 —

Harry and I had previously discussed the possibility that the major who had given us the orders to retrieve the "aluminum case" had been Major Holt. As he started relating the events it became obvious he was the one. The granite man with the hard, intense face was, indeed, Major Bruce Holt of the U. S. Air Force. He'd been wearing forest green camouflage fatigues when he met with the Phantom Teams at the helicopter base.

Bruce Holt began his narrative in a melancholy voice. "I had not always been gruff and mean. In fact, until a couple of months before this sordid business, my fellow Air Force officers knew me as an affable C-130 pilot prone to a practical joke now and then good-naturedly taking the same in return. I rather liked my life, maybe one of the few in Vietnam who did. That is, I liked it until I was grounded.

"As I walked to my Jeep, that evening after having given you guys your orders I was seething under my breath as I frequently was of late. That was another thing that was eating me, I had taken to talking to myself. Others were beginning to think I was loosing it. Well, they would have been too if they had not laid hands on the controls of a plane in all that time. That runt brigadier had grounded me after I made a hard landing and nearly totaled my C-130. I had been behind on the regulation amount of sleep required for pilots, something that was not at all uncommon, and I had sustained battle damage. My mission had been to resupply a forward fire base which meant flying across an uneven clearing at ten feet and having pallets of supplies pulled out of the rear with parachutes. We had taken ground fire and lost an engine. To top that off, the tires were flat on the starboard side. It was lucky any of us walked away from that landing.

"But Brigadier General Robert Diggens, who had shortly before put on that star, was intent on throwing his newly acquired rank around.

When Diggens had been a bird colonel he was almost a human being. It had always amused me the way higher ranking generals put down on brigadiers. Now, I knew why. They were jerks. The review of the incident should have been completed long before with me being returned to flying status. As it was, it was still pending. Worst of all, the longer it took, the more likely there'd be a negative outcome for me. It was maddening. This was war, and people shot real bullets. Planes were lost all the time. Now, I was flying a desk doing administrative work. That's not why I went full time Air Force. I did it to fly airplanes!

"I was in charge of issuing the daily orders that reassigned personnel, rotated pilots to R & R, establishing flight rosters, and a million similar things. These duties were for the most part handled by a competent career captain under me so I had only nominal oversight responsibility for most of that. In another role, I was in charge of a detachment that handled the air cargo that passed through the base. A lieutenant handled that function, but he was green and required a lot of supervision.

"Things that came under my direct responsibility were flights to and from CONUS, that's Continual United States. Many of these were flown by reserve units that were put into service for varying lengths of time to fly personnel and vital supplies to Vietnam and take various cargoes the other way. The reserves were used to augment air transport capability without having to increase the number of active duty units. This is something I understood since up until nine months before I had been a reservist in the 133 Airlift Group flying out of the Air Force Reserve Station at the Minneapolis International Airport. After several one week call-ups in a six month period it was affecting my job. While my employer could not legally fire me for my military duty, I could certainly be passed over for promotion. Finally I decided to go Air Force full time."

After a pause and a sip of water, he continued in a disconsolate tone. "After two months in Vietnam I was promoted to major and could see myself making lieutenant colonel. Not anymore. My career was over and so was the war. It was now spring of 1972 and President Nixon was drawing down the U.S. troops in Vietnam. On average, a thousand a day were leaving. This caused my work load to be almost overwhelming most of the time as I had to arrange transport for the troops. Nearly all were being rotated back to the States by air.

"If life wasn't bearing down on me enough, the Monday morning of the week you guys were ordered to retrieve that thing I had an unexpected meeting. At 0900 hours, out of nowhere, I found himself in a top secret meeting with an Army captain from Saigon accompanied by a heavily armed man also in Army uniform. The guard immediately assured himself that my office door had a lock and he locked it. With a nod from the guard, the captain rolled the combination tumblers of the locks on the briefcase that was handcuffed to his wrist when he arrived. He removed a sealed letter sized envelope and handed it to me. 'Yours to open and read,' the captain said.

"Slitting open the envelope I unfolded the two pages and began to read. As inexplicable as it seemed, I had been placed in charge of a project called *bright midnight*. The first paragraph consisted of a few sentences explaining the reason for the mission while only saying it involved extremely sensitive items, items vital to national security. The second stated that five small specially trained teams of four men each were being assigned to me to carry out the task of acquiring the items. It then gave a few general details about the background of those units and their capability. I wondered why, since the bearers of these tidings were Army, an Air Force officer, namely me, was being assigned the job. It didn't matter because I had been selected, I just wondered.

"The following paragraphs give the details that were important to me to accomplish the mission. It was clear now why an Air Force officer had been given the job. The logistics of the operation were the main part, and I was in logistics. The delivery of the objects of the mission to their final destination would therefore be under the direction of the Air Force. It seemed that retrieving the objects was a simple matter considering the capability of the teams that would be doing it so it must have made sense to someone to give the Air Force the lead in the operation.

"Toward the end of the orders was a paragraph, a short one, which said General Diggens had been informed that I had received a top secret mission and that I was to be given what support I needed. Almost as an after-thought, it mentioned that General Diggens was to verify and sign for the five items as assurance that they left the war zone.

"After ten minutes I looked up and the captain asked, 'Do you completely understand the order?' In answer I nodded my head and said, 'Yes.'

"'Good. Now fold the pages as they were when they came out of the envelope so I cannot see the content and hand them to me.' This I did. From his still open briefcase the captain took a small metal dish and a cigarette lighter. He struck a light and started the paper burning until he was forced to drop the remainder in the dish to burn out. He gathered the black ashes and thoroughly crushed them in the dish after which he dumped the residue in the wastepaper basket. After replacing the dish in his case he produced five eight by ten water resistant brown envelopes and another sheet of paper. 'Sign for the five envelopes. You can see the serial numbers from the envelopes have already been entered on the form. Verify that they are correct.'

"With that formality complete, the captain and his body guard departed. I watched through the window as the two men made their way to a waiting Huey on the tarmac. This being an Air Force base the helicopter was required to taxi to the main runway. Since Hueys don't have wheels it simply hovered at five feet and followed the line of other aircraft down the taxiway until it was its turn to take off. If a large flight of helicopters departed at the same time from an Air Force base, fixed wing aircraft were vectored clear of the area until they were on their way. With a single rotary wing craft, it was dangerous to have it popping up unexpectedly so it was required to follow the rules of fixed wing aircraft. At the end of the runway, almost out of sight, I saw the helicopter lift and peel off to the west. I was in sort of a surreal state of mind as I watched since this had been so sudden and so crazy.

"I remember resting my forearms on the desk as I carefully aligned the five envelopes in a neat pile in front of me. My orders were simple enough. Today was Monday and I had until 2400 hours on Friday to complete the mission. That gave me three days to organize the transportation assets needed and see to whatever other support was necessary.

"The fact that General Diggens would be the one to sign for the five items as they were leaving the country settled into my mind. I would be in charge of making sure everything went according to plan, and at the time of loading, the general would verify the serial numbers and sign the shipping manifest. What if one of them were to be lost after that dip of a general signed for them? One arrogant brigadier general would be on the hook for it. It was an amusing thought, but seemed like an impossible task. Yet, one never knew what could happen.

"Shrugging off the daydream, I reviewed schedules of Air Force transport planes due to depart for CONUS on Thursday and Friday. Planes were coming and going all the time, and I settled on a C-141 Starlifter scheduled for the late evening of Friday. There was also a C-130 scheduled to depart for Saigon shortly thereafter. Everything was open to change, but even though that would be cutting it close to my deadline, Friday was my best bet in case any of the items were delayed."

Here Holt paused, closed his eyes and rested. He took a few sips of water and rested again. "Is any of this making sense?" he asked.

"So far so good," I said, "except that you haven't told us anything yet."

"I'm coming to that. At 1400 hours on the third day, which would be Thursday, four senior sergeants of the Air Force Commandos reported to me. With the five of us in a locked room, I gave one of the envelopes I had signed for to each man as that man's orders. The fifth was mine. Each man would open his envelope and acquaint himself with the contents. These would not be burned—yet. They were not permitted to discuss their orders among themselves, though I knew each had orders identical to mine, the only difference being I didn't know where they would be going.

"At 1830 hours on Thursday the Air Force Commando sergeants and I drove to an isolated helicopter field some miles from the main air base. At 1900 hours the four sergeants and I met in an operations tent at the helicopter base, acquired our respective special teams and proceeded with the mission.

"However, by earlier that afternoon, I had become obsessed with what might be in the aluminum cases the five teams were to retrieve. At the same time, I was equally beset with the desire to upset something in the process so as to sting General Diggens and at the same time leave me in the clear. You can't imagine how angry I was with him. It didn't matter, though, because the process was designed to be ironclad, and it was.

"But, I couldn't help thinking that it would help to know what I was dealing with. There was no doubt it was valuable to someone. My list of possibilities included chemical, biological or radiological weapons that had been strategically placed to protect air bases or other important installations. It could be a super sophisticated listening device to detect enemy movements. Maybe it was a sort of beacon that could direct the smart bombs they started using. An electronic device would be valuable in the short term but would become obsolete quickly. A CBR weapon, on the other hand, would retain its value far longer. There was no way of telling until the first units had been delivered. They would certainly have a FSN, that is Federal Stock Number, on them.

"Along with my fixation on the contents of the cases, I had become enamored with the possibility of stealing one for eventual sale to the highest bidder. I saw it as recompense for having had my Air Force career ruined. And since I had quit my civilian job, that occupation was gone, too. I began to see how Vietnam managed to drive people crazy. Maybe, I had been getting close to that point before being grounded and this would have happened in any case. But, I put it off to the hopeless situation I'd been thrust into because of that surly General Diggens. Maybe I had done something to cause him to be reprimanded that I was totally unaware of. I thought of that as highly unlikely because you know how crap tends to run down hill in the military. As the week wore on, this caused me to hatch the plan of having four of the cases arriving in the afternoon, and one at the last minute. The last one would obviously have to be yours because the others would be coming in by helicopter to the helicopter base and trucked to the air base together.

"The truck with the first four cases arrived at the hangar at 1930 hours on Friday. I had arranged to have the crates already built and ready. General Diggens was on hand and verified the units and they were loaded on the waiting C-141. I made my apologies for the lateness of the fifth one, but I said there was nothing I could do about it. In fact, I told him that was why I had cut the departure time so close to my deadline. I had allowed time for something to go wrong, and it had. But, there was still time to meet the required timing. The general was gruff and snarled at me, which was nothing new. He left making it clear he was to be called immediately when the last one arrived.

"I had jotted down the Federal Stock Number of one of the cases so when the general was driven away in his chauffeured car, I set off for the ugly two story building that housed my office. There were still a few people working which was not unusual because there would be at least one person on duty all through the night. This was, after all, a combat station in a war zone, even if this was only a lowly administrative function. I passed a few pleasantries as I walked by one or another of the galley slaves laboriously pulling on his pen. Well, the metaphor was a little off. It didn't hurt moral, though, for them to see an officer putting in extra time, too.

"I had work to do, but I always had that. My purpose was to look up the FSN I had taken from the case. This was an instance where it was good that everything in the military establishment had an FSN. I hoped I never made a mistake and one day placed an order for fifty aircraft carriers, though in that case it was possible Congress would have something to say about it. As an aside, I knew of an incident where a harried sergeant had ordered a thousand commonly used fuses, but slipped a digit in the FSN. Someone higher up called him and questioned the item. Still rushed, he snapped that he knew what he was doing. The result was that an electronics company had to restart a production line and manufacture a thousand special vacuum tubes last used in radars at the end of World War II. The sergeant was demoted further than it should have been possible to be demoted.

"Now, I had a keen sense of anticipation as I expected to learn what this exercise was all about. The several volumes of FSNs were on a shelf near one of the men who was working late. I didn't have time to wait until he left.

"Walking over to the area of the shelf with a requisition form in my hand I said, 'There's something odd about this requisition Specialist Nonamaker typed up just before he left. Better safe than sorry.' I looked at the range of numbers in each volume. Picking the one that interested me, I laid it on an empty desk and flipped the pages. Finding it, the name was cryptic, but I understood the meaning well enough. In one respect it was the best of all worlds, it was valuable. The down side was it was too valuable. But, to succeed in my caper could have put me on top of the world. I let out a long breath as I tried to control my emotions. 'Something wrong, sir?'

"Suppressing the start I received from the voice, I said, 'No. Just kicking myself a little. I should know better than to question you guys.'

"I slipped the book back on the shelf, gave a brief smile at the airman a few feet away and returned to my office. I wrote down the number as I had memorized it before going to the FSN books and then compared it to the one on the note pad from my shirt pocket. I had remembered it correctly. Now as I thought about it, I knew for certain why *bright midnight* was classified top secret. Somebody had to have been nearly insane to have planted five nuclear land mines in South Vietnam. I doubted that the Secretary of Defense even knew about it which meant the people who did it would be desperate to safely and secretly undo it. I couldn't help thinking that General Diggens' selection for the mission was in some way connected with the possibility he had been in on the original plan. He would have been a junior player at the time, but would know well enough the sensitivity of the situation. Now that he was a general officer, he had the rank to accept custody of the devices until they were safely back in secure storage stateside. I was in the hangar waiting when you guys drove in and stopped at 2202 hours. I stepped out of the shadows as you piled out of the three-quarter ton."

Major, that is Bruce, Holt paused as if collecting his thoughts. I think Harry caught it too. Here was the part where he would reveal that he knew a lot more about this affair than he had hitherto admitted. His eyes became more alert and he spoke with a new crispness. His wife may not have noticed, but we were desperate for any clue.

"I remember snapping at one of you, and I think it was you, Wessen, 'Two minutes late, but close.' You probably remember what followed.

"'Where's the fourth man?'

"'Dead,' you replied.

"I remember being surprised. 'Accident?'

"'Enemy fire. The area where the case was buried is infested with Viet Cong. It's like they were expecting us. The case is in the truck.'

"I had been working on a plan whereby I could divert this last case, but it was flimsy and would have required four of you. With three it wouldn't work. I was defeated once again. I had you load the aluminum case in the wooden crate with the serial number plate facing up and then I called Diggens. He arrived in minutes, verified the SN, signed the paperwork, you guys nailed the crate shut and one of you drove the crate out to the waiting C-141 with a forklift where you loaded it on the plane. The only slightly odd thing, not so odd given the time of year, was the torrential rain. The general waited until the C-141 was in the air before leaving. I had remembered the C-130 that was scheduled to depart for Saigon a half hour later and hitched a ride on it having put in my papers for a few days leave. That's it."

I looked at Harry, he looked at me. That wasn't *it*. We both knew that. "Why did you tell Cutter and his friend that story about having flown to Anoka County Airport?"

"Come on! They were beating me to death. I didn't inflict these injuries on myself."

"Wait a minute," Harry said. "You told Vin that's what you told them. Maybe you told them something else."

"That's enough," Holt's wife shouted. "You asked him to tell what happened, and he did. I'm not asking, I'm telling you to leave this house. Now!"

"Yes, ma'am," was all I could say.

At the front door I told Harry I'd catch up in a minute, that I wanted a private word with Mrs. Holt. He looked a little skeptical but did as I asked. Turning to the woman I said, "I'm not sure if I impressed this on you at our first meeting, but if the men who are after that bomb find it before we do, they'll kill all of us, including you and your son, as a means of tying up loose ends. I'm certain your husband knows more than he's saying. May I encourage you to stress on him how important this is. One more thing. Calling the police won't help. The state police already know. Now, they want to find it so they can take all the credit for themselves. It just gets more complicated with every person who knows."

Without giving her a chance to reply I turned and walked away.

Driving away Harry asked, "What was that about?"

"I told her I was certain Bruce knows more than he's telling and if Cutter and company find it first we're all dead. You never know what will finally make him see the light."

"Well, what do you think about what he did tell us?"

"Two things, we have to find one General Robert Diggens, and he told a lot of lies. But, not everything was a lie. Whether or not he realized it, he laid out a compelling case for means and motive for having stolen the bomb. He only lacked the opportunity, or so he says. While under severe duress in the BWCA he managed to conger up a great sounding story about how he knew where the bomb was flown to, how the control tower was not in operation at night, how there was no security at the small airport, and how the truck with the bomb was only gone a short time. All of that was calculated to give his tormenters hope that they'd find the thing, and leave him in the clear as to not knowing where it was. That was a fine tale, but too good to have come up with on the spur of the moment."

"Yeah . . . . He took it. And, after he stashed it, got back to work, and when common sense had a chance to operate, he realized he had done a seriously bad thing. Like he said, it was too valuable. Which means it's still there, wherever he or someone I cahoots with him put it."

"Buried it."

"Had to have buried it," Harry agreed. "Furthermore, he had his plan in place before he learned what it was. After finding out he could have called it off, but he was still mad at the general. From there on it became a game, deadly, yes, but still a game. His taking leave starting that night really caps it. He needed the leave to cover his absence from Cam Ranh Bay for a few days. At the same time, it necessarily left him without an alibi. There must have been an investigation. I wonder how he handled that?"

We were on the freeway headed back to my neighborhood. Why did that seem like a dark place now? In my mind I saw an aerial view of the city with a black smudge over a small part of it with my house in the center of the darkness. Harry was driving and I was staring out the windshield. Somewhat lethargically I said, "They fooled with our minds to make us forget. Maybe they also implanted a trigger mechanism whereby if we ever came too close to remembering things we'd immediately have suicidal thoughts, and rub ourselves out."

Harry laughed. "In that case, I've got good news for you, old buddy. If *we* don't remember, *they* will rub us out, so you don't have to worry about a trigger."

It wasn't funny. "If you have any more good news, try your best to stifle it, okay?"

Ignoring my retort, he asked, "I wonder how old General Diggens would be, or even if he's still alive?"

As beaten down as I felt, we had to keep at it. "Well, let's see. From what you said that first night you came to my house, it's important to have a command in a combat zone if you want to make it to the higher ranks. So, let's say he served in Korea as a second lieutenant. That would make him about twenty-three in 1952. He got his first star in 1972 which would make him forty-three at the time. That's possible, I guess. That would put him in his mid-eighties now. Could be he's still among the living, though I'm beginning to feel that state of existance is highly over rated."

As we neared my home, I asked, "What are you going to tell Cutter? Tonight's your night to report in, isn't it."

"Yeah, it is. Guess I'll tell him he's got company the best we can tell from the listening devices. I'll have to tell him we talked to Holt, and that the stupid fools nearly killed the only real lead we have, and that they can't beat on him again or he'll be dead. And, I have the feeling his wife is close to calling the cops, maybe even the FBI, and letting things fall where they may. She's close to having nothing to lose, and somebody like that is erratic and dangerous."

— 25 —

Saturday Evening

Henni Froom was there to greet me seconds after I rang the door chime. "Hello Vin. I hope my call didn't come at a bad time for you because I've been thinking about your interesting situation."

As I entered the living room it set me at ease as it always did. He and his wife had a way of decorating that was uniquely theirs, yet made everyone who entered the premises feel it was magically changed at the moment of their arrival to suit them.

"Hi Henni. Your call was a little unexpected, though knowing how you like to research things it shouldn't have been." He showed me to the sofa area in the living room just beyond a planter and trellis covered with vines that went to the ceiling that separated the entry from the rest of the room. As I sagged heavily into an easy chair I said, "You didn't call at a good time. It's not that I was so busy only that things have taken a turn for the worse. If you have some further thoughts on this cursed thing I'm all ears."

Henni expression was empathetic. "The volume of business where I work has picked up and I've been working extra hours or I would have had something for you sooner. Or, maybe I sensed things weren't right and that prompted me to call. As you know, I see that people have many more abilities than is commonly acknowledged. You said things had gotten worse. How bad is worse?"

"We backed off for a couple of weeks hoping we'd remember something useful. We didn't come up with anything and they became impatient. Now they are expecting reports every two days where we show progress or they'll start hurting our families."

"Oh! Mean bunch. Let's see if there is anything I can offer. In the past, I haven't been into studying dissociative disorders but have taken it up because of your case. These are sometimes called psychogenic disor-

ders that deal with memory loss. I'll tell you some of what I've learned,
and let me know when you become bored."

He paused and all I could thing of to say was, "Proceed."

"Okay. Yours is a case of memory loss of some type. Disallowing the
case of severe physical brain damage, which it seems we can do, there
are the following main types of loss that could encompass what you are
experiencing. First, there is amnesia which is the simple failure to recall
events. The causes of amnesia can include head trauma, but is also commonly caused by alcoholic intoxication, or even intolerable psychological stress. This last type is called psychogenic amnesia caused by severe
stress, such as being a prisoner of war, kidnapping victim, or victim of
child abuse. Amnesiacs forget who they are, but remember how to walk,
talk, count, drive, and so on. Usually, amnesia vanishes as quickly as it
appeared. This isn't really what you're concerned with, but stay with me
and I'll try to put it together.

"Next there's fugue which like amnesia involves forgetting but it's
characterized by leaving one's home and identity for periods of up to
years. This disorder is always caused by psychological stress. Also like
amnesia, people dealing with a fugue state often awaken, that is return to
their former self, as quickly as they left. After the fugue state has passed,
people generally don't remember what happened during the fugue.
Again, not really what you have, but there are some elements that you
can identify.

"Finally, there is multiple personality disorder. This dissociative disorder is characterized by the massive separation between self and ordinary consciousness. People with multiple personality disorder usually
have two or more distinct personalities that are opposites like one being
restrained and dull, and the second uninhibited or impulsive."

He paused to get my reaction so I gave it. "None of them fit."

"Not exactly, and I don't think multiple personality disorder is involved at all. I only mentioned it as the extreme case. However, all of
those conditions are normally brought on by extreme stress or trauma.
Let me give you an example. There's the case of a man who walked between the twin towers the morning of September 11, 2001 shortly before
the first plane struck. Soon after that he disappeared. Six months later he
was found living in a homeless shelter in Chicago. The trauma of what
happened that morning in New York put him into a fugue. Now, this case
and others like it come to be because of unexpected events beyond the
person's control. What if someone with malice aforethought set out to

cause an amnesiac state which, as you tell it, is what they did to you? And, also from what you said, you, on some level, agreed to it.

"One way to look at it is you're not in either a state of amnesia or fugue now, but were in such a state while on your missions. Then, when you were caused to snap out of it, so to speak, you remembered nothing and that would be normal for such a state. And, while in that state you didn't remember your real life. That would have been important because if you were ordered to do some immoral act that you would normally never agree to, that normal life was not operative. That situation is exactly what they would have wanted for the teams. After the mission you would not only have no memory of it but would also dismiss having had anything to do with it because you're not that type of person."

I interjected, "This isn't working. In the detailed flashback where I remember us digging the thing up, I was my normal self. Waiting for the initial briefing at the helicopter base, I even remember thinking about things I did as a child to escape boredom—I remembered myself remembering my past. That doesn't sound like amnesia or a fugue state. If I hadn't had that flashback, I'd say they did something to physically remove the part of my brain that could connect to those memories. As it is, it seems they didn't actually damage my brain. Could they have done it with hypnosis?"

"I doubt it. That's too uncertain. But, I haven't finished. What I just said is a possibility but I don't think it's the correct solution. I think what really happened is in your training you were given a heavy dose of unit *esprit de corps*, patriotism, a heightened sense of your own abilities, etc. While you were on the missions, you were as normal as you could be. After all, they selected you because of your particular talents in your normal state. They wouldn't want you to be somebody else while on the assignments. It was after you returned that you were set up to forget probably using a combination of mild hypnotic suggestion, drugs, and trauma. At least that's what you implied the first evening you came to me. They used that to produce what amounts to a fugue state, without the leaving home part. Tell me everything you can remember about what happened after you returned from a mission."

"We were immediately debriefed, and I mean extensively debriefed."

"How long did that take?"

"I don't know because we were taken to a room with no windows. The debriefers, really more like interrogators, either one or two, would change off in shifts. We had no sense of the passage of time."

"Did they debrief you together or individually?"

I had to think about that. "It seems like while they were getting the information we were mostly together. When we were in forgetting mode we were alone. At the start it seemed to us to be chaotic. One of us would say something and immediately one of the interrogators would shoot a question at another one. He'd hardly have time to reply and the first man would direct a question to yet a third like 'What he just said is a lie. Tell me what really happened.' And, if what one man said contradicted the statement of another they'd really jump on us."

"What about forgetting mode? How'd that go?"

"They'd start out with the main parts of the mission, like 'Did you capture the enemy general?' I'd be expected to answer 'That didn't happen.' It seemed to go on for a long time. If I screwed up, there'd be punishment in the form of an electrical shock. It was not that severe, but after several doses, you really tried to avoid it."

"That's part of the trauma. The shocks combined with time depravation would be enough to do it. And, the shocks may have been a lot worse than you're remembering."

Here we stopped for some minutes. Then Henni said, "You didn't mention drugs."

"There were none that I remember, but after it was all over we were really tired and allowed to sleep for as long as we wanted which was twelve hours a day for several days."

"They could have given you drugs in food and water so we can assume they were used. There are plenty of them available. You could fill a good sized pharmacopoeia with just the drugs used to treat mental abnormalities. Add to that, it's likely a lot of drugs used to treat psychogenic conditions were developed by mad scientists working on projects just like we're discussing. So, we're back this. Before the mission you could have been told that the coming events would be grotesque, outrageous, fantastic and dangerous. But, that you were the best of the best and were up to it. During the debriefing they used a combination of hypnotic suggestion, drugs and trauma. It added up to a balanced system of memory loss that was very effective."

Something popped into my head. "You know, I have a kind of independent confirmation of your theory. It's off the subject, but maybe if I tell you it'll help us. When I was a young engineer I worked for a company that made anemometers. We had come up with a device with no moving parts to measure wind speed and direction from zero to over a hundred knots. We approached the U.S. Navy with the idea for use on helicopters. As some background, normal aircraft air speed is measured with Pitot tubes. These do not work below about forty knots. The reason one has a helicopter is because it can fly at speeds less than forty knots. This leaves them without reliable air speed data in that speed range. As a result the Navy was interested and we conducted a series of tests at the Patuxent River Naval Air Test Station in Maryland, commonly called Pax River.

"The first time I was out there was shortly after the failed rescue attempt of the hostages in the U.S. embassy in Terran, Iran, in late April, 1980. One of the test pilots in the group I was working with had been a helicopter pilot on that mission. After I had been introduced around, one of the Navy civilian engineers mentioned in a hushed voice that that certain pilot I had met had been on the rescue attempt and that he had been so thoroughly debriefed that he wasn't sure that he had even been on the mission. It then occurred to me that he had that cast to his eyes like he was looking a mile a way in a ten foot room.

"As a further aside, something went very wrong on that mission and it wasn't as simple as was reported in the newspapers and on TV. Since then, I've learned and put together other facts and know that to be the case. All the official reports of that incident are lies to cover up very bad things. But, going into that now would take too much time. My point here is to show that if they would have had to fry that pilot's brain to keep him from telling what really happened, they would have. But, they had developed methods that would do the job and leave his mind largely intact to the point of still doing his job as a test pilot. They probably learned the techniques, at least in part, from what they did to us."

Henni's eyes were wide. "Wow! That's some story.

Henni went to the kitchen and returned with two cans of beer. He held up one to me questioningly. I accepted it and popped the top. "We did remember some snippets about being in what had to be a hangar and using forklifts to shift around some crates." Then I told him about Bruce Holt and that he said he was on an unscheduled C-130 flight that landed at the Anoka Airport, and how he had subsequently denied it.

Dismissing the denial part, Henni said, "That's interesting. You remember I thought the bomb was around here someplace. I have no idea why I thought that, but maybe it is. Why the Anoka airport, though?"

"That makes sense to me. In '72 that airport was wide open. You could drive into it any time of day and at night. In the wee hours of the morning, the control tower wasn't operating and there'd be nobody about to ask questions. He'd glide in making little noise. Taking off he could ram the throttle home, and make all the noise he wanted. By the time anyone got out to look, he'd be long gone. That part works."

Henni accepted what I said in silence. I knew he had more to say so I said. "And, now for the other shoe to drop. You have something more, don't you?"

He smiled. "Yes, there is more and that is, to use a rather gross term, brainwashing. Today there are powerful drugs that do strange things to the mind. That's not surprising because there are a lot of people in the world with strange things going on in their heads and powerful drugs are needed to keep them at least sort of sane." Here he laughed. "I could mention several high government officials in that respect, but we won't go there. The thing is, the effect of brainwashing can be done much more easily now than in the past, even as recently as the Cold War. As you mentioned, they might have been experimenting with these drugs on you. The danger with that is there might be some deeply planted key word or phrase that will make you do something when it's activated."

"As in something destructive?"

"No. I was thinking more of making you blab everything you knew about the mission. There is the possibility that you were set up to be sort of a history device. At any time in your life someone with the trigger words could turn you on. You'd reveal the information and probably wouldn't remember that you had. They'd know something that you did not know and you wouldn't know that you told them."

"Kind of the worst of all worlds, huh?"

Henni nodded. Again we sat in silence each taking a swallow of beer from time to time. Finally Henni said, "Some time you must tell me the long version of that Iranian hostage story. I love conspiracy stuff like that."

"If I live that long!" I retorted. The fact that some American Gestapo dirt could deprive me of my life hit me again. Harry and I should take the fight to them, make them talk and work our way up the chain of command and rid the earth of that cancer! If we died along the way, well, it'd be over. But, we wouldn't die, we'd snuff 'em out! All of 'em, all the way to the top! That thought had come to me more than once lately.

Brushing the thought aside, I was about to say something when another flashback hit.

The pistol was aimed at me from the shadows. "Do it or die!"

"No."

"One last chance, do it or die!"

He had me. His gun was drawn, mine was holstered. I was standing in the light and he was invisible. His voice was the only cue I had as to his location, and he was constantly shifting his position. He had me. I did as I was told.

My eyes were shut and beads of perspiration appeared on my forehead. Henni said nothing. Once again I was rocking back and forth holding my face in my hands. This wasn't the same as when I saw Night Hawk die. This was when I died. Not really physically died, but close enough. To others it would seem like something that happens in life, not something we want or enjoy, but something that happens, like losing a chess game when we thought we would certainly win or being laid off from the best job we ever had. Maybe this was the incident that made me avoid games of all kinds. I associated losing with dying. On another level, I might have forced myself to forget as a defense mechanism to keep from going mad.

Finally Henni said, "Another flashback?"

I nodded. "The worst so far. It was when I died. You and I both accept that I can't understand your spiritual locution about peace. Similarly, you can't understand what I just said to you. I'm here breathing and talking so obviously I didn't die. But, I did. I don't know about the others in our teams, but for me my memory loss is due as much to my having died as it is to what they did to us. There's a warrior thing in me that doesn't allow what happened to me to happen. But, I let it happen. If I had fought at that instant, I would have surely died. Having chosen not to fight didn't change that. I died but my shell went on living."

Henni was shaken. "This is tough," he finally said. "Was it part of the mission?"

"Oh, yes." I told him what had come to me. It didn't seem so horrific in the telling. It wouldn't, of course, because words are not the reality. "I don't know what led up to the incident or what followed, but I'm sure it'll come to me, probably in a dream."

— 26 —

Sunday

We found it an odd coincidence that General Diggens as well as Bruce Holt would be from the Twin Cities area. Two of the main characters in this plot that was both whimsical and foreboding coming from the same locality was enough to give one pause. We located Diggens in his lakeside home on Forest Lake, some twenty miles northeast of St. Paul. Harry and I had called ahead and told him we thought we had served in Vietnam at the same time he had and were doing a personal history of the war. After a few questions we established that he had to be the General Diggens that Holt had mentioned, though we didn't mention Holt. He was delighted to get our call and invited us out.

We were met at the door by a man five foot eight or nine inches tall who looked to be seventy, though he had to be at least fifteen years older. His hair still had a tinge of dark brown and his strong square face had few wrinkles. He did not have a stomach hanging over his belt so watched his diet and exercised. In his younger days he had been a strong, big boned man. His hand shake was firm, to the point of pain.

As we followed him through the foyer I noted the hand of a woman who knew her business when it came to decorating. The wall hangings and accent pieces were artfully put together. He led us to his study and offered us iced tea which we accepted. It was clear this was his space. The many mementos of a military career told of a successful life and now a mellow retirement. The saying "old soldiers never die, they just fade away" came to mind.

When we were settled, he said, "You must have been Air Force and served at the air base on Cam Ranh Bay if we served together. What unit?"

"We served in Vietnam at the same time," I replied. "That's mainly what we have in common. And, actually, we were in the Army. The two or us were only on the Cam Ranh Bay air base for a few hours. And," here I paused, "it's those few hours that we want to talk about. It concerns you, an Air Force major, the two of us and a MADM. That's M-A-D-M., normally all caps. Do you recall anything about the confluence of those people and that object"

His first reaction was of surprise, then something like horror, and finally he threw back his head and brayed a hearty laugh. After a few seconds he said, "I knew the ol' gal wouldn't disappear forever. You know, it's sort of like a man who goes away on a business trip for a couple of months. He becomes lonely and has a tryst with his host's wife. Even though she may have more to lose than he does by revealing the affair, he spends the remainder of his life wondering if one day the woman will show up and tell his wife. Well, that's been the case of me and the MADM. Only, she's not an old girl, she's still sweet sixteen. Plutonium ages very well."

"Half life of 24,000 years," I interjected.

"Sounds about right. If she were to come calling it would be the crack of doom."

"As in a mushroom cloud," I suggested.

"Precisely." He had a quizzical expression as he examined first me and then Harry. "What on earth caused someone to poke a stick in that hornet's nest?"

Harry related how we figured it started the summer before when I slipped and revealed my Phantom connection, and how he had been contacted some weeks ago by some unsavory characters. Back and forth the two of us outlined what had happened with the general asking a question now and then. Prior to the meeting we had decided on a few particular things that we wouldn't tell, especially Cutter's name and our knowing who he was involved with.

Finally I said, "I think you can see that we're all in this now that it's started. It's out there somewhere and we have to find it first. The thing that caught us most off guard is the second set of snooping devices in my house. I can see that the state troopers would like to take credit for finding the thing, or that if the FBI has gotten wind of it they might have done it. But, in some way none of that sets right with me."

The general had a wry smile as he said, "Your suspicions are probably well founded. Have you considered that the Vietnamese may have become involved?"

Harry and I both could only offer blank expressions.

"It's a long story so let me begin at the end to answer how the Vietnamese would know about the present hunt. The crowd now occupying the White House are really a bunch of ghetto hayseeds, if that metaphor makes any sense. What they used to say about the Clinton White House applies to these guys ten times over."

I stopped him and said, I didn't know that he meant.

"Oh. There was the little anecdote that went, 'How does a boy scout troop differ from the Clinton White House? The boy scout troop has adult supervision.' The present denizens of the mansion are all communists and they foolishly think that means they and all the other communists in the world are just one big happy family. That's totally untrue, but thinking it is, they aren't careful with their security around others who they think subscribe to their political ideology. I'd guess it didn't take a week after they started looking for the MADM for Russia, China, and especially Vietnam to knew what they were doing. The big guys don't let the little guys have nukes if there is any way to avoid it. All the little guys want them because it gives them a higher standing in the world. Look at Israel and Pakistan. As a result, Vietnam doesn't have any, but definitely wants some. And, their appetites have been whetted because they almost had it. Therein lies the long story."

I shook my head as I said, "You're telling us that this is another legacy of that most pointless and stupid of all wars?"

"That's what I'm telling you, but that war wasn't as stupid and pointless as you may think. Since retiring, I've been doing some writing and along the way a few things have occurred to me to cast that war in a different light. What I am about to say doesn't bear directly on the present problem, but it may help you understand that these problems may in some way be justified because of that war.

"I'll be brief so if you don't follow the logic of what I say, you'll have to ask questions. The Vietnam War only has meaning if it is seen in the larger context of the Cold War. After the Second World War, the USSR, and the communists in general, started eating up countries with abandon. Of course Poland was given to Russia as part of the West's dealings during the war. Korea was divided on the thirty-eighth parallel at the end of the war. Hungary fell in '47 and '48. Czechoslovakia went communist in 1948. The communists took over China in 1949, and Cuba went in '59. Along the way we fought the Korean War from 1951 to '53. We ended exactly as we started, but South Korea did not fall to the communists. The next big test came in Vietnam. That war is called as you said, pointless and stupid, a tragedy, and similar things. We ultimately lost it. In fact, one commentator said it was the only time in history where an army won every battle and lost the war.

"But, here's the point that is generally overlooked, in fact it's always overlooked. If that war is looked at as a battle in the larger war, that is the Cold War, then we lost the battle, but won the war. Notice that Cuba was the last country the communists took over easily. When we weren't fighting a hot war we were sparring in various ways with the Russians. We were in Vietnam for ten years. Yes, the communists eventually won, as they were preordained to do because of the location of the country, its long narrow shape, and the lack of a central government worthy of the name after the demise of President Diem. That was a country not unlike Iraq. It was not a people, but a collection of intransigent, truculent factions, tribes, religions, and ethnic groupings. President Diem did a fair job of holding the country together, but, like Saddam Hussein in Iraq, he had to use heavy handed methods because that was all that would work. The U.S. didn't like Diem, in no small part because he was Catholic, so he was assassinated with the complicity of the CIA. After that, South Vietnam never again put together a government that could manage the country.

"In that ten years, though, world Communism was pretty much held in check. They had to see that if they pushed the U.S. too hard in other parts of the world that we'd go nuclear. In fact the nuclear option was seriously considered in Vietnam. I can't prove it, but it's entirely possible that we leaked the information that we were considering using nukes. The other important thing to keep in mind is during those ten years the USSR was experiencing serious internal erosion, especially economically. No one could see the future after Saigon fell in 1975. However, five years later Reagan was elected president and he went after what he called the 'evil empire' with a vengeance. His military build-up forced them to respond and in the process they went bankrupt. The years the U.S. spent in Vietnam were pivotal years. It's impossible to say what else would have happened if we had simply stayed out of it, but that war might very well have been a real bargain in spite of the blood and treasure we expended on it."

Harry asked, "So where in that story do we pick up on the possibility that the Vietnamese put listening devices in Vin's house?"

The general looked at the ceiling as he ticked off something on his fingers. He appeared to be having an argument with himself. Finally, he said, "It's been forty years, more or less, and a lot of archives are opened after that time. My quandary is that what we are discussing is highly classified. And, while you guys didn't sign an oath of security, I did. I don't know the whole story and you mentioned things I never heard about. My feeling is that if you two could retrieve your blocked memories you'd know more than I do. But still there are background things that you would never know. I think I can tell you some of that and not get into trouble.

"If you read any reasonably well researched history of the Vietnam War you'll find mention of Operation *Duck Hook* in the fall of 1969, Nixon's first year in office. To the Pentagon, it was known as Operation *Pruning Knife*. This operation was aimed at a massive air assault on North Vietnam and included the nuclear option. And, don't think that was so off the wall. Nearly all the war materiel the North Vietnamese and the Viet Cong used came from China. By land most of it came through a critical mountain pass on the border between North Vietnam and China. A nuke could have been used to close that pass. There was no city of any consequence nor population to speak of near the pass. It could have been done rather surgically, with the radio active fallout being within acceptable limits. Then if the harbors had been blockaded, and we maintained air superiority over the country, the supplies would have stopped and so would have the war.

"However, it wasn't long before the plan was discarded by Nixon as he stressed the need for more negotiation. *Duck Hook* is the only official mention of the possible use of nukes in Vietnam that one is likely to find. But," here he gave a broad smile, "that was by no means the only time it came up. All the senior officers who had been through the National War College knew how to win the war. It's just that the civilian leadership wasn't listening. McNamara as Secretary of Defense looked at the war in the same way an MBA would, that is, he thought it was only a problem of properly applying sound business administration principles. In addition, the strategy of 'body count' was doomed to failure. Ho Chi Minh said it, 'You will kill ten of us for every one of you we kill and it will be you who will tire.'

"The war could have been won by conventional means given the will to win. Absent that, the next option was to introduce at least one tactical nuclear weapon. I became involved in an operation, really a plot, to do just that. It would be tricky because the only plan that had any chance of success was to make it look like the North Vietnamese had used it. By extension, that would mean China was behind it because the North Vietnamese didn't have nukes. We would posture that we were ready to retaliate in kind, but were too civilized for that. Instead we would demand they meet us at the bargaining table with them under the massive world opprobrium of having done such a despicable thing.

"The plan was to place several, up to five, MADMs around South Vietnam ostensibly to protect key U.S. military installations. After the Tet Offensive in January 1968, this looked like a good idea and would be the reasoning the North Vietnamese would learn about from their spies. But, only one of the MADMs was to be real, the rest fakes. The real one would be set off in such a place so as to make it look like it was intended to destroy a U.S. military installation but for some reason went off prematurely, that is, just a little too far away to do extensive damage. It was to be equipped with a detonator that could be activated in a couple of ways. One used a coded radio signal as a fuse so it could be exploded any time we wanted. Another was a tilt sensor so it would detonate if it were moved."

"Wait," Harry said. "We were the ones who dug it up and it didn't explode."

"Yes. But, you were directed to remove a certain sensor cable from the top of the MADM as it laid in the ground and replace it with what looked like a cap to screw on over an electrical connector to protect the connector pins. That cap effectively disabled all the trigger options. However, if that cap were later removed, the thing would explode twenty minutes later. To avoid that requires that someone cut into the case in the right place and disable the triggers."

Harry gave me a questioning look. "Yeah," I said. "It's true. That major running our operation give me the cap with the instructions that it be used exactly as General Diggens said. I put it on while Night Hawk went to get the two of you. In our rush to get the thing out of the ground and on the truck you didn't notice it."

Here I looked at Diggens. "There would have to be a battery in the system to start the detonation sequence. That would have gone dead by now, especially knowing the battery technology of forty years ago."

The general shook his head. "Not true. When you pressed that cap onto the connector and screwed it home, you compressed a spring in a way that enabled, that is cocked, a clockwork timing mechanism but didn't start the clock running. If the cap were to be removed, it would allow the mechanical clock to start the count down that would cause detonation after twenty minutes. True, you couldn't detonate it by means of a radio signal at this time, but removing that cap would do it. I assure you, you can take it to the bank, if it still exists, that thing could be detonated right now."

Something else occurred to me. "The whole plan wouldn't have worked. It's well known that nuclear material used in bombs can accurately be traced to the reactor where it was made by means of trace isotopes. A dozen countries would have been sampling the fallout and traced it to the U.S."

He smiled again. "Yes and no. Yes, what you said is true if you don't care if someone knows where the material came from. Face it, in most cases where nuclear weapons might be used everybody knows who the belligerents are. You could assume one of the antagonists wouldn't blow up his own city just so he could blame it on his enemy. But, this case was different. It is possible, though very expensive, to purify and then falsely contaminate the fissile material so it would not appear to come from one of our reactors. And, I'm not talking about removing americium 241 which is a natural byproduct of the decay of plutonium 239. It's the other trace materials that are difficult to remove and don't affect the usefulness of the Pt 239.

"If it had been used, the U.S. would have denied it, and opened its nuclear reactors to foreign inspectors to verify it was not ours. Then they would have turned to China. We knew that China would have given up South Vietnam rather than reveal the extent of their nuclear program to the world so we win. And, if you ask anyone in the business if nuclear material can be falsely contaminated, they will vociferously deny it." As an afterthought he said, "It would have worked if the president had had the guts to do it."

"So, you say it's booby trapped and it was specially made so as to be untraceable to the United States. Why and how do you know all of this?"

The general thought for a moment. "I suppose since I've gone this far I might as will continue a little further since it doesn't matter now. I know those things because I was involved in the operation from the start. Something like that takes careful planning lest the opposite of the intended result occur. Being a colonel then, I was assigned along with an engineer from one of our nuclear labs to figure out all the things that could go wrong and how to compensate for them. We weren't too worried about placing the device because we would put it in a place where we had control of the territory. But, if we intended to remove it at some later time, things could have changed a lot. So we took into account that there would be hostile forces when the time came to retrieve it just as you seemed to have encountered. If they found it before you got to it, the tilt sensor would detonate it when it was moved so the plan to have them detonate a nuke would be forced on us all. If they took it away from you after you had dug it up, the trip mechanism under the connector cap was the key. It is human nature to want to see what the thing is all about. Someone would have to unscrew that connector cap. If the MADM wasn't used the intent was to have it returned to an old nuclear test range in the U.S. where the engineer in charge would disable the device, you know, in case he made a mistake it wouldn't destroy a lab and half a city."

Here he stopped and looked at his hands. "But," I said, "something went wrong, something that all your careful planning had not considered and compensated for."

He nodded but remained silent.

I persisted, "What went wrong?"

Without looking up he replied, "Deep down, I knew that would happen, that we would never use it. Furthermore, we knew the North Vietnamese had gotten wind of a nuke hidden somewhere in the vicinity of Cam Ranh Bay. As I mentioned, that information may have been intentionally leaked. It was difficult to see how such a small team as yours could retrieve it successfully. That was quite a feat. We could have gone in with a battalion and gotten it, no problem. But, then hundreds of people would have known about it. Anyway, you managed to get it. I checked the serial number on the name plate, it was the only one I cared about, the live one. I watched as the crate was nailed shut, saw it loaded on the C-141, and thought by some miracle we had succeeded. It was nearly a week later when I was called into a top secret meeting and told the fifth crate contained a jet engine going back for overhaul."

He looked up his eyes flashing as he slammed his right fist on his desk. "Of all the luck—that ruined my career! That major was there, he saw the name plate and the SN, too. But, I was the one who signed for it. Of course there was an investigation. The receiving end had multiple witnesses of every move that crate made after the plane arrived in the States. It was accepted that it went missing before it was loaded on the plane, and that the switch was extremely cleverly done. That meant the thing was still in-country. That was the only explanation."

"But," I said, "that was one of the contingencies you planned for, to have it stolen by the North Vietnamese. The only thing not according to plan was that they did not have the curiosity to unscrew that cap."

"Yes, yes. Except, it was supposed to be stolen before I signed for it!"

"You mentioned an investigation," I said. "In a case like this, wouldn't that be deeply classified?"

"Sure, but, if these people are who you think they are, they could get at all the files for missing nuclear weapons."

"Oh," I replied. "This would be a *Broken Arrow* situation like in the movie."

He smiled. "Yeah, the Pentagon has several code names for these events of which one is *Broken Arrow*. There are a few famous cases, and several more that are known and considered closed for one reason or another. For example, a lot of publicity surrounded the event that took place on December of 1965. An A-4E Skyhawk fighter fell off an elevator of the aircraft carrier USS Ticonderoga. At first it was reported that the plane with a hydrogen bomb aboard was lost five-hundred miles out at sea. However, it was later revealed that it was lost only miles from the Japanese island chain of Ryukyu. There was a diplomatic storm-fire over it because of Japan's anti-nuclear law prohibiting the introduction of nuclear weapons into it's territory. That law included the United States. Another reason for the first false reporting of the location was that the USS Ticonderoga was returning from a mission off North Vietnam, thus confirming the introduction of nuclear weapons into the Vietnam War zone. The nuclear bomb the A-4 was carrying was never recovered. Cases like the above were posted on the Internet as well as elsewhere. The truly baffling ones like this are held to the highest security levels.

"We liked the MADM because it only weighed something over 350 pounds with carrying case, while the actual munition itself only weighed 150 pounds. It could be adjusted to have an output from one to fifteen kilotons of TNT equivalent, though this one was fixed to maximum output only. These warheads, designated W-45, were intended for several uses so a lot of them were made—a total of three hundred fifty. Some were used on surface to air missiles or as the business end of surface to surface missiles. Others, like the MADM, were intended for demolition or as an atomic land mine. The MADMs were put into service in the nineteen-sixties, and the last ones were decommissioned about 1990, except maybe for the missing one."

The general, consciously or not, was slipping off into unrelated areas so I stood up and went to examine some of the pictures that adorned the walls. One in particular took my interest. It was a black and white photo of a B-29 with the crew posed by the nose. The emblem on the nose was of an American Indian wearing a full feather headdress and the name *The Ojibwe* under it. I pointed to it and asked, "Was this your plane?"

"Yeah, that's my ship, and a good one she was too. We all made it through for reasons I can't imagine. A B-29 was a sitting duck for the Migs over North Korea, but day after day we went out. After the F-86 Saber arrived with its gyro stabilized gun sight it got a bit better. They took down the Migs at a seventeen to one ratio. But, there were a lot of Migs."

Something stirred in me. "Where did the plane's name come from?"

He chuckled. "I'm one-sixteenth Ojibwe. One evening shortly after I took command of my ship, we were tipping a few and I let that little tid-bit of information slip. After that there was no stopping it. We didn't have crew briefings, we had powwows. It was all in good fun so I didn't mind much. From the way planes and crews were being lost, we all expected to die, anyway. After the war ended and the crew disbanded, the nickname died away. I was glad enough about that. Occasionally, I'd meet someone I knew back then and it'd be mentioned for old time's sake."

What was it about that name that tugged at me? It was connected to something else and I knew it did not involve the Korean War. I went to the next pictures and the general gave a short story for each one.

After some minutes of that, I asked, "What can you tell me about Major Bruce Holt?"

I had turned so I could see his reaction when I mentioned the name. He reacted by giving only a slight jerk of his head. "It's a funny thing that the two of you both hail from this metro area. He's living in Hopkins now."

After a pause, Diggens said, "You have me at a disadvantage. I seem to remember a Holt, Bruce, I believe. But, I don't recall in what context."

"We've both mentioned a major in connection with the shipment and disappearance of the fifth MADM. That's his name. You must remember him. He certainly remembers you. In fact, it was though him that we found you."

"Yes. I remember a major, but I didn't connect the major of that incident as Bruce Holt. When was it that he told you about me?"

"Yesterday. And, we were both there. There's no mistake. You grounded him for making a bad landing with a C-130 that had sustained battle damage. After all this time, he's still angry at you for that. As I said, it's odd that you're both from this area."

"Actually, that's not true. I'm from Wisconsin, near Madison. My wife was from St. Paul. After I got out of the Air Force, we settled here because her family was all in the area. Mine was pretty well dispersed around the country."

After a pause he continued, "What did Major Holt have to say about the missing bomb?"

"About the same as you. You both admit seeing it in the crate, seeing the crate nailed shut and then the crate being loaded on the C-141. That was the last anyone saw of it. Harry and I were apparently part of the team that retrieved it from the mountain, and I guess we were there to load it on the plane. Do you by any chance remember either one of us? We are assuming that was after Harry got the scar on his face so he would have been memorable."

Diggens shook his head. "No. And I agree, it seems reasonable that I would remember such a mark. But, since I didn't remember Holt as the major, I may have forgotten that, too. The ravages of age, I guess."

He stood and it was clear the meeting was over. "I've given you some background information that is classified so I do hope you will treat it with caution."

At the front door we turned to thank him for his help and suddenly he went a little rigid as he looked piercingly at both of us. "It didn't leave Vietnam to come this way. Surely it made its way to China all those years ago. It can't exist anymore. That's why I was willing to give you the information I did. What on earth would make those guys who are leaning on you think you know where it is? And, if you could tell them where it is, how would they expect to get it?"

With what I hoped was sufficient hardness in my expression I replied, "Because, in spite of what he told us yesterday, Bruce Holt told *those guys* that he flew the C-130 that was carrying it from Can Ranh Bay to the Anoka County Airport. That's why." We turned and walked to the car leaving him standing on his front stoop.

— 27 —

Harry was driving as we left General Diggens' house. After a mile Harry said, "He's lying, too. The background stuff is probably mostly true, but he left out a lot, just like Holt. I wonder if they're comparing notes. And, that part about the booby trap, if true, really makes this whole thing scary."

He kept rambling on, sort of thinking out loud. Finally I said, "Stop talking. There's something about the word Ojibwe that keeps nagging at me. Let me relax and see if I can remember something."

I closed my eyes and let the sounds of the car take over my consciousness. There I was with Night Hawk when I found him dead. "It's coming, another flashback."

"I've got a pocket tape recorder. Want me to turn it on?"

"Yeah. I'll tell it as it come unless it comes too fast. I remember being beside Night Hawk." I rambled on as the thoughts came to me saying anything I remembered hoping it would make sense.

Night Hawk was dead, and I could be so at any moment. Nothing could be done about him so I had to do what was possible to help Blue Dog and Nine Lives get clear of the mountain. A situation like this is all action. Your senses are more alert than normal, your actions smooth and sure. Scrapes and bruises go unnoticed. The only goal is staying alive to take another breath. There is no sense of time, or of how you will do what you have to do next. The battle is enjoined, you are committed, it must be played out in a dance of death and life. There's nothing heroic, or brave about it. The battle comes and when it's over, it may never have happened. A comrade is gone leaving an empty place until a replacement arrives. Then it starts again.

There was movement in the direction from which we had come. Switching to full auto, I emptied my magazine to the sound of thrashing in the bushes. Someone had been hit. A new magazine loaded, I took two from Night Hawk and slid back. It was imperative I move fast before they could encircle me. After putting enough vegetation between me and the area I had covered with my last burst, I was up and running, slipping, falling, rolling, and up again. The terrain was exceptionally rugged though there weren't many deadfall trees to impede my progress. That was to the advantage of my pursuers as well, but only if they were desperate enough to make a mad charge as I was making a similarly desperate retreat.

The rain was coming faster as I halted after fifty meters in an attempt to gauge the location of the enemy. I unscrewed my silencer and slipped it in the pouch provided for it. Having no indication where to fire I sprayed a half magazine in a one-eighty arc. The idea was to get them to follow me and not Blue Dog and Nine Lives. That didn't seem to have been a problem since there was return fire from where I had left Night Hawk and from up hill, too. The shots were not well aimed since none of us saw the other. They were shooting at the sound of my shooting. It was obvious though, they were trying mightily to flank me so I was up and moving again.

By this time the rain was a torrent. It wasn't cold rain, but I was soaked to the skin and had been for some time. The necessary energy required to keep my body temperature up was draining me. The feverish activity had warded off the effects up until now. I didn't want to start shivering, but there were not many options. From behind a tree, I sent another burst up hill. At first there was no return fire so I fired the way I had come. In a second the hillside erupted in firing from the way I had come, up hill and the way I was going. My plan had been to move more or less parallel to the road, though that was hard to tell with any certainty with it's many switchbacks.

There seemed to be one option left to me, and that was toward the road, and that was where they wanted me to go. If there was an enemy force waiting for me there, well, that was it. So, down hill I went, slipping and sliding more than before. I made good progress since gravity has that way about it. If it's down you want, it'll jump in and lend a hand. A time or two it seemed as if it might be too much help as I lost control of my descent. With no fanfare, I landed on the faint trail that was the road. Immediately, I saw fresh truck tracks in the mud. The truck had made it past this point.

As if at a jump instruction in a computer program, I came to the decision point of going over the far edge of the road and taking my chances in the ravine. From my earlier brief perusal of that option I decided against it. The obvious one was to start down the road after the truck in the hopes I could overtake it and we could combine fire as we rapidly withdrew. That was rejected because the truck would be traveling faster than was safe, which was certainly faster than I could run. Those on the hillside would be descending on the road either behind or in front of me, or both. That option was rejected. The remaining possibility would be to do what I was least expected to do, start back up hill and hunker down while they passed me. I liked it—always do the most unexpected thing you could. I ran fifty meters on the road, and started back up the hill. The vegetation on the road combined with the rain would make my tracks hard to find by all but the most experienced trackers.

The noise of the rain made it impossible to hear where the enemy was. Maybe they had anticipated my move and had stopped to await my return up hill. I stopped and sat down with my back to some thicket growing on the down hill side of a low ledge of rocks. It appeared the truck was on it's way so my mission had changed from drawing off the Viet Cong to staying alive myself. With that in mind I carefully screwed the silencer back on my M-16.

Between gusts of wind I thought I heard a muffled command to my rear. Then nothing, might have been my imagination. Putting the moment of rest to use I began eating an energy bar. After each bite, it put it in a pocket of my jacket so as to have both hands free in case of need. Behind me there was the scuff of a boot on rock, and a body rolled past me an arm's length away. He was game. Bruised, he gathered his weapon and started moving again looking to his left and right as if keeping track of others.

I froze in place. To shoot him, or to even move was death as clearly there were others nearby. In seconds my almost guest was out of sight down hill so I was up, and seeing nothing I could identify as a threat, started up hill again veering off in the general direction of the road as it headed out of the mountain. The terrain guided my direction so no map or compass was necessary. I knew within a hundred meters where I was at all times. That didn't mean the terrain was at all recognizable from my trip in. The rain had slacked off again. There was no movement to be seen so if they had gotten ahead of me and set up an ambush, I was dead again.

The road was at least three times longer than the straight line path I was trying to follow. I wondered if Nine Lives and Blue Dog had made it out yet. Maybe, and maybe not. Just in case, I changed my line of travel slightly in the direction of the road. There was light between the trees ahead as if I were approaching a clearing. More cautious now, I eased up to the opening to discover it was not a clearing as such, but a drop off. Below me a stretch of road was visible, and between me and it was a ledge with three VC lying on rocky outcroppings waiting in ambush.

It might be a trick to cause me to concentrate on an open target and forget my own safety as I positioned myself for a shot. I had no time to ponder the situation as movement on the road revealed a truck slowing at a washed out section of road. It would have to slowly negotiate the water covered rocks hoping not to be washed off the road and down the canyon or become hung up on a rock. At that point they'd be dead.

Putting my M-16 on single shot, I eased into position and started shooting. It was down hill and that type of marksmanship is always tricky. My advantage was they were close enough to make missing diffi-cult. In three shots I took out the three ambushers. Immediately I pulled back to a point of concealment only to have bullets chip off the rock I had braced against to shoot. The sound of the shot told me the shooter was not far to my right rear. I eased back a step at a time making no noise, moving, stopping, listening, then another step. He came past me not ten feet to my right. I froze.

The rain had slacked to nothing but the sound of a renewed down pour approaching from behind the ridge could be heard. The revving of the truck engine came to me clear enough indicating it had successfully negotiated the water. From what I could recall, that would be their last obstacle so there was a good chance they'd make it out. Now, it was up to me to save my backside, and that could be trying with the enemy all around. There was movement at the ledge from which I had fired as if someone were looking for a body, my body. I caught glimpses of him through the leaves as he moved about.

He paused in his search where my view of him was nearly complete. He seemed unconcerned that the truck was getting away. He carried an M-16 like mine except no silencer. Though unexpected, that was not im-possible since they used captured equipment whenever possible as in this man's weapon and the field telephone in the hooch. My concealment was nearly complete but taking no chances my gun was up ready for a fast shot. I had no desire to kill for no reason, though I'd take him down with no compunction to stay alive.

He seemed fascinated by the sight of the three dead men below. Then, he did an odd thing. He transferred his rifle to his left hand grasping it by the upper part of the barrel as the stock swung to the ground.

"You found it," he said in precise English with only a hint of accent which could only mean he had spent a lot of time in the States. "Those were good men we lost as was the man you lost. None of them need have died if *The Ojibwe* had given more warning."

Slowly he turned toward me. He was totally soaked as was I. The water changed the tone of his clothing and I could not determine if he was wearing a South or a North Vietnamese uniform. He was too far away in the dim light of the overcast day and the heavy foliage to see insignia distinctly. I was uncertain whether or not he could see me. It didn't matter because with his weapon in that clumsy position there was no way he could hit me before I had several bullets in him. "We've been searching for it for some time. It never occurred to us that it would be on this side of the mountain. Most unexpected."

What was he talking about?

"It doesn't matter because now that it has been found we need each other to complete the mission. With the truck gone, those pursuing you will regroup further up the mountain so your egress should be without incident."

My mind reeled. What was this? It sounded like he knew me or at least had been expecting me. The rain came across us like a curtain. Either he made a fast move or a branch gave way under the torrent. Not taking a split second to think, I was firing in a searching pattern—at where I had last seen him, to the left, to the right, then low. If he were thrashing about wounded it would go unheard above the thunderous rain.

I eased back slowly at first, then at a run for ten steps after which I stopped and took in my surroundings. If the enemy were close by, it was as unlikely they would hear me as it was I'd hear them. With the truck away, their main quarry was lost. They knew there had been something valuable buried in the hollow and wanted it as badly as we did. They had failed and lost a number of men in the effort. Would it be worth losing more in an effort to track down the rest of us because they had no way of knowing how many Americans there were. After all, they had Night Hawk's body and his weapons as booty. All of that would have made sense if it hadn't been for the man who had spoken to me. That part I blocked from my mind in an effort to keep my senses sharp in this most dangerous of all games.

It took two hours of silently negotiating the mountain side to arrive at the point where we had stopped in the morning to await daylight. For a monsoon day the rain had not been as heavy and unrelenting as it could have been, for that I was grateful. Some time before I had unscrewed my silencer and stowed it so as not to draw attention to myself as I slogged along the saturated road, or what passed for one. My M-16 was slung over my shoulder, muzzle down. It would not be too unlikely for the local inhabitants to see an American combatant walking this way. There could be Viet Con, and likely were, in some of the huts. However, they could expect that if they killed me, there would be a vicious reprisal on the village.

The afternoon was wearing on by the time I arrived at Highway 1. I had a reasonable hope that some U.S. truck would happen along and give me a lift. After a half-mile of walking in solitude, a truck approached from my front. Past me it ground to a stop and backed up.

"Duce!" the driver said as he stopped beside me. He had been expecting two men.

It was Nine Lives. "Yeah," I said. "Where's Blue Dog?"

He was leaning toward me, left forearm on the bottom of the open window jamb, and part of his head out of the side window. His right hand hug over the top of the steering wheel. "In the back. Where's Hawk?"

"Dead."

"Ah, gee! Such a good man. Well, get in, we'll find some hot chow."

That was it. If we were to grieve, it wouldn't be now. Another nightmare to endure later. Life had that sort of an edge to it.

He found a place to turn around and headed back to the helicopter base. He turned up the heat in the truck which felt good since it was still raining and I was wet through and through.

Nine Lives looked at me, "You sure he's dead?" It was the logical thing to ask. None of us cherished the thought of becoming a POW.

"Yeah. Took one in the head. Could have happened to any one of us at any time. This business sucks."

I asked the obvious question. "Did you manage to get out with it?"

"Yeah. That's why Blue's in the back. He's guarding it. He said he knows what it is, but won't say how he knows."

The air was dripping with expectation as I waited. In a grim sort of tone he said, "Says it's a nuke. One ready to go boom. Says it's all there. No secret codes, nothing. Only the right electrical signal to the right place. Fifteen thousand tons of high explosive right behind you ready to scratch your back. Go figure."

We still had dibs on the tent from the night before so we parked the truck beside it and I changed into my other set of clothes, pausing from time to time to put bandages on the more severe scrapes and cuts I had sustained. It always amazed me how beat up a guy could get when his only concern was staying alive long enough to take another step. I didn't expect to stay dry for long, but it felt good for as long as it would last. I'd wear a poncho in the area while we were getting some grub. We had our appointment to deliver the truck and the case to the major at the air base at 2200 hours.

After we had eaten, I gathered the others around and in whispers related to them the strange incident where the guy had spoken to me. We were accustomed to being sent on missions where there seemed to be no logical reason for what we were expected to do. This one set a record, though. We were always told not to discuss reasons or supposed reasons but I had a feeling there was enough wrong with this one where we'd better do some figuring or we'd be dead.

"Okay," I said. "If you're sure the thing is a live nuke, that means things are out of control."

Blue Dog was adamant. His previous team had been given training in using tactical nuclear weapons though he refused to say if they ever deployed them. He joined our team because his last mission had gone bad and he was the only one to come back.

"It's a tactical nuke that in this configuration is used as a land mine. The part the Vietnamese guy said about them not expecting it to be on the side of the mountain where it was buried is significant for this reason. If it had been intended to be used in the normal way, it would have been placed on the other side as they had expected. If you look at a map you'll see that Cam Ranh Bay runs parallel to the general coast line with the ocean side of the bay nothing more than an enlarged outer bank connected to the mainland on the north end making it a long peninsula. The main military facilities are on the southern end of that outer arm. To stop an attack on the peninsula, the bomb would have been placed to interdict the enemy approaching the point where the peninsula connects to the mainland. The mountain would have shielded the U.S. military facilities from the blast effects.

"But, it was placed on the side of the mountain facing the bay. That can mean only one thing. Whoever placed it intended it to look like a nuclear attack on the U.S. base. The main port facilities would have been seriously damaged but not destroyed. Neither would the runways at the air base be made unusable. The planes and hangars would have been swept away by the shock wave, though. I would conclude that it was intended to start a tactical nuclear war and make it look like they used one first."

We discussed it for awhile longer but what we thought didn't matter. We had to follow orders to conclude the mission by delivering the case to the air base. A few helicopters had come and gone but none with the other teams, and no sign of other aluminum cases. At 2045 hours, we started out. We were allowing, we hoped, plenty of time to make our rendezvous at 2200. At the gate to the base we were stopped and a call was made, I figured to the major. We were waved through.

It was a large base so it was a few miles from the gate to our destination. The roads were paved and the runways were, too. Nothing else was hard surfaced so in the dark it would have been inadvisable to deviate from our directed route since off the pavement, mud ruled. We approached a point where our route of travel went between two buildings. There was a five ton truck parked to the side facing us leaving just enough room to pass by on the driver's side. Nine was driving. He slowed and as he did the driver's side door of the five ton opened and a man stepped down. He waved us to stop. I tuned around and in a low voice alerted Blue Dog that we may have trouble. I could hear movement in the back. Blue Dog was exiting our truck to cover us as our motion ceased.

"Kill the lights," the man said loud enough to be heard above the rain. Nine Lives did as directed. Immediately the lights on the larger truck came on. "Get out!" the man demanded. The voice was familiar. It had been raining on the mountain, too, and I was almost certain it was the same man. Nine and I did as directed. Obviously there was at least one additional man who operated the light switch. The first man approached us stepping into the light off toward the building on my right. The truck light was coming from his right rear so I couldn't see his face. He carried a pistol aimed in our direction. The passenger side door of the five ton truck opened, visible from light reflected off the buildings.

"You are ordered to transfer custody of the case in your truck to me."

That was not how Phantom worked. We only took orders from our controller who for this mission was the major.

Blue took that moment to act. Using his silenced nine millimeter, he shot twice at the man getting down from the truck. The next two shots put out the headlights on the five ton. I dove for the ground at the same time drawing my pistol. I rolled toward the building and came up and shot once where I had last seen the man. Nine Lives said only, "Mine." That was so I wouldn't shoot again and inadvertently hit him. I heard him connect with the other man body to body and the two went down. I couldn't see much as my eyes had not yet dark adapted from looking into the headlights. How Nine managed to hit the man I never knew, but the scuffle on the ground ended after only a few seconds with a "thump."

"Got him," Nine said. "Any more?"

"Don't move, I'm going around back" I said as I bounded along the side of the five ton truck. There was no sound from inside the covered back of the truck. Ducking low, I went around the back to see up the passenger's side. There was a dark shadow on the ground, unmoving. I approached it in a quick dash and with my pistol at the ready, kicked it. No response. I reached down feeling the carotid artery. No pulse. Swinging open the unlatched door I stepped back. Nothing. Stepping forward, I covered the interior of the truck's cab with my weapon. Again, nothing.

"Blue," I said, "a flashlight to check the back of the truck." Blue was beside me in seconds as I heard Nine move. He'd taken a post near the back of our truck. At the rear of the five ton, I stopped at the passenger side corner. Nine ducked low and went to the other side. Keeping his head down he raised his hand with the light and flipped it on illuminating the inside of the truck. I was poised with my gun held with both hands covering whatever might be waiting for us.

"Empty," I said. That meant there was no human form, though there was a crate end on to me. The light went out. There seemed to be no further eminent danger. The three of us met between the two vehicles.

Nine said, "The one I took down is still alive, but out cold."

"Let's go," I said. "We're almost late for our meeting."

— 28 —

The building shown on the sketch turned out to be an aircraft hangar with the main door open. The only lights were a row shining down just inside the door. We pulled to a stop at 2202 hours. The major came out of the shadows as we piled out.

He looked at us and said, "Late. But, pretty close."

I didn't have time to mention our delay before he continued. "Where's the fourth man?"

"Dead," I replied.

The major gave the slightest start. "Accident?"

"Enemy fire. The area where the case was buried is infested with Viet Cong or more probably North Vietnamese. The case is in the truck."

It seemed to take the major a minute to process the information, though I didn't see why it should. Then he nodded. We gathered around, close. Three muscular, trained fighting men armed to the teeth with knives and guns pressing in caused him to became alarmed, as was the intent. "What's this?"

"We have a problem," I began. I related the incident on the mountain. The mention of *The Ojibwe* caused him to interrupt me.

"You're sure that's what he said?"

"Yeah. I'm from Minnesota and that's the name of the Indian tribe in Northern Minnesota and Wisconsin. Sometimes they're called the Chippewa."

He nodded and said, "I know. I'm from Minnesota, too. What did he say about this guy he called *The Ojibwe*?"

Then, I related the attack we had sustained less than a half mile from the hangar. "I'm not sure what's going on other than we are fairly certain that that aluminum case contains a tactical nuke. And, there are people close at hand who want it. The questions are, who are they, are you one of them, and what is anybody going to do about it? We have no idea who the good guys are."

We could see the major was in a quandary as he considered his options. Finally he said, "You guys are secret ops, right? I mean, you do illegal, or off the books stuff all the time, things that are never intended to see the light of day."

We nodded.

"Okay. I know who *The Ojibwe* is. It surprises me that he's involved, but it does explain some odd things that have been happening. That means I have to make this thing disappear without the trail leading to me or him. Are you with me?"

We could only agree because he was our handler and he had the final say as to what we did. Our bosses at Phantom Command knew our mission, but in cases like this where tactical control of us was released to another, they had no choice but to let the man on the ground make the decisions.

"Okay," the major continued. "There's a C-141 out on the tarmac that's nearly done loading. It's scheduled to depart at 2230. I've purposely delayed the final cargo so it can't leave early. The fifth case, this one, is to be loaded before the final cargo. But we need a slight change of plan. Here's what we'll do." With that he told us the plan making changes as he went because it was obvious he was making it up on the spot. It had to work the first time. It seemed an odd thing to do, but war sometimes doesn't make sense. No, that's not right. It never made sense so why should it now?

With our instructions we went into action. There was a government issue fork lift parked near the wall of the hangar. Nine Lives, as instructed, went to it, mounted the machine and started it. He brought it to the back of our truck and raised the forks to the height of the truck bed. Blue Dog and I slid the case out of the truck onto the waiting forks. From there he drove to a crate made extra large to accept packing between the aluminum case and the crate. The three of us heaved the case off the forks and lowered it into the crate. With my sleeve, we wiped off the tag with the FSN and the serial number on it. There were Styrofoam blocks of packing material handy and we wedged them in around the case. The cover to the case had been constructed and was at hand.

The major nodded his satisfaction and walked to the wall where there was sort of a podium with a phone where shipping documents and other records were finalized. He made a call. After the call he said he would leave for a few minutes and told me what to say if the general showed up to sign for the last case before he returned.

With that, we began the second part of this strange improvised operation. Nine Lives hustled to the second building to the right of the hangar and found the one where equipment was crated for shipment. As the major had said, there were several completed crates waiting for shipment. Following instructions he measured them and selected the one that most nearly met the dimensions of the one containing the aluminum case we had delivered. Starting another forklift identical to the one in the hangar, he picked up the crate he had selected that contained a jet engine being sent back for overhaul. It had the top nailed on and shipping papers in a clear plastic sleeve stapled to it. He had been told to remove the shipping papers, and replace them with others the major had hurriedly assembled in the hangar. He then found a stencil set and stenciled "5 of 5" on all sides of the crate.

At the same time, Blue Dog walked around the hangar to the back and found the two and a half ton truck he was told would be there. He drove it to the tarmac in front of the building where Nine Lives had acquired the second forklift and the crated jet engine.

I was directed to find some cases of C-rations and five gallon cans of water in a lean-to attached to the hangar. I was to load two of each into the back of our three-quarter ton truck. These items were used by flight crews making the long haul to CONUS. The military made sure to see its men were fed, though when given the chance, a lot of guys chose to buy their own food. After that I was to wait by the crate with the aluminum case in it with a clipboard containing shipping papers and have a hammer and nails handy.

The only lights on in the hangar were those above the main door so as I made my way to the lean-to for the supplies I entered deepening shadows. As I walked among the planes, a few F-4s, some Mohawk reconnaissance planes, and other assorted fighters, all parked at odd angles to maximize the number the building could house, I became concerned and drew my pistol. The door to the lean-to was standing partially open. Beside it was a switch for, I assumed, the light within. It was. The light inside the fifteen by thirty foot area was a single spot light shining to the right leaving the space to the left in shadow. Sweeping my gun left and right the building appeared to be clear of threats, though there were numerous places where someone would be crouched behind a pallet of supplies. The light shown on the items that concerned me, a half dozen five

gallon cans of water, and a pile of Cs. Holstering my gun I grabbed a can
of water in each hand and proceeded to our truck. On the second trip I
hefted two cases of rations, about forty pounds each, and turned. At that
point the spotlight was in my eyes and from behind it came a voice—that
same voice again.

"You will do as I tell you or you die now. As soon as you arrive at the
front of the hangar you are to kill that major."

A hand holding a pistol aimed at me was visible for an instant from
the shadows as if done purposefully so I would understand the threat was
real. "Do it or die!"

"No."

"One last chance, do it or die!"

He had me. His gun was drawn, mine was holstered. I was standing
with the light in my eyes and he was invisible. My hands were encum-
bered with the cases of rations. His voice was the only cue I had as to his
location, and he was constantly shifting his position. He had me. I acqui-
esced. "Okay."

"I'll be behind you so don't try any heroics."

I was beaten like I had never been beaten before. When I submitted to
his demands something in me died. It was my duty to take the bullet. The
shot might have alerted Blue Dog, Nine Lives or the major. The mission
was all important, and killing our handler clearly was not part of it.

I turned toward the door and nudged it open as it was off plumb and
tended to swing three-quarters of the way shut. Clear of the door I could
hear the shuffling of his feet as he followed. With a snap the light went
out. I kept telling myself, there was nothing I could do. Without the load
in my hands I might have had a chance.

His voice behind me was a sneer, "You fancy yourselves as being so
good, you Phantom guys." More shuffling as he stayed within easy range
of me, but not close enough where I might drop to the floor and lash out
at him. "You managed to get clear of the mountain, but there's no bushes
to hide in here. . . ." His voice trailed off.

A subdued groan, was followed by the clatter of a gun on the concrete. Without thinking, I threw the cartons to the right, drew my gun
with my right hand and threw myself to the left bringing my gun around.
Between the shadows thrown by the planes my nemesis was on the floor
his gun a foot from his outstretched hand. My one shot at him earlier by
the trucks must have struck home. I kicked the gun and it spun across the
floor toward where the cases had landed. Covering him with my pistol, I

checked for a pulse. He was still alive, though unconscious and would probably die.

On my knees I closed my eyes and endured an over whelming pain. I had agreed to throw the mission to save myself. The fact the no one need even know about this didn't change anything. With a good biblical up-bringing, actually, somewhat surprisingly, as a Catholic, I was well aware that Christ had made the willful desire to commit a sin equal to actually doing it. I had actually consented to his demands without the slightest protest. Even if one could argue that we were not expected to give our lives so wantonly, it was what I expected of myself. I had never intended to let the team down—for any reason.

But . . . from every outward appearance, they had not been let down. It was now my duty to continue with the mission as if this had not hap-pened. I stuck his pistol behind my belt in the small of my back and stacked the cartons one on the other. They weighed a ton. Hardly able to stand with my load, I made for the front of the hangar stashed the food in the truck and looked for the major. He had not returned. It was possible he had suspected the other man would be close and try to kill him.

— 29 —

I stopped talking because there was nothing more to say. This flash-back ended just as suddenly as the first. When I hadn't spoken for a full minute, Harry asked, "Then what happened? There must be more."

Shaking my head, I said, "Of course, there has to be more, but that's the end of it for now." We had arrived in the New Brighton area and I told Harry to exit I-35W at Highway 96. I knew a place we could pull off and park that would not draw attention. He pulled over on a side street and stopped where large trees shaded the street where I had directed him.

"We need the rest of the story," Harry said. "Can't you just pull it out. Why do we only get it in chunks?"

"You were there too," I retorted. "And, you haven't been any help."

"I told you about the second time we got chow and about forklifts and cases. That was right."

"But, until I put it into the narrative, it was useless. Listen, this isn't helping."

"You're right. It seems that Diggens was in on the plot to steal the case, though, so he knows a lot more than he told us. The thing about *The Ojibwe* settles that. A handle like that sticks and it's obscure enough that it's unlikely it would be anybody else." After a pause he said, "That part about selling out the team in exchange for your life really hurts, doesn't it?"

I nodded. "It does. It might be that I've been blocking the whole thing to avoid facing what I did, or consented to do. My friend, Henni, alluded to that. In fact, he mentioned that we were debriefed with a combination of hypnosis, drugs, and trauma because we were set up to do things that we just wouldn't normally do. In normal life we saw ourselves as being the type of people who would draw the line at doing what they wanted us to do."

"Yeah," he said wistfully. "I never looked at myself as being a particularly virtuous guy, but there's always that point where I'd say, 'That's going to far, that's not right.'"

That said, I pushed him, "Now, it's your turn. You recalled the forklifts and crates. Kick yourself in the butt. What did you do with them?"

He shrugged. "I must have driven the forklift if that's what you remember the major telling me to do."

"Darn it!" I said. "Of course you did! Where did you drive it?"

"Well, I drove out to where I was beside the truck driven by Blue Dog. Oh yeah . . . that must be it. Over the years I always remembered driving the forklift in the rain like sort of in a dream. That must be it." He trailed off.

"Okay. Care to let me know?"

"See, after I came up beside the truck we both drove with no lights parallel to the front of the hangar ten yards out until Blue Dog could see you in the hangar, but due to the rain thundering on the hangar roof and the poor visibility, you wouldn't be able to see the truck. No one in the hangar could see me on the forklift because I was on the opposite side of the truck from you. We stopped fifty yards before I came to the open hangar door. There we waited for something but I can't remember what."

"We were waiting for the general to come and sign the shipping document. Was that it?"

He shook his head. "That doesn't fit."

"Wait," I said. "There's more."

I waited five or ten minutes before a government sedan pulled into the hangar and a brigadier general stepped out; the driver waited in the car. I stood at attention and saluted as he approached. After returning the salute, he looked around surprised to see me alone, and said, "Where's the major?"

"Taking care of other business. He said he picked up a case of dysentery, and told me what to do if you arrived before he returned, though he promised to be back as soon as possible if you cared to wait."

The general looked at the case in the crate and examined the label on it. "The case is awfully scratched and dented. And, it's dirty. Are you sure this is right?"

"I wouldn't know if that's what you expected. This is the case we were instructed to bring to this hangar on this air base for shipment out of country. It's here. The FSN and SN are correct, aren't they? The major said they were."

"Are you getting testy with me soldier?"

"Sorry sir, but I lost a good man on that mountain, not that we didn't take out a bunch of Viet Cong along the way. That case cost a lot of blood. I don't want to sound glib, but what is it about war that you don't understand?"

"That's enough, soldier!"

I was over the line and I knew it. "I apologize sir. Night Hawk, that was the man's legend, was the best of the best. Never saw anyone better then him—took a ricochet in the head not ten feet from me. A man doesn't get over something like that right away."

The general could see the pain. "All right. Apology accepted. But, how could that be? There're no Viet Cong in that area."

"We heard talk at the helicopter base that there were Cong in those mountains. We found a listening post manned by two of them. At least they weren't wearing standard South Vietnamese uniforms. What else would we expect? And, if they were friendly, why were they all shooting at us?"

He was about to say more and then didn't. It was obvious that what I had said was different from what others had told him. He took the clipboard that I held and checked the FSN and the serial number again. Then he hashed out the lines of the form beneath the ones listing the five cases and signed it. As instructed, I tore off the top sheet and placed it in a clear plastic sleeve, handing him the second sheet. He motioned to me to finish the crate. I nailed down the top and stapled the sleeve to it. As this was going on, there was more activity on the tarmac behind the C-141. The remainder of the cargo was being made ready to load. It might have been that the major had left to get that under way.

The general appeared apprehensive as he glanced around the hangar. "How long has he been gone?"

"Sir, he left only a few minutes before you arrived, said it couldn't wait."

"Well, might as well get the job done. You the forklift operator?"

"Yes, sir."

"See that C-141 out there?" he said pointing.

"Yes, sir.

"Take the crate out there and load it. They're waiting for it."

I mounted the forklift, lifted the crate off the concrete floor, and had just started for the flight line where the C-141 waited. As I was leaving the hangar on the forklift, a two and a half ton truck pulled to a stop ten meters from the building directly in my line of travel. The driver, who happened to be Blue Dog, wearing an Air Force wet weather coat, leaned out and said, "Yo! Can you tell me where I find building 129C?"

My response was to say, "Yeah. Keep going straight ahead to the end of this building, then between the buildings. It's at the rear."

He responded, as scripted. "Yeah, thanks," but did not immediately move the truck. Instead he busied himself flipping through pages on a clipboard. He wasn't looking at the pages but watching his review mirrors.

I angled the forklift to pass behind the truck as was normal practice to avoid being run over should the driver suddenly move forward. Under these conditions of heavy rain and darkness, no one would fault such a move on my part. On the far side of the truck I was immediately behind Nine Lives who drove the other forklift with the nearly identical crate on its forks. He immediately sped off toward the C-141 and became visible to the general in the hangar past the front of the truck. With Nine Lives well on his way Blue Dog started moving the truck and I paced him staying masked by the truck from the view of General Diggens.

Out of sight of the general, I parked my forklift with the crate containing the case on its forks between the buildings and watched for the other forklift to make it's return trip. We met in the gloom and Nine Lives and I changed places. I continued the return trip to the hangar as Nine Lives waited on my forklift with the case.

The general still stood at the open hangar door just far enough inside to stay dry. He was intent on watching the C-141 as the rear ramp lifted, and the plane started to move. The huge transport lumbered down the taxiway. At that moment the scream of four jet engines gave notice of a KC-135 tanker aircraft taking wing. That was standard procedure. The tanker took off first and proceeded to a refueling station where it would rendezvous with the C-141. Once at altitude the tanker would fuel the cargo plane for the first leg of its long flight to the United States.

The difference between airliners and large military planes is that airliners can take off with a full load of fuel, though in an emergency they cannot immediately return and land without dumping fuel to lighten the load. That's because they are designed to take off with a much larger gross weight than is safe to land with. Air Force transport planes are not designed to take off with a full load of fuel. Since the fuel tanks are in the wings of nearly all planes, the weight of full tanks while the plane is setting on the ground will break the wings off a C-141. It's the way the plane was designed. When in flight, the fuselage is supported, held in the air, by the wings. The wings are strong for forces in that direction. The weight of fuel in the wing is evenly supported by the aerodynamic lift over the entire area of the wing. On the ground, the entire weight of the wing must be supported by the joint where the wing is attached to the fuselage. As a result, military transports take off with a minimum amount of fuel and have their main load of fuel added in flight.

A few minutes after the KC-135 was on its way, the C-141 thundered down the runway and was off to its destination. Without so much as a nod to me, the general got in his car and was driven away. That might have been the end of it, but the major was only getting started. No sooner had the general departed when the major reappeared. A minute later Nine Lives and Blue Dog appeared on the second forklift with the original crate on the forks.

With all of us assembled, the major said, "Now we begin phase two of the mission."

I stopped talking. Harry said in a irritated voice, "I suppose that's it again."

"What do you expect for nothing, your money back!" I snapped. "You aren't being much help."

With a smug expression he replied, "I got you started again, didn't I?"

"Whatever. Anyway, I'm tired. This isn't much fun for me."

"Yeah, I suppose not. Sorry if I got pushy. It's just that we seem to be getting so close. All we, oh, sorry again, *you*, have to do is remember what happened after that and we'll probably know where it is."

"At this point, I'm optimistic that the rest of the mission will come. I only hope it has a happy ending. In the meantime, we have to start thinking about what we do when we have the rest of the story. Your turn."

"We might as well go to your house, that okay."

I agreed.

As we drove Harry started itemizing the situation. "We have Major Holt, General Diggens, the State Troopers, Cutter and cronies, and maybe the Vietnamese guy in on this. I'd bet anything that if the Vietnamese are involved, it's in the person of the guy we kept running into back then. You left him passed out on the hangar floor, but he didn't die—count on it. Since it's likely he was from the South Vietnamese Army, and had close contact with the U.S. When it was all over he came to the U.S. and was given U.S. citizenship to protect him from communist reprisals. That not withstanding, he never forgot about the big prize and has kept up his contacts with his mother country. Oh yeah, we also have the ex-FBI guy, what's his name? Fred something?"

"Fred Clements. And, hanging overall of this as if we didn't have enough of a problem finding the thing, is who told Cutter about Holt? If not you, then who? And, why? If anybody knows where it is, Holt does."

"As to who told, only one possibility, your PI outfit. They were the only other ones who knew that name. So I ask the obvious question. How much do you know about that organization? How did you come to pick them?"

I shrugged. "From the yellow pages. I didn't want a one man outfit so I dismissed the ads with two lines. Opposite that, the ones that had whole page ads seemed too flamboyant, too expensive. So, I picked one with a moderate sized block ad. Very clever, don't you think?"

Harry chuckled. "I wonder what it's like living the logical life you do."

"I don't know how logical it is, but I like it to make sense. That leads me to the job you will have for tomorrow. First thing, go to other PI outfits and ask what they know about Metro Investigations, the guys I use. It must be a small community and one or the other will know about them."

— 30 —

Monday evening

It was a hot day for June and the sun was still high at six in the evening as it approached the longest day of the year. The air conditioner was doing it's job, for that we were thankful. The single "ding" of the door chime indicating someone was at the back door didn't surprise me. Before opening the door I pulled the curtain back. It was Harry all right with a bit of conspiratorial smirk on his face. I took that for a positive sign.

"Am I in time for dinner?" he asked immediately. "I've been beating the hot pavement of this city all day, and I'm ready to drop."

The tone was definitely upbeat.

"We've just finished, but there's probably a few scraps we can find for an indigent man before he retires to his domicile in a cardboard box under the bridge."

He chuckled as he entered. "Did all right, if I do say so. Not a ton of new information, but I got a few questions answered."

Camilla was into the whole sordid affair as deeply as we were, so it made no difference if she heard what Harry had to say as she put food on the table.

"That hits the spot," he said placing the half empty glass on iced tea on the table. "Well, to business. You're logic in selecting a PI outfit was a little off. Metro Investigations is the biggest, by far, in this area. They had a relatively small ad in the yellow pages because they don't really have to advertise at all. They have a majority—one guy said seventy percent—of the sleuthing business around here. And, with the messes people manage to make out of their lives, it seems that employers have applicants for even relatively minor jobs screened through private investigators. With all the divorces, child support, alimony, second and third marriages, and stuff like that, to say nothing of addictions of various kinds, it's hard to know who will make a good employee. That is only good news for the PI industry.

"But, that's not so bad. You picked a big player. Nothing wrong about that. You know, I'm getting the hang of this and I kind of like it. A person starts cold and gets a few facts or even gossip. At the next place he can act like he's reasonably well informed and only looking for a little bit more. I even played the out of town card a couple of times. Some were put off but others didn't mind helping since it was unlikely they'd get any business from St. Louis."

Harry tended to do that—that is, string it out keeping himself as the center of attraction. As he paused, I said, "Harry, the chase, as in cut to."

"Oh yeah. The guy who runs Metro Investigations is one Bren Nugent. I could play with you but I'll just say it. He happens to be General Diggens' son-in-law. I talked to a guy who worked for Metro many years until he quit and went into business for himself so he knew quite a bit. Nugent worked at the place summers while going to college. That's when he met the daughter. He's a rather smart fellow all around. More than one person said that. After graduation he went to work for the CIA as a field agent. When Diggens was near retirement, Nugent quit, came to work for his father-in-law and in a few years took over the firm. There was a hint that he quit the CIA under less than optimal conditions."

By this time the food was ready so we let him eat in peace with only small talk here and there. He was a good eater and the relish with which he put it away made me think he hadn't even stopped for lunch. I was trying to factor this new information into what we already knew. A few pieces were falling into place so as Harry finished I offered some speculation.

"If we assume our lead about Holt was compromised when I called Avery Fallon to locate him, that would mean, or at least could mean, that Cutter and company had my phone bugged already when you first contacted me."

"Sure," Harry interjected. "If it was your slip last summer that got this whole thing started, they began the search for our Phantom team with you. So, of course they'd be watching you from the beginning."

"But, I called Fallon, not Nugent to get info on you. And, like I said, I may be wrong, but he appeared to be honest in not having talked to the Secret Service guys."

"Yep. You could be right because the former employee said they take extreme measures to be sure their ship doesn't leak. Confidentiality is the most important product of any of those places, and Metro takes it to the limit. They have a program where a small group has nothing else to do but snoop into the personal lives of their own employees. They watch for all the stuff, like missed mortgage payments, too much gambling, you name it. All the information concerning the investigations is computerized so people with the right access code can follow the progress of any case they want. They can even put in key words and see where they turn up. For example, being so large it happens that both parties to a dispute could hire them. They have to know this so they can avoid conflict of interest problems."

I nodded. "Cutter learned that first evening we spoke that I used a particular PI firm. They went to the top guy, flashed the creds, and demanded to be notified if I asked about anyone else. It was easy, and he didn't have to tip his hand by talking to Fallon. Fallon played it straight, like he knew nothing because he didn't. Nugent, for his own reasons, didn't want to run afoul of the Secret Service because of his past, whatever that is. Fifteen minutes after I asked about Holt, Cutter knew and got there ahead of me."

"Not quite." Harry said. "If your phone was bugged, Cutter knew about Holt so wouldn't have had to be in contact with Nugent."

"But, I had Fallon call me at work the next day with Holt's address. I doubt my work phone is bugged. That means Nugent has to be in on it."

Harry leaned back. "That fried chicken was excellent, Mrs. Wesson."

Camilla acknowledged the compliment with a nod and said, "As interesting as the connection between Metro Investigations and Diggens is, how does it help?"

"Let's see how it could help." I said. "Nugent was in the CIA. His father was a high ranking Air Force officer and when that went sour became the head of a snooping company. After Cutter and Divner paid Nugent a visit it would make sense he'd compare notes with his father-in-law. They both worked in sensitive areas of the Federal Government. If Nugent had never been told about the missing nuke on Diggens' watch while in the Air Force, he heard about it now. That may be the reason why Diggens so readily agreed to meet with us."

"Which means," Camilla interrupted, "Diggens was prepared for you and you can't really trust anything he told you."

"Except," Harry cut in, "the part about it being easy to detonate. There doesn't seem to be any reason why he'd fabricate that. If anything, he'd say it was totally worthless by now so why should anyone be interested in it? And, Vin's flashback corroborated a lot of what Diggens said."

I shook my head. "That's kind of beside the point. He knows after what we told him that it's unlikely anyone but the two of us will succeed in the hunt. He did everything he could to give us incentive to bust our necks finding it. And, the Diggens-Nugent duo run the biggest snooping, bugging, surveiling and following outfit in these parts. They plan to watch us find it and at the last minute snatch it for themselves for reasons we cannot guess."

Camilla asked pensively, "What if he was right about it being so easily detonated, though?"

"We make sure nobody removes that little connector cap, that's all."

Tuesday afternoon

We decided we'd have to talk to Nugent. One of the PIs Harry visited had a group photo with Nugent on it so Harry knew what he looked like. Of course, his phone number was not in the phone book, nor was there any useful personal information about him on the company's website. After work Tuesday afternoon I drove downtown and parked in a ramp near the Metro Investigations offices. As planned, Harry had taken a taxi, leaving his car at my house.

We met as arranged on the sidewalk outside the parking ramp. Harry had arrived early to size up the situation. He found that the building housing the main offices of Metro had an under ground parking garage, so it was not possible to wait in the parking lot for Nugent to walk to his car. As expected, drivers without a special magnetic card were not permitted to enter the parking garage. However, if one went into the building and took an elevator at least ten floors up, he could select the parking floors and the elevator would deliver a person there with no special access code. There were two elevator banks in the building on opposite sides. Since I had been there to see Fallon, I knew which side to watch. However, we had to split up to watch both sides just in case Nugent used the other side. Harry watched the most likely side since he had seen the photo of the man. If he worked late we could be there for hours, but we saw no other choice not knowing where he lived. The biggest challenge was deciding what to say upon first approaching him to convince him to hear us out.

Two hours passed slowly as we waited. It was hard because men seen loitering around in the parking area might be reported to Security so when someone arrived on the elevator we had to be seen walking purposefully either to or away from the elevators. Shortly after six, I flubbed up. One elevator was on the twelfth floor and the other had just arrived. A man entered the garage from the elevator as the door opened. I was walking away from the elevators ten steps in front of him. He hurried to catch up with me and asked what I was doing. I said I had forgotten something in my car and was going back for it. He was a stickler, kept asking me questions and eventually went back to the service phone and called Security. Those PI guys are really paranoid. I ignored him and when out of sight hustled around to the other side of the block where Harry was posted.

"Find him," were his only words.

"No. Some jerk took exception to my being there and went back to call Security. If Nugent doesn't arrive in the next couple of minutes we'll have to bail out."

The elevator "dinged" and as the door opened a woman stepped out and behind her was a man. "That's him," Harry said.

Luckily, the woman went to the left and Nugent to the right. Harry approached him alone since we didn't want to make it appear he was being assaulted. Also, Harry was accustomed to meeting strangers and immediately gaining their confidence and putting them at ease. Though, it was doubtful whether any amount of smooth talk would help in this case.

As Harry approached I could hear him begin his pitch. "Mr. Nugent, my name is Harry Auston. I've spoke to your father-in-law, retired General Diggens, and he suggested you might be of some help to me in an extremely urgent matter." That was not quite true, but he had to set the hook with nothing more than a sound bite.

Bren Nugent stopped momentarily, faced, and appraised Harry. It was evident Harry was wearing expensive clothing and was well spoken. Harry immediately added, "Please forgive the scar on my forehead. Some people fine it disconcerting. It's the result of combat in Vietnam and is unrepairable."

Nugent was starting to turn as he said, "Your appearance does not concern me and my father-in-law never mentioned you."

Harry increased his stride to come up along side Nugent as I maintained a discrete distance behind.

Harry, made another appeal. "Has General Diggens ever mentioned a missing nuclear bomb to you? It's urgent. We have to talk."

Nugent, approaching a dark blue Mercedes, pressed the button on the key fob. The car chirped and the driver's door unlocked. He reached for the door latch with his left hand and said, "I have nothing to say to you."

We had discussed something like this happening and had decided under the circumstances some amount of force would not be out of line. Harry grabbed his left forearm and pulled it away from the door. He reacted by turning and pulling his right hand back preparing to punch Harry, but I was already there and grabbed his wrist.

"You can do this the easy way or the hard way," I said, "but, we must have a few minutes of your time."

He struggled briefly, but both Harry and I were strong men who had stayed in shape. After a few seconds of seeing the futility of the situation he relaxed a little. He scanned around obviously hoping someone from his firm would happen by. We were concerned about that too so I immediately asked, "Does the name Sal Khruz mean anything to you?"

"Of course not. Why should it?" was the terse response.

I was going with the two names we had gotten out of Cutter in the wilderness before asking him about Cutter and Flavian. If he recognized either of those names as the Secret Service guys who had visited him, he might assume we were on the wrong side of things. If he did not recall them it wouldn't matter anyway.

"How about Seth Goldman?" I asked.

I was startled as he whipped his head around and looked at me. Recovering, I continued, "You know, Seth Goldman as in the president's National Security Advisor."

There was almost a wild look in his eyes. "I *know* where he works. How in blazes do you come to mention him to me?"

Harry glanced from him to me with the strangest look of bewilderment on his face.

"Because," I replied, "he's one of the men who's looking for the lost nuke, and from the little we've been able to learn we don't think it would be a good thing if he found it first." After a second is said, "By the way, I'm Vin Wessen."

I could see him putting it together. "I see. Vin Wessen and Harry Auston? wasn't it? Yeah. The Secret Service agents."

"Not really Secret Service agents," I corrected.

"Okay," he said." You can let me go. I won't run away. We have to talk."

Looking at Harry I could hardly suppress a smile. "Where do you live. Could we meet you at a public place, a park, shopping center, or some such that is on your way home."

He thought. "I live in North Oaks. Try this. Go out I-35W and exit at Highway 96. Go east to Lexington Avenue. A few blocks east of Lexington, on the left is a small park where the Shoreview city offices are located. Meet me in front of the city hall. Do you think you can find that?"

"I live in Shoreview, so I know where that is," I said. "We'll see you there. I'm parked in the ramp across the street so I'll be a little behind you."

"Don't get lost," he said as he slipped into the driver's seat. "This is important."

As his motor cranked and caught, I rapped my knuckle on his window. It lowered. "Do you suppose Harry could ride along with you? He could fill you in on some of the background along the way and save a lot of time."

He grimaced ever so slightly but said, "Sure. Why not?"

The window closed and as Harry walked around the car, I said, "Tell him whatever you think will help, but don't discuss Diggens."

Harry nodded. From the start of this fishing expedition, we didn't really know what we hoped to learn from Nugent other than get a better reading on Diggens. And, I wanted to be there for that. Besides, with Harry in the car, he couldn't call the police and have us arrested for annoying him. North Oaks, where Nugent lived, was a way up-scale gated community north of St. Paul so he was certainly among the "finer" members of our society. It happened to be half way from downtown Minneapolis to where his father-in-law lived, too. It might be he simply wanted to live there, and it might mean he spent a lot of time with his boss.

— 31 —

When I arrived the Mercedes was empty. Harry waved from where they were sitting at a picnic table. As I approached, Harry said, "I filled Mr. Nugent in on Phantom, what you have remembered from your flashbacks, and what happened in the wilderness. I'm not sure I got it all straight about the Boundary Waters, but he gets the idea."

Nugent nodded. "Please call me Bren. He also mentioned your friends Cutter and Divner, who had previously visited me, the State Highway Patrol, the assassin, and my head is starting to hurt."

We were all silent for a moment. Then I asked, "What can you tell us about Seth Goldman? That name seemed to connect with you."

Nugent was apprehensive. "I was in the CIA, but you already know that. For a considerable time I worked for Goldman so I know him well. There is so much about the Federal Government that is classified that it's hard to know what I can or should say."

"Well, try putting it into perspective. Think of a million people, including yourself, being swept up in a mushroom cloud."

He frowned. "I have been thinking about that. If I knew any of this was real, I'd have no problem, but you know how it is."

"No," I replied. "*You* don't know how it is. Our families have been attacked, and if we don't make progress they'll be killed. And if we fail to find it, they'll kill us. And, since we are required, as a means of keeping our families alive, to make a report to them every two days, we will most certainly tell them we talked to you. That means after us you will be next on their list to deliver or die. They have no scruples. They intend to get it. In case you aren't putting this together, we have from the time we make one report to them until the next report is due to locate the thing and expose it to the world. They said that we must make real progress from one report to the next, beyond that, they don't care how we do it. That doesn't mean they aren't watching us every minute they can."

Harry and I had seen it several times now. After someone finally internalized the gravity of the situation they almost collapse into nothing. Nugent pulled himself up with what looked like the last act of his will. "If I believe you guys, I feel I must be nuts. Yet, I have never encountered two men so intense, so desperate, that I can hardly not believe you. What can you offer for proof?"

"You have all the tools you need. When you get home look up the incident in the BWCA, about the two women who were bound and gagged on the small island, about the plane that made the illegal landing up there, about the dead assassin who supposedly died in Iraq some years ago, but didn't. My name is connected with all of it. I could give you other names, but until we are more sure of you, I won't. One name you know is retired General Diggens. After we are through here, you might think otherwise about mentioning this to him."

"Tell us about Goldman," Harry said

He nodded. I hoped this meant he was coming around. "Goldman is a monster. If—and it's still a big if to me—he managed to get his hands on a nuke that was untraceable to the U.S. he'd use it, probably on the U.S. As you might expect, in an agency like the CIA we are given a lot of pep talks by way of indoctrination. After all, we might be asked to give our lives for our country so we have to be made to see that the sacrifice would be worth it. We are also taught many scenarios about how an enemy might attack us. The scariest one is where the leaders in Washington become dictators."

He pause to see if this surprised us. Since it seemed he was expecting a response, I said, "It seems to me that with every passing year they are headed more and more that way. We are hardly free anymore."

"Yes, but I mean in the brutal sense like rounding up certain religious sects and starving them to death in concentration camps, putting tracking bracelets on everyone. That sort of thing."

I didn't want to get into politics so I encouraged him to continue with what Goldman might do.

He continued. "To take over, suspend the constitution, declare martial law, etc, you need a defining event. For instance, if the San Andreas Fault in California made a really big shift and destroyed everything from Mexico to San Francisco, tens of millions of people would be homeless. To handle that would require total governmental control of the people, the economy, the press, all of it. But, mother nature is too unpredictable.

They have to create the defining event. A nuclear bomb detonated in a major city would do it. He'd do it. It's as simple as that.

"If this thing is real, they probably learned about it from you guys and now see it as the means to their end. However, I don't see any way I can help you."

Harry asked, "What can you tell us about your father-in-law? He admitted to us that he was part of the team that put together and implemented the MADM project in Vietnam. He was also there with us when it disappeared. He described in detail how it can be detonated even after all this time. Has he ever mentioned any of this to you?"

"Not a word. He mentioned that due to Air Force politics his career was cut short, but that it was a blessing in disguise. He had a much better life settling down and running the firm."

"Nothing else?" I prodded. "When we were there it seemed to make his whole day as he told us the stories behind some of the pictures in his study of his days in the Air Force. I would say it was the love of his life."

"Well, yes, there was one time. It was Christmas day a year or two after I joined the firm. He had partaken a little too liberally of the Christmas cheer and had retired to his study. After an hour or so, his wife asked me to check on him. When I entered he waved me in and was in good humor. After a few minutes of small talk his eyes rested on some of his memorabilia. It was then that he showed a side of himself I had not seen before or since. He had really enjoyed the Air Force especially after becoming a general. At that point he was beyond pretending he was a bird with the concomitant dangers associated with flying. He allowed as being a brigadier was not unlike being a second lieutenant in some respects, both being the bottom rung of their respective scales. Still, he had great perquisites and a lot of respect. He was young enough so he could see himself getting his second star, and with luck, even his third.

"Then there was the business of the nukes. When he was assigned to it at the beginning, he knew it had the potential of being the sting of death. Significantly though, it was his handling of the acquisition and deployment of them that went a long way toward getting his star. Their decommissioning should not have been a show stopper. He knew well enough that there was only one that mattered, that being the live one. So how could that have gone so wrong? He thumped his fist on the desk saying that he had checked everything and watched the forklift deliver it to the C-141, then waited until the plane was in the air. With mid-air refueling, the plane didn't land until safely in the U.S. Yet, it had disappeared. Revealing that much he told me I should never tell the story to anyone. He reminded me that having been in the CIA I knew about security. That's it."

He didn't say more, though Harry and I both thought he wasn't through. Then he said, "I remember thinking at the time that something didn't ring true about what he had said. Granted, he had a little too much to drink, and yes, it probably did end his career, but not for the reasons he said. I could see he wasn't in the mood for me to question him on it so I let go. It never came up again."

Harry said, "Goldman and company obviously have access to the documents associated with the investigation of the disappearance of the bomb so they would know that the general is bitter. How could they use that?"

None of us had an answer. Then, something that had been nagging me came to mind so I asked, "What made you say that Goldman was a monster?"

Nugent was once again apprehensive as he answered. "Let me say that I was involved in some operations that he directed to take out terrorist cells in foreign countries. In the area where I worked we used military special forces to carry out the missions, so the work was not particularly dangerous for me though I was away from home a lot. At that time he was in a position where he didn't have to get his hands dirty either, but the scuttlebutt was that in his younger days he was a firebrand field agent. At times I could tell he was itching to be in the thick of it. Let me further say that he got results by accepting a much higher level of collateral damage than civilized people would accept. If you think the news media reports all of the cases where U.S. special forces cause a ton of civilian causalities, you're wrong. It got progressively worse until on my last operation there were two hundred innocents killed. I knew he was too connected by that time for me to do anything about it. Since my wife and father-in-law had been encouraging me to get out and come to work at the PI firm, I did. The fact remains, if he had to destroy a U.S. city to get what he wanted, he'd do it."

Harry was absent mindedly kicking at some pine needles on the ground. "I infer from what you just said that now that he's moved into the big time Goldman really should be taken out, as in permanently, for the good of humanity."

Nugent nodded. "I hadn't taken it to its conclusion, but, yes, that's a valid statement."

I looked at Nugent. "You are yet another person we have had to let in on this affair and we wouldn't have done it except to spare our families of almost certain retribution if we fail to make progress. Unfortunately, you haven't added anything that can help us. I'm not blaming you. But, please don't tell this to anyone. The more people that know the more dangerous it becomes for all of us."

"How about your flashbacks?" he asked. "Nothing more there?"

"They come in spurts when least expected. There are two things about them. The first is that they are incredibly detailed. I remember not only the events, but what I was thinking at the time. The other thing is a new one takes up right where the last one stopped. I can't explain it. My friend who knows a lot about such matters said that is not unexpected. He said it's all in my subconscious mind, that is, my spiritual part, my soul. All that's needed if for my physical brain to give the signals to release it. If I know where the darn thing is, the information is in my head. I only hope we can jog it out in time."

I looked at Nugent. "Will you help us?"

He shrugged. "Sure. But, I don't see how."

"Well, first, did you have the CIA field training, as in martial arts, weapons training, and such things we all assume a field agent has?"

"Of course. And, I stay proficient with a 9mm pistol."

"I'm not sure it'll come to that but I'm glad to know. The most important thing, though, might be in the area of information. Harry and I both remember something about carrying a heavy object in sand, a gravel pit or something like that. We're not even certain that was connected with the operation we're interested in. But, if the nuke was delivered to the Anoka County Airport via a C-130, as the pilot at one point said, and he was only on the ground for a short time, that gravel pit would be within five or at most ten miles of that airport. We would go on the assumption that it was buried under a tailings pile, something the person who hid it would know would never be disturbed again. Can you find the gravel pits that were in use in this area in 1972?"

We had not mentioned names where possible and this included Holt. We assumed he told Cutter about Holt, but that he had no idea why he was important. If he didn't know Holt was the pilot, we intended to keep it that way.

"My next request will be difficult in fact it may be impossible. See if you can get more information from your father-in-law. He was in this from the beginning so it's hard to see that he would simply be ignored by the people looking for the bomb."

He shrugged again. "I'll see what I can do. I don't see that I can mention it without making him suspicious unless he brings it up."

We were getting up from the picnic table when Harry said, "One more thing. There's Fred Clements, the man who went to the BWCA with Vin. See if you can find out if he really was let go from the FBI, or if it was made to look that way so he could work under cover."

"I'll give it a try and get back to you if I learn anything."

Without making any show of shaking hands we were about to part when Harry said, "Wait."

He was on one side of the picnic table and Nugent and I were on the other. "Over your left shoulder, Vin, is an Asian man walking a small dog. He came past once before while we were talking here. It could be the same man I saw in the sporting goods store. The general said the Vietnamese might be in on this. I wonder if he's Vietnamese rather than Chinese or Japanese? It might explain why he's been shadowing us."

None of us had a comment, though Nugent clearly took it in with interest. With that we went our separate ways.

The meeting had been discouraging. Other than being able to tell Cutter that we had tracked down another player and Nugent's connection to Diggens, we had nothing. And, I'd be surprised if he didn't already know about Nugent.

I made a right turn onto Highway 96 headed west. Just past the stoplight at Lexington Avenue on the right, was the National Guard base for the metro area. As I saw the collection of army vehicles parked along the highway something came to me. I swung right onto the road east of the compound and pulled over. "Something's coming," I said. "Turn on you tape recorder."

Harry pulled it out of his shirt pocket and fumbled with turning over the tape. He had started it before he got in the car with Nugent and let it run. As a result, it had run to the end of the tape before we took our leave from him. Now he flipped over the tape, slipped it in, snapped the recorder shut and said, "Okay. All set."

A full minute passed as we sat in silence. "That's funny, I thought sure I was about to remember more. But, wait. I do remember—it's different, though. The thing that comes to me is that we were all given a dose of the sleeping drug. Somebody had a mitt full of those spring-loaded syringes. That would be just great. The reason we can't remember where it is, is because we were asleep the whole time."

"No!" Harry said emphatically. "Not asleep, groggy. I remember that. We were coming out of the effects of the drug and were awake enough to do some lifting and carrying, but were not lucid enough to take in our surroundings or have any real sense of what we were doing. Yeah. That's it. It was a heavy load that we were carrying and it seemed like we had to carry it a long way. The going was hard because of the loose sand. Where were we?" He paused holding his forehead in the palms of his hands. "Where was it?"

Harry leaned back and closed his eyes. "You know," he said. "Over the years I've had recurring dreams that were all different, but had a common theme. I'm being chased by something big. One time it was an rhinoceros, another time a Mac truck came up behind me as I was driving. Things like that. Just before I'm to be run down and squashed, I wake up."

"Okay, Harry, you drive. When we come to Highway 10, take a right and head out on 35W to Lake Drive. Then find someplace to pull over. I want to see if the driving will start another recall."

Harry did as requested. Once on 35W it started to come, another detailed flashback.

— 32 —

After the C-141 had departed, and the general drove away, we were assembled with the major in the hangar. We had made the switch of the crates and had the crate containing the nuke on the forklift. The major said, "Now we begin phase two of the mission."

The three of us exchanged glances. I said, "It's been a long day for us, sir."

He held up his hand. "Understood. And there is little the three of you will have to do before you can stand down. That said, we now uncrate that case," he pointed at the one on the forks, "and load the case into the three quarter ton truck again. Go ahead, do it."

We loaded the nuke sans crate after having moved the C-ration cases and water cans to the front of the truck bed. With the other two in the back of the truck, I drove with the major seated in the passenger seat.

"There's a C-130 loading at the end of the tarmac. I have orders to override that cargo and load this truck with its cargo instead. You will load the truck tactically. The four of us will go along on the C-130."

Tactical loading simply meant that I was to back up the ramp into the hold of the plane so the truck would be facing the rear for rapid unloading at the destination.

Stopping near the C-130 the major said, "Find the load master for that plane and have him come here. When he arrives you stay outside."

Stepping out of the truck, I flipped my poncho over my head and went to the plane.

Who's the load master?" I asked.

"Here," a master sergeant said.

"There's a major in the truck who urgently needs to talk to you. Go to the driver's seat. You can get out of the rain."

The sergeant nodded and I scooted around to the back of the truck. Nine Lives lifted the tarp that covered the rear opening and extended his hand and heaved me up into the back. We were squeezed in around the case. We could hear voices in the cab but the pounding of the rain in the canvas top precluded understanding what was said.

We heard a few expletives, the sergeant opened the door and we heard it slam shut. I took that to mean I should resume my place as driver. Opening the door, he waved me in. Fifteen minutes later I was backing into the plane. Inside, the Air Force loading crew set about lashing down the truck.

I was out of the truck by this time. The load master said, "We need to lash down any cargo you have in the truck."

The major responded, "Consider it done. That's all you need to know. Your job is finished."

With the loading crew gone, the major now took on the flight crew producing more top secret orders. The pilot was a captain as was the co-pilot. "That's all we take on this trip," the major said. "Time to take off."

The pilots shrugged, took their seats, and after the usual check lists, and what not, the engines started to turn. The three of us settled in web seats along the port side, forward in the cargo bay. There was a passage way from the cargo deck to the flight deck on that side. I, at least, was interested in learning anything I could about this strange flight. From that location it was possible we'd over hear something. The major had strapped in on the bench seat behind the pilots.

This was getting scary now that I thought about it. The aluminum case in the back of the truck on this plane was the one we had extracted from the side of the mountain at such a high cost. It was the case the general had signed for. But the crate I had placed on the C-141 contained a jet engine. The thing about it was that the four of us, my team and the major, knew there had been a switch, but, of course, the general did not. When the five crates arrived at their destination, there would only be four aluminum cases, and the general would be on the hook for five. Stuff like that happened, but this was starting to bother me.

Oh boy, something else occurred to me. The major was not around when the general signed for the case and I pretended to load it on the plane. That would make the general and me the last two people to actually see the case before it went missing.

While in the Quartermaster Corps, I had heard a story about something like this. It was in South Korea in the late fifties. There were two U.S. Army installations, one on either side of the peninsula. Each had a fire engine. For one reason or other one of the trucks had been lost, probably sold to the South Koreans so some senior sergeant could pay off a gambling debt or something. Anyway, each time a fresh new lieutenant arrived to fill the position that required him to sign for a fire engine, there it was, shiny as could be. However, the sergeants would ferret it from one side of Korea to the other as needed for a new lieutenant to take over the property. I never heard the result of that situation when the deception was finally uncovered. Possibly, a lieutenant bought a fire engine. It was known to happen.

I wondered what the general would do. It was obvious those cases were valuable. He would eventually figure out that the major had made the switch, so what was the major's plan to stay out of trouble? I hated it when I started thinking. It never did me any good, but once started, I couldn't seem to stop. So, the major was in charge of a top secret operation. That gave him a lot of power, enough to take possession of this C-130 and direct it to his own purposes.

Ah, ha . . . that was it. That's what had been nagging at me from the time I learned we would switch crates on the general. It was a legitimate operation up until that time. At that point a top secret operation had turned rouge. The general didn't seem at all pleased that the last of the five cases had arrived so late. He even seemed confused about there being Viet Cong on the mountain. Why was that? The C-141 was on the tarmac all loaded except for this one relatively small item. It was late, dark, and raining, the conditions under which unexpected things happened. The way the general stayed around until he saw the C-141 actually take off hinted at the fact that he was worried that something might be wrong.

We were strapped in as power was applied to the four turbo prop engines. *Up, up and away in my beautiful balloon . . .* Only this was no joy ride. We took off to the northeast and now were turning to starboard. The engines throttled back to normal cruising power and we leveled off. It was then that I heard voices in the cockpit.

It was the major's voice. "Captain, there has been a change in destination. You will not be going directly to Saigon, you will get there, but not before a detour. My top secret orders are for you to take this plane where I will now direct you." After that the voices became incoherent as the pilot, copilot, and the major seemed to keep interrupting one another. Soon after, the voices became more hushed, and with the noise in the plane, I understood no more.

With those in the cockpit engaged, I turned to tell my companions of my suspicion. "I don't know how you see it, but I think the major has taken a huge step into *Twinkie land*," I said. Only I had been present when the general had signed for the crate so I laid out the situation as I saw it. After ten minutes we were in agreement that we could be in danger from the major. With the three of us permanently out of the way, only he would know about the switch. However, he seemed to know about the Phantom teams, and how off the books we were doing illegal things. It was possible he would feel he could let it go at that, but we had to stay alert, and that would be hard seeing how fatigued we were.

After fifteen minutes of flying, the plane tipped and we turned to port, out to sea. It seemed to me like we had turned enough to completely reverse course. In a couple of minutes we encountered buffeting. From snippets of radio communications I gathered the turbulence was not weather related. We were in the slipstream of a larger aircraft about to be fueled. The rear bottom of the plane in front and above us was faintly illuminated by the reflection of the light shining on the top of our C-130 by the man piloting the refueling boom. Loosening my seat restraint, I drew close to the passageway to the cockpit. Sure enough, we were being fueled. It made sense. When I found the load master on the ground the plane had been packed full. Since the trip to Saigon was only a couple of hundred miles, they would have had a light load of fuel so as to carry more cargo. Now, we had a light load so the fuel tanks could be topped off. The C-135 that I saw taking off to fuel the C-141 had obviously been ordered to stay on station and fuel us, too. The logic of this was we were going to take a long trip.

Shortly after disengaging from the C-135, the major came back to us. "There's food and water in the truck. Get something to eat and drink. Don't waste the water."

The major returned to the cockpit, I assumed to keep tabs on the pilots. From what he said about the water, we decided we'd be flying for awhile so pulled our packs out of the truck and spread out our wet clothes in the cargo bay lest they get moldy. It was part of the training.

We had eaten six hours before, but decided to take a crack at the C-Rations. There was no doubt a person would not starve to death eating C-Rations, but they were hard on the system. Generally, after a few meals of them, you would avoid eating until you were over hungry and then eat more than was good for a person. That was to stave off having to endure the experience again for as long as possible. The food was designed for men in combat where the ultimate in energy was packed into every bite. If you were waiting for something to happen, as was normal for the Army, it was hard to eat more than a part of a meal.

For the uninitiated, C-Rations came in five different meals, some better than others. Each box was one meal for one man—a very big man. One can in the box, the largest one, about the size of a can of peas from the grocery store, contained the main course, so to speak. The worst was roast pork because it contained so much lard. Others were beef, chicken, ham, and spaghetti and meat balls, though, sometimes that was hard to discern what the last one really was. After that there were a variety of side dishes. In one of the meals was a can containing two crackers about a quarter inch thick along with another can about a half inch high containing peanut butter. The idea was to spread the peanut butter on the crackers. Each cracker was made by taking a two foot tall biscuit and compressing it with a twenty ton press to the thickness mentioned. That in itself would be a meal under normal circumstances. One meal contained a can of chocolate cake. It was the densest cake you could imagine, but better than other items. There were other treats that are just as well not mentioned. Then, there was a packet of sundry items. It contained small envelopes of dried coffee, tea, sugar, salt, a can opener, and a packet of toilet paper. In normal circumstances one of these meals could easily keep a man going for a day.

The odd thing about it was that the first time a person ate a C-Ration meal it tasted pretty good. One of the guys from basic training managed to abscond with a couple of meals and took them home with him on leave after his training. His intent was to garner sympathy from his family when they tasted the horrid stuff that was so much a part of his training. But, as I mentioned, they, having never encountered such a thing before thought it was the greatest picnic lunch they had ever tasted. So much for trying to inculcate army life into the minds of civilians.

We each grabbed a box without looking knowing somebody had to get a pork box. After we ate we settled down. It was after midnight and we were tired. There were no windows in the cargo bay so it was impossible to tell if we were over sea or land. They had done this to us before. We'd load on a plane and fly. We'd sleep and would be awakened shortly before we landed. Sometimes they even applied the sleep potion that I had administered to the VC on the mountain. It came in different duration doses so you could sleep for up to twenty-four hours. When you woke up from a long sleep, you were groggy for several hours. You'd be awake and functioning, but remember little about what you did. If they wanted you awake and sharp there was an antidote that cleared your mind in less than ten minutes. Going into Phantom we didn't know any of this, of course, it came to light as the need arose. There was nothing we could do about it. It was not as if we got to pick what we wanted to do, or what was done to us.

The temperature in the cargo bay was acceptably warm so sleep came easily. I hated the thought that we'd all fall asleep but there was no stopping it. We slept.

I awoke by slipping in and out of dreams. My confusion lay in the fact that the dream world was identical to the awake surroundings. It was dark but not totally black. A small amount of light came from my left. Turning my head I saw the top of the passage way leading to the cockpit. There were four steps up from the cargo bay floor to the passage way that entered the cockpit above and behind the pilot. It came back to me slowly as my thoughts swam through a viscous fluid. My watch said 0020 hours so I had been asleep for only an hour or twenty-five hours or my watch was wrong. That last possibility took awhile to ruminate in my brain. My next sensation was an urgent need to relieve myself. I released my restraining harness, stood, unsteadily holding the bulkhead, and made my way to the station reserved for the function of my need. Considering the time I took to do my job, I realized I had not been asleep for only one hour.

Returning to my companions, I shook first Nine Lives, and then Blue Dog. They came out of it in due course, and made the same trip I had taken. We knew what had happened and also knew we could be in a different part of the world from when we went to sleep. As the thinking process slowly ground along it became apparent the major could have reset our watches while we were out so it was impossible to tell how long we had slept. While standing, we could see into the cockpit and out the windshield. It was night wherever we were.

We returned for the uneaten rations we had each started since, not having eaten for some time, we were hungry. Rather than drinking from our canteens, we poured water from one of the Jerry cans into empty food tins. Who knew what the major could have put in our canteens? This sleep thing had been done to me twice before and this time I was more alert coming out of it than the other times, though not a hundred percent. It remained to be seen whether or not he'd come around with the antidote. Walking around to the far side of the truck I came upon one of the pilots strapped into a web seat near the back of the plane, sleeping like a baby. It was hard to think things through other than to sense that something was wrong. Returning to the others, they sat with silly expressions on their faces. Clearly, I was in the best shape. Maybe my system had acquired a certain immunity to the drug.

I had a moment of horror that was real. If one of the pilots was back there, where was the other one, and who was flying the plane? Easing up the steps into the passageway from the cargo bay to the cockpit, still unsteady, I saw the pilot seat on the left occupied by a pilot who was also asleep. The other contained the major who was awake. He hadn't noticed me so I quietly returned to the cargo bay. There was no point in trying to figure out what was going on since thinking beyond that required to stand up and sit down was most trying. The other two were alternately sleeping and looking around with blank expressions.

I knew the best thing I could do was drink plenty of water to help metabolize the drug. The problem was Blue Dog and Nine Lives were still too far out of it to make that point stick. They drank what they wanted, but couldn't be coaxed to indulge beyond their natural inclination. I drank again and again.

An hour after I had awaked, the light from the cockpit darkened and I turned my head. It was the major blocking the illumination as he approached. I maintained as blank an expression as I could which wasn't at all hard.

"You're awake. How about the other two?"

"They still sleep . . . they still want to sleep for most of the . . . time . . . I guess."

"Get them up and walk them around. In a half hour, I'm going to need you guys. Nothing special, just some strong backs to do some lifting and carrying. Got it?"

I gave an exaggerated nod, "Yes, sir."

"Good." He returned to the cockpit.

Blue Dog and Nine Lives were reluctant to move around, but I shook them, talked to them, and pulled them to a standing position. They finally drank more water, but soon plunked into their web seats again. I gathered up the clothing we had laid out to dry. Everything was dry. I hoped I put each man's clothing into the correct rucksack.

It wasn't long before the hum of the engines lowered and the nose pitched down ever so slightly.

"Strap in!" the major called.

We did. Shortly thereafter, we felt the slight jolt as the wheels made contact with a runway. If the major were piloting the plane—and it seemed neither of the other pilots were awake—he was very good. The plane shuddered as he applied the brakes, but I didn't hear the engines surge as reverse thrust was applied. We turned, I assumed, onto a taxi-way. I wondered where we had landed. Well, why not? I silently un-latched my harness, stood, and eased myself up one step toward the pas-sage way. There were a few lights visible through the windshield, but nothing distinct. We clearly were not at a large airport. He had extin-guished the landing lights and was using the glow from security lights to guide him. The plane rhythmically rocked from side to side as we rolled from one patch of concrete to another. We turned again and after some distance, I saw a row of general aviation hangars on the left. He seemed to know exactly where he was going. We slowed nearly to a stop and I almost lost my balance as he revved the engines on the port side and we swung around, turning nearly in place. Then we stopped and the engines wound down.

Blue Dog and Nine Lives were awake, but still not doing too well. I knew the feeling from the other times. This must have been the first time for them. And the major thought it would be largely the same for me.

In seconds he was in the cargo bay and switched on dim lights. "Re-move the truck's tie downs, fast!" The order was sharp enough so my two companions swung into action. In a minute flat we had the truck ready to go.

"Now, listen to me the three of you," the major said standing only a couple of feet from us. "This is still a top secret mission, and we are about to enter into the most dangerous part of it. You must deposit the case as I will direct. I will kill the lights and lower the ramp. I will drive. The three of you will be in the back of the truck. Pull down the rear tarp and keep it down. You must under no circumstances be seen. When I stop you will remain in the back until I tell you what to do next. Now load up."

I was in the truck first and gave a hand to the other two as the lights went out. We heard the ramp lower and we were off. The road was paved and in good condition, better than any I had encountered in Vietnam. The major was pushing it. I was at the front of the truck bed on the left and not visible to the major if he turned his head and looked out of the rear window. There was something I wanted to do, but was having a hard time remembering what it was. Wind rippled the canvas, and I put my hand on it. What was it I wanted to do? Just because I had consumed a lot of water didn't mean I was normal. Wind blew on my neck and I reached over to see it's source. There was a crack between the canvas and the cab of the truck. That was it. Try to look out and determine were we were.

The canvas gave a few inches and from what I could tell it was in the wee hours of the morning because there was no other traffic and all was dark except for a street light now and then. We went up a rise and I saw the light strips of concrete of a large expressway passing under us. In the distance was a lighted green sign with white letters on it. Unfortunately we were too far away to make out what the sign said, or even the language. This effort fatigued me and I closed my eyes to rest. That was how it was coming out of that sleep drug.

The next thing I knew the major was in the back of the truck shaking us. We all woke up to varying degrees of consciousness. "Okay. We're at out destination," he said.

— 33 —

As with the other times, the trance-like state passed quickly as if I had blinked my eyes. I remembered most of what I had said, but there was nothing I could do to bring back more of the experience.

"Did you get it?" I asked.

"Got it all." The tape was rewinding as he spoke. "What do you make of it?"

"Clearly, we were in on it the whole way. Why, oh why, did it have to end with the major saying we were at our destination. All we have is a small airport, good roads, street lights, an expressway with green signs and white letters, which could be in Anoka or anywhere in the world."

Harry had turned off Lake Drive in Circle Pines and parked as my recall was progressing. I could see he was pondering something. "We have two conflicting stories," he said. "The first is the general and the Ojibwe reference. It seemed that since the Vietnamese man on the mountain mentioned that term with such familiarity, they were both in on at least recovering the bomb, if not doing something nefarious with it. Now, we have *the major* doing the switching of the crates and flying it someplace a long way from Vietnam. That makes him the thief. And, we are as certain as we can be that the major in question is none other than Bruce Holt who for his own reasons is not at all interested in finding the nuke."

Harry paused, so I said, "That could mean that Holt feels that it's not possible that anyone will ever recover it."

Harry frowned. "No. According to your last flashback," he held up the tape recorder, "we were with the darned thing the whole way. He said we'd have to do some lifting and carrying so we lugged it somewhere. According to Holt's accounts, that place was near the Anoka County Airport. There's no active volcano or anything remotely like that in the area." He was shaking his hands as if trying to make a point. "There's something wrong with all of this!"

I felt as frustrated as he did. There was nothing to do but go home. We said little as he drove, both of us were mulling over the situation. When we pulled into the garage I saw Camilla enter from the door off the patio. Her face was ashen.

I opened the door and before I could step out she almost screamed, "Jimmy was beaten up real bad by a big man with a scar by his mouth. The man said to tell Uncle Vin that he wasn't making enough progress!"

Harry followed the two us to the back door. In the house I managed to get Camilla to sit on the sofa. She was frantic. "Vin! This has to stop. Those are devils. They have to be killed before we're all dead."

As she dabbed here eyes with a handkerchief I said, "Yes, he has stepped over the line and this is now war, though I doubt he recognizes the seriousness of what he's done. But—look at me," she lifted her head, "you have to understand that we must see this thing through. There are a lot more where he came from. Putting him out of commission, permanently or not, won't end this. Do you know how bad Jimmy is?"

"Oh, he'll live and I don't think there any broken bones, just bruised up a lot. Pam called me from the emergency room wanting to know what was going on."

"Did she call the police?"

"She called 911 and the police were there first so they know about it."

"Did she tell them about Uncle Vin?"

"I told her not to, but they will be doing their police thing and will press her and Jimmy to find out who did it."

Harry was in the kitchen seated at a dinette chair. "This is a major complication," he interjected when there was a lull. "How could Cutter be so stupid. If the local cops become involved, they'll keep pushing and it will hit the news. Goldman will back off until it quiets down and then be back. Who's Pam?"

"She's my sister-in-law. They live in Blaine, north of here."

"Can she be counted on to keep her mouth shut?"

"No."

The front doorbell rang. We looked at one another. Harry said, "Cops."

I nodded, "Most likely."

Opening the door I saw a policeman.

"Mr. Vincent Wessen?"

"Yes."

"May I come in?"

"Why not?" I stepped in and made introductions. "My wife, Camilla, and a friend of the family, Harry Austin."

"I have a few questions to ask you," this male member of Blaine's finest began.

I did not ask him to be seated, since I knew he'd refuse. After all, when he sat down I might remain standing and that would put him at a psychological disadvantage. Cops always remained standing unless it was something that would take a long time, and then they only sat down when they were certain you were already seated.

"Your nephew was beaten up by a large man this afternoon and your name was mentioned."

"We've heard."

"Care to explain what's going on?"

I paused trying to think of consequences then decided to load him down with the whole works. "The man who beat up Jimmy is Flavian Cutter. Care to guess who he works for?"

No response.

"He works for the president of the United States. What he did was extremely stupid, but then he has not proven himself to be particularly bright so that was not unexpected. But, it means he's being pushed very hard to get results. Do you care to guess why he beat up Jimmy?"

No response.

"Because there is a weapon of mass destruction loose in this town and Cutter thinks I know where it is. He and his bosses want it because they are terrorists and will likely use it in a U.S. city so they can assume dictatorial powers. If you apprehend Cutter, please know that he will have legitimate looking Secret Service credentials. They are not. To verify that call the state police, ask for the top guy and mention Flavian Cutter and you'll have his full attention. I recommend not contacting the FBI because they are by definition Federal and connect directly to the top. We don't know if any of them can be trusted. The state police are acting as if they can't."

His complexion became shades whiter as I spoke. "You have to ask yourself, where in the grand scheme of things does the great metropolis of Blaine reside? Does being ground to mush under the wheels of a battalion of egos on steroids make a point? What I'm saying is that there is a growing circle of people who know about this, but nothing will happen until Harry and I find the thing, and we don't know where it is. But, we're working on it."

He was groping for words, "That's why you didn't want to say any-thing, isn't it?"

"Yes. The fewer people that know about this the better. If you want to help, find Cutter and throw him in a cell, not that he'd stay there long if he has a chance to make a call. Investigate it like it was a simple case of a beating by a drunk or a bully from the neighborhood. Don't go nuts but try to keep it out of the papers and off TV."

He drew himself up. "Okay for now. But, I'll have to tell my superior at some point."

I nodded. "People have already died over this thing and more will die. There is nothing you can do that will make it any better. Give me your card so I can contact you if needed. Include a home number because things tend to happen at inconvenient times."

This he did.

"By the way, they tend to run a tidy ship. If you insist on making noises, they will not hesitate to silence you. You get it? Permanently. This is way beyond your pay grade. If at some point we need you, we'll call."

With the door closed, Harry said, "I have to say, you handled that about as well as was possible. The part about the tidy ship was nice."

Harry and I were seated in the living room while Camilla prepared a late supper when the door chime sounded. We looked at each other.

I answered it and there stood Fred Clements. "Mind if I come in?"

I laughed. "Why not. By all means come on in. There might even be something to eat since we're about to have a late supper."

A little unsure of himself after my greeting, he tentatively stepped into the house. "I hope I'm not interrupting anything. It's just that I haven't heard from you for awhile. How are things going? I mean on finding the you-know-what."

"Have a seat," I said. "We were just discussing the you-know-what. We seldom talk about anything else. We think we may be getting closer, but still there's nothing we can act on."

"Is there anything I can do to help?"

Harry looked at me, then at Fred and asked me, "How about the gravel pit?"

"Why not? Fred, you recall when we found Holt and his son in the BWCA after the plane took off from the lake, he said he told them he had flown a C-130 to the Anoka County Airport?"

"Yes, I remember that. But he said he never left the plane."

"I know. After we got back from the north country we talked to him again and then he denied leaving Vietnam at all. But, we were thinking, what if he did land there, and, as he said, the truck was gone only a short time. What if he, or someone, took it to a gravel pit and buried it in the tailings. It seems there would have been machines like big backhoes or bulldozers at such a place. This was back in 1972. Do you know of any such place in operation back then?"

He leaned back thinking. Before he said anything, Camilla called us to the table. All she had on such short notice were cold cuts to make sandwiches. There were pickles, mustard, and sundry condiments. Fred agreed to a sandwich. As we were all putting together the makings, Fred said, "The area around the airport is flat with a high water table. There are a few hills, but that is a sandy area. I don't think it would be good for gravel."

"How do they build freeways?"

"They haul in whatever they need from as far away as necessary."

"That's no good. The only thing we're left with is the TCAAP, you know the Twin Cities Army Ammunition Plant. And, why would he take it there?"

After we had eaten, and Fred was about to leave I said, "Think about it. Harry and I both have a strong feeling that it was buried because we have vague recollections of a gravel pit, though they could be associated with another mission, and it could be a sandy beach. And, if Holt transferred it to another truck, it would be hopeless. Within twenty-four hours it could have been anywhere in the country." I wasn't about to tell him about my flashback where we were in the truck with the major after we left the plane.

Fred left saying he'd be in contact in the next day or so whether or not he came up with anything.

— 34 —

After Fred left, the three of us slumped in stuffed chairs in the living room each lost in his own thoughts. Finally, Harry asked, "Did you mean it when you told the cop I was a friend of the family?"

Camilla and I both smiled. She responded before I could think of how to answer. "Harry, with a friend like you we don't need enemies, but there seem to be plenty of others who have already taken that title of enemy."

Curling up the edges of his mouth ever so slightly, he asked, "Do I take that to mean yes?"

"Yeah," I said. "As the saying goes an enemy of my enemy is my friend. When this is over we have to get the families together and have a celebration. I'd like to meet your wife and kids."

This was one of the first times in a long time when I was genuinely feeling relaxed, though there was no reason why I should have been. Then, I began to sense it, that feeling I got as a flashback was coming on. I held up my finger, "We're in the back of the covered truck and it's backing up an incline."

"Into a warehouse, I bet," Harry said as he leaned toward me.

"Hush," Camilla said. "Let him keep going. Start your recorder, if you have it."

Harry slipped it out of his shirt pocket and pulled a fresh tape from his pants pocket. In a few seconds he said, "Okay."

"Up an incline, now leveled off. The truck stops, we push aside the tarp covering the back. It's dark, only faint reflections. Wait. I hear a pump or motor or something, probably a door closing. It stops and dim lights come on. What we see is familiar. We're back in the cargo hold of the C-130."

I heard a subdued but harsh statement, "No! You left part of it out. What happened after we arrived at out destination in the last one."

Then another retort. It was Camilla. "Stop. Don't upset his train of thought. Maybe it'll come."

What happened before this? Of course, we know that. The three of us were out of breath having run so hard. The major ordered us into the back of the truck and we pulled down the trap. Oh, yeah. By this time the case was gone. You remember that. Then he got in and drove off. I was still awake but feared I'd fall asleep again so I pulled aside the rear tarp to see what I could. After a couple of miles we passed over an expressway again and were immediately in a residential area. It looked so civilized with neat houses and mowed lawns. We crossed a four lane street at an angle to our line of travel. The intersection had a traffic light and we went through on the green without stopping. We immediately passed a commercial area. There was a prominent sign for a fast food place but I can't remember what it was. After that it was dark. We turned a few times and in what seemed like fifteen minutes, we were backing up the ramp. The engine stopped, the ramp was raised, and the major was at the back of the truck and snatched aside the tarp.

"Re-lash the truck and be ready for take off in three minutes."

I snapped up my head as if from sleep and said, "Yes, sir."

The others had fallen asleep so I shook them awake and told them what we had to do. Our job wasn't as neat as the guys at the Air Force Base had done, but it looked as though it would stay put unless we hit severe turbulence. The hold of the C-130 was big enough for three of these trucks, and the major had stopped it about in the middle, though a little too far forward by my thinking, but he was the pilot. The plane started to move with the major in the copilot's seat again.

I knew what had to be done, but had to be careful about it. It seemed to me the major would try to kill us some time in the next hours, certainly before we arrived at our destination. And where would we be going? It could be anywhere, but one possibility was he would return to Vietnam, deliver the C-130 to the destination where it was headed before he commandeered it, and continue with his life as if nothing had happened. If he had put in for a few days leave starting the day after the five cases were shipped he would return to duty after the leave with no one would knowing where he had been. It was unlikely he intended to steal the C-130. There would be people who would take that with less than good humor. It would make him a wanted man no matter where in the world we went. Yes, it seemed most likely we were headed back to Vietnam. It occurred to me that my thinking was coming back. All the water I had guzzled was having the desired effect. I wished the other two were doing as well.

We were strapped in by the time we started our take off run. Once again, I was taken by the guy's professional handling of the plane. It would take, say twenty minutes, to reach cruising altitude where he would engage the autopilot. After that he'd be back to take care of us. I wanted to take care of him in the most gruesome way, but couldn't get carried away. We all needed him to fly the plane until at least one of the normal crew was awake enough to take over. If he killed them it would be even more difficult.

From what I had seen earlier, the pilots were both sleeping. In order to get back into his real life, though, the major would have to leave them alive because he had to deliver the plane and the two pilots someplace where he could disappear and make his way back to the Cam Ranh Bay Air Base. Dead bodies complicated things, except for us, that is. After all, Night Hawk was dead and there was nothing that would be laid at the major's feet about that. It would be harder if we all died, but not impossible. After all, we had succeeded in our mission of recovering the case.

Wait, no we didn't, not really. When the crates on the C-141 were opened, our case wouldn't be there. It was a sure thing the serial numbers could be traced and someone would know ours was the missing one. This would take some delicate handling if we were to stay out of prison.

It was time to act. It was dark in the cargo bay and I had to work by feel. I dug through my rucksack and found a spare set of boot laces, about the only weapon the major had not removed. I returned to my seat beside my companions who were asleep again. They had taken the seats closest to the cockpit, so I was sitting in the third back. I was alert for movement coming from the cockpit. About on schedule, the light in the passage way darkened as someone came our way. He didn't turn on the lights in the cargo bay.

My restraining harness was unbuckled and hanging in such a way as to give the appearance that I was strapped in. We all had our bush hats on and were about the same size and build. The other two were asleep, and I maintained the same posture. The major stopped by Blue Dog, the one nearest the front to the plane, and did something. I thought he might tie his hands and feet, but there wasn't enough movement for that. Then, he was in front of Nine Lives. It was then that I heard the muffled "snap!" The sound was familiar, but I wasn't placing it.

Through slitted eyes I saw boots stop in front of me and I didn't hesitate. I thrust out my foot and caught my toe behind his shin. At the same time I leaned forward thrusting my hands at his waist. Startled, he fell back. The rear of the truck was a few feet off to the right so he landed on unobstructed deck. Out of my seat, I grabbed his right boot twisting his toe toward the left leg. To relieve the stress he flipped over as I lunged landing with my whole weight on his back. He had started to get up on all fours, but his weight combined with mine plus my downward momentum caused him to crumble under me. Straddling his torso with my thighs, I grabbed his head, turned it to the side and slammed his head into the deck with both of my hands. He no longer struggled but I saw his right hand pulled tight in a fist. I pulled his hand under and up into this back in a hammer lock.

The snap sound I had heard when he was in front of Nine Lives now registered. It was the sound of a spring loaded syringe. He had one clasped by his fingers and had pressed the rounded end with his thumb before I had knocked him unconscious, thereby injecting himself with the sleeping drug that he had intended to administer to me.

I could feel the adrenaline flowing and was at last at the top of my game. With hardly a thought, I peeled the syringe from his fingers, grabbed the boot laces out of my pocket, and wound a lace around his thumb as tightly as I could hoping to cut off the flow of the drug to his body. Some of the drug would have entered his system, though I could only hope it would not be enough to keep him unconscious for hours.

The implications were obvious. With the two real pilots asleep, the major would be the only one to fly the plane. With him asleep, too, we'd have no pilot. He was psychopathic enough to decide that if he couldn't win, nobody would. He had used the drug because he realized that bullets were not a good thing for a plane in flight. Our weapons were likely hidden in some unlikely place on the plane, but they weren't my immediate concern. If I couldn't find the antidote syringes to bring around at least one of the pilots, I'd need him. And, surely he would have hidden the antidote against a situation such as this.

If we were returning to Vietnam, and it seemed now that was the only scenario that made sense, we had a long plane ride ahead and we'd need a midair refueling or we were dead. That took a competent pilot who was totally recovered from the drug. Even if I were to get on the radio and declare an emergency, it was unlikely I could land the plane without leaving a smear of wreckage across the landscape. But, it was more complicated than that. My crew and I *had* to return to Vietnam, and report to our controller after our mission. Anything less would indicate that we had been the ones who had gone rogue and killed or at least disabled the officer we had been assigned to for the mission. Being off the books the way Phantom teams were, the possibility was always there that a team would go into business for itself. There were stern warnings that even a hint of such a move would result in our being hunted down and assassinated.

These thoughts had been percolating through my mind for the past half hour so now they were the energy driving my actions as I bound the major's wrists behind his back with the remaining lace. Flipping him over I removed his boot laces and used them to fetter his ankles. I found a pocket knife on the man and used it to cut a strip out of the back of his shirt and used it for a gag. I had no intention of listening to any more of this man's arrogant commands. After a thorough search of his person I found no syringes of the antidote. In fact he had no identification on him at all, only a small wad of cash.

The first order of business was to revive my team mates. With no effort at civility, I splashed water into the face of Nine Lives and slapped him soundly on the cheek. He snapped his head back seeing me standing over him with a dripping canteen in my hand.

"Why'd you do that? Who you think you are, Duce?"

"I need you guys awake. We're in deep trouble."

"Not me, think I got another jab of the juice." His head rolled over and was asleep in seconds.

I shook Blue Dog, and he didn't even respond. My boot slipped under me as though I had stepped on a round object. Picking it up and examining it I realized it was a used syringe. I had been right about the syringe the major had been clasping in his hand. It also meant Blue Dog and Nine Lives would be no help to me.

My guess was the major had intended to drug us and dump us into the back of the truck. Then, while the plane was still on autopilot he'd remove the tie-downs on the truck and lower the ramp. He'd take over the controls and do a severe pitch up so the truck would roll out the back with us in it. When he revived the real pilots, he'd say it had been his orders to drug them and deliver the truck, its cargo, and the three of us to a secret location. That done, it was now time for them to take control of the plane and head back to Saigon where they were headed when he took command.

I went to the cockpit for a quick check and didn't like what I saw. The pilot in the left seat was still asleep, but if he were to awaken even a little and touched the control yoke it would disengage the autopilot. I knew that much. Scanning the sea of dials I found one that said something about fuel. It stood at less than half so there wasn't much time. I wanted to restrain the hands and feet of the pilot but doubted that could be accomplished without disengaging the autopilot myself. I needed the antidote!

It was spooky knowing I was the only person awake on a large airplane flying through the night on autopilot. The plane would tip and pitch now and then. Immediately the automatic sensors and hydraulic valves would adjust the control surfaces and the plane would fly level again. I had to hope we were not flying into severe weather. What would happen if we ran out of fuel I had no idea. Probably, the automatic system would pitch the plane up to compensate for the lost altitude until it stalled and we'd spin in, totally out of control. Of course, I'd be at the controls when we were coming to the last of the fuel and would take over myself. I didn't look forward to that experience. But, that's the way I was—I'd give it my best try.

There was a flashlight in a holder on the bulkhead which I unclasped and took to the cargo bay. My first stop was by the copilot. I splashed water in his face and slapped him resulting in a moan and some thrashing about of his arms as if to push me away. It would take too long for him to come out of it naturally.

Where would the creep have put the antidote? There could be a hundred cubby holes on a plane this size. I had to assume he was a C-130 pilot with a lot of hours because he handled it so professionally. That meant he was thoroughly familiar with every inch of the plane so could have hidden things behind an access panel or something like that. I thought hard. Since he had been expecting us to carry the case, he had to plan that one or two of us might not be awake enough. That meant, there had to be antidote syringes. Since he didn't have them on him, the next best place was in the truck cab.

Hope was beginning to wear thin as I looked in all of the obvious places. The glove box held the maintenance log book and a few scraps of paper. I felt all around in it for loose panels, not that there would be any secret compartments. The truck had seen a few days, probably having been built at the time of the Korean War or even before. Some part could have come loose over time and could be bent back to provide a hiding place. No luck. Nothing was obvious under the seats or behind them. The roof was canvas so there was no place there.

As I stood beside the open door, a part of our training came back to me. Put yourself in the place of your enemy if you want to know what he'll do, or did in this case. We were dead tired when we finally took off from Cam Ranh Bay, so he knew we'd fall asleep. That meant he could administer the drug whenever he wanted with the requirement that we'd be slowly waking up when we landed. During the flight he also had a lot of hours to plan what he'd do after reaching his destination. As far as I could tell he had not been carrying a gun which meant the sound of shots in the area where we left the case could not be tolerated.

Whatever his thinking, since takeoff I had accounted for three syringes of the drug and none of the antidote. They had to be around someplace. I swept the beam of the light around. He had the flashlight at that time, too. There, I saw the place. The old seat cushion was worn on the side toward the door from a million men getting in and out. The fabric had been ripped a little. Would it be there? Hopefully, after he returned the truck to the plane, he was more concerned about getting back in the air than retrieving unused syringes. To be sure, I was, at that time, pretending to be a lot more groggy than I really was.

With the major's pocket knife I slit the fabric beyond the tear, and peeled back the cushion of the seat, and there it was. It was still in the sealed plastic sleeve, so was good. I knew immediately who to use it on, the copilot strapped into the web seat behind me. I was hoping the pilot would stay calm and not disengage the autopilot for the time it took to revive him. In seconds I had the antidote injected in his thigh. It took ten minutes of confused conversation before the man was fully awake. With him drinking water, walking around, and eating parts of a C-Ration, I told him the story. He seemed to understand what had happened, and was ready for duty.

With me walking directly behind him, we headed for the cockpit. He settled in his seat and clasped his five point restraint.

"Can you tell where we are?" I asked. "And, how is our fuel state?"

"Not so fast. From now on, you have to stay out of my way so don't speak unless spoken to. Is that clear?"

"Yes, sir," I replied.

"Our fuel is getting low, but not dangerously so—yet. Do you have something that will revive the pilot?"

"No sir. And I doubt I will find anything not knowing any of the likely places on the plane he could have hidden them."

"How long before he wakes up without it?"

"I don't know except that from the time he begins to wake up until he is fully awake it will be a couple of hours, and he hasn't started to wake up yet. And, as he comes around he could thrash around. Could that be a problem?"

The copilot's cheek muscles twitched as he clenched his teeth not liking the news. "Yes. It definitely would. Can you unbuckle him and pull him out of his seat?"

"Can do."

I reached over and undid the clasp on the restraints. The copilot, whose name was Raskin, was making calls on the radio as I tussled with the inert body of the pilot. He only weighed one-seventy more or less, but the seat was clearly designed to be entered and exited by a fully ambulatory man. I was sweating profusely as I dragged the body through the passage way to the cargo bay. In the bay there was room to move and it went better. With him strapped in a couple of seats back from Blue Dog, I returned to the cockpit.

Raskin glanced over and pointed to the pilot's seat. With me strapped in he said, "We're over Canada. That makes sense because we were headed for CONUS when the major put our lights out. I've contacted our tanker station in Alaska and gave them a story about a faulty fuel gage and that we're getting low on fuel. They'll send a KC-135 out to meet us. There'll be some explaining to do, but they dare not let us go down simply because we screwed up on our fuel load. Faulty gage or not, we should have calculated our fuel usage and not gotten into a fix like this."

I smiled. "And, that's not the only explaining we'll all have to do. A little missing fuel is one thing. More importantly, where have we been for something like two days?"

He nodded. "We should have arrived at Saigon a few hours after we took off. There will definitely be questions."

Something came to mind. "Maybe not as bad as you think. Before he talked to you he had to show the top secret orders to the load master and have him empty the plane so we could drive on. The load master would have had to do something with that cargo no matter how much he was threatened to keep his mouth shut. The trick will be for you to find him and get together with your stories. It seems pretty clear to me that this whole diversion was not in the original plan."

Raskin didn't reply. He obviously had things on his mind so I said. "It looks to me like you have things under control up here. I'll check on the passengers, maybe bring the drink cart up the aisle. Might have to touch up my eye shadow first, though." He nodded with a smile.

Pausing a minute, I asked, "Is there any rope or chord aboard? I have that major tied up with boot laces and that bothers me."

He told me the location of several lockers where I might find something. The flashlight was laying beside me so I took it along. Knowing how someone coming from the cockpit made his movements known by how he blocked the light I eased onto my stomach and slid the short distance back. As my head came even with the front of the cargo bay I switched on the flashlight.

Blue Dog and Nine Lives hadn't moved. The pilot was still in the seat where I had left him. All three strapped in along the port side of the plane to my immediate front. The major was not where I had left him on the deck at the rear of the truck and he was nowhere in sight. Snapping the light to my left to shine along the front of the bay I found it was empty. I cataloged the situation in an instant. I could see along the side of the truck on the port side of the plane. He could be in the back cargo space of the truck and I wouldn't see him because the tarp that covered the back was hanging down. He could be on the opposite side of the truck, in the front of it, or in the cab. I could see under it as far as the rear axle, but no further.

Attacking as fast as possible was the key to a situation like this since I had no other weapon. Switching off the flashlight, I rushed in a crouch along the side of the tuck to my front, grabbed the rearview mirror in my hand, and heaved myself on and across the hood. I came down on the truck's left side at the location of the front wheel and rolled over. I fell, not because that was my intent, but because I had landed on something. I shined the light to where I had landed and looked into the blazing eyes of the major. He was still bound but had been rubbing his bonds on the rusted edge of a panel of the truck. The gag was still in his mouth.

Pulling him by the feet to the front of the cargo bay, I left him and started searching the lockers the copilot had suggested. In the second one I found what I needed and did a proper job of restraining my antagonist. Leaving him lying in the deck, I lashed him to one of the web seats on the starboard side so he wouldn't sneak away on me again. I also found a piece of cloth that I tied over the major's eyes. In time I found our weapons and slipped my nine millimeter in my waistband, and the silencer in my pocket. The rest of them I transferred to the back of the truck.

Searching the rest of the storage compartments with greater care, I eventually found where he had cached the remaining syringes. There were two of the sleep drug, and four of the antidote. I put all of them in my right shirt pocket, buttoned the flap down and returned to the cockpit.

— 35 —

"Do I have to ask the captain's permission to come onto the flight deck or something like that?"

"Not necessary, but it's a good idea to let me know you're coming so you don't startle me. If that were to happen during refueling or landing, that could cause a disaster."

"Understood."

"By the way, why did you wake me up rather than the pilot. He's a lot more experienced then I am when it comes to refueling. If there's a lot of turbulence, I'll have my hands full."

"Like I said before, when a person is coming out of the sleep drug, it's common for him to thrash around. I was afraid that if he did that he might disengage the autopilot long before he was capable of flying the plane, and the machine was doing a lot better job of flying the plane than I could have done."

"That was good thinking." He noticed the gun in my waist band. "What's that for? Shooting inside a plane in flight isn't too smart."

"When I returned to the back, the major was a long way toward getting free of his bonds. If he had, he would have had the gun and we'd all be dead, whether or not shooting was a good idea. I could easily take him as long as he wasn't armed, but if he were to get free, I can't dodge bullets. He's pretty resourceful."

"I've got a lot of questions, but we're about to meet our gas station in the sky so I'll be occupied."

The radio exchanges began. I looked out of the windshield at total black. In only minutes Raskin was easing up under and behind a large airplane. It seemed like magic how he managed to become attached to the flying boom hanging behind the tanker. I watched his hands and his expression as he held the gently swaying plane in line with the ship above. He spoke, they spoke, both ways with cryptic words and phrases.

It was an intense business. I had heard that it took only a second for the plane being refueled to bounce up and ram the plane above sending both to the ground the short way. Finally it was over. The man flying the boom stowed it into traveling position as they eased apart. The final comments were more relaxed.

Alone in the sky again, I said, "That's something most people wouldn't believe. I have to hand it to you, that's impressive flying."

"Yeah. I guess it is kind of off the wall, isn't it. Two planes under separate control flying that close together for that length of time. By the way you never really said just what it is the three of you guys do. And how much do you know about what this joy ride has been about?"

"I've been thinking about that. First, how much can you tell me about where we went? While you two were asleep the major flew the plane, and he knows how to handle this plane like a pro. We landed, deposited our cargo, and took off again. The question I have is where did we land? You see, the three of us were coming out of the drug the natural way, as I said, which leaves a person confused and muddled for a long time. We helped him, but were not awake enough to have any sense of where we were. In the future that might be important for all of us."

"Before he put us under we were headed for CONUS. But the first leg of the trip is always the same because we have to pick up a tanker out of Alaska. We were in control for that. From there it could have been any-where. From our location when I took over again and the fuel remaining, I'd say it was in the mid U.S. especially the four state area of the Dako-tas, Minnesota, and Wisconsin. That's as close as I can come."

"As for us, we're a special team that does unorthodox things."

"You mean Phantom?"

"For a secret force, it seems everybody knows about it."

"That's just it. It's like a shadowy myth. Nobody knows anything about it."

"It might seem odd to you, but because of the missions we do, we're sort of expendable and by extension, now you may be, too. We have to figure out how to get out of this. Our mission was supposed to end, as far as we knew, when we delivered a certain commodity to the air base using the truck in the back about an hour before we all took off in this plane. Of course, it's possible that all of this was part of the plan from the be-ginning, but I don't think so. After the mission, the three of us were to report to our handlers and be debriefed which is standard procedure. If the trip in this plane was not part of the plan, we are way late in reporting in. So the question will be, where have we been? It could be because the three of us went rogue, or the two of you are the villains, or of course the major. We all know he was the one with the orders, but will anyone believe us?"

"From my position, it may not be so bad," Raskin said as he adjusted something with the autopilot. "With the U.S. pulling out of Vietnam so fast there's a lot of confusion. This is a National Guard plane and we were due to head back to CONUS in a week, anyway. At times, we've received orders to go someplace and when we arrived they've said, 'What are you doing here?'"

"Am I getting this right? You could show up at Saigon with the three-quarter ton truck and the three of us rather than the cargo you were supposed to take and you could bluff your way through it?"

"Yeah, I think I could. The cargo we were supposed to haul is probably there by now, anyway."

I nodded my head. "That's good. My suggestion is this. Set your course for Saigon where you were going in the first place. That's where we meet our handlers. We might even be able to stretch the truth enough by saying we were forgotten by the major and couldn't find transport back. When we are assigned to someone like the major, it is his responsibility to close the loop and finish the operation. That includes making sure we arrive back at our base. We could say he didn't know that. We'll have time to thoroughly search the plane for the top secret orders, if they still exist. They would help all of us."

"Nope. I doubt they would. They only said to do as directed by the officer in possession of the orders."

"Very clever."

"What do we do with the major?" Raskin asked.

"We'll put him in the truck before we land and take him off your hands. I think that's about all you should know. Will we have any trouble getting off the air base?"

"Act like you know what you're doing and they'll just wave you through."

I had it in mind that we'd dump the major in a bad part of Saigon. He had no identification on him so he'd have fun. Then, we'd ditch the truck within walking distance of our destination, or maybe just drive it in. I wouldn't have had Blue Dog and Nine Lives put to sleep again, but seeing as the major got to them before I knew what was going on, it may be a help to them. By the time they woke up from a second dose, they'd remember nothing about our time on the ground. I remembered little enough, and intended to play it as though I had a second dose, too. Unless, that is, we could fake our way through with the story about being forgotten at Cam Ranh Bay.

Raskin looked at me. "When will the pilot wake up?"

"I found another antidote syringe so we can do it any time."

"Better do it now. I need a stretch. Besides, we'll have to refuel again and I'd rather have him do it."

I had really been out of it this time so when the recall ended it took a few moments to realize where I was. Camilla and Harry were looking intently at me.

"Do you remember what you said?" Harry asked.

"I think so. Why do you ask?"

"You told everything about what happened except what we did at the destination, and where we were. How could you have left that out?"

"According to Henni, there might be some damage in a part of by brain. The memories are in my mind, but if the proper part of my physical brain isn't working, I can't get it out. Didn't I give some clues from the streets I described, though?"

Camilla leaned forward. "If we assume it was the Anoka County Airport, we could look at maps and using the few things you said, maybe we could narrow it down to an area to search."

We were tired. Harry left for a motel and we decided to call it a day.

Wednesday after work

Bren Nugent had called me at work about quitting time and said he wanted to drop in on his way home from the office which would be between six and seven. I called Harry so he was there when Nugent arrived at seven-ten.

After introducing him to Camilla, he began. "I went out to talk to Bruce Holt. I know you thought that would be counter-productive, but people in my line of work are practiced in interviewing people. No offense, but that's not your line of work."

I nodded, he continued.

"He actually supplied information that may be useful to you. He said that he was grateful to you for coming to his rescue in the wilderness, but nonetheless, you scare him. He remembers you and the guy with the scar—you Harry," he said nodding to him. "From what I gather, what you guys did both in recovering the bomb from the mountain, and then on the trip in the C-130 was in your line of work, at least back then. For him, what he decided to do was all a desperate slide into darkness. You see, he assumed General Diggens intended to steal, or divert, a nuclear weapon for personal gain. He literally put his life on the line to stop it, that is to steal it from the thief."

I held up my hand so he'd pause. "I have no basic problem with grown up boy scouts. The question is, did he tell you what he did with it?"

"No. He said he can't remember and that it's your fault."

"Everybody wants to dump on me. So, lets hear his explanation of what happened. It seems like he is at least admitting, again, that he flew to the Anoka County Airport."

"Not really. He remembers being put in charge of recovering the five cases scattered around South Vietnam. He also remembers he had intended to have the fifth case arrive later than the other four, but isn't sure why. He seems to remember that there were odd things happening that made him suspicious. After packing up and loading the first four, he went back to his office and looked up the FSN he had seen on the cases and learned they contained MADMs. Now he was really worried. When you arrived with the fifth case, you said something to make him realize he had to act. From there on it is pretty much a blur for him."

I interrupted him, "You still haven't said why his lack of memory is my fault."

"Yes, I was getting to that. After the mission he came to after being drugged and abandoned in a very bad part of Saigon. He had no identification, no money, in fact no clothes except for the boxer shorts he was wearing. At least in his mind, he associates you, that is, the only alert Phantom man on the plane, with his being dropped in such a terrible place. Apparently he was beaten, and nearly died. After he was found, he was in a coma for several days. That's why he can't remember anything, at least according to his account of things.

"After he recovered enough to answer questions, he was interrogated about the missing nuke. He was asked if he had flown the C-130 to the Anoka County Airport because he kept mumbling something about that while in the coma. He told them they were wrong. He probably mentioned it because he liked that little airport having done a lot of recreational flying from there. Anyway, while in the BWCA he told Cutter and later you that he had flown the C-130 to the Anoka Airport because if

Cutter had seen the file on the investigation he would have remembered that airport was mentioned. He hoped they would conclude they had what they needed and would stop beating him.

"You see, his story is that he can't remember anything, that it's your fault, and anything he did say to anybody at any time was put together from things his interrogators *asked* him about, not things that he *told* them."

All I could say was, "That's one cleaver SOB." As an after thought I asked, "Did you think to ask him about other things they asked him about while he was being questioned?"

"Yes, I did. It's part of what we investigators do. He said there was a cryptic phrase he had uttered while unconscious. It was this: 'Twin Towers: 90 by half.' They pushed him hard on it, he said, like it was a clue to where the nuke was. But, in the end, they let it go as random utterances that made no sense."

I had my eyes closed thinking.

Harry asked, "Is there more coming?"

"No, but something occurs to me. What if Holt planned some sort of code that gave the location of the MADM for reasons we don't know? There are twin TV broadcasting towers in Shoreview. They would have been easily visible from the Anoka airport and may have been a convenient landmark when approaching the Twin Cities while still a long way off."

Camilla was shaking her head. "What is it?" I asked.

"Back about then they were building one large candelabra antenna in Shoreview that would have had several TV transmitters on top. But, as it was nearing completion it fell down killing a lot of men. That was one tower, not two so could not be the twin towers he meant."

"Okay," I said, "to the computer."

Camilla had the newest computer in the house so we used that one. I put "Shoreview Twin Towers" in the search engine and in a few minutes had it. "The single candelabra tower fell in September 1971. The replacement twin towers were operational in 1973."

"That leaves out the towers as a likely landmark," said Nugent.

"Yeah," I replied. "But, that was only a suggestion of why he used that name. By spring of 1972 the twin towers would have been under construction. If he were leaving a code for the future, he would have assumed they would eventually be successfully erected and standing for years. He was right—if those are the towers he meant."

We trooped back into the living room. Harry began. "We both remember being on the C-130 coming out of Can Ranh Bay, and it being refueled in the air. Since Holt was in charge of the C-141 shipment he was the one who laid on the C-135 for mid-air refueling. It only took a radio call to tell the refueling ship to stay on station and refuel the C-130, too. I remember a little about being on the ground. From your flashbacks, you remember the whole flight pretty well. The real pilot put our landing in the four state area. Holt mumbled about Anoka. By his own admission he was intimately familiar with that airport. I say we must assume it was the Anoka County Airport, and Holt was the pilot who landed the plane. Therefore, if 'twin towers' mean anything, those in Shoreview are the ones."

Nugent got up. "I've got to go. I found nothing helpful in the subject of gravel pits around that airport."

"Just another second," I said. "Knowing Goldman as you do, what would lure him out of his ivory tower in Washington? I mean, what would get him to come here so we could grab him?"

"I don't know because he's one of those guys who likes to run things but never gets his hands dirty."

"Think about it, especially about his weaknesses. Okay?"

He nodded and left. With Nugent gone I said, "'Twin Towers: 90: by half.' I'd bet it was to be a code, but one way or another, part of it's missing."

Ignoring my comment, Harry said, "It's Wednesday evening and time to call Cutter with a progress report. What should I say?"

"I'd like to tell him I'll cut him to fish food for what he did the my nephew. But, all you can say is we got the message. We know he did it. You could say that distracting us like that is counter-productive and not to do it again. If we have to spend all of our time protecting our families, we won't be working on what he wants. Even though Jimmy gave a good description of him say the local police have no leads. We don't want to scare him away and have new people getting involved."

"That sounds good. What about the hunt?"

"You could say we've both recalled detailed parts of a mission where we were drugged and flown in a C-130 a long way. You could also say that we remembered Major Bruce Holt as having been on that mission, that we interviewed him and he didn't remember much because after the mission he was beaten and in a coma. Since Cutter almost certainly has seen the report of the investigation, he knows about Holt and his coma."

"Ah . . . ." Harry interrupted. "That's where they knew about Holt. You know, we never did get around to asking Nugent if he was the one who told Cutter about Holt."

"Yeah," I said. "Those guys probably knew about Holt all along but didn't bother with him until they learned he was of interest to us. This is all sort of making sense now that I think about it. That file on the investigation is probably six inches thick, in fact, it may be five file cabinets full. When I was driving back from the north country, only Divner was awake. I dug at him a little, saying that Holt had told us what he had told them, and that is was too vague to do them any good. I stressed that they had clumsily failed and that they'd probably be shot and replaced.

"He was confident that wouldn't happen because they were a small group that hailed from their days in Chicago. They were all trust worthy because they all knew where the others had bodies buried. I think he meant that literally. That also meant there were no replacements. From that we can conclude that with such a small group, they didn't want to spend months sifting through all of those files after all those years looking for clues about where the bomb was hidden, especially since the investigators had failed to find it immediately after the fact. Instead, they went out and found who they thought buried it. And that happened to be us."

"That means," Camilla broke in, "that if we scare Cutter off, the replacement would only be a hired hand paid to do a certain thing, like kill one of us and then leave town." She shuttered. "That sounds so clinical, doesn't it? So like them."

"Okay," Harry said, "then I could say we are pretty sure Holt was honest in telling them he flew it to the Anoka Airport, and we've concluded he did it on the spur of the moment to keep it from being stolen by enemy forces. That means there was no elaborate plan to take it from the plane to a waiting truck for shipment to who-knows-where for sale to terrorists or anything like that. Therefore, we are going on the assumption it is buried within several miles of that airport. All of our efforts will be concentrated in that area."

"That's good but say a ten mile radius," I added. "Oh, and add that we have a clue, 'Twin Towers: 90: by half.' See what his reaction is to that."

Harry nodded and was about to punch in the number when he stopped. "I think we should ask him how he plans to recover the thing. It might throw off their thinking. After all, if it's buried, and it weighs four hundred pounds, it will take machinery to dig it up. That requires permits, signatures, and all kinds of stuff especially if it's on public land."

"That's good," I said.

Harry made the call to Cutter. We had checked the number and it was a cell phone from Maryland. I attached a tape recorder pickup to the phone so if there was any question about what Cutter said we could review it.

After the call, Harry's eyes were smiling. "When I mentioned that code he brusquely said to stop with such nonsense, that he'd cut off my hands if I wasted time on anything so stupid."

Camilla's laugh was more of a sneer. "It doesn't take a genius to figure out that they've spent a lot of time on it and gotten nowhere."

"How did he take the rest of the report?"

"He stopped short of setting a deadline, but I got the impression it won't be long before he does, probably at my next report. If they intend to use the bomb to create an incident and from there to martial law and ending at a dictatorship, they probably have a backup plan. If they go to *Plan B*, I'd guess they'd make a quick sweep and kill all of us involved in *Plan A*. It would be set up to look like one of us went on a killing rampage as a statement against homosexuals or something like that. Any disagreement?"

There was none.

— 36 —

Harry left. I was tired and ready to call it a day when I noticed Camilla at the kitchen table with a map laid out. "What ya doing?" I asked."

"Looking at the location of the twin towers in relation to the Anoka Airport. As luck would have it the airport is on one side of the street map and the towers on the other."

"Yeah. That's the way it always is. The most important battles in history have been fought at the intersection of four maps during heavy rain."

Ignoring my comment, she continued, "I've had to use the map that covers the whole nine county metro, but it should do." Camilla knew where the towers were located because at times we walked in the park where they were located.

I was still sitting in my favorite chair with my legs stretched out and leaning my head back. "See anything interesting?"

"Nope. The main runways are north-south and east-west. The towers are off to the southeast so that doesn't seem to mean anything."

"Try drawing a line from the airport to the towers and extend it a long distance in both directions." I could hear her rustling through a kitchen drawer looking for a ruler and pencil.

After a few minutes, when my mind had drifted far from her little endeavor, she said, "I don't see anything that makes sense there either. We have to use the rest of the code, though. What does '90: by half' mean?"

This was not the type of game that appealed to me at the moment, but I knew when she started on something like that, there was no stopping her. "Well, to a pilot, 90 would mean 90 degrees as in due east. Is there anything east of the twin towers?"

"No. That's not it. It's not around the towers. That's too far."

When she said "no" in that tone of voice it was pointless to argue, it was settled. Sometimes she was even right when she got in that mood. I loved her dearly, but she could be stubborn.

"Even a short distance east of the towers would be too far to drive, bury the bomb, and return to the airplane in the time you said it took."

"I didn't say how long it took, only the time I was awake enough to be aware of the passage of time."

"When you first relayed the flashback, you seemed pretty darned certain it was close to the airport, so that's what we go on. Besides, you remember passing over expressways, not traveling on them, and you would have had to have used the local freeways to make it to the towers and back in time."

She continued, as I knew she would. "The towers were a land mark, if not as seen from the air, at least on air maps. Even if the candelabra tower fell, the air maps would have been updated to include it as a navigation hazard. As I recall, it would have been considerably taller than the towers that are there now. And, due east of the airport makes no sense because then the towers don't have any meaning."

"How about due east of the airport until you're directly north of the towers? That would be 90 degrees meaning east and then 90 degrees to that line headed south to the towers."

"That's dumb. That would take two nineties, and there's only one. And, then what does 'by half' mean?"

See what I mean? No reasoning with her. I decided to go to bed knowing she'd be at it half the night.

The earthquake was about to roll me out of bed. Not only that but it had turned on the ceiling light in the bedroom and it was blinding me. Besides that I recognized Camilla's voice in the state of excitement. Strangely, she was not trying to wake me up and get me out of the house before I was buried alive. Instead she was on her knees bouncing up and down on the bed shouting "I found it! I found it!"

Next, she was squeezing my cheeks with her hands, her mouth only inches away saying, "Vin, wake up! I found it."

Finally, I was able to say through puckered lips. "Okay. You found it. Found what?"

"The bomb, silly. The ding dong stupid bomb."

I had been in the deepest sleep I could remember and was having a hard time coming to. "Okay, give me a minute, will you?"

She had thrown back the blanket, and was pulling me to a standing position. "Well, be sure you don't unscrew the cap over the electrical connector," I said still in a stupor.

"No! No! I didn't find it as in I have it in the house, but I know where it is."

As she excitedly rattled on, I staggered to the kitchen. At the sink, I splashed cold water on my face, and finally sank heavily into a dinette chair.

At last it was registering. "Let's see it."

"You were right about drawing a line that bisected the towers and the airport. Then you draw a line 90 degrees to that line also through the center of the airport. Now look at this, the towers are exactly three inches away from the airport."

"How many miles is that?"

"Doesn't matter because half of three is one and a half inches. One and a half inches perpendicular to the line through the airport is right here." She had the point of her pencil on the spot.

I leaned over and saw in faint letters "Lochness Park."

"Wait," I said. What's located one and a half inches the other way from the line?"

"Yes, I checked that. It's the east bank of the Mississippi River. And, no, they didn't dump it in the river. That's because, you have to know what Lochness Park is."

I knew, alright. It was a sanitary landfill that had been closed for many years. Since the water table was so near the surface in that area, the landfill had been built up rather than in a hole. It was now roughly the shape of a truncated pyramid rising above the tops of the tallest trees in the area. In fact, the lake in that park, Lochness Lake, was man made as they dug out the sand to form the walls of the landfill. Several years ago I had flown RC model airplanes there. That was until the infinitely wise authorities decided to convert it to a park where people could run their dogs off the leash. Now, it was nothing but dog poop wherever you stepped, to say nothing of frequent dog fights. Ya gotta love this society. Recently they added a Frisbee Golf course in it so it was too overrun with people to fly a model.

"She continued, "You remember a gravel pit, but it wasn't a gravel pit at all, it was that landfill in the process of being closed. I remember a certain amount of controversy about it back then. That was in the early seventies. I'm pretty sure it was closed by 1975. That should be easy to verify."

That did make sense. If Holt parked the C-130 near the east gate of the airport, we would have driven east out of the airport gate that was never closed back then, and south a half mile and then east on County Road J. That would have taken us over I-35W which angled from northeast to southwest in that area. Continuing east we would have intersected Lexington Avenue. North on Lexington we would have crossed 35W again. A couple of miles north of the interstate was that park. Since Holt flew a light plane out of the Anoka County Airport, he would have flown over the area frequently, and would have known about the landfill. Maybe he even swooped low a couple of times to see what was going on. That also accounted for my remembering running in sand, and the smell of garbage. No doubt, that had to be it.

"It fits," I said. "Now that we know where it is, what do we do?"

We decided to go to bed and try to sleep if that were possible with the excitement. Surprisingly, the solution to the puzzle was like a sedative after weeks of tension and frustration. We fell asleep easily.

Early Thursday morning

My alarm had gone off five minutes before and I was wondering if I should call in and take another day off. People were beginning to notice that something was wrong, and it was getting harder and harder to ignore their questions. I decided that a day at work wouldn't change anything. And, I had better go in today because when we got serious about doing something with the information we had, things would go crazy. It was then that the back door bell started to ding like it had become possessed. It had to be Harry, or I hoped it was because anyone else would be worse.

At the door I pulled back the curtain and, no surprise, it was Harry. I unlocked the door and opened it. He didn't give me time to say a word.

"I got it, remembered a bunch of stuff like one of your flashbacks. Not so full of detail but every time I say it out loud more fills in—been talking to myself for hours."

By this time he was in the kitchen headed for the dinette table. I didn't normally make coffee in the morning, but I had a jar of instant in the cupboard. Holding it up I said, "Coffee?"

He nodded. "Here's what I got and it's about the part you skipped over. What got me started was the dream about being chased by something big. Now I know it's a bulldozer. Yes. I do remember that clearly. And, I always remembered a bad smell. It was a garbage dump."

"How about a landfill?" I asked.

"Yeah. That's just what I thought. Let me tell you what I remembered in my dream last night and immediately after it while I was still half asleep.

"The three of us practically fell out of the back of the truck like a bunch of drunks that had been hauled back to base after a night on the town. He, I'm assuming it was Holt, had backed the truck up an incline as far as he could go without getting stuck. This was a large operation, a quarter mile from side to side, maybe twice that, and it was all raised above the surrounding land so it wasn't a *pit* at all, but more like a hole in the top of a hill.

"The major told us to carry the case to the place the 'dozer was filling in. There was one large bulldozer pushing sand up the incline to the edge of a cavity. There were spot lights on tall poles arrayed around the area so it was easy to see what was going on.

"We had maybe one to two hundred yards to carry the case, all 350 to 400 pounds of it, and in our condition that was going to be tough. As soon as the major had given us our orders, he was running so as to maneuver himself behind the 'dozer.

"We lowered the tail gate and slid the case out. It had to be one man on one side and two on the other. The sand was lose and that made it even harder lugging the thing. I glanced over to see the major catch onto the rear of the huge machine as the operator stopped and began another push of sand toward the edge of the cavity. After thirty yards we stopped and changed places so each of us had a turn being on the side with only one man. By this time the operator was unconscious and the major was in command of the tracked vehicle and had it stopped. He waved his arm to speed us along. We complied. After a few more switches, we were within twenty feet of the edge and stopped. That was close enough. Glancing into the cavity in the hill all I saw was trash, another odd thing that didn't compute at the time, but now that we know it was a landfill it makes perfect sense.

"We were exhausted. Blue Dog even sat on the case and wiped sweat out of his eyes with his sleeve. The sound of an engine having the throttle slammed open made you and me look up to see black diesel exhaust pouring out of the stack of the dreadnought bearing down on us. The major had left the engine at idle as he slowly brought the machine in behind us as we concentrated on carrying the case. I remember you yelling, 'Trouble guys. Move it!'

"Still dopey from the drug, we were stunned as the blade grew ever closer and larger. The head lights mounted above the blade glared at us from the growling machine and the spot lights on the poles gleamed off the broad shiny surface. Each of us grabbed one of Blue's arms as we helped pull him along, almost dragging him. As I remember, you did more pulling than I did, seeing as you were the most awake. We stumbled along. The blade changed course to match our move. We pulled harder, all the time yelling at Blue to get his dead backside moving. Ah . . . those aren't the exact words, Mrs. Wessen, but you get the idea."

Camilla had joined us soon after Harry began his story.

"Blue finally realized the danger and started to run as a shot of adrenaline put him in high gear. 'Spread out!' you yelled. That made an impression as we each ran in a different direction. The sand was even softer there than it had been near the truck, but even at that we could out maneuver the 'dozer. I had no idea how fast the thing could go, and maybe Holt didn't know how to put it into high gear, but we could stay out of the way if we worked at it. At last the machine stopped and reversed. We came together a hundred yards behind it and watched as the aluminum case was pushed over the brink to take its place among the garbage. Then he backed up and pushed two piles of sand over it. After that he backed up to where he had taken control of the bulldozer."

Harry looked at me. "If you had been just a little worse off, we would all have been pushed into the cavity along with the case and covered with sand. The major had opened the throttle a few seconds too soon and that saved us. After we were all running in different directions I instinctively reached for my pistol to find the holster under my left arm empty. I'm sure you guys did the same. You can tell how effective the drug was even when we were partly recovered from it. It was totally second nature to maintain an awareness of our weapons and we hadn't thought to check.

"We knew we were in a dangerous spot. Not functioning at full mental capacity, we weren't a Phantom Team, and with no weapons we weren't even decent soldiers. It seems to me now, it was more the instinct for survival than anything else that caused us to make for the truck. I see now that that was the right move. We had to complete the mission which meant getting back to Vietnam to report in to our superiors. If we over powered Holt and escaped, we'd be three soldiers massively AWOL who could easily spend the rest of our lives in a military prison.

"We were all breathing hard as we reached the truck. Helping Blue, we managed to pull ourselves in the back of the truck, and raise the tail gate. Looking back the major jumped off the machine and jogged our way. This much we could understand. He had used a spring loaded hypodermic needle to put the operator out with the sleep drug. Just before he jumped off he gave him a shot the same way with the antidote. In five to ten minutes he'd wake up with a headache and wonder how he had managed to fall asleep. By that time, we'd be long gone.

"If Holt had intended to bury us, he had failed, so we pulled the tarp down and pretended to fall asleep as if everything had gone as planned. We could only hope that now he'd drive back to the plane, load up and go back to Vietnam where it was so much safer."

I placed a cup of instant coffee in front of Harry. He had that smug look that he was so good at. "Now, I'm pulling my weight, too, huh, guys? All we have to do is find a landfill that I'd guess has been closed up for about twenty years, am I right?"

Smiling, I said, "Right you are Harry. The landfill is now called Lochness Park. Camilla found it last night from the clue. But, your recounting of what we did with the case is perfect confirming evidence."

Harry looked dejected. "You're kidding, right?"

Camilla shook her head. "Here, I'll show you how it works."

In two minutes Harry had to agree. "Anyway, if I see the place, I think I'll be able to get us pretty close to where it is. As I remember, that's a lot of territory even if we know what park it's in."

"I have to go to work," I said. "How about spending the day thinking about what we do now. I've worked it out this far. Cutter has to assume the state police know something about it from when the trooper stopped us outside of Ely. That was too messy with wounded men in the car and Secret Service credentials for them to simply drop the incident. That means Cutter would have to further assume that if we told him where it was that we'd also tell the state cops so that as soon as he dug it up the cops would show up to nab him with the goods. For now, don't go near the place. In fact, spend some time wandering around another park or some open place pretending to take sightings on land marks and stuff like that."

Harry nodded. "Yeah, that makes sense. I wonder if they've spent any time working out what they'd do once we remembered where we stashed it?"

"We have no other choice than to assume they have done a great deal of thinking about that, and it involves bad things for us. Oh, something else. From the caustic remark Cutter made about the 'stupid clue,' we can assume they've been trying hard to find the bomb from the clue without needing us. They certainly made a try with Holt. Maybe we have to give them clues that even they are smart enough to figure out."

As I was leaving I saw a self satisfied smile on Camilla's face. After all, she *had* figured it out.

— 37 —

Thursday evening

Harry joined us for supper. He was becoming a member of the family out of necessity. I had to hand it to him for sticking with it and neglecting his business. However, he was smart enough to know his business wouldn't mean much to him if he were dead.

The meal passed quickly with little conversation as the acuteness of our position added a pungent taste to every bite. After the table was cleared, Camilla said, "I think we can agree that if we tell the state police where it is and they recover it, Cutter and his goons will know we thwarted them and take reprisals against us."

Harry and I nodded our concurrence and Harry added, "And, we can also agree that we can't simply tell Cutter and his pals where it is and let them have it. That would be dangerous for the country and they'd have to get rid of us to keep us from telling the story. On the bright side, if they used it immediately and assumed dictatorial control they could ignore us because by that time they would have taken full control of the information media. However, they might kill us anyway out of spite."

We moved to the living room and I said, "Over the years there have been times when I became paranoid about some of the missions we ran, thinking someone might rise to a position of power and decide to even a score with us. As a result, a few years ago I looked into the assassination of JFK in 1963 and the convenient deaths that followed in its wake. In the first year after the assassination there were fifteen suspicious deaths. In the thirteen years after it there were about a hundred. Most of these were people whose only fault was being in the wrong place at the wrong time. I remember reading that Lloyds of London looked at the lives of those people from the first year and estimated the odds of all of them dying within a year's time. The odds were millions of billions to one which meant these were not accidental deaths. And, those were the good old days. What I'm leading up to is that we have to get this right, even if we are amateurs."

After a moment, Harry said, "If there are a limited number of people who 'know where the bodies are buried' what would happen if they all went down when the bomb was made public?"

I answered, "We don't know how many there are, and even if we did, how would we do that? Let's see, how many we do know about? There's Seth Goldman, Divner, Cutter, the driver for the assassin who called himself Jimmy Hook, General Diggens, Nugent, Holt and the other one Cutter gave us a phone number for. Who was that, Sal something? And, don't laugh, the president of the United States. Of course, Bren Nugent thinks the world would be a much brighter place even if Goldman were the only one we managed to permanently sideline."

"From the training," Harry said, "we know to do the unexpected, so let's call Cutter tonight with something, anything, rather than waiting until tomorrow."

We all agreed that was a good idea. Than, it became a matter of figuring out what to tell him. After an hour of haggling, Harry was ready to make the call when I stopped him. "If we give him all that information and they are even a little bit lucky, it would be as bad as telling them exactly where it was. What would happen if we called John Witherton, had him leave Ely early tomorrow, and we use his meter and find the thing for sure?"

"I wish he would have let you keep the meter."

"He didn't precisely because the state troopers didn't want to be left out. What do you think?"

Camilla said, "Can I say something?"

"Sure."

"What would stop Witherton from immediately telling the top brass of the state police where it was? They'd rush out and dig it up taking all the glory while letting us swing in the breeze as we already agreed we would?"

"For every problem, there's a solution," Harry said. "We'd simply have to take Witherton prisoner until we had the whole thing worked out."

"That could be difficult because he might have 'helpers' when he shows up. But, we have to do something. How about this? We forgo the unexpected call to Cutter and call Witherton tonight. I'll say we have some possibilities, not good ones, but better to take a chance than do nothing. Plan to go out on Saturday which would make the state guys have to think about overtime pay for 'helpers,' and leave the impression we really didn't expect to be successful, anyway."

Harry said, "If we really did find it, though, we couldn't let Witherton go and expect him not to blab."

"Boy, this is really messy. What would happen if Goldman and maybe one or two of the others were to go down? Would we be safe after that?"

"I suppose that's the best we could hope for because if we dug it up ourselves and dumped it somewhere, we'd still be on the hook to Cutter to find it."

"Okay," I said. "The only safe way to do it is to let them find it, have them caught by the state police just as they dig it up, and have them either killed or blamed for being terrorists."

"Do you suppose the state police will go along with something like that?"

"It's possible. From what Witherton said, there's no love lost between state police and federal agencies."

I called Witherton and he agreed to drive down on Friday so we could go prospecting on Saturday. I asked if he could arrive in the early afternoon so we could discuss things without it getting too late. I knew that didn't make much sense, but if he called me on it, it wouldn't matter because of the plan I was putting together.

Then, Harry called Cutter after we agreed to give him a lot less than we had originally planned.

"Cutter? Harry Auston. We've got something. Let me review where we are. We are 99.9% certain it's in the Minneapolis metro area and that it was flown in a C-130 to the Anoka County Airport."

There was a pause. "Yeah. Most of what we've been going on up until now was from stuff Wessen was recalling. Now, I've been remembering things, too. We were in the back of a three-quarter ton truck driven by the pilot who we think was Holt, but that's neither hear nor there. We didn't drive too far before we stopped in a gravel pit, only it wasn't a pit, it was more like a hill that was being dug away. Three of us carried it a couple of hundred yards to where a bulldozer was filling in an area, maybe a place they were finished with digging out and were back filling with overburden or something. Anyway, our truck driver commandeered the 'dozer, pushed in the bomb, and covered it up."

There was a long pause after which Harry said, "We strongly think the twin towers play into finding the exact location, though."

I could hear a strident voice as Harry pulled the phone away from his ear. The comment about the towers was made precisely to elicit that reaction. With any luck, Cutter would discount the rest of the information because of it. Later we could say we had given him good information if he had only taken it seriously.

That was it. Harry hung up.

We tentatively decided Harry would go with Witherton to Lochness Park on Saturday. If they did find it, they would give no indication of that as if they were being watched, which they probably would be. Then, they would go to another place and do more searching. It would have been nice if we could have found a dog or two so they wouldn't be conspicuous as they tromped around dog poop heaven, but we couldn't cover everything. After Harry left I called Nugent on his cell phone. He had just left the office and was on his way home. He agreed to stop by.

Nugent arrived a little before seven. The guy worked long hours unless he took two hour, three martini lunches. He parked his Mercedes roadster out front. It was way out of place for my neighborhood. Maybe the neighbors, especially the woman in the second house down the block, would think I had a rich uncle.

The front door was standing open and I watched as he approached. "Come on in, Bren," I said before he could land his finger on the doorbell button. He entered, impeccably dressed as always. The collar of his expensive pastel blue shirt was open with no tie, and his subdued hounds tooth sport coat coordinated perfectly with darker blue nicely creased slacks. Black shoes gleamed from beneath the trouser bottoms.

"Anything new?" I asked.

He shook his head. "How about you?"

"Yeah, might be," I said. "If we have it figured right we know the general area where the object of our search is located. With the proper equipment, we are reasonably sure we'll be able to pin point it. That's the main reason why I called. We've figured that it's necessary to lure Goldman here, in fact to the actual site of the excavation while it's being dug up in order to connect him to it."

Nugent pursed his lips as he thought. "Assuming, as you suggest, that we can pique him enough to assure his presence at the location of the discovery, and I think it may be possible, I don't see how we can make the case that he's involved in any of this. He's slippery by nature and he occupies a position of power where he can manipulate rules that would apply without extenuation to you and me."

He was well spoken, I'd give him that. It probably had to do with the job he had. Precision of language was probably what made the difference between profit and loss, or winning or losing in court cases where he testified. He had a point, though, one I had dwelt on long and hard.

"Yes," I replied, "I see that it isn't good enough to simply catch him in possession of the device. He would simply say it was part of his job of "security" as in National Security Advisor. And, if his cohorts could come up with Secret Service credentials that were as good as genuine, they could appear this time with Department of Energy IDs also just doing their jobs. We need a better plan than that."

We had been standing by the front door as we spoke so I said, "Might as well come in and set a spell as we work on this."

He nodded and we proceeded to the end of the room with the sofa and easy chairs. There was a tinge of a grin on his mouth as he said drolly, "If they were to detonate the thing on the spot, I suppose that'd make the case that they were involved in the plot. Or, in any case it would make their complicity moot."

With what I hoped was an equal amount of dryness, I responded, "I had hoped to step back from such an exacting application of justice since we, too, will be in the near vicinity at the time." After a pause, I continued in a more somber tone, "I've come up with a few ideas if you can draw him out of his ivory tower to the place and at the time we need."

"Okay, when and where do you need him to appear, and when should I make my plea?"

"We expect to locate it in the next few days so this being Thursday evening, and as much as I hate to do it on Sunday, make sure he's available in the Twin Cities, ready to go early Sunday morning. Do you know how to contact him?" Unless there was no other way, I wasn't willing to reveal the special phone number Cutter gave us in the wilderness when he thought I would abandon him there to die of thirst. "And assuming you do reach him, may I ask how you're planning to entice him to come?"

"I'm pretty sure I can find him and that he'll take my call. I made him look good on some important operations. Regarding the hook, I know enough about the case to weave a web of intrigue so he'll be interested. I can use the fact that he's the only man in the federal government that I know who's in a position to do anything about it, and that if the locals handle it, I know from experience in this town that it'll be on the news in an hour. He'll accept that easily enough."

He had it figured as well as I could have hoped. "You could mention that in some way the Vietnamese are involved so he thinks he has competition. But, I hope you're aware that you can't mention nuke or anything like that. Our snooper friends at the NSA probably have those flag words in the watch list on a permanent basis."

He thought for a full minute as he was composing his spiel in his mind. "Yes, that can be handled. His response will depend on how personally committed he is to recovering the thing. If it's the main operation concerning him at the present, he'll pick up on any number of hints I might drop. Otherwise, the direct approach may be the only way. I'll call him on my cell phone so it doesn't involve you. Is there a room where I can make the call in private? With calls like this I operate the way I operate and I don't like the idea of someone breathing over my shoulder giving me suggestions. It throws me off my stride. Do you understand that?"

I understood perfectly since it was the same for me. I led him to a little bedroom across the hall from the main bathroom. As he entered, I said, "It's too bad you can't record the call because I'd like to know how it went. Harry will be calling Cutter with another report soon and I wouldn't want him to be at cross purposes with what you said."

He nodded. "With a push of a button I can record it on my phone. I do that with most business calls."

That took me by surprise. "Isn't that the same as wire tapping? I'd think in your case when your investigations frequently end up in court that you'd have to be careful not to do that."

"No it's not. Wire tapping is where someone records a call between two people and neither of them knows it's being done. If only one knows about it, it's legal. If it ends up in a court case, it depends on the biases of the judge if he'll allow it as testimony."

"But," I replied, "why is it that whenever I call my insurance company or something like that, they always say the call is being recorded?"

He smiled. "That's mainly to keep the callers from becoming abusive since most such calls involve problems. Other than that, it reminds the caller that in case of a dispute they have a record of the call and he doesn't. So forget about challenging them."

"Yet, another case where the little guy loses," I mused.

He nodded and closed the door to the bedroom.

It seemed to take forever as I sat in the living room waiting. The call, or calls were going into fifteen minutes when he opened the door. His face was inscrutable. He could see my face which I'm sure expressed, "Well?"

"I got him on his cell phone as he was driving home. It didn't go as well as I had hoped, but after he thinks about it for awhile and talks to his guys on the ground here in the metro, I think I'll be able to coax him out here. The timing it the big problem."

"Can I hear the call?"

He pushed the "Power" button and after feeling through his menus for a few seconds he handed the phone to me. I placed it up to my ear.

After a series of clicks and beeps as a call was being transferred, I heard, "Yeah."

"Hi, Seth? This is Bren Nugent, been a long time."

After a pause, "Bren Nugent?"

"Yes, that's what I said."

"Boy, it has been some time. Say, I'm a busy guy, I'm in heavy traffic, and I really don't have time for old times sake. Okay?"

"Wait a minute. Don't hang up. This is no nostalgia call. I've stumbled on to something big, really big. I'm running a large PI business if you recall. Can you take a few minutes to hear me out?"

The sound of a condescending breath, almost a snort, could be heard. "Make it quick, okay?"

"I'll get right to it. During routine business, which for me is investigating things, I ran across something, call it a plot, to recover a lost item. I can't say certain words over an unsecure line, you understand, so say this is a very valuable and dangerous item. It seems to be located in the Minneapolis metro area. Suffice it to say, it would be something the Department of Energy would take a keen interest in, in the military side of their business, that is. It's portable and in the wrong hands could be a national threat. I'm calling you because you're the only one I know who's in a sufficiently high position to handle this without all kinds of undesirable side effects. One of those is if I were to notify the locals, even the Bureau, it'd be on the news in an hour. They leak like a sieve as I've learned from hard experience."

It seemed like the line was dead with no sound from either side of the conversation. Finally, Bren said, "Are you there? Did we get disconnected?" There would have been evidence of being disconnected, they both knew that. But, it was something to say on Bren's part. Clearly, Goldman was thinking.

"I'm here," he replied slowly. It wasn't hard to understand that Goldman was trying to mesh his plot to recover the MADM with what Bren had told him. "I need everything you have, and as soon as possible, got that!"

He was hooked. Bren cleared his throat and made a few noises until finally he said, "Well, yes, I can see how you feel. But, I have this information as part of a confidential investigation. I can't simply be broadcasting stuff around especially since it would appear that the Vietnamese government is involved. I forgot to mention that. In addition, I can't attach it to an email, that'd too insecure. I feel we must meet."

"Fine. Stuff what you have in a briefcase and hop on a plane. I'll meet with you first thing in the morning."

Now it was Bren who let the line go dead. When he finally spoke his voice was firm. "No." He drew out the word. "That will not do. The situation is here, it must be handled here. You don't have the details, but if you did you'd understand."

"If I draw the proper inferences from what you said, we can't sit on this. And, I simply can't get away tomorrow. How about if I send you someone?"

Now, Bren was hard, "No! We have history. It must be you and nobody else. I wouldn't have any idea if the man you sent really came from you. I've already run into false federal IDs with this thing. I'm in this a mite deeper than you imagine. I have information, and it seems to be getting around that I have it. Besides, Saturday or Sunday would work the best as I now see it. Saturday would be okay, but I expect to have further information by late that day. It looks like the best would be first thing Sunday morning in Minneapolis."

"I don't know. I have a funny feeling about this. You sure you're not stringing me along?"

I seemed like Bren had been expecting such a comment because he was ready with an instant retort. "I suppose there's no way you can be sure, but in our time working together, did I ever, even once, lead you wrong?" An instant passed before he continued, "Not once! It's real, and it's here. If you want to hear about it on the evening news, that's up to you."

"Okay, okay. Don't do anything rash. Give me a number where I can reach you. I have to see about schedules and make some calls. I'll call you tomorrow. Agreed?"

"Fine."

It was impossible to tell who ended the call first, probably they both clicked off at the same time.

I handed the phone to Bren as I smiled. "He's hooked. And, it does appear that this is quite high on his list of priorities. Right now he's probably calling his henchmen and will learn that it was Cutter and his buddy who flashed the 'fake federal IDs' at you. That will do two things. The first will cement the idea that the thing you were talking about is his MADM. The second is that Cutter will pay you a visit. How do you plan to handle that? He will also wonder how you came to the conclusion that the IDs were fake."

Bren shifted uncomfortably. "First, about the IDs, that's simple. I'll say the two men presenting them didn't fit the profile. After all, I flashed a CIA badge enough times. I know how it's done. As far as Cutter's concerned, I'll put him off and refuse to say anything to anyone except Goldman in person. Do you really think he'll show up on my front step?"

"More like your back door when you're alone in the house."

— 38 —

Friday

At work I was having more than the normal amount of trouble concentrating. The past few weeks had put a decided stress on my mind as I tried to keep from making mistakes with my attention continually drawn to other matters. Today it was positively surreal. Here I was making drawings and ordering equipment to upgrade a chocolate refining line at the Hershey factory in Hershey, Pennsylvania. The other half of my mind was grappling with what to do about a live nuclear weapon, one the president of the United States seemed intent on using to eradicate an American city. The two endeavors were hardly on the same metaphysical plane. Yet, the mundane had to be accomplished lest I give myself away and the glaring horror of the possible were to come to light.

When 3:30 arrived I left work even though I had less than a full day in. I'd make it up next week if there were a next week. Home at 4:15, I saw Harry and Witherton on the patio. Harry had called me shortly after noon and said they'd go out together and check a few places.

"How'd it go?" I asked expecting that they had spent a pointless day walking land where we knew it wasn't.

Harry spoke first, not an abnormal occurrence for Harry. "We went to the places you suggested. At the ruins of the old homestead in Rice Creek Regional Park we planted a steel stake near the foundation where the house once stood." We had agreed they would plant stakes at a couple of places in case anyone were watching them.

He continued. "We walked the park on Golden Lake in Circle Pines and on a whim spent some time at the old landfill in Lochness Park. After that we walked the seaplane base on Lake Drive. We planted a stake there too."

My eyes if not my whole expression showed surprise. We had agreed they wouldn't go to Lochness Park today. I didn't look at Witherton for the moment, remaining intent on Harry. There was a tinge of "Who made you leader of the band?" in what he said. Harry had been letting me take the lead, I assumed, because he had gotten us into this by taking the money. And, with him commuting from St. Louis and me living here, I was the closest one to the action and made the decisions as the need arose, though, he was an equal player more or less. It came to me in a flash that he had not offered nor had I asked for my share of the money he had been given. Time enough for things like that later. What was done was done, and what they had done today was probably what should have happened, anyway.

"And . . . ?"

"Nothing," Witherton interjected.

That was comforting from the point of view that we didn't have to tie up Witherton to keep him from spilling the beans, but bad news from the standpoint that we were all wrong on where we thought it was.

Harry caught my mixture of expressions, though it didn't appear Witherton had. "I know," Harry said, "we agreed to say away from the most likely spots until Saturday to keep the timing on the mark. But, Bren called as we were leaving and said Goldman let him know in no uncertain terms that he'd be here Saturday morning, not Sunday. It was as if he suspected he was being put off and intended to do the unexpected to throw off other people's plans. Sounds like something we'd do, huh? So, I made the decision we had to locate the thing before he got here. But, guess what? No bomb."

"But," Witherton said, "there were some indications of x-rays on the meter at the landfill. Considering the hours we spent before and after that with the dumb needle acting like it was glued on zero, I'd say that's our best shot."

"Yeah," I replied, "but you must remember that most of that refuse was accumulated during the nineteen fifties and sixties. That was the beginning of the nuclear age when everything from luminous dials on watches and dozens of medical procedures and devices used radioactive isotopes. For example, radiation therapy for cancer was far more common then than it is now. When the machines using the isotopes were phased out, the isotopes were removed before disposal, but that left a lot of low residual radioactivity that ended up in landfills. How about tracking?" I asked.

Now Witherton laughed. I had told Harry that I suspected the state police had put a tracking device in the meter and that we'd take a look before we went out on Saturday. The case was meant to be taken off to replace the batteries. And, I had noticed the first time we used it that it had a fiberglass case rather than a metal one.

Witherton continued, "When Harry said we had to check the batteries I didn't think much of it other than that he was acting like we were going into a combat situation, you know, like he had reverted back to when he was nineteen. We went to your basement—nice model airplanes hanging from the wall by the way—and sure enough, he found it, removed it, too."

"What'd you expect?"

"Knowing the two of you, nothing but that."

I sank down in a chair and asked, "What do you want to do now?"

"Another dead end," Witherton said. "You said the chances weren't that good when you called me. I might as well go home."

"No," I said thoughtfully, "why don't you stay in town tonight. I'll have to do some thinking about this. There are a few more possibilities that we might as will try in the morning."

"Sure, be glad to. I'm being pushed pretty hard. I wish I had never been caught up in this. Now, I have to call my bosses and say we failed again. They have everything set to call in the TV helicopters and who knows what. If anything turns up, call me even if it's in the middle of the night."

I nodded. "You can count on it. We have your cell phone number, but as soon as you're settled, call me with your hotel phone just in case."

He agreed and walked around the house to the front where his state patrol car was parked. If he showed up many more times the neighbors would start thinking we were being investigated for drug dealing or something.

I went into the house and watched him through the lace curtain on the front door to be sure he drove off. Harry had followed me in and then motioned me to follow him out the back again. He led the way to the end of the house behind the fence. We sat on the lawn leaning back against the wall.

In a whisper Harry said. "I found it, but he doesn't know it. Once I got to the landfill, things really came back. I could see in my mind where we parked the truck and it connected perfectly with the lay of the land as it is now even though it was considerably altered since our long ago visit. It's amazing that it's so different yet so much the same. In spite of the trees growing on the sloped sides and all that, there are two views in my mind, the one then and the one now. I could sort of place them over one another and see where the bulldozer pushed it into the pit. I can tell you it's buried only about ten feet under the present surface."

"Why didn't he know you found it?"

"Because we didn't walk that part. If you remember, the main part of the landfill is sort of an out of shape truncated pyramid with an uneven top. But the east side was extended to the south to make what now is a nice flat surface about two-thirds as high as the rest of it and only half as wide going to the west. That was the last part to be filled in and where we dumped the bomb. He asked about it, and I said that we had checked local records and found that part was only started several years after this business with the bomb so it couldn't be there. It made sense to him. But, if we call him and have him bring his x-ray meter in the morning, I know I can pinpoint the location in ten minutes. I am certain of it."

My mixed emotions were back but the other way around. It now seemed like it actually existed and we knew where it was. Before this, there had always been the possibility that the whole thing was nothing more than some sort of collective fantasy.

As we walked to the back door, I asked, "Did Bren say what time Goldman would arrive?"

"No," Harry answered. "Maybe I should call and find out."

As we entered Camilla said, "I've made some bologna sandwiches and coffee. You might as well sit down and have something to eat."

There were carrot sticks and sliced apples to go with it. The front door chime sounded and Camilla went to it. We could hear the first words. "Hello, Mr. Nugent. They were just about to call you. Please come in and pull up a chair."

It was clear Nugent had other things on his mind besides a bologna sandwich.

Before he could say anything, Harry got right to the point, "When is Goldman due to arrive in the morning?"

"Early," Bren replied. "Probably touch down at six, maybe six-thirty. Is that important?"

"Very, I said. Please, everybody sit tight while I make a call, okay? It'll only take a few minutes."

In a back bedroom I punched in the number for Dutch Tuley. It rang three times and was answered with a bored, "Hello."

I recognized the voice. "How's it going Dutch. This is Vin Wessen. When are we going fishing?"

The voice lightened up. "Hi Vin, been wondering if you'd ever call."

"Well, we'll go soon but first I want to spice up your life a little. I have two questions. First, do you have the backhoe parked in your yard as of right now?"

"Yeah. But, that ain't spicing up anything."

"Question two, are you and it available for me to hire the combo for tomorrow morning?"

A pause. "Ya oughta do a little better planning, ya know that, Vin."

"I know, but this sort of came up faster than I had thought it would."

"What ya want to dig, anyway?"

"That's the spicy part. When Harry and I were there, we mentioned that we were being pushed to remember something from our army days. We finally remembered what it is. Are you ready? I want to dig up a nuclear bomb that we buried forty years ago during the Vietnam War. It's a very long story and best told while in the middle of a twelve pack while hanging a line over the side of a boat. Wha-da-ya say?" I wasn't worried about using flag words like "nuclear" for the NSA snoopers because this thing would be finished before anyone could act on it.

There was a chuckle. "I always thought there was a bit of a crazy look in your eyes, Wessen. You sure you aren't screwing with me?"

"I most surely wish it were that simple. I am as serious as I have ever been in my life. Remember Joab Feinstein from last summer? Well, his boss, Seth Goldman, is our problem now. And if you thought Feinstein was nasty, this guy is far worse. Goldman will be there in the morning, too."

It was like a shot, "I'll be there—when and where!"

"Say five-thirty tomorrow morning. Here, I'll give you directions. It's easy to find."

With the call done I returned to the kitchen. "Okay," I said. "I'll have a backhoe on site at five-thirty in the morning. What airport is Goldman coming in on?"

All eyes focused on Nugent. "He didn't say."

"It's important. If he's coming in a government biz jet, which I assume he is, tell him to come to the Anoka County Airport. It's close by and there will be less chance of traffic delays."

Bren agreed and got up to go to the back room to make his call, as I expected he would. He paused as the front door chime sounded again. I rolled my eyes as Camilla once again answered it. Who else? Fred Clements.

Her clear voice with a sound of mirth filled the room. "Come on in, Fred. Everybody's here."

Fred hadn't met Nugent so I made introductions.

"Good," Fred said. "This will be easier than I thought. Now listen up all of you." He whipped out his wallet and presented his ID. "I'm FBI, lately working under cover, but still with the Bureau. You can all sit back and have a nice night's sleep because the FBI is now in charge of the case. And, you Wessen, will tell me where the cussed thing is. No holding back our I'll see your sorry butt is dumped into a prison cell for the rest of your life."

So much for the down on his luck ex-FBI agent. I should have known better. The only thing that bothered me was how we had gotten this far without him taking over.

Bren was edging to Fred's side so I engaged Fred's attention. "Therein lies the big problem, doesn't it, my old 'lying like a rug' friend? You stinking Feds all think the end justifies the means. Has it ever occurred to you that if the rest of us lacked all moral sense the way you do, that we'd beat your brains out like you deserve?" I didn't care if what I said made any sense since my purpose was to make him mad so Bren could step away and call Goldman.

Fred's face turned red and he reached for his gun in his shoulder holster. Harry was fast as he caught Fred's wrist before it had a firm grip on the gun, and stepped in front of him. His left fist landed in Fred's belly followed by a cuff with the palm of his hand to the side of the head. Disoriented, he tripped on an accent rug and landed hard on his rump.

"Stay there," I said.

I scooped up Fred's gun and laid it on the kitchen table far out of his reach. "Okay, Fred, enough of this. The glory game has to stop. The state cops could already have the thing in their possession if that's the way we wanted it. You should try seeing the bigger picture. The first thing you must know is that your threats will not get you and any other FBI freaks the information until we decide to give it."

Fred was still seething, but refrained from saying anything.

Bren rejoined us and said it was set that he'd land at Anoka in the morning.

Fred was calming down as it occurred to him just how far out of the loop he was. "Who's landing at Anoka?" he asked.

"The president's National Security Advisor," Bren replied in a deadpan voice.

"Did you mention our latest development?" I asked.

"Most certainly did. Is your cell phone turned on?" he asked Fred.

"Yeah, of course. Who wants to know?"

"Probably your boss and his boss, you know, right up to the top."

I returned to the kitchen to finish my meal. The rest followed. I seated Fred between the table and the wall after putting his gun on top of the refrigerator. After we were seated Bren continued.

"Like you'd expect, he didn't like the Fibbies elbowing their way in. I managed to convince him that we'd be able to keep things under control on our end if he did what he could from his end. For some reason, he believed me."

"Coffee, anyone?" Camilla asked with a broad smile. She was enjoying this a lot more than anyone else. I supposed it was because all the stress over the past weeks was starting to lift. The end was in sight. Everyone accepted coffee.

As she was serving, the twitter of a cell phone demanding attention emanated from Fred's pocket. All eyes riveted on him in a way that he knew he had no choice other than to answer it.

"Clements."

All he did was listen until he finally said, "Yeah," and snapped the lid closed. Twitching his mouth he said, "The Bureau has been called off from the top to the bottom, the latter's me."

We finished our meal in silence. Then I said, "Fred, something may happen in the morning. If it does, do you want me to call you? It will be as a courtesy for the help you gave me in the BWCA. Is that okay?"

He nodded and I continued, "Good, because I need to get this place cleared out so I can think. We aren't out of this by any means. By the way, we still haven't located the thing with any certainty other than a pretty good idea of where to look."

He got up and left.

With Fred gone, Bren looked at Harry and me. "Is that right? You don't know where it is?"

"We are ninety-nine percent sure," Harry said.

Bren caught my eye. "I have a bit of information and I'm not sure what it means. Is it safe for the rest to hear?" He was looking at Harry and Camilla.

"We're all in it to the end. What do you have?"

He began in a hushed voice. "When I had dinner with my dad-in-law last night, he wanted to talk about the MADM, though it took him awhile to get around to the subject. He remembered the Christmas when he had a little too much to drink and didn't know how much he had said. I laid out what I knew and he became apprehensive. After a lot of disclaimers and such, he said that in the remote chance the bomb still existed, and if we did find it, there was something about it he had not told you—something important. I pressed him and he refused to tell. What do you think?"

"Could you call him and say we have found it, and to let us know what's so important? I'd think the twenty minute fuse activated by removing the electrical connector cap would be the most important thing there was."

He shook his head. "Not until we actually have it in hand and he can see it will he tell. It's the last secret."

We sat in stunned silence. Finally, I asked, "Any ideas?"

"Only one. There must be something about it that is even worse than the twenty minute timer, something that is so uncivilized that he will not reveal it. He was in on the design, not the mechanical part, but the strategy of what would set it off. And, I'm guessing that he won't tell the world the entire plan until there is absolutely no other choice."

"It can't be a tip switch or a shock fuse or anything like that," Harry said. "We rolled that baby down the hill to the truck bouncing it off rocks and aiming it for trees to stop it's forward motion so we could plan the next move. We really abused it and no detonation."

"How will we be able to convince him that we have it in hand?" I asked.

"I will call him on an unlisted number he has. He has voice recognition equipment so it must be me."

"Okay. Pick up Goldman and if we have it before you arrive, I'll call you and then you call him."

Bren agreed and left. Harry would spend the night in the spare room.

— 39 —

Just when I thought we might have the situation under control at least a little, out of the blue, we get that news from Bren. The last secret had to deal with the device itself so it was either another fuse that would detonate it, or it could be an explosive that would blow it up with no nuclear reaction and spew radioactive contamination on everybody at the site. Of course, there could be a canister of poison gas or something of the sort that would disgorge its contents on us if we did the wrong thing. I was deliberately staying away from the possibility it contained a star drive from an alien space ship that would split the earth in half.

I could understand his reticence. There would be no deniability about it being one of ours in spite of the pains they took to purify the plutonium back then. It was bad enough to have it get out that the U. S. had tried to introduce a nuclear weapon into the Vietnam War, but now to threaten the American people with that very same weapon would set off a fire storm. My countrymen by and large would like the first possibility. They felt it was fine to blow other countries to bits with our bombs, killing them by the tens of thousands, destroying their economies, and poisoning their land and water with spent uranium munitions leaving twenty-five percent of their babies with hideous birth defects. They don't even get too excited about terrorists killing a few Americans in the U.S.—just don't let it happen to me.

Enough! There was insufficient information on which to even make a guess about what the general knew. It would wait for morning. I went to the master bedroom and sat on the edge of the bed. Fatigue like I had not experienced since those long ago days in the bush fell on me—again. The difference, then to now, was that then the fatigue only needed sleep to dispel it, and sleep came easily. Now sleep wasn't enough even when it came.

There's a thing about good news and bad news that affects the physical as well as the mental part of us. Good news leads to hope, lifts the
sprit and all seems better. Aches and pains are less noticed, the whole
person seems lighter with more energy. The opposite is true of bad news.
And, the bad news just kept coming. I was on the precipice again only
this time I could feel myself losing my balance as if there were no alternative to my falling, falling forever. The abyss was there, to pull back
from or to achieve release in succumbing.

I awoke with a start. It was dark except for the dim illumination from
the street light across the street filtering thought the drapes. I was lying
on the bed fully dressed with a blanket thrown over me. I looked at my
watch, 2:14 a.m. Camilla lay asleep, or so it seemed. For the briefest
moment things were set aright and there was a deep sense of peace.
Then, it came to me like touching a bare 240 Volt line. The bomb would
detonate. Whether when we pulled it out of the ground or later, I didn't
know. Whether by accident or intent, I didn't know either. The feeling
that I would be part of the fire ball was compelling, but not certain. I
closed my eyes and was asleep.

When I awoke, it was a little after four. There was no time to waste.
Staggering across the hall I rousted Harry out then went to the kitchen to
start a pot of coffee. Back in the bedroom I went into the bathroom and
flipped on the light. Normally, I blade shaved, but this morning, not
trusting myself I used the electric. Then I put on clean clothes and met
Camilla and Harry in the kitchen. Sipping the hot coffee I called Witherton telling him to hit the deck and meet us at Lochness Park by five. I
told him Harry thought of something they might have missed the day
before and we needed his instrument to check it out. He complained
about it was awfully early and I replied that we wanted to be there before
the dog people arrived. I suspected he'd be there with a dozen state
troopers.

At ten minutes to five Harry and I left in Harry's car, after all, it was a
rental. It was only a twenty minute drive to the park and half way there I
punched in the number for Clements. He answered on the second ring
and I told him we were headed out to Lochness Park where we had some
expectation of finding the bomb. I knew he would not refrain from in-
forming his bosses the second he had the information. Having been
called off the case by the National Security Advisor wouldn't stop them
from showing up.

Not to leave any of the players out I fished out the card from the member of Blaine's finest who has visited us and punched in his number. When he finally answered, I told him it was going down at the park.

When we arrived there was a state trooper car stopped partially blocking the entrance to the park. I lowered my window and so did the occupant of the trooper car. It was Witherton.

"Going to be a nice sunny day," I said. "Are there any other troopers here?"

He nodded. "There're two others in the park."

"If you want to come with us, have one of them come out here and keep other traffic out."

He made a call with the radio in his car and a minute later another trooper car rolled up the tree lined lane from inside the park. I got out and walked to the car. The trooper of about sixty looked tired as if he had been called two minutes after I had spoken to Witherton. Clearly, they were not calling in just any troopers but old timers who were connected to the top echelon of the state police. This meant he had previously been briefed on the situation. I told him a man by the name of Dutch Tuley would be arriving with a backhoe in tow shortly and that he should let him come in but keep dog walkers out. I also said the president's National Security Advisor would show up after that and that he'd come in whether or not the trooper tried to stop him. He understood. I also thought to mention that Bren Nugent should be let in too, though he'd likely be with Goldman.

At the north edge of the parking area in the park was a berm of dirt to keep vehicles in the parking lot rather than driving into the foot of the landfill mound. In the not too distant past there had been a parking lot there, too. We drove around the berm and down the paved trail to the foot of the mound. Without a word we got out. Witherton had the instrument in the car with him so he didn't have to open his trunk. We walked up the road that led to the top of the landfill.

Each of us had his own thoughts. Harry and I were worried we'd find it, and Witherton likely was worried we wouldn't. Even though the birds were overjoyed by the prospect of the beautiful new day with calls of all kinds filling the air, I was filled with foreboding. This was a cursed business if ever there were one. Harry had recalled little of the mission, and any other part of our missions in that far away land so long ago. For me it only got worse as the days, and more notably the nights, passed. It was here and we'd find it. Even though the case had been built to mil spec, it had been buried a long time and there was no telling what deterioration had set in. Then, there was the ominous message from General Diggens. What else could there possibly be to worry about? One only had to assume that given fertile and devious minds, it could be any number of things—all bad.

Half way up we bore off to the east. We were walking in waist high grass and weeds now and they were saturated with dew that a heavy rain could not equal. It was summer and the day would be hot, but still the wet was cold on our legs and feet in the dawn.

"Hey," Witherton said, "yesterday you said this part wasn't even here when you buried the bomb."

Harry answered. "Yeah, I got thinking since things had changed quite a bit since we unloaded it, that it made sense to check out this area after all."

"But . . . but . . ." he stammered, "from the way you said it in your call this morning, it sounded like you knew where it was. I've alerted a lot of people and I'll look like a fool if this doesn't pan out."

"You worry too much," I replied.

Harry was a step in front of us and since I stayed with him, so did Witherton. "What does the meter say now?"

"Well . . . it's moving a little like it did a few times yesterday on the other part of the hill. No, wait. It's moving a lot all at once. Wow! It's really moving. I have to change the scale since the most sensitive one has the meter on the peg. Wow, gain! This must be it!"

I looked at Harry. Turning all around he said, "Yeah, I think this is about it."

"Keep walking," I said to Witherton.

He did. "Now, the reading is falling off. Sure. Where Harry's standing, that seems to be the strongest reading."

We heard the down shifting of the automatic transmission of a larger vehicle and I assumed it must be Dutch as he started up the partially paved road. Soon the top of the backhoe came into view and then the cab of the pickup. I waved and the vehicle changed course and headed our way.

I had Witherton pacing off in several directions to locate the point of the strongest reading. Finally, he looked up from the instrument and announced, "This is the spot to dig."

Dutch pulled to a stop not three feet from me. He had his window down and his forearm resting on it. "We just found it," I said. "So, the sooner you can get in action, the sooner we get that nasty thing out of here."

"Say it ain't so. And even if it is, I mean, this here's a park. How can I go digging holes without a permit or something."

Witherton came over and looked at Dutch. "On behalf of the whole Minnesota State Police Department, I give you permission. And as this guy said, it's well that we get started because this is the big time. There will be a cloud of news helicopters overhead before long and all that goes with it." He walked ten paces away and said, "This is the point of the strongest x-ray signal so here's where to start."

Dutch drove a distance away, stopped and alighted from the cab. I walked over and said, "Better lock the cab in case this place becomes overrun with newsies." He did. After unlatching the chain hold downs from the backhoe, he crawled into the operator's seat of the machine. It started with a cough and ran smoothly. After letting it warm up he drove off the trailer and to the place Witherton was standing and started to work. I took a long handled shovel from the bed of Dutch's pickup.

To the east the sun was up but still shielded by a row of trees. A dot in the sky soon turned into the image of a helicopter. It was starting. All the time Witherton was on his cell phone giving a blow by blow account of everything that happened including the arrival of the first news helicopter.

We stood by and waited as Dutch worked. The engine throttled up as he dug each bucket of earth and then backed off as it was dumped. In twenty minutes he had a decent hole eight to ten feet deep. With a slope on the far side from the machine so someone could walk down into the hole. I held up my hand motioning him to stop.

"Time to see what it reads in the hole," I said to Witherton. "Better give it to me so you don't get too dirty. You'll be in front of some cameras before long."

His expression was a study. He hated to relinquish his hold on the all important instrument, yet from years of discipline, did not want to appear to anyone, least of all the news cameras, in anything but a perfect uniform. He handed it to me.

I descended into the hole with the instrument and the shovel. At the bottom of the hole the pungent smell of old garbage greeted me. I turned a full three-sixty and found the strongest x-rays coming from the east. Setting the meter down, I jabbed at the dirt with the shovel and heard a dull scrape of steel on aluminum. In a minute I had the side of the case partially exposed. I looked at Dutch, he nodded. After I was out of the hole he began again. It was necessary for him to start at the surface and dig down on top of it, but it went fast. As Dutch worked I returned to his pickup and found what I wanted, a length of chain with a grab hook on one end and slip hook on the other. Finally after a few shallow probing scoops with the bucket, Dutch motioned me into the hole again.

Witherton had taken possession of his now unneeded piece of equipment, but was glad to have it back. After all, win or lose, he was responsible for it.

In the hole again, I dug six inches of earth away and uncovered part of the case. It was lying so the main lifting handle was on the side. More digging for me. Finally, I managed to engage the slip hook in the eye and motioned Dutch to bring the bucket over the case. I looped the chain over a tooth of the bucket and engaged the grab hook. He pulled the chain tight and I held up my hand for him to stop while I scampered out of the hole. Slowly he began lifting the bucket gradually moving it to the west to tip the case out of the earth. He had to move it fore and aft a few times to get it free of the soil. I could imagine him thinking he could be vaporized any second. The dirt was piled to the northeast of the hole and he set the case down on the west side.

Witherton stepped to it with the meter. He snapped the scale knob a couple of notches in the less sensitive direction. Suddenly, realizing he was in an x-ray field, he stepped back not realizing the extreme sensitivity of the instrument he held. Even right next to the case the exposure was only on the order of a tooth x-ray at the dentist's office.

Harry was beside me. "That's it. Seeing it really brings things back. There's no question we handled a case that looked exactly like that one." He looked at it carefully scratching off clods of dirt with his fingers. "Yeah, that dent is where it hit a rock while rolling down the hill. It hit hard and we looked at each other wondering if we had broken something. No question, this is it."

Nodding I agreed with him as I punched in the number for Nugent. He answered on the second ring. "Where are you?" I asked.

"Still at the airport, but there is a Lear Jet that just landed and is taxiing my way. I assume that's him."

Before he could say anything else I said, "We've got it out of the hole and setting here in front of us so get here as fast as you can, and call your father-in-law. If there are any other tricks in this thing, we have to know about them . . . now!"

"Will do," and the call ended.

Turning to Witherton, I said, "Tell the guys at the entrance to the park that not only will there be the National Security Advisor arriving in about fifteen minutes, but also to be sure they let in a man by the name of Robert Diggens, general, retired. In fact, they are to give him an escort up here."

He looked at me questioningly.

"Just, do it!"

There were four helicopters in the sky and a couple of news vans sporting dishes on the roofs pulling up the grade into the landfill. The Blaine police were in evidence helping with traffic. It had started in earnest. A state patrol car pulled up and Witherton said, "That's the head of the state police, be nice."

"As long as he behaves himself."

"Is that it?" he snapped as he approached.

Witherton went ramrod straight and replied, "Yes, sir!"

"Okay, you know the drill. The Blackhawk will be here in a few minutes and we're off with it. It'll take the DOE boys some time to arrive, but they'll be vectored to Ripley where we'll arrange a change of custody. I've had the governor lock down all the National Guard's heavy stuff so the Feds can't get a hold of any of it."

Oh, boy, I thought, this didn't look like it was going at all according to Goldman's plans. I knew about Ripley, that is Camp Ripley, a few miles north of Little Falls in central Minnesota. It was the only military base in the state worthy of the name, and significantly, it was a National Guard base so under the control of the governor.

I decided to call Nugent and see how he was doing. He answered on the firs ring. "Yeah."

"I's me. Where are you?"

"Turning off 35W on to Lexington. Be there in five."

"The state guys are ready to grab it and zip it off to Camp Ripley."

"Means of transport?"

"Blackhawk." There were a few terse comments in the background.

"How long before the chopper arrives, can you hear it yet?"

"How should I know, the sky's full of news 'copters." More hurried comments.

"Can you put it back in the hole. Say there is a danger of x-ray exposure and it's not safe."

"Come on! The state dicks have been preparing for this for weeks. They've researched that and know it would be a bogus ruse."

"Well, we're here." There were shouted commands followed by the revving of an engine, followed by even louder curses. There were no sounds of shooting, which I took for good. In a face to face standoff with the Feds, the state authorities had no rights and they knew it.

The whapping of the blades of a heavier helicopter overcame the incessant buzzing of the news helicopters. After all, the networks needed only enough machinery to carry a camera and maybe a cameraman, even though with things becoming more automated all the time, the cameraman was frequently left behind.

— 40 —

A Blackhawk swept over the trees from the south, flared immediately to a hover, and maneuvered to the north of the hole. I glanced at Dutch and caught his eye. He only shook his head and pointed to the road that led up to the plateau where we were. Two black Suburbans hove into view bouncing over the uneven terrain. The lead vehicle skidded on the wet vegitation as it attempted to stop traveling ten yards farther than intended narrowly missing Dutch's backhoe. The driver slammed it into reverse and spun the wheels into a hole in the soft earth. The rear door jarred open a crack but was stopped by a tangle of weeds. The driver began rocking the car forward and back and at last extracted himself. The door swung full open with a loud creak as it caught on the vegitation when the big vehicle backed. The Blackhawk was down and four soldiers jumped out and headed to the growing congregation of people.

The Suburban stopped twenty feet away and a small man jumped out. "Seth Goldman! The president's National Security Advisor. I am here as his personal representative to take possession of that case," he said pointing at the object of everyone's attention.

The chief of the state police stood his ground. I noticed Cutter and Divner getting out of the second Suburban. They were carrying automatic rifles out in the open. I wasn't sure how well either of them would do in a shoot out with the injuries they had sustained in the recent past. But, they appeared to be game. A half dozen more state trooper cars were now on the scene stopped on the trail on the west edge of the plateau. Some of the men were opening trunks and arming themselves with heavier weapons.

After the near miss by the big SUV, Dutch began slowly maneuvering his machine away from the hole and drove it up onto the trailer. He wouldn't likely be able to get out of here in the near term, but was clearly determined to be ready to go as soon as he could.

"The procedure in a case like this is clearly defined," the chief of the state police said firmly. "It was recovered in my jurisdiction and I will transport it to a safe place until Department of Energy personnel arrive. After proper identification and proof of their qualifications, it will be duly signed over to them for removal by the best means for proper disposal. I don't know who you are, and with what authority you are acting other than what you say. Badges and other identification can be forged. In fact, forged documents constitute one of the largest problems we in law enforcement face."

There! That ended the conversation. Maybe. A Jeep type of vehicle came roaring down from the upper part of the landfill mound. It too skidded to a stop, only without over shooting more than a few feet. The man who got out was Diggens. Troopers converged on him having been caught off guard that someone would make it up the steep black slope of the mound.

"Let him come!" I yelled. "He's the man who made this thing."

That got everyone's attention. We walked towards one another. "What's the last secret?" I asked just loud enough to be heard above the still running Blackhawk engines.

Brushing past me, he walked to the case pulling a slip of paper from his hip pocket. Using his sleeve, he wiped the name plate clear and studied the plate and the slip of paper. "What's the x-ray count? Who's got a meter?"

Witherton shouted, "I have."

"Bring it here!" He snatched it away from Witherton and examined it as he nodded his head. It seemed he recognized the model of the meter because it probably dated from the time that the bomb had been built. Using the meter he held it over the case, and then backed away, then advanced to the case again. He looked at me. In a subdued voice, he said, "That's the live one, alright. There can be no mistake."

Finally Goldman had had enough. "Who is this man. Get him out of here." Cutter and Divner had moved up behind Goldman, and state troopers had moved up behind them. All the pieces were in place for things to turn ugly. Several news teams were being held back by Blaine police and a few troopers to the top of the rise to the north. They had parabolic dishes pointed at the group so they could hear what was being said. I assumed that with modern software they could pick it out from the sound of the Blackhawk engines.

Diggens turned to face those near him motioning them to congregate around him. In a lowered voice he said, "Those parabolic listening dishes on top of the rise must be silenced. What I have to say cannot go out on the news, at least not yet. What I am about to say is vital, life and death vital, for a million people. Tell them it's national security, whatever. Do it."

The state police chief turned to one of his lieutenants at his elbow. "See to it Hank."

In a minute there was a commotion at the top of the rise, but the dishes disappeared. Now, there were the state police chief, three of his troopers including Witherton, Goldman with Cutter and Divner, and Harry, Nugent and me clustered around Diggens. Other troopers, Goldman's driver and Blaine police stood a little further back.

Diggens began, "I was in on the design of this device. It is a nuclear bomb with a destructive capacity roughly equal to the one dropped on Hiroshima at the end of World War II. It has several, shall we say, anti-theft devices built into it."

He took a step to the case. "The cap screwed on to this electrical connector is a booby trap," he said pointing to it. "There is a spring loaded plunger under the cap so if the cap is unscrewed it will pop off when the last thread is reached. That will start a mechanical timer running that will detonate the bomb with full force in twenty minutes. Luckily, it is still in place. We can control that booby trap simply by not removing the cap. But, that's not the biggest problem."

He had their attention. "Now hear me well because this is no joke. There is another booby trap that we cannot control. When this device was deployed it was buried in the ground and that last trap was activated. There is no way it can be deactivated. It operates like this. Are you listening." They were listening, I was listening.

"When the case is at fifty degrees which is the temperature of the earth, the device is safe. As soon as it reaches a temperature of sixty degrees a timer starts—a twenty *day* timer. Since this is an atomic land mine, there was always a possibility that the enemy would discover it. This timer was intended as a means of being sure the bomb was not captured and reverse engineered by the enemy."

I glanced at Goldman. The wheels in his head turning. Assuming half the time on the timer had been expended, ten days would be plenty of time to position the bomb and have someone remove the connector cap and produce the event I was sure he intended.

Diggens continued, "There is no way of knowing how much of the twenty day interval has been used. These are all mechanical timers that require no batteries so we must assume they still function. The problem we must face is that it was buried in Vietnam for a couple of years with less than a foot of dirt on top of it. It is likely that on some hot days with the sun beating on the ground above it, the temperature rose to sixty degrees thereby running the timer for some hours. The sun is up, now, and the device is rapidly assuming the temperature of the air. That is easily warm enough to start the timer. How much time is left before it detonates nobody knows. The squabbling about who has possession of it must stop!"

All of us in the group around the bomb were torn. We wanted to run like we were being chased by mad dogs, but that meant those with nerve enough to stay would be the winners, or the losers if the timer reached the end. Harry was standing beside me. I pulled at his sleeve and we backed off a few paces. In a whisper I said, "I know what has to be done, but don't know how to initiate the process. No time to explain. It'll be clear, just go with me."

Harry gave me a quizzical look and saw that I was serious so he nodded. We had done this many times, and I was pretty good at revising the mission plan on the fly if the original plan came apart. Harry was good too and would see what had to be done.

About to add something, he was interrupted as Goldman shouted. "Then, it's settled. I take it."

"No you don't," retorted the state police chief. In case you haven't noticed, you're out gunned five to one. I take it."

The sound of a two bladed helicopter made it's presence felt. Even though it could not be seen it could definitely be heard. A second later a Cobra gun ship appeared over the trees to the east. Goldman put his phone, probably government issued, encrypted, to his ear. "Show 'em who's in charge."

The gun ship circled once and coming from the south fired a burst from the chin mounted chain gun. It tore up the foot of the hill leading to the higher ground where the media people were. It had been a lifetime since I had seen that and it still left me awed. Everyone but Harry and me hit the ground. As the Cobra pulled out and orbited again to make another pass I fell beside the police chief. I whispered into his ear, "He clearly has you out gunned. So, you're both wrong, I take it. But I need you to back me up. It's obvious Goldman is out of control. Ricochets from that chain gun have probably killed people. That means he doesn't care about the repercussions from what he just did because the president is about to assume dictatorial control." That's all there was time for.

This time the gun ship came in low slapping dirt on everyone with the rotor down wash. Then, he was gone taking station higher up. The news helicopters seemed to suddenly have found other stories to cover because the Cobra had the sky to itself.

Something had to be done, and done now. While everyone else still on the ground, I stepped quickly to the aluminum case and started unscrewing the connector cap. Why was it always me? I hoped the spring was not so strong that I couldn't hold it. I was pressing the cap down as I turned it. Finally I felt the pressure on my fingers—the last thread had been passed. The spring was manageable. Holding the cap down I swiveled around and sat on it using my right cheek to hold it in place.

Harry was in horror again but in a heartbeat pulled into action. "Listen up!" he yelled.

I looked at him and with my hand out, palm down, motioned him to keep his voice down.

In a tone that all could hear he continued, "That man and I are working together. He has unscrewed the cap to initiate the twenty minute timer. He is sitting on it to keep it in place so the timer hasn't started yet. You touch him, the cap snaps off and this hill becomes a mushroom cloud. Stand back!" Harry was a quick study.

They did. "Now," I said, "there is a Learjet at the Anoka airport in the form of a C-21, the military version, all fueled up and ready to go, is that right, Mr. Goldman?"

He nodded.

"All of you will combine your resources to transport the case with me on it to the back of that black SUV. It will transport it and me to the airport and the waiting jet. Then you will load it and me on to the plane. We are leaving town. Anyone so much as touches me and I will roll off starting the timer. Is that clear?"

"Wait a minute," the state police chief said. "There isn't enough head room to get it into the Suburban with you on it. The Blackhawk is a better bet."

"Nice try," I said. "No. We'll make do with the Suburban. My friend can drive that one, whereas he can't drive the Blackhawk."

From ten feet away Harry said, "I'd sure like to give it a try, though."

"Shut up, Harry."

"Won't work," Goldman said. "The door of the plane is too small."

"Wrong again. You came to town with the intent of transporting this case away with you. You certainly saw to it that you had the part cargo, part passenger version of the C21. And, that version has a plenty large door." I paused for a few seconds. "No more games. Let's get on with it, and back off the guns."

The chief of police motioned to the four soldiers from the Blackhawk. Harry went to the lead Suburban and motioned the driver out. He probably let the man know he was serious by letting him see his gun. Even if armed, the driver would not have been prepared with his gun drawn, and he would not survive a bullet coming though the door.

While Harry was positioning the SUV, I motioned to the police chief to come to me. Pulling his ear next to my mouth I said, "I need you to see to it that Goldman and his men, not including a Mr. Nugent, who is with us, are all incarcerated for at least six hours. I need that much time. No phone calls, nothing." Then I remembered. "Strip them to their boxers because they have communication devices in their belts, shoes, watches, etc. If you can't do it, have the Blaine police do it. Got it?"

He nodded.

Harry backed the Suburban to within a few feet of me. When he alighted from the cab, I saw him pocket the keys. Nice going. He supervised the state guys. Goldman and his men stepped back. Soon there was some arguing and I lost track of it except to hear the distressed, demanding voice of Goldman.

They had to detach and remove the rear seats that were left on the ground. The four men from the Blackhawk were all well muscled but still it was a heavy lift for them. I could only wonder what the newsies were thinking. Here was a man sitting on a case of some kind and he was being lifted into the vehicle along with it. It must have looked like a tribal chieftain being carried in a Sudan chair. I glanced that way and there he was again, the Asian man, who by now I knew had to be Vietnamese. Our eyes met with a flash of recognition. Then it was gone and I had to divert my attention to not falling off the case.

It was cramped and I had to bend my head and shoulders over to the point of some pain, but I fit with it under me. Harry eased the rear doors closed and took his place in the driver's seat. The chief of the state police took the passenger seat which was good.

I spoke to him. "Chief, be sure we have an escort to the airport. We don't want an accident."

"Already handled."

"You're a good operations man." As the SUV started to move I continued. "There are a couple of other things. We'll need your four strong armed guardsmen at the airport, too."

"Already seen to."

"Have the two pilots from the Blackhawk come with them."

He turned his head to me for the first time. "And, why do you want them?"

"Fair question. I have to assume the pilots of the Learjet are in league with Goldman so you'll have to find out which one of your pilots has experience flying fixed wing planes. I intend to throw one of the pilots off the plane and have your man take his place. It works both ways. If I had gotten on the Blackhawk you would have flown to Camp Ripley daring me to detonate the bomb, right?"

The chief was facing the front as he keyed his radio ordering the Blackhawk pilots to hop over to the airport.

"What if neither of them has fixed wing experience?"

"You'll have to decide which one has the most overall experience. I need someone who knows flying to watch the compass and such things to be sure we're headed in a southwesterly direction. I intend to deliver the bomb to the Nevada Nuclear Test Range. Goldman indicated the C21 had been refueled, so it will have plenty of range. Don't worry, we'll do everything we can to make it look like you were in charge and doing the only thing possible under the circumstances."

— 41 —

The drive to the Anoka airport seemed to take an eternity. I was sweating even though Harry had the air conditioner running full blast. My windbreaker didn't help, but it was needed to hide the gun behind my belt in the front. The pistol was gouging into my waist from my being bent over, but the jacket hung loose making sure there was no revealing bulge. The blinking lights and sirens of the trooper cars before and behind were mesmerizing. They had all the streets blocked so we drove through regardless of the lights. They weren't even using the emergency vehicle trick of changing the lights to favor them as if it were too risky, which it probably was.

At the airport, trooper cars swarmed around the jet. It seemed like the pilots were going to refuse to open the door. A loud speaker from one of the cars ordered them to open up or they would be arrested. It took a few minutes but finally they must have assumed they were not going to be allowed to take off. And, with Goldman notable by his absence, it was obvious something had gone wrong so there was no reason they should rot in a jail cell.

The door opened at the rear of the plane and as soon as the steps were down, two troopers rushed into the plane. Both pilots were ushered out in front of the troopers. While that was going on I spoke to the chief. "The plan is to find the best runway in the test range and land. Two guardsmen, one of the jet pilots, one of your pilots, Harry and I will be going along. After landing, and unloading me and the bomb, the plane will take off with everybody else."

"What about you?"

"Part of the job that I certainly didn't want, but landed on me. I'll try to wedge my hand under my butt and screw the cap back on. Failing that, I'll run. I figure I can run two miles in twenty minutes. Got a better plan? Maybe we should trade places."

Harry smiled, the chief didn't.

I added, "I had a premonition last night that the bomb will detonate, but I'm not sure when."

I didn't know if he believed in my premonition, but the crew was ready to transfer me to the plane so there was no more convincing I could do. Harry had the vehicle stopped near the plane and they opened the rear doors of the SUV. Someone had scrounged up a forklift which would help immensely as long as it didn't malfunction. They slid me out onto the forks. The operator had probably been told the case contained conventional explosives, all the same, as close as he was, he was sweating and concentrating like his life depended on it. The Suburban was driven away and the forklift turned, the forks lifted to the level of the floor of the plane at the cargo loading door and they slid me in. Easy. Unloading would the fun part.

The cargo door was at the front of the passenger compartment, hinged at the top, with no stairs so that was where I stayed. I motioned to Harry to come in first. Opening the door to the cockpit I had him swing it back and then nudge the case in front of the door's edge so it was wedged open. I intended to be able to see and hear everything that went on in the cockpit.

Outside the chief circulated among the troopers having a short conference with small clusters of three or four. I couldn't hear what was said, but from time to time there were rapid gestures and brief glances at the plane. While this was going on Harry foraged around in the back of the plane and soon came forward with some nylon chord, a six pack of bottled water and a half dozen power bars. He handed me two of the bars which I put in my shirt pocket and I took one of the bottles. He lashed down the case to lugs in the floor.

Harry had no sooner finished his task when the chief of the state troopers stuck his head into the cargo loading door and motioned Harry over to him. Harry crouched at the door and the chief made as if to whisper something into his ear. But, instead he grabbed his wrist and pulled him off the plane. Immediately three troopers bounded up the steps and just as fast closed both doors.

As two of the troopers nudged past me on the way to the cockpit I said, "How are a couple of road cops going to fly a jet."

The second one coming past me said, "Don't sweat it. We both have fixed wing time, and I have jet time. We'll manage for such a short hop."

So that was it. They planned to fly to Camp Ripley after all. Obviously, none of them thought for a minute that the two timers in the bomb were real, or if they were that they would still function after all this time. General Diggens had said they were purely mechanical devices and would not degrade with age. Yet, I was still sitting on the case. Why had they not simply yanked me off the case and thrown me out of the plane like they had done with Harry? I smiled to myself. They were not entirely sure and were hedging their bets. As soon as the plane landed they would clear the area the best they could and then the last trooper would pull me off the case and drive like crazy, with or without me. If the twenty minute timer fizzled, as they expected it would, they would be back assuming they had twenty days to do their publicity stunt and then transport it to Nevada. I always hated to have to figure out what others were thinking because it was such a risky business. This time, though, it seemed to be the only explanation after the comment of the short hop.

The third trooper sat down in the front passenger seat which was about half way back because of the cargo space and belted in without giving me a glance. They were awfully confident of themselves. The engines spooled up, and through the windows I could see trooper cars moving so as to unblock the path of the plane. We taxied to the north end of the north-south runway. Being summer and clear, the light winds were from the south. At the north end of the runway, the pilot turned his head and said, "Hang on!" like he meant it. I was the only one not wearing a seat belt, and the only passenger he cared about.

We accelerated down the runway, rotated and were airborne. As I had suspected we started coming around to the north. I always hated it when I was right in such an obvious prediction. Couldn't they have flown south across the city and then slowly, sneakily made a wide sweep around to the north? Of course it made total sense, their thinking I was helpless. Pulling my gun from behind my belt I pointed it at the trooper in the seat to my left. He saw the movement too late. I motioned to him with my left hand to produce something and he knew what I meant. Cautiously, he pulled his gun from his holster and I pointed to the floor behind the case. He casually flipped it in that direction. Now I motioned for him to lay on his stomach facing the rear of the plane. I think he could see the safety on my gun was off and my finger was on the trigger. He was very cautious.

That done, I said in a loud voice, "In the cockpit, change course and make for Nevada. I have a gun and the trooper back here subdued. I will kill all three of you if that is necessary and fly this plane myself even though that may make it a short flight." The pilot in the left seat swiveled his head around and saw the muzzle of a 9mm aimed at his face. "Do it now!"

Maybe it was the shear daring I exhibited in taking control of the situation at the excavation site that made them believers, but the plane slowly started to come around.

"Now," I said, "you on the right, very slowly pull out your weapon and hand it to me butt first." This done I repeated the task with the pilot and had both guns laying between my feet.

The pilot swiveled his head around again and said, "You're one crazy loon with a handful of missing screws."

I shook my head and said, "If you only knew just how many. I was one of the guys that buried this thing in the park were we found it this morning. We did that to keep it from the North Vietnamese at the time. And, that's only part of the story. The Vietnamese still want it so bad they can taste it. Their point man was there among all the people in the park and nobody even noticed him. You might wish you had a chain gun on this plane before the day's out."

The copilot craned his neck around to look at me. "What nonsense are you babbling about?"

"I'm saying this is way above your pay grade. In fact, it's above the pay grade of the chief of the Minnesota State Police. We thought everybody would act at least a little rationally, but it appears the egos are too big for that. That's enough story telling. What I want out of you . . . ."

I heard the scrape of a shoe to my left and snapped my head around. The trooper had his feet under him, turning and moving fast. I wouldn't have thought I still had it in me, but apparently I did. In a flash I whipped the gun around and fired twice. One bullet caught him in the right shoulder and the second in the right knee shattering the bone. He went down with a thud. The gun was instantly back on the cockpit.

"One more stupid move like that and we all become vaporized, got it? That man will have to bleed until we get where we're going. There's nothing else to do. Now, let me continue what I was saying before I was interrupted, What I want out of you two is to fly to Nevada. Find the atomic test range. It's northwest of Las Vegas a hundred miles or so if memory serves. I want to see bomb craters out of the window, is that clear? No craters and we keep flying until we run out of fuel. After we find the craters, we put down at the nearest available air strip, road, whatever. There must be someplace to land in the area. By the way, anybody use a radio and he loses his brains all over the windshield. Any questions? Now I'm really ticked off."

At a cruising speed of 520 miles per hour it would take us between two and three hours to get there. The plane gave a slight dip due to air turbulence, and it occurred to me, weather permitting we'd get there. The only thing I had going for me was it was a suicide flight if anything other than a nice smooth landing happened at the end. How crazy were the two men in the cockpit to follow their superior's orders, I had no idea, but it worried me. Even though Harry had managed to get the case tied down, I wasn't. All it took was a wild maneuver and I'd fall off the case and before I recovered they could be on me. Staying totally focused for three hours would be nearly impossible. It was even possible these guys were working for Goldman. He planned to blow up something, so in the worst case the bomb could be pushed out the door and detonated on whatever was handy. If I remembered right, we'd be flying close to Denver. That would be a perfect spoil sport maneuver.

I watched the angle of the sun and the instruments in front of the pilot. We seemed to be going in about the right direction. The two doing the driving seemed to have decided I was too crazy to deal with while in the air. The one in the back kept groaning which was getting on my nerves. That I could handle but what I couldn't was the fact that his left arm was stretched out toward where he had tossed his gun. I knew if that stupid fool made a move for it I'd have to kill him. It wouldn't be the first time I had with malice of forethought killed . . . . Where did that come from?

I switched my attention to the cockpit. The pilot on the left was looking at me with pure hatred. "What's your problem?" I snapped. "What makes you want to blow yourselves into a bunch of ions? Why can't you believe this is a real bomb, or at least err on the side of safety in case it is? The fact that you didn't throw me off the plane like you did the other guy tells me you aren't sure."

He stared at me for a full minute before answering. "Maybe I've had second thoughts. Maybe you are bona fide crazy and get a thrill out of killing people. You've killed before." He caught the momentary wince in my eyes. "Yeah, I'm right. So, you plan to kill all of us no matter what happens!"

A flash from the past occurred as he was talking. It wasn't a narrative like the past recollections I had had, but more of an awareness. Yes, I had killed, and it wasn't always or even most of the time the enemy. Our Phantom Team was the special one, the one sent to take out, kill or maim, mostly maim, inept American field commanders. What I had done to the trooper was a rehearsed movement. A commander who couldn't walk or write had to be replaced. Then the time came when we had done too many friendly commanders and were becoming a threat.

The purpose of the mission where we ate the snake was to have us not come back. It was so poorly planned and the objective so indistinct that we would spend an inordinate amount of time in enemy territory. I now recalled how we discussed the ridiculousness of it before, during and after the mission. They intended for us to be discovered and killed, or tortured to death. It was a one way mission. That explained the consternation that met us when we finally showed up.

Things happened fast. I had not noticed that the groaning had stopped, nor that I had lost concentration and was looking with glazed eyes at the bulkhead. The pilot had unlatched his seat belt and lowly come to a half turned position where he clapped his hands together in a sharp snap so I'd instinctively look at him. The sharp sound brought me out of my stupor, but I had other built in instincts. Subconsciously, I knew that my greatest threat was a hand near a weapon on the floor to my left. As my head turned I saw movement and hardly realizing my arm and hand were moving as my gun came around and the bullet went though his head. His hand with the gun in it fell limply on the floor as the weapon tumbled free. The pilot was half out of his seat as my arm immediately came back around and the muzzle went right into his partially open mouth. I could feel it scrape on his teeth and the resistance of the muzzle digging into the back of his mouth as his momentum carried him a few inches more in my direction.

I slowly shook my head. "Why are you guys so eager to die? Whatever they've promised you, it isn't worth it. The indoctrination must be intense for you to be willing to throw away your lives so easily."

It came back to me that Harry and I had discussed that very thing a couple of weeks ago. The difference was that was a long time ago, we were part of a war and we were too young to know better.

"Fly the plane," in continued. "Live to tell about it. You've had a little training, but when we had ours we were in a for real hot shooting war." I felt a swell of anger inside me as the words tumbled out. "We knew we'd be eyeball to eyeball with the best trained advisories the enemy could throw at us and we'd die unless we were better than they were. We trained like our lives depended on it, because they did. How many of your class died in training? Huh? I can answer that, none! It happened all the time for us. We were good or we were dead!"

Our eyes were locked while I was yelling at him. He seemed unable to move. I gave a poke so the barrel of the gun tore the skin at the back of his mouth. With that he slowly slumped back into this seat spitting blood. I couldn't let it go. "I've killed men for no reason other than they had the audacity to think they might be better than I was. They died before they could draw a weapon. I put you in that category! Fool!" I was still yelling I was so mad. "Your nerve, your stupidity!"

It felt good. What can I say, it felt great, a catharsis had over come me. I had it all recalled, all those shadows from the dark nightmares were made light. I took no joy in what I had done back then, but now I could start to cope, to come back and have a real life—if I survived the next hours.

From their movements it was obvious my outburst cemented in their minds that they were dealing with a for-real crazy man. Okay, so I was crazy. I was also operationally the most competent of the three of us. That thought caused me to become more focused in the immediate future. No one except Harry and the state police chief knew exactly where we were going . . . . Oh nuts, the police chief, that meant everybody knew, at least anybody the chief chose to tell. But, it was possible he wouldn't tell anyone. If the word got out what we were carrying and where we were headed, the military would take charge and the chief would be out. No, he wouldn't tell. He put three of his people on the plane and expected they would over power me and bring his bomb back to him.

"You, in the left seat, the head driver," I said. "How close will we come to Denver on out present course?"

In a level professional tone he replied, "We'll pass over the outer suburbs."

"Then change course so we miss those suburbs by at least twenty miles. Do it now."

Time dragged and my butt was really sore where I sat on the cap holding the plunger down. It was not a strong pressure, but not being able to shift my position made the little discomfort become almost intolerable. The copilot had been unfolding and refolding charts for some minutes until he seemed to be studying one closely. "We don't have the best air charts of that area, but what I could find shows that the area where you want to go is restricted air space. It's all part of the Nellis Air

Force Range. I can't imagine nobody will notice us sashaying into their secret country club. And, the place we want is Yucca Flats. I know a guy who was stationed at Creech Air Force Base near the little town of Indian Springs. That base is thirty or forty miles to the south of the test range so they'll know about us."

"Well, get it landed before anyone figures out what's going on. Maybe go in low like you had engine trouble, radio trouble, pilot had a heart attack, be creative. Keep the radio on, but no transmissions unless we're challenged. When we're stopped, I dump it out and jump out after it."

"Why'd you do something like that?"

"Somebody has to move the case out of the line of travel of the port side wheel so you can take off again, stupid. I stay there."

That ended the conversation. We slowed to three hundred knots and descended to two thousand feet, that's above sea level and lower than the peaks on either side. In fact, we were weaving our way through the terrain. It was bare black rocks and unbelievably rugged. "Okay," the pilot said. "We're in restricted air space. We should be over Yucca Flats in minutes."

Coming out of a cut between two mountains we saw craters, hundreds of them. The area was as cratered as the moon. The copilot said, "Most of them are subsidences that occur over under ground tests."

"Enough!" said the irritated pilot. "There are no air strips here, not even a paved road."

"There are plenty of roads, we can all see that. Pick the one you like and put it down. We are going to land here. I will not allow this nuclear device over a populated area if I have to kill both of you, got it?"

The pilot had the flaps partially down, and made a wide circle, lined up with an east-west road, headed east and I heard the wheels come down. We were fifty feet up and, "Oh, no!" There was a missing part of the road visible at the low angle, that was not apparent from above. He surged the engines, and settled again. I grabbed an over head hand grip and held on the best I could, but that wasn't good enough. When the wheels hit the hard pack road, I was thrown off the case and into the bulk head beside the cockpit door. It didn't matter from the point of view of the twenty minute timer because the clock was running on everything now. On my knees beside the case I slid to the rear of it and held on to anything handy as the plane jolted and bounced down the road. As it stopped I grabbed my gun that had slipped my grasp, laid it on top of the case, and with my pocket knife slashed the nylon chords on the case.

Snatching my gun, I said, "Stay strapped in your seats gentlemen. I'll be out of here in a minute."

They didn't move other than turning their heads. I unlatched the door the reverse of the way they had latched it when they had boarded. With a shove it swung out and up by means of its air springs. The engines were still idling and the sound swept through the cabin along with a blast of hot air and dust.

"This is how it will be," I said. "The timer has already started but less than a minute ago. I'll push the case out and jump out myself. If I detect any movement in the cockpit I'll start shooting. Nothing changes except you don't have a chance to take off. But, you won't care because you'll be dead. Do you understand? Answer, both of you." They did.

I thrust my gun behind my belt in front, and slid the case to the door watching as it tumbled to the roadbed below. Immediately, I drew my gun again. I kicked out the three guns, the remaining bottles of water and what was left of the package of power bars.

"Okay," I said. When I'm out I'll roll the case away far enough to clear the wheel. Then I back away from the plane. You close the hatch and take off. If I see any suspicious movement while I'm in a position to see any, I start shooting. Got it? I'll have four guns."

The pilot relied, "Yeah we've got it but we might not get this thing up again. That road ahead doesn't look so good."

"There's no place to turn around and the timer's running so make the road good."

With that I jumped out and gave the case a couple of rolls into the shallow depression that served as a ditch alongside the road. Immediately I snatched up another gun and backed away, out of the jet blast but where I could see the hatch. It swung down and immediately the engines spooled up. The power increased until the wheels started to slide with locked brakes. With brakes released, I watched the plane accelerate, slowly, impossibly slowly it seemed. It must have felt to the pilots like they were being held back by a ten ton weight. The plane rocked and bumped as it gained speed. If he was any good he knew what to do. It was a standard short field take off to clear a low obstacle. Run with full flaps and red lined engines until flight speed was reached, and then pull the nose up just enough to get the wheels off the ground, level off until well above stall speed and then gain altitude.

I didn't wait to see if they made it as I ran back to the case and grabbed the plastic loops that had held the six-pack of water bottles to-gether, three loops still holding a bottle. In the same motion I scooped up the power bars, stuffed them in my pockets. I checked my watch. At least two, maybe three minutes were already gone. There were craters all around, and structures every way I looked, though all were at least a mile away, most more. The main thing was to put distance between me and the bomb so I started jogging to the west staying on the road. The sun was still high and I was heading into it making things indistinct. The plane had become airborne and disappeared. Well, that was the last of them. Now all I had to do is get as far away as possible and in some sort of cover by the time it detonated. If I could run at four miles an hour I'd cover a mile in fifteen minutes.

— 42 —

My throat was parched and I longed for a drop of water, but didn't dare take the time. I had been running for fifteen minutes when I came to a dry water bed passing under the road through a three foot culvert. That would have to do. Not sure I wanted to be in the culvert in case it caved in, I'd sit next to its outlet on the side opposite to where I had rolled the case. There was no way to tell how far I had come, and I did not intend to stick my head up. If it detonated full in my face the x-rays would fry my brain before the blast wave arrived. Panting as if my lungs would fly out of my mouth I pressed my body against the sandy bank. The time came, no bang. Five more minutes passed, no bang. I shifted to a kneeling position with the sun to my back and opened a bottle of water. It all went down in a single draught.

Now what? There were two possibilities. Either in the fall from the plane, to say nothing of the way those two guys tumbled it down the hill in Vietnam all those years ago, the timer had been damaged and would not set off the bomb. The other was that there had never been a timer. However, there was always the possibility it become stuck and only ran intermittently so it could go off at any time.

It was hot and since it didn't seem like there would be anyone looking for me, I'd have to get out of the sun, wait until evening, and then try to walk out. On the bank of the water course, I shielded my eyes with my hand and saw the structure to the southwest somewhat more clearly than I had while running on the road. I had come a respectable distance. It made sense to follow the dry water course now in case the bomb decided to go off after all. It would be slower going, but generally in the direction I intended.

Twenty-five minutes later I was walking around a concrete structure that might have been a bunker of sorts for bomb tests. I found a place to sit down in shade and also with a solid chunk of concrete between me and where I thought the bomb should be. I had to be more than two miles away by now. I ate one of the power bars and drank another half bottle of water. It seemed there should be planes flying around but not one could be seen or heard. It might be that they'd let the case sit exactly where it was for twenty days to see if the other timer worked. I had to believe word had gone ahead to let us dump it off with no interference or we would have been intercepted.

Watching the clear sky a speck of movement caught my eye. At first it appeared to be a hawk or vulture, but its course was too steady for that. Then I realized it had to be a plane though there was no sound. It passed over and the silhouette seemed a little out of whack until it registered. It was a Predator drone. Okay, that made sense. Some sort of alert had been sent ahead and with the jet on its way someone was checking to see if the bomb had been deposited as planned. A few minutes later I heard the thin whine of an engine. Peaking around the corner of the bunker the Predator was back, this time low, under a thousand feet and it passed directly over the case. They had terrific optics in those spy planes, but there was nothing like getting a close up look so detailed they could practically read the serial number.

The specter of what must be happening is certain halls of power amused me. People were digging through old records, checking design specs, comparing the images taken by the Predator against the files, finding old engineers long in retirement—all in a scramble. Any decent commander would err on the side of safety and not let anyone approach the case until everything about it was known. That meant there was not likely going to be anyone coming to rescue me, which I supposed was all right. There was a chance I might be able to walk to the southwest until I reached Highway 95 and hitch a ride.

Hours passed more quickly than I had expected. I'd decided to rest out of the sun until close to sunset. Running away from the case in the heat of the day had taken a lot out of me. Then I heard the rumble of jet engines to the west. The sun was within a half-hour of setting and long shadows were stretching toward me, though I was still blinded from seeing the source of the sound. I was a half mile south of the east-west road where we had landed and now I could see the plane. It was the same one. Those nut cases! They had refueled in Las Vegas and waited until the sun was low, the better to give shadows to obstructions. The logic was if they could land and take off once with the sun high, they should be able to do it again now. They were going to collect the bomb after all.

As I thought of it, the two pilots were strong looking men. With extreme effort they could manage to heft it into the plane. Or, if they had brought a ten or twelve foot plank with them they could slide it up into the cargo hold a lot easier. They'd win after all. And if I did manage to get out of this moonscape, I'd be the villain with the killing of a state trooper as only the first of a thousand charges against me. Nobody ever said life was fair. On the Team we'd said that to one another many times as we were out in the bush, wet to the skin, hungry, bitten by bugs, and in mortal danger. So it was again. Nothing new there.

I gave them ten minutes to load it and stood up again. There was nothing I could see. Maybe it was too far and maybe the land rose slightly obscuring the road. Anyway, I soon heard the roar of jet engines again. That was really discouraging. I risked my life and that of my family, and guess what, they win and I go to prison. Dejected I slumped down against the concrete wall again. I had my eyes closed as I thought about how they would relate their harrowing ride "across the endless sky" like the line from the western song *Ghost Riders In The Sky* with a crazy man.

My sight went from the nearly black behind my closed eyelids to a bright red. Instinctively I opened my eyes and everything was brilliantly white. In seconds it returned to normal. My sight quickly readjusted and I knew what had happened. Waiting ten seconds I stood up and looked in the direction the plane had gone and saw the mushroom cloud ascending skyward. It had been a low air burst so it had not swept up a lot of earth, but the sight was still over powering. The light was such that I could see the spread of the shock wave as it swept to the left and right. Almost too late I saw the sand whipping as if came at me. Ducking my head, the whomp caved in my chest as the nuclear breaker lashed against my metaphorical shore. Sand pelted my face and dust swirled about me almost throwing me headlong to the ground. Heaving in a few heavy breaths my respiration returned to normal. Normally there is a return surge as the ascending hot air drew air up into the mushroom. At my distance, it was a brief wind far less than the shock wave.

I continued to watch the roiling hot air ascend. Either the twenty minute timer had gotten stuck and with the jostling of getting the case back on the plane it had started again, or the twenty day timer had run out. I couldn't help thinking that it was beyond happenstance that it had gone off at that precise moment. The hand of Providence was in this one way or another. It didn't matter right now, though. What breeze there was would make any fallout affect the area more or less away from me. Since the plane had taken off toward the east and I had decided to walk to the south or southwest, I had nothing to fear from the radioactive residue of the explosion.

Immediately I walked fifty yards to a north-south road and started jogging south. There was no question that with the bomb now detonated, there was no safety concern as long as the fallout zone was avoided. It was hard to keep from thinking about the plane and the two state troopers that had been ionized. Why in the name of God didn't they let it be and have someone who knew about those things dispose of it. At the very least it would have been the prudent thing to let the twenty days run out before coming near it. This was certainly a remote enough place that could have been cordoned off if that were even necessary. It didn't seem like there would be much reason for anyone to come into this area.

But, more to the point, what drove people like that? What happened to their common sense? In fact, now that I thought about it, they weren't that different from a lot of people I knew. Telling those guys to leave the bomb alone was like telling some kid not to use drugs. It never made sense when a person first thought about it. But, with some reflection, it was all too understandable. We live in a society where any absolute is hated, whether it involved truth or morality. Everybody had to be their own authority on things like that. Philosophers called it names like positivism, existentialism and others. In those theories, life and in fact nature had no meaningful completion but was only a process. When an individual made up his mind on something, that was truth for him. If he were ever put into a position where he had to admit he was wrong his mental world would crack in two which in too many cases led to making a corresponding end to his physical life by suicide.

In the case of the three troopers, they must have decided that total allegiance to their superior was a moral imperative, something far beyond a simple duty to follow lawful orders. It became a mystical, almost spiritual unity of purpose, more than simply the feeling that they were the good guys and the rest of society were law breakers. The added benefit that if they were stanch in their loyalty they could expect added rewards was there, but was not what drove them. They had the uniforms, the code, the frequent positive attitude meetings, and many other elements to cement their fidelity. Theirs was probably an extreme case of it, but it was pervasive. What kept society somewhat sane was that most people had too much to lose to let their rules get too far out of line with the main stream, not that the main stream in some cases was at all moral.

When a particular person's rules got him fired for using drugs on the job or something like that, there always seemed to be a friend, relative, or government program to help him out. He suffered, but was never left with nothing, he always survived. There was no final accounting for his moronic set of rules.

As I alternately jogged and walked, thoughts about killing a state trooper were ever present in spite of the fact that the detonation of the bomb had proven I was justified in doing what was necessary to get it away from population centers. As a personal practical matter I hoped that the pilots had said nothing about the third man during their refueling stop in Las Vegas, and that was likely. They would want to take the problem home and have Minnesotans whipped to a lather by such an atrocity, all the better to mask that they had stolen the bomb for personal aggrandizement. If they had revealed the dead man in Las Vegas, they would not have been back so quickly due to all the formalities associated with a shooting death, especially the death of a law officer. And they wanted to return to the test site to collect their booty as soon as possible. I had correctly guessed their motivations and actions before and felt more comfortable now that I had thought it out.

During my normal life I frequently jogged around the neighborhood, and that was when I did a lot of thinking so it was no surprise that all of these thoughts descended on me now. While I had been siting by the bunker I had been mostly in denial as I watched a few of the little desert critters go about their business.

Twenty minutes after had I hit the road, the beat of helicopter blades became noticeable. In a couple of minutes a light shape like a blond bumble bee could be seen coming from the southwest. It passed a half mile to the east and abruptly changed course and headed right for me. It was nice to be found, but not nice in that I expected I'd be arrested for the crime of setting off an atomic bomb out of season, and without a license. It flared ten yards from me and set down on the gravel road. It was a jet ranger or something like that, I wasn't very familiar with the types of helicopters. The pitch of the engine fell and an arm out of an open window motioned me over. Walking over I saw the face of the Asian man from the crowd at the park, now up close he was familiar from somewhere else.

"Vin Wessen?"

I nodded.

"We meet again after many years. Do you remember the last time?"

It was déjà vu, though not completely. That term means the feeling of an experience once had, but is really new. Here, I knew I had seen this man before, but was at a loss to know where it was. It hit me that he was a lot older, yes, he had said ". . . after many years."

He had fine features, and not an aggressive expression. My memories of men like him were from Vietnam, and he reminded me of hundreds of men of that general appearance. The main difference was his thoroughly American though accented speech. While in country, if any of them spoke English, it was barely understandable. I shook my head, "It's not coming to me."

"On a mountain side during the monsoon rain. How about that?"

It hit me and my expression betrayed me. He smiled broadly. I tensed, not from fear of him, but from fear of memories. I almost stammered as I said, "I wish you hadn't found me."

He was wearing a tropical sport shirt rather than a military jumpsuit. I had to give the bugger credit for persistence if nothing else. I yelled, "You're too late! Nobody gets it now. Poof, it's all gone."

He yelled, "The door's not locked, get in, and make it fast."

I walked up to his open window. "I'm not sure what you mean."

"Of course you don't, but there's no time to waste. I was never after the bomb. Now, get in!"

His words were like staples punched into my skull and all I could think of was flying was faster than walking so I grabbed the door latch, opened the door and piled in as I heard the engine picking up speed. The door was barely closed and we were airborne.

"What's going on?" I asked.

He whipped his head around and yelled, "A nuclear explosion, or did you miss it? Buckle in on the left and don't bother me!"

He pointed his craft to the southwest staying just above the sagebrush which immediately began to make the hair on the back of my neck start to crawl. Why that direction? My new "friend" of Vietnamese extraction glanced back at me and yelled. "Watch out to the left and tell me if you see anything else in the air, especially helicopters. Something will be coming from Creech Air Force Base any time. We must avoid them."

This was over the top. What the heck was going on? Who was this guy? Why avoid the Air Force? Nothing made any sense other than my being intimately involved with the first above ground nuclear detonation since 1962 was understandably upsetting certain people. Well, I suppose, that was sort of over the top, too.

We were approaching some rugged black mountains like the ones I had seen coming into the test site. He had the helicopter aimed at the lowest point between two peaks. Most of the time I kept to my assigned task of scanning the sky to the left. "There," I yelled, two helicopters, OH-6s I think."

"Watch their direction of travel. Don't take your eyes off them!"

The helicopter shuddered as we encountered turbulence. My line of sight to the OH-6s was cut off by a wall of black rock within spitting distance of my window. I yelled, "I can't see them anymore, but as long as I could they seemed to be headed north."

"Okay. Good. Hang on for a rough ride."

It was obvious he was a proficient pilot, but it seemed he was either trying to make me soil my underwear, or he had recently escaped from a mental institution having been incarcerated for bearing a death wish by any means possible. And, immolation in the twisted wreckage of a helicopter was his most cherished hallucination of accomplishing his goal.

As we sped along we were in shadow as twilight advanced making it difficult to determine our general direction of travel as he dodged between spires of rock, flew down arroyos and used the terrain in any way possible to mask his presence. Flying nap of the earth was hardly the word for it, he was flying below the earth level most of the time. As the twilight advanced, his flying seemed suicidal and I was about to bring this to his attention when he pulled up and started flying level, though only high enough to clear the highest ground.

It was after dark when he gently settled the craft on the ground somewhere in the vicinity of Las Vegas. We had approached it from the southwest at tree top level so I had only seen the sky glow from millions of lights, and we had not flown long enough to get to any other comparable urban area. He proficiently flipped a number of switches and the engine stopped. Unbuckling he told me to do the same. Out of the helicopter he said to follow him. We had set down on a general aviation airport, and he walked straight to a gate in a chain link fence and to a waiting sedan. He pressed the key fob switch and the locks popped up with no accompanying chirp. We got in, me on the passenger side and him driving.

He spoke for the first time other than curt instructions in the helicopter. "This may seem a bit nuts, but it is necessary. I want to get on the road east out of town as soon and as inconspicuously as possible so don't speak and distract me. There'll be time enough."

I had been correct, we were in the environs of Las Vegas. He drove with extreme caution never breaking the speed limit by one mile an hour, making sure to stop fully at every stop sign, and if there was any chance of not getting through an intersection on a yellow light he didn't chance it. I began to worry we'd be stopped by a suspicious cop as the only car obeying all the traffic laws. We weren't. At last, we were on Highway 93 headed to Henderson.

My insane pilot, careful driver, and friend/captor appeared to relax as the lights of the city receded behind us resulting in the appearance of a more loquacious demeanor. "My name is Fong Cha but you can call me Eddie."

"Of course," I replied lightly. "It makes as much sense as everything else that's been happening. How's it going, Eddie?"

"Pretty good, how about you?"

"Been better, been worse. How are the wife and kids?"

"No wife, no kids."

"I find that hard to believe, a good looking guy like you. I'd imagine those slanty eyed chicks would be falling all over . . . oops. I said the wrong thing, didn't I?"

Eddie gave a low chuckle. "You're as outrageous as everything I've come to know about you. But then, I suppose it goes with the personality."

"Am I to assume you planted the second batch of bugs in my house?"

"You may. Anyway, it's been my job to keep track of you. We'll get into that but, first I should say a few things about our time together so far. The atomic blast is causing a growing stir as the full meaning of it is settling into the heads of both the military and civilian authorities as well as the general public. An atomic bomb lighting up the sky with no hint of a prior warning really caught people flat footed. I can only guess that the delay in getting someone out to the site of the explosion was first and foremost the unexpectedness of it and then deciding who was in charge. When that was figured out, whoever was in charge had to decide what to do. Creech Air Force Base is the closest, but Nellis here in Las Vegas is much larger and far more important. Then, who had assets hot and ready to go? I was a little surprised a response appeared as fast as it did, though they'd assume there wouldn't likely be anything to find. But, there was something to find wasn't there? You! And what a prize you would have been. Now do you understand why I was flying low . . . ."

"Flying like a mole would fly," I interjected.

"Yes, low," he continued. "I was a helicopter pilot in Vietnam and have kept my hand in. Not bad for an old man, huh? But, let us not get sidetracked. There will be a lot of questions asked and unless you want to be the center of an international media circus, stay with the plan I have mapped out. The only thing that will work is to get you back to your home as if nothing happened, and do that as quickly as possible. I instructed Harry Auston as to what he should do before I came after you. I told your wife that you were safe, to talk to no one, and you'd be home in a day or two. Then the mendacity starts all around including you. It will be extremely important that all of you stick to your stories."

We drove on into the night. There was enough traffic so we weren't conspicuous by our presence. "Where are we going?"

"The goal is to get to Flagstaff. We should get there in a couple of hours, maybe a little more, before the traffic thins out too much. From there, if things go right, I plan to fly you home. It'll be faster than driving, but not as fast as on a jet. We'll probably do it in stretches."

He was concentrating as he spoke like he wasn't sure about the next step. "I don't want to interfere so stop me if I'm out of place, but you're sort of making this up as you go, aren't you?"

"That's the only thing I can do. It's not like anybody planned any of this. I have one helper who does a pretty good job with travel arrangements and things like that."

He took a cell phone from his pocket and pressed a speed dial. After twenty seconds he said, "Lu, I made the pick up on time but it was close, and we're on the road. How does it look for the next pick up?" He glanced at me. "He's checking on Flagstaff." We waited and sped on into the night. "Yeah, not too bad. How about the pilot?"

I always hated it when someone else was working an operation on the fly. When I did it, experience showed that I could make the decisions needed, and if things went off kilter, I was the one to get things back on track, that was my strong suit.

Finally, he punched off his phone. "He found a charter service in Phoenix that can supply a Beachcraft King Air. That goes at about 250 mph so four or five hours to Minneapolis. The pilot is a feeder airline pilot putting in his time at minimum wage until he gets enough hours to move into the big money on the major routes. We caught him during a three day down time from his real job, so he'll pick us up at Flagstaff and take us the whole way."

— 43 —

More road stretching off into the night. To pass the time and keep crazy pilot, safe driver awake, I asked, "How did a nuke get into South Vietnam? General Diggens told me some of it. More curiously, what was your role, the part that started out with you trying to kill me, and now having you save me? . . . I think."

"Oh, I am trying to save you, and I never was trying to kill you. I'll get to the story, but first I have to reiterate, I still don't think you have comprehended the seriousness of all this. A nuclear weapon of any type going off in the atmosphere in these uncertain times is enough to cause world wide panic. We know of several countries who have a few nukes and they would love to set one off just to demonstrate to the U.S. and Israel, to say nothing of their neighbors, that they should back off. Now that we've been seen to do it they'll think it was to make them back off, but instead they will respond in kind. This has already made it on to the world news so everybody knows about it. The thing to remember is if anyone were to find out that you were directly involved in the explosion, it would force the U.S. president into one particular story while his administration might have several other explanations that they see as being better where world consumption is concerned. From here on it's all politics. None of the world opinion makers cares what happens to you. In fact, the first impulse of that White House crowd would be to eliminate you. I hate to see people wasted like that, plus I have a professional and personal stake in keeping you alive. So, if you can be kept from muddying up Washington's spin on this, you have a chance at living.

"There'll be a feeling in some quarters that since you did manage to get it to detonate in an unpopulated area, and a nuclear test range at that, it's worth some expense to keep you alive. Of course, those at the top will feel you should not have detonated it at all."

"Hey, I didn't detonate it, I was trying not to detonate it. I just happened to be the only one who believed what I was told about the timers. And, if the timers had been disabled, the troopers would have gotten away with it. Then what?"

"The troopers would not have gotten away with it. If it had not exploded when it did, they would have been blown out of the sky with long range air-to-air missiles before they left the test range."

"How does that make me the bad guy? Everything was under control."

"Once again, politics. How is the chief of the state police of the grand state of Minnesota supposed to explain the disappearance of three of his troopers? And as we know, they have disappeared in the most extreme sense imaginable. He's supposed to take the fall for that? Not likely. You are the designated patsy. You took charge of things in the park where it was found. As a matter of fact, you are the one who dug it up. The media spin will be intense, but will do the job—if you can be kept out of it."

"Wait a minute. The three troopers will not be coming back even in body bags. That means they were in on it as much as I was. They can't spin that away."

"Let it be. You don't know what a compliant press can do. If the president were a Republican, it would be different in that you would be toast. The media would dig and dig until we'd all be in prison or better yet, dead. As it is we, that is those I work for and myself, will have our hands full keeping you from becoming a crispy slice of bread."

There was more. "Why were you keeping track of Harry and me?"

He looked at the road rising out of the night to our front as if to distance himself from what he was about to say. "I had no choice. Others had found you. By you, of course, I mean one of you since you were all connected."

"I don't know what that means, and just who are you? And, why did you say you had a personal stake in keeping me alive?" In the glow from the instruments I saw him nod.

"Have you heard about the witness protection program under the U.S. Marshals?"

"Yeah."

"I do something like that. The CIA is in every country on earth using locals to feed them information, for a fee of course. Some of them are highly placed in the governments, the military or are technical experts. If they are discovered working for us they would in many cases be killed so they and their families are expatriated to the U.S. and given citizenship. In fact, I was expatriated to the U.S. like that after the Vietnam War.

"Being talented individuals, they frequently find jobs in sensitive positions in the U.S. Since they are not really in hiding, it's always possible that their home countries will find them and make agents out of them to spy on us. We keep track of these people by constantly accessing their personal records such as finances, travel, etc. When something alerts us to undesirable activities someone like me steps in."

"Wait," I broke in. "Isn't accessing people's records like that illegal even unconstitutional?"

"Technically yes. But the constitution no longer has any practical force in this country. Surely, you know that."

"That means you had the computers watching me, too, and Harry I suppose."

"That's right. We saw Mr. Auston's financial situation going bad but that in itself wasn't too alarming. But, when he got a sudden infusion of cash from no discernable source, I was on the case. You always had been my charges since we had history together. I picked up on Auston too late as I found Blue Dog was already dead. Now it's important that we keep you and Harry alive."

"That doesn't make sense, either. I can't imagine Goldman, Cutter and the rest of those guys caring a twit about keeping anyone but themselves alive."

"That's not what I said. We don't work for them. Some parts of the government must operate from one election to the next outside of politics or the country couldn't function. Your case was very low priority since for decades there had been no warning signs until, that is, Auston got the money. As such, you didn't even know I existed. There are other high profile cases where the subject knows me. There's no avoiding it. These types of expatriates tend to know one another—it's a relativity small community. If you were to go down, it would make them lose trust in me and even, in some cases, come after me with evil intent."

The fog around all of this was starting to dissipate. "Speaking of our history together, you were the one that spoke of *The Ojibwe* on the mountain in Vietnam. How about telling me what that was all about? What you said at the time made no sense and still doesn't except that you were referring to General Diggens."

"Let me fill you in on the story. Retired General Diggens told you a little so I might repeat some of it. Some American generals were behind the plan to plant and use at least one nuke in Vietnam and blame it on China. They planted one, the one your team recovered. The other four were inert. The generals were chagrined when the war was winding down and there had been no chance to use it. Perhaps from the beginning they saw this possibility and made a sixth unit, also inert, just in case. With the U.S. involvement in the war ending it was obvious that South Vietnam would be getting less aid from the U.S. while North Vietnam would be getting more aid from China. The result on the course of the war was obvious. Therefore, there was a plan made to transfer the live MADM to South Vietnam and let us use it. I was an officer in the South Vietnamese Army then. It was not traceable to the U.S. so China would be blamed and that would change things a lot. If the South could capitalize on this, we could still win. Maybe, seeing the changed situation the U.S. would step up aid to the South again. Therefore, the plan was to have the Phantom Team dig it up and have South Vietnamese soldiers steal it, that is, have it transferred to them."

"Wait," I said. "Why didn't the South Vietnamese simply dig it up themselves? Why involve us?"

"We tried. Oh, how we tried, but we couldn't find it. Your team was our last chance. None of us even thought Phantom really existed. Well, sure enough you did exist, and you did find it."

"That doesn't make any more sense than any of the rest of this. We drove in as far as we could on that old road that hadn't seen any use for years, and then proceeded on foot. The hollow where we found it was the only place the team in charge of placing it could have dug deep enough to bury it."

Eddie laughed. "The fickleness of war. You were given the standard maps the U.S. had available which, if you had checked, were made in the nineteen twenties and thirties. The same maps were given to the guys that buried it. But, we were South Vietnamese so we were smarter. We had newer maps, spoke the language like natives because, of course, we were, and we talked to the locals. Since your maps had been made a new road had been built up the other side of the ridge. Of course, it didn't show on your map and the new road was the only one the people in the area thought about when we talked to them. That meant we were looking on the wrong side of the mountain."

"That's a nice story," I said irritably. "Then, why was the mountain infested with Viet Cong, or were they North Vietnamese Regulars?"

"They weren't Viet Cong, or were they NV. They were ARVN, South Vietnamese regulars. The heavy rain made everyone's uniform wet so it was hard to tell."

"No. That's wrong. The two soldiers at the listening post in the hollow where we found the case were wearing North Vietnamese uniforms. The cut was enough different so I could tell. And, I was close enough to be touching the guy as he answered the calls on the field telephone. That's what seemed so odd, really. I had thought the Easter Offensive had cleared out those guys. VC were every where, but not NV."

"I can't speak for those two men, but it was possible they were wearing captured NV uniforms. Things weren't going so well for us in the South. Many ARVN soldiers closed with the enemy for no other reason than if they could beat them back they could strip the clothes off the fallen enemy and use them for themselves. The unit insignia were to be replaced by ARVN ones, but sometimes there wasn't time, to say nothing of needle and thread, for even that."

He could see the conflict going on in my head, and in my gut. I was shaking my head. "If that's true, why were they trying to kill us. They did kill Night Hawk!"

"They had orders not to injure anyone. Night Hawk was an accident. You knew he was hit by a ricochet, didn't you?"

"Yeah," I said slowly. I was reliving once again that fight on the mountain. "Wait, a minute. How about the ambush laid for the truck when it came down that switchback road?"

"They were to shoot the engine to stop the truck and we were to make a stand-off until we could convince them we were all on the same side." He closed his eyes briefly and breathed deeply. "We never imagined that Phantom could be so lethal, so totally invincible, so unpredictable—just a handful of men."

"Then, I killed three South Vietnamese soldiers," I said. I was so weak I was glad I was sitting down and strapped in.

He nodded. "Not your fault. As I have learned, you could not have been told it was a sham operation or the team would not have functioned, which means you would not have found it. I'll go into a little more of what I've learned about Phantom if you want."

"No I want to hear the rest of this. What was the deal with the five ton truck between the buildings?"

"When we failed to take possession of the nuke on the mountain, I hotfooted it back to the base. You managed to nick me so I needed some medical care, but mostly I had to be on hand for a last attempt to take possession of the live nuke. I was waiting for you in the five ton truck. The sixth unit, also inert, was in the back of that truck in its crate. We now planned to make the switch there. The fake unit even had the same serial number as the live one. General Diggens was directing all of this from his desk, of course. It was to be a simple transaction, but once again, we were usurped by the Phantom mentality. What Diggens and I didn't take into account was the system of orders for Phantom. When given a mission, only your direct handler could change orders which in this case was Major Holt. No other orders from any senior officer would affect you.

"Having failed in the switch, and being wounded more severely this time, I tried, and failed, once more in the hangar. When General Diggens arrived to sign for it, he assumed the switch had been made successfully and the live nuke was on its way to the South Vietnamese Army. I would have alerted him to the fact that he was shipping the live nuke instead of the inert one. But, I was unconscious on the floor in the back of the hangar. This you know."

"Yeah," I said, "Diggens did comment on how dirty, scratched and dented the unit in the crate was. He expected to see a pristine one that had, in fact, never been out of the crate." It was at last making sense.

I related what I had learned. "Major Holt, or course, knew nothing about the big picture and when appraised of *The Ojibwe* being involved in trying to steal it, assumed he must step in and do the right thing. That is, he had to steal it from the thieves. There was an investigation into the missing live nuke as everyone expected, but those generals in on the master plot made sure it stayed within bounds. The fact that a jet engine was in the fifth crate arriving back in the States rather than the inert MADM caused some consternation, even among the generals in on the plot. But, in the end the real one was intended to be lost so the whole investigation was finished and put away. What happened to the sixth unit in the back of the five tone truck?"

"I have no idea. It was only a case with some inert material inside to make the weight right. It was lost as so much materiel is during a war."

"That's some story," I said. "There is even precedent for a nuke being "lost" in order to transfer it to a foreign power. I looked it up on the Internet. In the 1960s, 587 pounds of highly enriched uranium was classified as missing from a nuclear facility in Pennsylvania that is known to have found its way to Israel. They in turn fabricated weapons from it. The only difference here was that of a ready to detonate bomb."

We both paused for over a minute, then the Vietnamese man, Eddie, continued. "The fact that South Vietnam never used the nuke seemed odd to certain generals, but they could only assume something had happened to make that impossible. The result of all of this was that Diggens had no problem telling you what he did about the incident because he thought if you did find a MADM it would be the inert one. On the other hand, since Holt had no knowledge of the sixth unit or of the planned switch, to him it was a real nuke, which it was, and the only thing he could think of to save himself was to keep his mouth shut."

"What about the timers? Within twenty days after the incident on the mountain, there should have been an explosion someplace if the South Vietnamese actually had taken it."

"That remained unexplained. Some thought that the enemy might have gotten lucky and managed to disable the timers, or that they were damaged and failed to operate after the beating your guys gave the case. But more likely, it was assumed that the South Vietnamese Army didn't grasp the meaning of the twenty day timer and buried it in the ground somewhere so the case cooled and the timer stopped. Then, due to changed tactical circumstances they could not get back to recover it. If someone later happened upon it and it exploded, well, too bad. It was a communist country then."

I couldn't resist picking away as was my nature. "There's still a problem. If General Diggens thought we were looking for the inert MADM why did he tell us about the twenty minute timer, and then rush to the park and at the last minute tell about the twenty day timer, too?"

"Maybe I'm wrong about why he told you about the twenty minute timer, and then at the last minute the twenty day one. It's possible that since there was no explosion in Vietnam he thought this was the real one."

In other words, he didn't have a clue. "So, what happened with Blue Dog. Why was he killed?"

"It was too bad about Blue Dog, in a way worse than Night Hawk. At least Night Hawk died in battle. If I had picked up on what Goldman was doing in time I could have seen to having Blue Dog arrested and kept out of circulation, under humane conditions, of course, for as long as this thing took. I, as well as the terrorists, recognized that we didn't dare let three of you get together."

"Why were we considered such a threat? We're just ordinary men. This has been bothering me for a long time."

Eddie answered, "Individually, yes. But when in a team, you were something no one ever realized could exist. By the way, the algorithm that was used to pick each of you out of all the servicemen at the time has been destroyed. It was considered too dangerous. If four of you got together unsupervised, you could have toppled empires."

After a pause he continued. "They were thinking that it was possible that all the great leaders in history were not so special by themselves, but they had gotten together with three or four others like you guys. One was the more charismatic of the lot and he's the one history records. Maybe it was that way with Hitler. In all the years leading up to the Second World War he had to make daily decisions and could make few mistakes. This was possible if he had such helpers. And they were way in that background, truly phantoms. Later, his generals might have learned of them and through jealously killed them or he became arrogant and dismissed them. Either way, the thinking is that he might have lost the war because without his 'Phantom Team' he lost his ability to make the right decisions in a timely manner."

He stopped talking as if uncertain if he should say more. "What are you thinking?" I probed.

"How much are you into philosophy? There is more, but it goes deeper."

"Try me," I responded thinking about what Henni had told me.

He nodded. "In the Bible, in Genesis, it says God made man in His own image and likeness."

"Wait," I said. "Are you going to dump some of this born again Christian rapture stuff on me?"

"No," he replied. "I'll leave my personal religious leanings out of this. I mentioned the Bible because this country has Christian roots so everyone recognizes the Bible and Genesis. If I mentioned a Hindu manuscript, nobody would know what I was talking about to say nothing about neither that religion or other religions has as one of its doctrines what I will refer to."

I nodded so he continued. "That means, if you believe we—that is our souls—are created spirits rather than simply the result of fortunate chemical accidents, we have immense potentials that we never use. This in turn means there are some of us who can access this or that dormant ability but only when the right stimulus appears. The best inference or guess that anyone can make is that you guys are special in a way that does not manifest itself until you're put together with others like yourselves. And this is the strange part, even then, it doesn't manifest itself completely until the team becomes involved in a dangerous situation.

"And, these abilities aren't directly related to, for the lack of a better term, warrior traits. There are two distinguished abilities. One is what could be called a knack, or natural talent like some people have the knack of playing musical instruments, or learning foreign languages. Your knack was in thinking quickly, in fact acting without thinking, in a dangerous situation. The second was the team thing, and then only with others like yourselves. Any comments on that?"

"Yeah. I'm one of them, and I was on a team. I can recall actions in detail that we were in. There was nothing special about us. We were scared, scrambling, hardly thinking, acting by instinct and reflex. There were times when I thought I was dead the next second and then something happened like a hand-hold appeared. I didn't make that happen, it was there for anyone to see and being desperate I grabbed it, used it, or did whatever was the natural thing to do. It was like I had a guardian angel helping me when I needed it most. I didn't do anything so special."

He chuckled. "You've stated the situation as well as anyone else, and several have tried. You're saying you guys have nothing more than the best darned guardian angels in the whole world. I think you're selling yourself short. It's probably more like those hand-holds, as you called them, would have been there for anyone except the vast majority of people wouldn't have seen them as an asset. What do you think?"

"I agree to a point except there have been times when it was like playing Russian Roulette only in my case four of the chambers had bullets in them and I got one of the two empty ones. No hand-holds.

"I can go back and analyze situations and can see absolutely that it was considerably better than a fifty-fifty chance of my being killed, yet here I am."

"I wouldn't have believed it."

— 44 —

Early Sunday morning

The twin Beech was waiting for us at a general aviation airport in Flagstaff. After a stop at the men's room we piled in and were off minutes after midnight. We'd be in the Twin Cities by dawn. I slept.

The wheels squeaking on the runway pulled me out of deep sleep—no dreams. It was the start of a new beautifully clear day that I hoped wouldn't fall apart on me. I saw the sign for Thunderbird Aviation and knew we were at either Flying Cloud Airport in Eden Prairie or the Crystal Airport. I put my money on Crystal. Not bad, I thought. It was good to stay away from the Anoka Airport. Who knew what reporters might be camped out there.

Fong Cha, Eddie, looked at me as I sat up. "How do we travel from here?" I asked.

"With any luck, Lu had a rental agency drop off a car. We'll see."

We taxied to the tarmac in front of Thunderbird and the pilot killed the engines. Eddie told the pilot he was free to return to Phoenix when he was ready. The car was there, and we made our way to I-694.

As we were driving I asked, "What about Seth Goldman?"

"What do you mean, what about Seth Goldman?"

"The obvious, he tried to put his hands on an atomic bomb to blow up an American city."

"Nothing will happen to him because you don't know anything about him trying to snatch such an item let alone what he might have done with it if that's what he were trying to do."

"There's something unfinished about that. He attempted to pull off the crime of the century."

Eddie nodded then said, "Here, I'll interject some of my religious beliefs, where I deliberately didn't last night. In the gospels there's the parable where the land owner finds an enemy has planted weeds in his wheat field. When his servants ask if he wants them to pull up the weeds, he says no, because in the process they will up-root much of the wheat, too. So both weeds and wheat are left to grow until the harvest when the weeds will be burned, and the wheat stored in his barn. Well, to me this seems like that. We can't set ourselves up as judges and kill a man because we know what he meant to do. The human race—the wheat field—will have to get along with that particular weed until the harvest—the Last Judgement. What do you think?"

"Undoubtedly that's what will happen, but it's hard to watch the weeds win all the time."

"We'll always have the weeds. What's needed is hardier strains of wheat. In the present society, the wheat is most anemic so the weeds flourish."

"Yeah, no argument there. And, Bruce Holt will have lied his way to safety. I wouldn't be able to lie my way out of having stolen a cupcake and he makes off with a fully ready to explode atomic bomb, and he's in the clear. Life isn't fair. Have you ever noticed that?"

He didn't answer and we drove in silence. I turned my head and he caught the motion out of the corner of his eye. There was a slight nod and his eye glistened with what appeared to be the start of a tear. I was struck with the reality.

"I'm sorry," I said. "When I asked about the wife and kids last evening you said there weren't any, that is, now. But, you had a family in Vietnam. And, they perished in the war. I'm very sorry."

Nodding more noticeably he replied. "You're right. Life can really suck at times."

After a few more miles to lighten the mood and change the subject I interjected, "Wait a minute, won't Seth Goldman have to at least account for a jet airplane that's missing never to be found?"

It was the top of the hour and Eddie, without a word, switched on the radio. The first news story began: "The White House is saying nothing more about the atomic explosion yesterday afternoon. In the event any of our listeners missed the announcement, here it is, 'A low yield atomic bomb detonated in the atmosphere in Nevada under controlled conditions yesterday. While decommissioning the device the technicians encountered an unexpected difficulty and rather than take a chance took it to the nuclear test site in Nevada. After waiting for optimum weather conditions a robot with manipulator arms was being used to put the munition in a safe condition when it exploded. The radioactive fallout was minimal and all of it came to earth harmlessly on the test range.' That's it. Not a word more.

"In another odd event from yesterday, supposedly not connected to the atomic explosion, a business jet owned by the U.S. Air Force was flown to the Anoka County Airport. There three Minnesota state troopers took possession of it for the purpose of extraditing a prisoner from Arizona back to Minnesota. Over a remote area of the southwest an in-flight emergency occurred causing the plane to crash killing all three troopers. Our deepest condolences go out to their families.

"Through unnamed sources we've learned that the big event at the Lochness Park in Blaine yesterday morning was much ado about nothing, or at least not much. It had been leaked that some nuclear material was being recovered from the landfill. That landfill has been closed since the seventies. It turned out that the aluminum case that was dug up with much fanfare contained military airborne camera equipment. It contained a small amount of radium in the sighting mechanism used to aim it at night—as much as on a luminous wristwatch of the time. While the cameras were state of the art back then, they are good for little more than to be displayed in a museum now.

"The weather today will push the pleasant meter right off the scale. . . ."

Eddie switched off the radio. I was stunned. It was like the end of an inning of a boring baseball game, no hits, no runs, no errors. Nobody left on base.

He looked at me. "Nice and neat. All you have to do is keep your mouth shut."

"Will Goldman start looking for another one of those things I know nothing about?"

"I doubt it. He and his cronies thought this one was lying about ready to be picked up and most importantly it was a complete weapon easily detonated. It's unlikely they'd get that close to one again. After what happened the Department of Defense and Department of Energy will tighten security on those devices to the limit. Besides, there're easier ways to take over the country, especially now. This country has been sliding toward some form of totalitarian government for years. It seems to me that the pace has picked up a lot in the past few years. With half the people dependent on a government check of one kind or another they aren't about to vote for a change back to the self reliant rugged individualism of your forefathers. Your schools teach nothing about reality. I would like to teach a class about what happened to my homeland when the communists took over. It's not something you want. Regardless of the outward appearances, life in Vietnam is hard and the people suffer in many ways just like they always suffer under authoritarian regimes.

"The best guess is they would have used the thing of our interest to destroy Washington D.C. which is the symbol of where all the government largess comes from. With that gone a majority of the American people would have believed there was no country anymore. The United States would be split up into several regions—a social Balkanization—while they maintained overall political control. The end result would include Mexico and Canada. For example, the Southwest would go with Mexico, while the Pacific Northwest would join with Western Canada. The New England states would join with Eastern Canada. That's been talked about for years."

In what seemed like only minutes Eddie was dropping me off in front of the house. The lawn needed mowing but other than that nothing had changed. I had only a couple of vacation days left so Camilla and I wouldn't be taking that trip to the Canadian Rockies like we had planned. Life would go on.

A couple of weeks later I drove into the garage upon arriving home from work. I wasn't well yet, that is, in my mind, but there was no chance I'd seek psychiatric help—too many secrets. Like Eddie said, it would blow over if we all kept to our stories and didn't say anything at all unless there was no other choice. As I walked up to the back door there was a package wrapped in brown paper with a red bow on it. UPS left packages at the front door, not the back, and never with a bow. If it was a bomb, I didn't really care. I took it in leaving the back door open and letting the screen door slam behind me. I set it on the kitchen table and considered it. Camilla was there slicing and dicing something or other.

"What's that?" she asked.

"I don't know. It was setting on the back step. The bow is odd on a package like this. It sounds like there're cans of liquid in it."

Not saying more I ripped off the paper to see a twelve pack of beer and a small white envelope taped to the side. The card inside said, "Gift of homage to the Great White Warrior, signed Big Buck."

I chuckled as I handed it to Camilla. "I like a guy with style."

"I heard that!" came a voice from beyond the screen door in back.

"Come on in, Fred."

He did. I looked at his smiling face and said, "Hey, I've got an idea, why don't I offer you a can of beer."

"That would most certainly be hospitable of you."

We sat at the kitchen table as we each popped a can. "What brings you around, and with gifts, even. I though you'd be sore at me."

"Not at all. You got my job back for me."

"Huh? When you were here last you said you had been working under cover the whole time."

"I stretched the truth a little. Remember that first night we talked you promised me my job back, a raise, a reward and that I'd be a hero. You mentioned that it could be made to look like I had been working as a security guard at Northtown as a cover. When I learned what was going on I paid my former bosses a visit with just that story. It was a hard sell, but I made it. If Goldman hadn't pulled that stunt of calling off the FBI I would have been a hero. Still, that wasn't my fault, and the FBI would have been blindsided if I hadn't come forward. They appreciated that. So, the outcome, while not perfect, wasn't bad at all."

It was good to see that someone came out of that abysmal affair the better for it. Harry and I had not contacted one another since the event, and it was likely we never would. We were tired of the whole business and needed time to recover—except I still had Fred in my kitchen. I didn't dislike him but would rather he had not come.

Before I could think of a polite way to ease him out the door he said, "It was some wild ride, though. I was part of a Phantom Team for awhile, wasn't I?"

So, that was it. This was one of the things we weren't supposed to talk about but I was sort of stuck. "Fred, in all honesty it's impossible to determine whether or not you were part of a Team. That's because a special algorithm was used to pick men to be on the Teams, and that has been destroyed. Nobody wanted to do that again. You did a good job, I'll say that."

I stared at the top of my beer can not knowing if I should say more, but in consideration of how he had dropped his life to go with me to the boundary waters, I continued. "Remember that night in the park, that first night when I clipped your legs out from under you? I heard no special sound due to the train passing by nor did I see any out of the ordinary movement. Yet, I knew what was going to happen, and did the only thing that could have been done to save your life. I acted only on premonition. If you think you can do that on a consistent basis, than you are Phantom."

He was conflicted as if he knew he didn't have it, but wanted desperately to believe he did. "Well, I prefer to think I would have been picked for a Team. At the very least, watching you and Harry work, especially you in the boundary waters, really made an impression on me. As I've thought about it, it's not that you did any single action that was superhuman or anything like that. You just did the absolutely best thing at each moment. It's changed the way I look at my job, and I must say for the better. What I'm saying is I came to thank you for that experience, the training, if you will. That being said, I'll be on my way. If you ever need anything, feel free to ask."

He rose to leave and I accompanied him to the door. I extended my hand, which he took. "Well, Big Buck, I appreciate the kindness and will remember to call when in need."

He smiled broadly and walked out the back door.

THE END

He was conflicted as if he knew he didn't have it, but wanted desperately to believe he did. "Well, I prefer to think I would have been picked for a Team. At the very least, watching you and Harry work, especially you in the boundary waters, really made an impression on me. As I've thought about it, it's not that you did any single action that was superhuman or anything like that. You just did the absolutely best thing at each moment. It's changed the way I look at my job, and I must say for the better. What I'm saying is I came to thank you for that experience, the training, if you will. That being said, I'll be on my way. If you ever need anything, feel free to ask."

He rose to leave and I accompanied him to the door. I extended my hand, which he took. "Well, Big Buck, I appreciate the kindness and will remember to call when in need."

He smiled broadly and walked out the back door.

THE END

www.ingramcontent.com/pod-product-compliance
Lightning Source LLC
Chambersburg PA
CBHW012229010726
47494CB00002B/416